The MacKinnon's Bride

TANYA ANNE CROSBY

PUBLISHER'S NOTE: This is a work of fiction. Names, characters, places, and incidents either are the product of the author's imagination or are used fictitiously. Any resemblance to actual persons, living or dead, business establishments, events, or locales is entirely coincidental.

COPYRIGHT © Tanya Anne Crosby

Published by Oliver-Heber Books

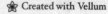 Created with Vellum

For my beautiful mother, Isabel, who gifted me with a love for storytelling.

SERIES BIBLIOGRAPHY

THE HIGHLAND BRIDES

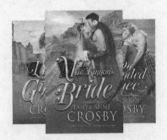

The MacKinnon's Bride

Lyon's Gift

On Bended Knee

Lion Heart

Highland Song

MacKinnon's Hope

These books are

ALSO AVAILABLE AS AUDIOBOOKS

MEDIEVAL SCOTLAND

MEDIEVAL SCOTLAND

PROLOGUE
CHREAGACH MHOR, SCOTLAND 1118

Iain, laird of the MacKinnons, descendant of the powerful sons of MacAlpin, paced the confines of the hall below his chamber like an overeager youth.

So much hope was affixed upon this birth.

Now, at last, thirty years of feuding with the MacLeans would come to an end. Aye, for how could auld man MacLean look upon his grandbairn and not want peace? After a year full of enmity from his bonny MacLean wife—a year of trying to please her only to meet with stony disapproval and wordless accusations—even Iain felt burgeoning hope for how could she look upon their babe, the life they'd created together, and not feel some measure—some small measure, of affection?

Despite the past hostilities between their clans, his own resentment dissipated in the face of this momentous occasion, and though he couldn't say he'd loved her before this moment, he thought he might now, for she lay abovestairs, struggling—and a heinous struggle it was—to gift their babe with its first wondrous breath of life.

She was havin' his bairn.

Ach, but he was proud of her.

As difficult as the birth was proceeding, she'd borne her pain with nary a scream, nary a curse, though he'd

TANYA ANNE CROSBY

never have begrudged her either. In truth, her shrieks might have been far easier to bear. Her silence was tormenting him. He couldn't help but be nerve-racked by the thought of his young wife in the throes of her labor, for his own mother had died just so, giving him life. Guilt over it plagued him still.

Iain lengthened his stride.

What if the birth killed her?

What if he killed her?

'Twas a fear he'd borne from the first day he'd lain his hands upon her in carnal pleasure, and it wouldn't be eased now until he saw her face once more. He would welcome even her sullen glances this moment. He'd bear them for the rest of his days if only she'd live through this punishing birth. In fact, he swore that if his touch was truly so unbearable for her, he'd touch her no more. He'd grant her anything her heart desired—anything—and if she desired him not, then so be it.

If she died... where, then, was their peace?

Damn MacLean, for he'd as lief be—

The glorious sound of a babe's newborn wail resounded from above, a rapturous siren that froze Iain midstride.

He found he couldn't move, could do little more than stare at the stone steps that led to his chamber, joy and fear holding him immobilized.

It seemed forever before he heard the heavy door above swing open and then the hastening footsteps.

Maggie, his wife's maid, appeared on the stairwell. "A son, laird!" she exclaimed, shouting down happily. "Ye've a son!"

Those beautiful words freed Iain from his stupor. Yelping euphorically, he bolted up the stairwell, taking the steps two at a time in his haste to see his wife and a first glorious glimpse of his newborn son. "A son!" he said in marvel, passing Maggie as she hurried down to

2

spread the news. She nodded, and joy surged through him. He wanted to kiss her fiercely—aye, Even Maggie.

Not even the midwife barring him entrance at the door diminished his spirits.

The woman who had so long ago helped to deliver him unto the world thrust out her arms to keep him from entering his chamber. "She doesna wish to see you, Iain." The piteous look that came over her face sent prickles down his spine. "No' as yet, she doesna."

He braced himself to hear the worst. "Is she—"

"As well as can be expected. The babe didna wish to come is all." She lowered her eyes, averting her gaze.

The babe was no longer crying.

"What is it, Glenna?" Fear swept through him. Unable to help himself, he seized her by the arms and fought the urge to thrust her aside, to see for himself. "What o' the babe?"

She tilted him a sympathetic glance. "Dinna y' hear him, lad? Your son is a fine wee bairn. Listen closer," she bade him.

He did, and he could hear the babe's soft shuddering coos.

His gaze was drawn within the darkened chamber.

The midwife must have felt his tension, his indecision, his elation, his confusion, for she stood firm when he tried to nudge her aside. "Iain... nay," she beseeched him, "ye dinna wish to see her as yet... Gi' her time."

Iain released her and reeled backward, numb with misery. "She loathes me still?"

"Her labor was difficult and long," Glenna explained. "'Twill pass. Go now, wait below stairs. I'll come t' fetch ye anon... ye've my word." He hesitated and she added more firmly, "Do her this one kindness, Iain MacKinnon, for she doesna seem to be herself just now."

Iain was torn between wanting to grant his wife this favor, no matter that it pained him that she didn't wish to see him, and needing to hold his son. The desire was nearly tangible. "She truly doesna wish to—" His voice broke. "See me?"

The midwife shook her head.

"I... had hoped..." His jaw worked.

"Ach, but ye canna expect her to come aboot so soon, Iain! Gi' her time. Gi' her time."

"Verra well." His jaw turned taut. "But I'll no' wait long," he assured her. "I intend to see my son, Glenna. She cannot keep me from him forever."

The midwife's eyes slanted with understanding. "'Tis all she asks o' ye, lad."

Iain could not speak, not to assent, nor to refuse.

He turned and made his way belowstairs, cursing whatever prideful act had kindled the accursed feud all those years ago between her da and his own. He didn't even know, nor did anyone else seem to recall, what heinous crime had engendered such animosity. Like as not, it was naught more than the simple fact that his father's hound had pissed upon old MacLean's boot. Stubborn auld fools!

He didn't have long to wait. For that he was grateful. Glenna needed only call him once and he was there at the door, shocked to find his wife standing in the middle of the chamber with their babe cradled in her arms, face wan, her hair disheveled. He thought she wavered a little on her feet, but she came forward, her face without expression, to place their infant within his arms. The gesture moved him so that any protest he might have uttered over her being out of bed fell away as he embraced his child.

He stared down in wonder into his child's wrinkled little face.

Mayhap there was hope after all?

"'Twill be all, Glenna," Mairi said.

Iain barely heard his wife's clipped command, or the

door closing behind Glenna, so overwhelmed was he with the incredible gift his wife had given him.

His throat constricted as he examined his son... so tiny... so incredibly beautiful... He began to count toes, fingers, dared to touch the little nose, lips... skin so soft.

"A son!" he whispered in awe, and glanced up momentarily to find his wife at the window. "Mairi, come away from there," he said softly, his voice choking with emotion, "afore ye catch your death." His heart pounded joyfully as he returned to the inspection of his babe.

"I wanted to show ye something, Iain."

Her voice was lacking emotion, weary. He looked up to find her staring from the window, the breeze blowing gently through her beautifully mussed hair. A lovely halo surrounded her, he thought, the mother of his child. "You should rest," he advised her. "Show me later, Mairi. Get yourself back to bed now." She turned to face him then, and there was something indiscernible in her expression.

The hair at his nape prickled.

She tilted her head and smiled a little. "I wanted ye to see that bearin' your bairn didna kill me, after all. Here I am, ye see." She swayed like a drunkard, and guilt wrenched at his gut. "Two days it took me, but here I stand." She laughed softly, and choked on her emotion.

"Thank God." he said, and meant it fiercely. He peered down at their son, unable to endure her accusing gaze any longer. Self-disgust flowed through him. "Thank you," he whispered, unsure of what it was he was supposed to say. "I'll make it up to ye, Mairi. I swear it."

"I want only one thing from you," she spat.

"Anything—" He choked on the declaration, but swore he'd give her whatever she so desired. *Anything*. She need only ask for it.

"I only wanted ye to see me wi' your own eyes... to know the thought o' bearin' ye another—endurin' your touch." She shuddered and turned from him abruptly, leaning out from the tower window. "Sweet Mary!" she sobbed. "I'll never do it again! I'll not!"

Iain's arms went numb with the weight of their child. A sense of foreboding rushed through him. She leaned farther, and a shudder shook him. "Mairi, come away from there now!"

"I want ye to know."

A cold sweat broke over him. "Now!" he barked. "Get away from there, Mairi! Glenna!" he shouted and he started toward his wife with the babe in his arms, unsure of whether to lay the child down.

"The thought o' ye *ever* touching me again did this. You killed me, Iain."

"Mairi, nay!"

She flung herself from the window before he could reach her.

Iain staggered to his knees, clutching their babe against his pounding heart.

The babe.

His son.

He might have reached her had he not been holding their son.

Startled by his bellow, the babe began to squeal and Iain could only stare, stupidly, at the open window where an instant before his wife had stood.

CHAPTER 1
NORTHUMBRIA 1124

S omeone was watching; she could feel it.

Page froze in the midst of donning her undergown.

A twig snapped, muffled by the bracken of the forest floor, and she snatched down the hem, her eyes focusing upon the twisting shadows of the not too distant woods.

She could see naught through the midnight blackness, and naught more than silence reached her—a silence that settled like the night mist, formless and unnatural. Her teeth began to chatter, and for a long instant she stood there, chilled and wary, but she could hear nothing more than familiar night sounds: the croaking of frogs, the trilling of crickets, the distant howl of a wolf.

A quiver passed down her spine, for she had heard something. She was nearly sure of it.

'Twould behoove her, she decided, to hie back to the safety of the keep—perhaps to rethink the wisdom in coming out alone at night. All these months of slipping out without incident had made her lax in her guard.

Like a hundred nights before, Page had come out for her swim, without bothering to inform anyone of her destination—not that anyone would have cared, she assured herself quickly. The only blessed good to come of being daughter to a man who only wanted sons was that she had the freedom to do as she pleased. And yet it truly meant that nobody cared one whit where she went, what she did, or what became of her. And she didn't trouble herself to think tonight would be any different.

On the other hand, she cared. She cared very much, and she had no intention of becoming somebody's—or something's—prey.

She sat hurriedly upon the boulder beside where she'd lain her clothes, and reached down to pluck up her beaten shoes from the dewy ground. She donned one quickly, muffling silent curses as her wet foot impeded her progress, and then changed her mind about lingering long enough to dress.

Mist crept about her feet, nebulous fingers wrapping about her ankles, unsettling her. She didn't consider herself an overly fanciful person, but this instant, she might as well have been a timid church mouse for all that her heart was racing. Peering up at the sliver of moon that hovered above, she surged to her feet, bending hurriedly to retrieve the remainder of her garments.

Her eyes sought the metallic glimmer of her dagger beneath the pile of her clothing, and the downy hairs at her nape prickled when she failed to find it.

For the love of Christ, where could she have put it?

What good were clothes if she were dead. Dumping her gathered bundle, she lifted the other shoe to peer inside, thinking mayhap she'd placed the small dagger within it, but it wasn't there, and she stifled a curse, fearing God was like to banish her to purgatory for an eternity already for her irreverence. Damnation, but she couldn't help it.

Where could it possibly be?

Another twig snapped, closer this time, and Page decided she didn't need the dagger after all. No sooner was her decision made when there was a hideous outcry. In the next instant they appeared—three barely discernible figures scrambling from the woods.

She didn't linger to discover their intent.

Shrieking in fear, Page bolted, flinging the shoe behind her. An answering curse rang out, but she didn't bother turning to see what damage it may have inflicted —minimal, if any, she was certain, for the sole was soft and worn with age—more's the pity! She would've hoped to pluck out an eye with it.

Spouting oaths she didn't like to admit she knew, she ran with all her might towards the castle, crying out for aid, hoping Edwin, the gatekeeper, wasn't so inebriated that he thought her pleas a mere fancy of his cock-eyed dreams. Blundering sot! If he had been at his post to begin with, she might not be in this predicament— she mightn't have left the castle so effortlessly. And yet she knew the fault was not his, but hers. She should have known better—curse her rotten luck.

Her heart pounded faster with every stride she took.

Like a death knell, the sound of their footfalls came faster.

Closer.

She quickened her pace, surging forward with a burst of energy born of terror. Ignoring the pain that flared at her side, Page kept near to the stream lest she collide with the enormous oak tree that guarded the pathway to the castle. God forgive her, but she hoped they wouldn't see it and break their bloody necks for their efforts.

Her chest heaved. The pain in her side came sharper as she raced past the old oak. Still they remained behind her, their footfalls catching her shorter strides with too little effort.

She wasn't going to make it. She really wasn't going to make it.

Page wanted to weep with fear and despair.

Ahead of her, Aldergh Castle loomed, a distant silhouette against the ebony sky.

Distant and unreachable.

Like her father.

Her heart hammered.

She wasn't going to make it.

Still she ran, nearly toppling headlong into the water when the path curved too sharply before her.

Their voices chased her, indistinguishable and alien, like bats in the darkness of a cave, flying at her from all directions.

Judas, where were they now?

Ahead of her? Behind? Where?

She wasn't going to make it.

The stream wended its way before her, blanketed by a sheet of mist. A glimmer of hope sparked. Mayhap they couldn't swim? She didn't know many who could. Perchance she could lose them beneath the mist.

A hand reached out, brushing her leg and nearly snatching her shift, followed by a profusion of indecipherable curses when her pursuer realized he'd missed. But the shock of his touch made Page's decision for her. She couldn't afford to take the time to consider the consequences. Arms flailing, she hurled herself into the stream. Her legs followed like deadweight. She landed smack upon her belly, icy water striking her full in the face. The impact reverberated through her, numbing her senses, but Page recovered her faculties quickly. Ignoring the sting of her flesh, she swam with all her might toward the opposite shore, all the while listening for sounds of pursuit behind her. Relief flowed through her when there were none.

Thank you, God! Thank you! she prayed.

Even after reaching the bank, there was still no evi-

THE MACKINNON'S BRIDE

dence of her pursuers, only shouts and curses she couldn't quite decipher—coming from somewhere on the opposite shore. But she didn't dare feel triumphant. If they were even vaguely familiar with the lay of the land, they would know that, but a few furlongs ahead, the stream ended and they would once again meet en route to the castle. Page didn't intend to take that risk. Lifting herself from the water, sopping to her bones, she made instead for the sanctuary of the forest. They might expect her to run for the castle—as instinct was crying out she do. Logic told her she would fare much better doing the unexpected.

If she made it into the safety of the woods—and perchance climbed a tree—she could wait for them to tire of searching and then go home. They were likely no more than brigands—she their luckless prey. She was certain that, given the choice of searching all night for some faceless woman to rut with or seeking out more profitable victims, they would tire sooner rather than later and leave her be.

Encouraged, she ran, panting, her heart pounding. Her wet undergown clung to her legs. Running, she tried not to trip as she peered behind to make certain they were not following, and once again relief surged through her, for there was no sign of her attackers.

Euphoria washed over her.

She was going to make it, after all!

That, regrettably, was her last coherent thought, before she turned and collided with a tree.

At least Page thought it was a tree.

The impact knocked her flat upon her back and left her reeling. She lay there, stupefied, staring up at a Goliath of a man.

Mercy, but he was tall.

Within the instant, she was surrounded by the rest of them. Their faces a blur in her benumbed state, they seemed to be leering down at her, disembodied teeth shining in the moonlight.

"Ach, mon, ye've gone and made her daft," she understood one to say.

"Eh, she'll come aboot," assured another.

Scots.

Bloody damned Scots.

She could tell by their brogue, but that was her last thought before darkness swallowed her.

CHAPTER 2

The scent of grain surrounded her... golden fields abloom... Page was running through them... running... running...

For a befuddled instant, she thought she'd died and entered the hallowed gates of Heaven.

Had they killed her already?

Nay... she didn't think so.

A groan sounded in her ears and she thought it might be her own. Her body felt... squashed... broken, detached somehow.

At least she was able to feel.

Run, she commanded herself—run!

Her body jerked into full cognizance only to find that she was being jostled between them inside a meal sack—a meal sack. Tiny leftover grains stuck to her face.

She wondered hysterically if they were going to kill her now, stuffed as she was, like some pesky cat to be drowned in the river.

At least the sack wasn't filled with stones, she reasoned.

But it seemed they were moving away from the bank... into the woods... She sensed the darkness close about them and struggled in vain, screaming until her throat turned raw. Curse them. Her abductors seemed impervious to her struggles.

Hysterical laughter bubbled from the depths of her.

Her father's prophecy was about to come true. Judas! He'd always said she'd be her own ruin someday. That someday was now.

She should never have come out at night to wade alone. She should have brought Cora with her—now she was going to die for her recklessness.

What an empty-headed fool she was.

"Release me," she shrieked, tearing at the sack with renewed determination. "Release me at once!"

Heart pounding, Page twisted and fought like a savage, kicking and bucking against their hold upon the sack. "Release me this instant, bloody rotten heathens —let me go!"

They broke into fits of laughter—but didn't bother to comply.

Well, she wasn't about to make this painless for them. Twisting and turning, she vowed that when they finally released her, she was going to pluck out their eyes.

If only she had her dagger.

But it lay somewhere along the bank along with— Sweet Mary!

Her struggles ceased at once with the realization that she was half naked to boot. Pure hysteria welled within her. She couldn't have made it easier for them to ravage and murder her had she sent them bloody invitations.

And no one would miss her.

Her stomach wrenched.

Aye, she'd be fortunate enough if her father even noticed she was gone after a sennight. He was more attentive to his Scots guest than he'd ever considered being to her. Well, she thought despairingly, mayhap he would take note sooner, if only because she seemed to have the most unfortunate gift for getting herself into his ill graces—just as she had a genius for getting herself into trouble. She was ill fated, to be sure. He was bound to miss the mayhem.

Fueled with a fresh wave of desperation, Page began her struggles again, only to be jabbed with a knee for her efforts.

Damn their bloody heathen hides.

She didn't care if they bruised her body until every inch of it was blue, she wasn't going to simply lie quietly while they raped and murdered her.

The sound of new voices stopped her struggles abruptly.

Suddenly, without warning, the sack was overturned and she was tossed unceremoniously upon the ground.

Page shrieked in outrage.

Reeling, she surged to her feet, only to sway dizzily backward and fall back upon her rump to stare, dumbfounded, at the barest pair of limbs she'd ever laid eyes upon.

Strong male legs.

Bloody rotten luck.

Another giant.

Her gaze flew upward and locked with eyes that gleamed with amusement at her expense, eyes that were filled with arrogance and cool disdain. Sweet Jesu, she'd seen that look too oft to mistake it. Like everyone else, he'd peered down his nose at her and found her wanting.

Well, she didn't care what the dirty Scot thought of her. Particularly as he was likely to be planning ahead to her demise now that he'd changed his mind about the ravaging.

She didn't look much like an earl's daughter—more like a drowned wretch, Iain thought—save for the eyes.

Nestled within them he spied all the haughtiness of her breeding.

Impudent little wench.

Like some mad, cornered hare, she looked ready to pounce upon him. And yet, for the briefest instant, when she'd first peered up at him, a flash of pain had shadowed those soulful dark eyes. A trick of the moonlight, no doubt, for as quickly as it had appeared, the look vanished, replaced by that fierce glare of open defiance she now wore.

That and little else, he couldn't help but note.

A shudder coursed through him, for he hadn't missed her bold appraisal of his legs. Had she been the least bit nearer and chanced to peer up his tunic, she might have earned herself an eyeful. Despite her bedraggled appearance, he found himself fully aroused by the sight of her. Christ, that body—even cloaked in mist and shadows, her graceful curves were more than discernible. Even through the silken shadows, her perfect breasts rose to tempt him, dark nipples plainly visible, teased by the cold night air.

His brows drew together as he considered her state of undress. Garbed in little more than her sodden shift, she seemed completely oblivious, in her anger, to the sight she presented to his men.

Shaking his head over her foolishness, he made an effort to dispel the images that accosted him: long luscious legs wrapped about his waist... full, ripe breasts arched in passion, beckoning to his lips... He knew the taste of them would be like manna from heaven.

Bones o' the bloody saints, he was just a bloody man.

What sort of father allowed his only daughter to roam free at will? At night, no less?

"She was just where they said she would be," his cousin disclosed.

"So she was." Iain's voice was husky with lust he couldn't quite eschew.

He didn't want her, he told himself, shaking himself out of his reverie. No good would come of wanting such an impertinent wench.

He crossed his arms and glowered down at her. "D' ye make it a habit to bathe yourself afore God and man alike?" He wasn't certain why he'd asked the question; he knew she must. 'Twas how they'd managed to find her, after all, and yet he found himself oddly vexed over the notion.

She lifted her chin, denying him an answer, her dark eyes flaring with undisguised anger, and Iain tried not to chuckle at her mettle. Here she was, no more than a slip of a lass, challenging him before his men, when even his enemies dared not face him so directly.

Fools, all, for he intended to discover the name of the Judas who'd dared to hand his son over to the bloody English for barter. He planned to rip out the serpent's tongue and stuff it up his bloody arse.

The grim reminder of his business with FitzSimon's daughter turned his glimmer of good humor once more to rage. His jaw turned taut, and he asked her pointedly, "Have you no tongue, wench?"

Like the legendary phoenix rising up from its ashes, she stood to face him, her hands clenching at her sides.

"Have you no breeding?" she returned scathingly. "Scot!" She hurled the epithet at him with an imperious lift of her brows, and despite his anger, it was all Iain could do not to laugh outright at the unexpected insolence. "What concern is it of yours where I should bathe?"

Iain was incredulous at her brazenness, her foolhardiness. Were he any other man... Christ! Could she truly not know her folly? His gaze raked her from her wet, plaited head, down her long graceful limbs, wholly exposed by her wet gown, and on to her bare toes before returning to her face, carefully avoiding those delightfully tempting breasts, as he added, "You've an insolent tongue, wench. Need I remind—"

"Aye, well you shall have no tongue at all when my father hears of this," she returned boldly.

Although she had to overcome the urge to take a wary step backward, Page held her ground and drew herself up to her full height. For an instant he seemed bemused by her reply, and then he arched a brow.

Challenging her?

"Truly?" he asked, and his smile turned cold.

Page shuddered at the bold way he appraised her once more. No man had ever dared look at her so— with such undisguised lust. It sent a jolt of alarm racing through her. And to her dismay, the tiniest thrill.

Another quiver shook her.

Mayhap she'd lost her wits when she'd collided with his monolith of a friend?

She cast a glance at the others and found them all staring, mouths agape. Page hoped their idiocy wasn't contagious. They were half-wits. Every last one of them.

"Catching glowworms perchance?" she asked.

A ridiculous sight, the lot of them; their brows drew together in unison and they cast surprised glances at each other, then snapped their mouths shut.

"Bones o' the saints, wench! 'Tis no wonder your da lets you aboot in the middle o' the night," the leader said. "He's like to be hopin' ye'll lose your way in the dark."

Page's heart wrenched at the barb. It stung like the rude crack of a palm across her face. She swallowed her pride and blinked away angry tears, determined not to betray her emotions to these heartless barbarians. He couldn't possibly know how near to the mark he'd struck, or how much the truth hurt.

Nor would he care, she was certain.

Her eyes burned. "My father shall have you all beheaded for this insult to me," she swore, and couldn't help but note that his gaze roamed her body once more —this time more slowly and with a turn of his lips that both infuriated and appalled her.

Confused her.

Another frisson raced down her spine.

Forsooth, but the man had a mouth more exquisite than any man had a right to own. She blinked.

What the devil was wrong with her? How could she stand here contemplating lips, when her very life might well be at stake? Her honor at the very least.

Why, then, didn't she feel more afeared?

By all accounts she should be. Everything about the man bespoke danger—everything from his barbarously unclad legs to his fierce expression proclaimed him a savage Scot. If she'd thought his brutish friend tall, this one was immense, towering above them all.

And yet... something about him seemed harmless ... vaguely familiar, too.

Page narrowed her gaze, studying the shadowed contours of his face. She couldn't know him. Could she?

It was dark. Mayhap her mind was deceiving her. Then again, mayhap she was completely addle-pated from the injury to her head. Certainly she was mad to even wonder whether those lips were so beautiful in the bold light of day.

"Who are you?" she demanded, crossing her arms over her breasts, feeling wholly exposed to him suddenly, despite the shift she wore and the veil of darkness surrounding them.

He said naught, merely stood, staring, with that infuriating turn of his lips, and Page asserted, "Have you no tongue, Scot?"

For the space of an instant he seemed taken aback by the question, stunned even, and then he surprised her with the rich timbre of his laughter.

His men didn't seem quite so amused. And bless the saints, Page didn't know why he should be either. Her father would have slapped her face by now. Never would she have been so brazen with him.

"'Tis the MacKinnon you're speaking to," growled one of his lickspittles. "Ye'll be watchin' your tongue, wench, lest you lose it."

"MacKinnon!"

Startled, Page took a step backward—less in response to his warning than her shock. Her fear was at once forgotten in her indignation.

'Twas not simply any savage Scot who stood before her, but *the* savage Scot.

It was his child her father had granted safe harbor to as a favor to David of Scotland. The boy was to become a ward of the English court. Page had spent enough time with the youngster to know he'd been ill used. How dare this beast deal with his son so cruelly that his own king should be forced to intervene to safeguard him. Poor wretched child! 'Twas no wonder the cur seemed so familiar. Father and son shared the same look—albeit one morphed by age.

This face was hard and ruthless, despite the laughter that softened those exquisite lips. And ruthless was precisely what he was. Rumor had it, even, that he'd murdered his poor young wife after she'd borne him a son. "Blackguard!" she spat. "How dare you show your face here."

He arched a brow at her. "I came for my son, wench. Did you think I would not?"

Came for his son, indeed!

Page was so infuriated that she thought she would box his ears. She couldn't care less about the consequences, so angry was she.

"Aye, well, you'll be leaving without him," she returned. "My father will never release him to you." Whatever else he might be, her father was no imbecile.

Mayhap he held no tenderness for the boy, but he would never dare risk Henry's wrath by returning the wretched child to his vile father. "Have you not done enough to harm him already?"

The MacKinnon stiffened at her accusation.

Good. Let him feel guilt. If he had a heart within that overgrown chest. "Aye, disabuse yourself of the notion he'll be returning to Scotia with you, for your son is to be protected by King Henry himself," she persisted, when his eyes betrayed alarm. "Tomorrow he will be out of your hands and safe from you evermore."

The muscles in his jaw clenched, and he seemed momentarily unable to speak.

Page hoped he was feeling regret. The poor boy had come to them beaten and mute, fearful of even meeting her gaze. No matter that she'd tried to draw him out, he kept his silence still. "What have you done to that poor child that he fears even to speak? You should be deeply ashamed of yourself, sir."

He found his tongue suddenly, and Page winced at the thunder in his tone.

"What d' ye mean Malcom willna speak?" He advanced upon her, his look darkening, his arms falling away to his sides, fists clenching.

Page stumbled backward at his murderous expression, the obvious threat in his stance. "Y-you sh-should know," she stammered. She took another prudent step backward.

He continued to advance upon her, demanding, "What have you done to my son?"

Page gasped and took another leap backward, her hand flying to her breast. "Me? You! What have you done to him?" What gall that he should cast the blame for his son's affliction at her own feet. "He came to us just so."

"What in God's name have you done to my son?" he persisted.

21

The MacKinnon towered over her, glaring down fiercely, and Page thought she might never catch another breath. Her heart vaulted into her throat, strangling her.

He was too close.

She winced, noting his distressed expression, and was no longer quite certain the tales told of him were all true—leastways not those accusing him of misusing his son, for he seemed ready to rent her to shreds at the very notion that his son might be harmed.

The rest of the tales were quite easy to believe, for the man standing before her appeared more than capable of ripping the heart from any man—or a woman —with little effort.

Now she was afeared.

Her heart thrashed madly against her ribs until she thought the strain would kill her.

He spat a mouthful of indecipherable oaths, and commanded his men, "Take her! Bind her to the stoutest tree you can find. I mean to be certain she remains come morning light."

They seized her by the arms.

"Nay! My father will flay you alive, MacKinnon."

She shrieked in outrage when he dared to turn his back upon her and walk away, leaving her at the mercy of his men.

"Brute! Oaf! He'll gouge out your eyes."

He stopped abruptly and turned to assess her once more, this time without the slightest pretense at civility.

"He values you, then?"

Did he challenge her? Page thought her heart would burst with misery at his question. For a moment she couldn't speak to answer. "Of course he values me." She felt the burn of tears in her eyes, but refused to shed them. Tears were for the feeble, and she was anything but. Aye, her father had taught her well. She lifted her chin, daring him to refute her. "I am his daughter, am I not?"

He didn't respond.

Did he know? Could he possibly know? Was he laughing at her behind that turbulent gaze?

Rotten knave. She knew he must be.

"Good," he said, and continued to scrutinize her with narrowed eyes. "You say King Henry comes on the morrow to take my son? Where does he plan to take him?"

Page straightened to her full height, her lips curving with a smugness she didn't quite feel. "Aye, he comes, blackguard. And when he does, he'll—"

"What?"

Her heart twisted. What, indeed, would he do? Naught, she determined, for she knew Henry not at all and she doubted he would trouble himself for her benefit if her father did not value her. And her father did not. She swallowed the knot that rose in her throat and tried to wrench free of her captors. To no avail.

"Where does he think to take my son, wench?"

"My father will tear out your bloody hearts and I will stand by and watch and laugh."

Unaffected, he advanced upon her, demanding, "Where?"

Page loathed herself for cowing to him in that instant. "I-I don't know."

His gaze scrutinized her through the night shadows. Recognizing the lie?

"For truth?"

Her voice sounded much too feeble to her own ears. "Aye."

"No matter," he yielded. "Henry will never set eyes upon my boy. Silence her now, Lagan! I dinna wish to hear another bloody word come out o' her Sassenach mouth."

CHAPTER 3

Never in the whole of his life had Iain met a wench so troublesome—or so impertinent. He was mightily glad to know her father would deal with him come morning, because he couldn't wait to be rid of her.

The sooner the better.

And yet, much as he wished to summon FitzSimon from his bed at this hour, to ransom Malcom this very instant, if the wench spoke true, and King Henry arrived on the morrow, then that was one more advantage he could press if the need arose.

He'd never been one to waste opportunity. 'Twas said that, forsaking comfort, and in favor of celerity, the English king oft rode with a minimum retinue. Iain was counting on it. He had nigh forty men at his command —more than most traveled with at best—more than enough to give FitzSimon pause.

Tomorrow would have to be soon enough.

In the meantime, he was going to have to keep the mouthy wench bound and gagged, lest she drive his men to murder.

Or him to worse.

Of all the impudent, foolhardy... plucky females.

She'd actually defended his son. Against him! The notion was ludicrous, and yet...

She'd said Malcom would not speak.

Iain tried to consider the news rationally—for Malcom's sake. 'Twould serve no purpose at all to be losin' his wits now when he needed them most.

The fact that FitzSimon's shrewish daughter thought him responsible for Malcom's ills led him to believe that she, in truth, had had no part in his affliction.

Else she protected her da...

Though after the manner in which she spoke of him, Iain doubted she thought he needed protecting. She made her bastard da out to be some venerable champion. To hear her speak, she bore little fear of Iain's reprisal against him. On the contrary, she expected her da to flay him alive. He shook his head with wonder over the callowness of her words.

'Twas like to be the simple fact that Malcom was frightened that kept his tongue stilled. His son liked to think of himself as a man, but he was yet a child, with a child's heart.

Christ, but when he discovered the traitor...

His jaw clenched.

It had to have been someone from within their clan, for the bastard had left no witnesses, nor evidence, to betray himself. He'd simply come, like the proverbial thief in the night, stolen Malcom, and then had fled, leaving no one the wiser.

She had defended his son.

Iain shook his head in wonder. He didn't know whether to kiss her soundly for her unbiased defense of Malcom, or to strangle her where she stood.

Damnation, she was a sharp-tongued wench with a mouth the likes o' which he'd never known a woman to possess in his lifetime. He grinned then, despite himself, because he couldn't believe she'd been so barefaced.

Catching glowworms, indeed.

He chuckled. The looks upon his men's faces had been worth a king's ransom.

Aye, he was going to have to remain close to the wench, he resolved—but first things first. Right now he intended to retrieve her garments from the riverbank where she'd likely left them—he had to believe she had worn more clothes than those she bore upon her back just now. The last thing he needed was a bloody distraction.

He couldn't think straight while staring at those luscious breasts of hers. And damnation. Who could help but stare when she stood all but naked before him?

Which brought him to wonder yet again... what sort of man allowed his only daughter to roam the countryside free and naked as Eve?

Ach, but there were daughters who were governable, and daughters who were not, he reasoned.

Had she been his wayward daughter, Iain might have locked her safely within a tower until the day she pledged her vows.

Impertinent, sour-mouthed wench.

While the rotten lot of them lay snoring upon their backs, Page sat, shivering with her back against a tree, arms twisted and bound behind her and a sour-tasting rag wedged within her mouth.

Loathsome Scots.

Not that she could have slept anyway, for she was much too miserable with worry and regret. Forsooth, she should never have come out alone. Why couldn't she be content to simply sit within the solar and sew like other ladies?

Why couldn't she be what her father wished of her?

Then again, she reflected somewhat bitterly, the answer to that question might better be known if only she knew what her father wished of her.

The truth was that Page couldn't please him—never

had been able to please him. And what was worse, she wasn't certain she wished to try anymore.

She might not have to after tonight.

The thought sent a shudder through her.

What would they do to her once they discovered her father didn't want her? The truth was that her father would no more give up the boy than he would spit in the king's eye—not for her, he wouldn't.

Well, she told herself, she didn't care.

She truly didn't.

But her eyes stung with hot, angry tears.

Well, she'd soon enough discover what they would do ... if she didn't manage an escape ... so she set her wiles to that end. Trying not to deliberate on the dire possibilities should she fail, she regarded her captors.

To her dismay, the original four had not come alone as she'd first suspected. Worse, she couldn't precisely make out how many there were, for their limbs and bodies merged together in the darkness—like cadavers huddled together in a common grave.

There were a lot of them, she surmised.

They'd dragged her shrieking like a fishwife into their camp, and the lascivious looks she'd gotten from the lot of them had made her resolve never to look at a man full in the face again.

Overweening boors.

The MacKinnon in particular.

She shuddered, remembering the way he'd looked at her, the knowing look in his eyes.

Unreasonably, she found herself wondering what color his eyes were. Blue? Green? She hadn't been able to make them out in the darkness, but she was certain they wouldn't be so common as hers. Alas, but there was naught ordinary about the infuriating man.

He had yet to return.

Not that she cared one whit whether she ever saw his too comely face again, she assured herself, but—

27

well, damnation, mayhap she did, and frowned at the admission, her brow furrowing as she contemplated that fact. 'Twas only natural, she reasoned, that she wouldn't wish to be left alone with these men of his. She didn't trust them.

But had she anymore cause to trust the MacKinnon? a little voice nagged.

It wasn't precisely that she trusted him. Just that she didn't mistrust him quite so much—although why she should feel even thus toward him, she couldn't begin to comprehend. He was likely no better than the rest.

Soon after she'd been bound to the tree, he and the one called Lagan had departed camp. She imagined they were scouting Aldergh's defenses as a precaution.

Good for them, because her father was going to tell them to go to Hell, she was aggrieved to admit. It mattered not what she'd said, or what she secretly hoped, she wouldn't delude herself into thinking otherwise. They were stuck with her, didn't they know.

If she didn't freeze to death first.

Or if she didn't manage to escape.

She heard their voices long before she spied them and her stomach lurched as they came from the woods. The MacKinnon and the one called Lagan—the boor who had shoved the despicable rag into her mouth. They stood whispering beside the fire. Something else she could thank them for—setting her so far from the fire's heat, as wet as she was, and leaving her to freeze in the chill night air. Thoughtless, infuriating barbaric wretches.

The firelight flickered between them, casting its copper tint against their bodies and faces, distorting their images. Caught between the eerie glow of the flame and the obscurity of shadow, the MacKinnon cut a daunting figure, to be sure. Dressed in a black woolen tunic and cloaked in his belted breacan, he stood at least six inches taller than her father in his thick leather-lined boots. In a leonine display of masculinity, his dark wavy mane was unbound and fell below his shoulders, and his stance was one bred of confidence. He was a man born to lead, she couldn't help but cede.

Was he a murderer, as well?

The prospect made her throat tighten with renewed fear.

Her heart lurched. What would he do when he discovered her father wouldn't deal with him?

She couldn't even begin to make out their discourse, and then the one called Lagan left the MacKinnon's side to jostle another man awake.

He whispered something into the man's ear and the man rose at once, shaking off his slumber. Together the two spoke to the MacKinnon and then stumbled off into the shadowy realm beyond the fire's brightness.

Only Page and the MacKinnon remained still awake.

Starting at the realization, Page turned to look at him and gasped to find him simply standing there, watching her, the firelight playing upon his face, making his harsh features appear all the harsher for the contrasting shadows. She prayed he couldn't see her where she sat so far from the light, and was relieved when he turned and bent to retrieve something that lay beside the fire. Her relief was short-lived, however, for he pivoted suddenly and came toward her, and a shock of pure hysteria skittered through her.

Reacting instinctively, Page slammed her head backward against the tree trunk and swore a silent oath, closing her eyes, feigning sleep. She was being foolish. She knew it, and still couldn't help herself. She couldn't face him just now. She didn't know why, she just couldn't. Tears sprang to her eyes.

He values you? the ghost of his voice whispered in her ear, and the question tormented her. She had to remind herself he'd not spoken it aloud. 'Twas merely her imagination mocking her, making her the fool.

His footfall was light, but Page could make out the soft sound of moss surrendering beneath his leather-soled feet and knew the moment when he stood before her.

Bare limbed.

The thought accosted her from nowhere, and her heart gave a little start, beating faster as he crouched down beside her—at least she imagined he crouched. She could swear that he did, for she thought she felt the heat of his breath against her cheek.

A sigh blew across her face.

Or had she imagined it?

Merciful Lord, was he watching her so intently?

Nay... oh, nay...

Her heart began to flounder, and she tried not to panic, tried to pretend he wasn't hovering so close, scrutinizing her every breath, but failed miserably. She knew that he was, and was only grateful for the veil of darkness to conceal her when she felt the telltale flush creep up from her breast, to her throat and face, warming her.

And then suddenly her heart slammed to a halt, for he touched her—sweet Mary, the way that he touched her.

Her breath left her, and her body quivered as his hand cupped her face, the gesture so much a tender caress. She leaned her face hungrily into the warmth of his palm, and then realized what she'd done, and her eyes flew wide. She drew in a breath, and lifted her face to his.

Their gazes met, held, locked.

He didn't remove his hand, and Page, though startled by the embrace, could scarce protest with the rag still filling her mouth. Scarce could she breathe. Scarce could she think.

With a gentleness that belied his strength and size, he brushed his thumb across the hollow above her cheek, and Page closed her eyes and felt the sting of tears anew.

How inconceivable it was that this man, this stranger, her captor, would be the very first to touch her so gently?

"Dinna be weepin'," he whispered.

Was she? Page nearly choked on her denial. She hadn't even realized.

He removed the gag from her mouth and brought it to his nostrils. They flared at the stench and he glowered, tossing it away. She swallowed with difficulty. "Damn Lagan," he grumbled, and shook his head in disgust.

Page couldn't find her voice to speak, but it wouldn't have mattered, she wouldn't have known what to say.

So near, his face lost none of its masculine beauty.

It held her mesmerized.

He seemed so young to lead, she thought, despite that his hair proclaimed elsewhere; dark as it was, the shock of white at his temples stood out distinctly against the black of his hair. It was braided, she noticed for the first time—the silver at his temples. How old was he? His youthful face declared six and twenty, no more, but his hair bespoke some two score years and more. His cheekbones were high, his nose perfectly aquiline, and his lips... his lips were the sort to make a woman fancy stolen kisses. And his eyes... she still couldn't make out their color in the darkness, though she tried.

Her heart beat a steady rhythm in her ears.

"Ye've my word, lass, that ye'll no' be harmed." His voice was low and husky. "Dinna look so woeful."

He stroked her cheek, and confusion flooded her. Why was he being so gentle? Judas, but she didn't know how to deal with this.

Page jerked her face away from his touch. "I—I was not."

He arched a brow. "Weeping?"

He lifted his hand abruptly and Page flinched, thinking he meant to strike her for the denial, but he brought his thumb to his lips, instead, sinking his teeth there. Watching her, he sucked the salt of her tears from his flesh. "Were ye no', lass?"

A shiver coursed through her at his gesture—the way that he addressed her—the way he continued to stare. She tried to ignore the heat that suffused her under his scrutiny, taking refuge in her anger. "No. I was not."

"Nay," he agreed, still suckling at his thumb. "Of course not. You're much too... fearless. Are ye no'?"

He suckled his thumb an instant longer, then withdrew it from his mouth, and Page lapped at her lips gone suddenly dry. She swallowed convulsively.

"Still... ye've my word... ye'll no' be harmed."

Page closed her eyes, trying to blot out the image of him kneeling before her. "How gracious," she drawled, concealing a quiver. She opened her eyes once more, narrowing them, and her voice was steadier with anger. "In the meantime, my hands are bruising at my back."

His lips hinted at a smile—the rogue—a smile that snatched her breath away and made her heart flitter wildly. It should have made her yearn to slap his face instead. Curse him for that. And her, too, for allowing herself to lose her composure over a comely face.

Her wits were addled for certain.

"Some things are necessary," he told her without the slightest trace of remorse, "but verra well, I'll grant ye a moment's respite." He fell back upon his rump and reached behind her to free her hands.

"How generous... for a heathen Scot."

He merely chuckled at that, and it multiplied her confusion tenfold. What was wrong with the fool? Did he not realize he was supposed to be angered by her quips? Page wasn't certain what to make of him—less so by the instant.

He released her hands, and then slipped his fingers across the small of her back. She squealed in alarm, arching away from his touch. "What!" she shrieked, "do you think you are doing?"

He didn't bother to beg her pardon, nor to remove his hand. It burned her flesh even through her shift.

"You're wet," he announced.

"Am I really?" She recovered her composure and glared at him vengefully. "How peculiar. I wonder if 'tis because you abducted me wet from my swim... refused to allow me to dry... and then thrust me away in a damp corner far from the heat of the fire."

She tried to shrug away from his touch, to no avail. "Remove your hand from my person this instant."

His brows drew together, though his eyes glinted with unconcealed amusement. "You're an impudent wench," he said, with too little heat, but he complied at once. "Did your da beat you oft?"

Once again Page found herself aggrieved by his question. "Nay!" she countered, but she swallowed the ache that rose like a goose egg in her throat. In truth, her father hadn't cared enough even for that. She averted her gaze. "How dare you speak of him so!" she mustered herself to say. "My father... he would never..." She rubbed at her wrists, trying to ease the pain that flowed into them.

Naught could ease the ache in her heart.

"Well, then, mayhap he should have..."

Page glared at him.

"Let me see your hands."

It was a command, no matter that it was spoken so softly, and Page bristled. "I can see to them myself, thank you."

He sighed. "As you wish."

"Aye, 'tis my wish."

"You're a stubborn fashious wench," he apprised her.

"And you—" From the corner of her eye, she saw that he lifted his hands toward her, and Page flinched again. Aha! Now it began.

He moved quickly and she was staggered to find he merely placed a dry gown over her head. Her own gown, for the material was familiar, soft and worn with age. The scent was hers too.

And it was toasty warm.

He'd gone after it—but not only had he retrieved it, he'd gone so far as to dry it before the fire.

Shock filtered through her. Stunned, she allowed him to draw the gown over her body, smooth it down, and like a poppet, she thrust out her arms to place within the sleeves.

Her throat squeezed shut so that she could not speak. No one had ever elicited so many emotions from her as did this stranger. No one had ever looked after her so. No one had ever worried whether she was comfortable, or hungry, or lonely...

Her heart wrenched, and once again, despair threatened to strangle her.

She couldn't believe he was treating her so... kindly.

He was staring at her strangely... as though he would read her thoughts. And then his expression shuttered and his brows drew together, as he commanded, "Place your hands at your back."

Page recanted her opinion of him at once and gave him a glare he was like never to forget.

He cocked his head, and entreated, "Dinna make me force ye, lass..."

He could, she realized, and she gritted her teeth. Still, she couldn't make herself obey quite so easily. "You're a wretch, you realize?"

He chuckled, seeming impervious to her wrath. The

man wore his good humor like an accursed suit of armor.

"So I've been told," he confessed without apology. "Now place your hands at your back so I can bind them."

"Why can you not leave them free?" she protested, but obeyed nonetheless. Better to bide her time and choose her battles wisely.

It might help to know how many men she must do battle with and she wondered if he would tell her. "What have you to fear of me?" she asked, trying to sound casual. "You've fifty men and more..."

"Do I?" he answered noncommittally, peering up at her, his lips slightly crooked.

The wretch. He knew very well what she was asking and wouldn't even give her so meager a concession.

"As for your hands, wench, I'm simply no' foolhardy enough to allow ye to remain unfettered. I'll be needin' my sleep tonight and dinna have in mind to play nurse-maid to a foolish lass who doesna seem to know enough to keep her tongue stilled."

He reached behind her to bind her wrists together behind the tree, this time not so tightly. "I'm sorry Lagan was so harsh wi' ye," he said, testing the rope. Page cursed him for his small gesture. It only served to discompose her all the more.

She decided to ignore the apology—and the gesture, as well. "Surely you cannot expect me to sleep this way?"

"As I've said, lass..." He met her gaze. "Some things canna be helped." He proceeded, then, to adjust her gown so that her legs were covered, and Page bristled at his manipulations. She didn't wish to be appreciative— didn't want to be indebted to this man for any reason at all.

Did he treat his son so patiently? So thoughtfully? She couldn't help but feel a prick of envy at the notion.

Then, too, his actions only served to stress that her own father had lied yet again. The man before her no more beat his son than he would beat her. The thought both relieved and aggrieved her at once.

Only belatedly did she realize he was staring. "What are you looking at?" she asked peevishly.

His lips curved. "I should think it would be evident."

Page lifted both brows. "Are you wondering whether I'd make a tasty meal?" she ventured caustically. "Don't bother, you would find me bitter, I assure you."

His lips turned a scant more. "Tempting thought... but nay." His expression turned sober. He reached suddenly to brush a strand of tangled hair from her face, and Page fancied biting off his fingers, so much fury was she feeling. He merely held it there before her face, separating the damp strands between his fingers. "I was simply wonderin' at what ye were thinking, lass."

Lass.

The way he spoke the single word... as though it were laden with affection, made her shudder to her soul. "Naught," she lied, and nearly choked on her anger and her grief. "Only that my father—" He tucked the strand behind her ear, and her thoughts scattered to the winds.

"I know... he'll pluck oot my eyes," he finished for her, sighing, as he untucked the checkered blanket from his belt. He drew it from his back, and covered her with its formidable length.

To Page's dismay, it was warm with the heat of his body, and the bestirring scent of him rose to accost her; sunshine, horseflesh and man. Unreasonably, she found herself wondering whether his skin would be swarthy from the sun, or pale—somehow, despite the fact that she could not see him clearly through the shadows, she knew he would be dark from his labors in the sun.

She imagined him bare-chested, working... and then

realized he wore no breeches, and expunged the image at once, shocked by the realization. She felt herself grow warm even at the thought of him bared to the bottom. She found her protests silenced by the fierce pounding of her traitorous heart.

Until he stretched out before her suddenly and rested his head upon her lap. Then she found her voice at once. "What do you think you are doing, sir?"

He grinned up at her and had the audacity to wink, as well. "Sleeping, o' course." His long hair spilled over her lap, dark as ebony silk.

Mercy, he was bare bottomed beneath his tunic. "Not on me, you'll not."

"Ah, but ye've my breacan, lass," he pointed out quite reasonably, his voice silky. "Where else would ye have me sleep but here?"

"In a tree for all I care," she hissed, and squeezed her eyes shut. No use, the image accosted her behind closed lids with greater detail. "Stop calling me lass," she snarled, her eyes going wide.

His eyes glinted by the light of the moon. "Aye, lass," he agreed, "but then what would ye have me call ye if no' lass?"

He was mocking her, Page realized, and she found herself mute with anger and chagrin. She'd be hung by her toes before she'd reveal her name to the likes of him. "Oaf! Take your accursed breacan. I'll not allow you to sleep with me. Get off me."

His lips curved roguishly. "Ah, but I'm no' sleepin' wi' ye, lass. I'm sleepin' on ye," he pointed out, without the least compunction. "And nay, I'll not. What better way to keep you warm and free from harm?"

"What better way to watch me while you sleep, isn't that what you really mean?"

His grin widened. "That too."

"Arrogant wretch. I could spit upon you, you realize. And I might do that. Just you wait and see."

"Aye... ye could," he agreed, "but then I'd be sorely taxed and have to send Lagan to guard ye, instead and I'd be guessin' my randy cousin would take great pleasure in a buxom English lassie for a pilloo." He snuggled a little to prove his point, burying his face into her lap, nuzzling between her thighs. His chest expanded with his intake of breath, and he sighed audibly, sounding as contented as a child left to fill his belly with tarts.

Page's stomach floated into her ribs. Something deep inside her woman's core quickened at his brash male gesture, and heat trickled into her nether regions.

"Ach, but if ye dinna mind Lagan's wooing..."

He made to rise, and Page shrieked. "Nay!"

He chuckled, and lay back down at once. "I didna believe ye would relish the thought. G'nite, then, lass." He snuggled his head once more, like an innocent boy with his beloved mother.

But he was no innocent.

Nor was she beloved.

And he was lying within her lap.

Bare bottomed!

So was she for that matter.

"Overbearing brute," she spat, glaring at him fiercely. "The only harm I have to fear is harm from you."

"Then ye've naught to fear, at all," he countered, shifting indolently to his side and thrusting an oversized arm over her leg, cozying himself.

His arm was as big as her thigh.

"Anyway, ye've only the one night to endure," he assured her. "Tomorrow ye'll be safe again wi' your da."

She wanted to slap his arrogant face—wanted to sink her teeth into his flesh. What gall. "Get off!" she cried, and tried to free her hands. She muttered a fierce oath when they refused to come free from their bindings.

"Ach, wench, does your father know ye've such a rude tongue?" he asked her.

"'Tis none of your bloody concern. Beast! Rest yourself comfortable, why do you not?" She fought the urge to scream, knowing that the last thing she needed now was to wake his men.

"Dinna mind if I do," he murmured.

He had the nerve to close his eyes, dismissing her once and for all, and Page wished she could box his ears. She tried to move her legs, but he held her pinned irrevocably with his weight. She ceased her struggles only to summon every blasphemy she'd ever heard uttered. "Oaf," she hissed. "Swine! Knave! Scot!"

His lips curved into a smile.

Her brows collided. She tried to think of worse. "Beast! Demon! Black-hearted dev—"

"Ye're to be well commended on your mastery of the language," he said only.

"And you shall never get your son back," she swore in anger.

His expression sobered at once, although he still didn't open his eyes. "For your sake, lass, ye'd better be hopin' I do."

Page felt hopelessness seep into her very soul. She didn't know what to say. There was nothing left to say. She hadn't lied. The MacKinnon wouldn't get his son back. Her father wouldn't deal with him, and she was doomed. Doomed.

"If I thought ye would answer me true," he said after a long moment, "I would ask ye how my son fares." His eyes remained closed, but Page could see that his jaw remained taut. Worry was etched upon his features.

Curse him. For no matter that she might despise him, she found she couldn't bring herself to deny him the answer he sought. This one thing she could never withhold from an anxious father.

She sighed irascibly. "And if I were inclined to answer, I would say he fares well enough. He's not been abused, if 'tis what you fear—not by us. He simply will not speak, is all."

She could see the strain ease somewhat from his face, and found herself envious of his son, that he would have a father who fretted for him so. But then... fathers always valued their sons, did they not?

Her heart twisted painfully.

"Thank you," he whispered, and didn't deign to speak to her again.

Page averted her face, trying to ignore the stranger lying so intimately in her lap.

It was a futile gesture. Never in her life had she been more aware of another human being.

Safe again with her father, indeed.

The image was laughable. Security was something more than simply being free from harm. She knew that instinctively... and yet... she'd never truly known the feeling at all. Security was an alien concept, for it spoke to her of warmth and caring... a welcoming embrace... things she'd never known. She snorted and refused to look down upon him again until he was snoring beneath her. Fast asleep, and so easily. She ought to spit on him for truth. That would surely show him. She ought to drool all over him, too.

She writhed beneath him, trying to dislodge him from her limbs, to no avail. His weight, as he'd intended, made it impossible. Wretched, insufferable man.

She ought to scream in his ear—but that, she counseled herself, would only serve to wake the rest of his lechers, as well. Nor did she wish him to follow through with his threat and send Lagan to guard her instead. That one, she trusted the least of all.

And that brought her to another thought entirely... how pitiable it was that the one man who, by rights, should have been the most cruel was the one man who had been the most gentle.

It made too little sense.

Close upon the heels of that conclusion came her most nonsensical yet. It occurred to her, as she gazed down at her abductor's too comely profile, that she still hadn't yet determined the color of his eyes.

What would he do when her father refused to deal with him?

A frisson passed down her spine; fear?

She refused to acknowledge it.

Her last coherent thought before she dozed was not unlike that of a stray pup's, she reflected somewhat lamentably... for it occurred to her to wonder, then, if the MacKinnon would think to keep her.

God save her, but the foolish notion kindled just the tiniest spark of... something... Something so absurdly unreasonable, she refused to give it name.

CHAPTER 4

Though Iain forced his body to rest, his mind
worked ceaselessly through the night.

In his half-sensate state, he was wholly aware of
where he lay. He could hear the lassie's even, steady
breathing when she dozed at last, and her fitful slumber
when her dreams disturbed her.

He understood what those soft cries bespoke, for
his own nights were too oft plagued by demons—worse
since Malcom's abduction.

She was afeared, he realized, and guilt pricked at
him. Though she had too much pride to cower before
him while awake, in her dreams she could scarce keep
herself from it.

Despite that she was his enemy's flesh and blood,
Iain could only admire her. She'd masked her fear well,
had stood up to him like the fiercest of she-wolves. In
defense of his son, even. He only wished he didn't have
to resort to such measures that would cause her such
distress, but it couldn't be helped.

He would do anything to ensure Malcom's return.

He was full awake come first light, but loath to
move lest he wake her. For the longest interval he lay
listening to the easy rhythm of her breathing and savoring the delicate scent of the woman upon whom he

was so intimately nestled. He smiled, remembering the indignant tone of her voice when he'd dared insinuate himself upon her person.

He hadn't intended to be so bold—had only meant to sleep beside, not atop her—but the beguiling scent and sight of her had appealed to his baser instincts. And then, as he knelt over her, bantering words with her, listening to her stubbornly insist that she could fend for herself, that she didn't need his aid, and watching her stroke the blood back into her aching wrists, a strange tenderness had stolen over him. She wasn't so strong as she appeared, he sensed, and he fully intended to hasten the negotiations and see her safely returned to her father.

In truth, had she been any other woman, in any other circumstance, he might have liked to know her better.

His nostrils flared as he drew the essence of her into his lungs. His body reacted to her siren's perfume like a man famished and scenting Heaven's manna.

He opened his eyes and peered up into her face, trying to ignore the insistent burn of his loins.

She slept still, her head lolled forward. Touched by the faint morning light, her features were soft and delicate, hardened only by the memory of her stubborn temper. His lips curved slightly at the image of her standing before him, fists clenched at her sides.

Her father would pluck out his eyes, would he?

Vixen.

Her hair was the color of burnt umber. Tightly braided at her back, it was of undeterminable length, but the curls that fell loose about her face were long enough to sweep his forehead. The feel of it upon his flesh hardened him fully, and he had to restrain himself from drawing a lock into his mouth to savor. He reached out, instead, testing a soft curl between his fingertips.

Her lashes were long and sooty, he noted, darker than they might have been for one whose skin was so fair.

And her lips... they were her best feature, he decided, full and luscious... made to suckle.

His gaze shifted to her breasts. Rising and falling with her slumber, they were her next best attribute, he resolved. High and round and full, they were made to nourish a man's bairn... to whet a man's appetite... to be suckled and loved.

Bloody hell.

Iain snapped his eyes shut, constraining his thoughts, and shuddered. Lifting his head, he rolled free of her at once, telling himself that he had no need to be preoccupied with some wench's bosom—or her mouth.

Not now.

Certainly not hers.

Careful not to wake her, he knelt beside her, bracing his body against her so that she might lean into him, and then he reached behind the tree to unbind her wrists. Once liberated, she slumped sideways. He caught her and eased her down upon the ground to inspect her wrists for damage. He frowned as he examined them. Though he'd taken care not to bind them too tightly, they were chafed nevertheless. They must have pained her, and yet she'd spoken nary a word in protest. Gently he began to massage her wrists and hands, her fingers, and was surprised to find them coarse to the touch, not soft as he'd imagined. His brows furrowed as he turned them, considering their callused condition.

His gaze returned to her face to find her awake and watching, the strangest look nestled deep within her soulful eyes... eyes so deep a brown they recalled him to some cool, dark cavern. They drew him just as surely as his childhood sanctuary had—the great stone cairn that had lured him despite his father's admonitions and curses—with the promise of secrets to unfold.

What secrets had she to be discovered?

She jerked her hand free and scrambled to sit, scooting away. "Haven't you a bargain to put forth?" she asked him, her voice throaty from slumber. She lifted a brow. "Or have you changed your mind already, and decided you cannot part with me, after all?"

"Troublesome wench," Iain said without much heat. He shook his head, smiling despite himself. "You just dinna quit, do ye, lass? What do you think? That I'd risk my son for the comfort of some wench's lap? I dinna think so."

She rolled her eyes. "Of course not," she answered, hugging herself and eyeing him disdainfully. "I forget myself, but he's your son." And then she asked with narrowed eyes, "I wonder, would you do the same for a daughter?"

Iain merely stared at her, his sense of unease sharpening. "Of a certainty, lass," he answered after a moment's deliberation, his eyes narrowing thoughtfully. "I'd do the same for any one o' my clan. Would no' your da?"

She lifted her chin, cocked her head, and smiled slightly. "We shall see, shall we not?" Her smile deepened when he frowned.

She was provoking him, he realized.

Such a contradictory creature, she was, noble born, with mettle enough to vanquish a king's will, and yet—his gaze shifted to the hands she continued to stroke—those hands were more suited to a Highland lass than to a soft English miss. She followed his gaze, and seemed to understand his scrutiny, but she didn't bother to explain. He didn't bother to ask.

She wasn't his concern, Iain told himself.

And with that decided, he set Broc to guard her, and anticipated Lagan's and Ranald's return, pacing as he waited, all the while aware of the dagger looks FitzSimon's daughter cast at his back. He dismissed her for the time being, anxious for the bargain to be put forth.

It wasn't long before his cousin returned—without news of Henry's camp. It mattered not, Iain assured himself, he wouldn't need it. 'Twas a simple enough trade—the man's damned daughter for his son.

So why did he have a sense of doom creeping through his bones?

Something wasn't right.

He gathered the men he would ride with, leaving only Ranald to watch over FitzSimon's daughter. The greater their numbers, he reasoned, the better it would go for them. But he couldn't quite dispel the sense of unease slithering through him.

Nor could he banish FitzSimon's daughter from his thoughts.

Even as he awaited FitzSimon's emergence upon the battlements, her expression continued to haunt him. He kept seeing her face as he'd left her, proud but glum.

Something plagued him... something, though he could not put a finger to it as yet.

The bastard was taking too long.

Although Iain remained mounted, some crazed part of him paced before the barbican gates, shouting obscenities and rattling the damnable portcullis. He wanted his son back. He was desperate to have Malcom back.

And he was close—so close, and yet...

The man had been disinclined to meet face-to-face. He would, instead, hide behind stone walls and the bows of his men.

Nor did he appear much in a hurry to show himself.

Not the mark of a man who held great affection for his daughter and desired her return at any cost.

The realization lifted the hairs upon Iain's nape, and he found himself heartily glad for the slip of the lass's tongue. Though Lagan and Angus had scoured the area all night for the English camp, to no avail, the information might still work to his advantage—provided she'd spoken the truth and King Henry was, in fact, due.

Finally, when FitzSimon deigned to appear, Iain thought the man arrogant and unmoved. For one whose daughter had strayed into enemy hands, he reacted with too little concern over the news. Iain braced himself for the man's dubiety, telling himself that he might react the same without ample proof—perhaps he'd taken so long in showing himself because he'd been searching for his daughter within. With a wordless gesture, he demanded the lass's shoe from auld Angus. Angus complied at once, spurring his mount forward to hand it over. Seizing it, Iain prepared to fling it up into the ramparts. FitzSimon's declaration arrested his hand.

"So you have her, and what?" The older man shrugged, bracing his hands imperiously upon his hips. "What is it you wish of me, MacKinnon?"

It took Iain a full moment to comprehend the import of the question. Like the instant Mairi had flung herself from their chamber window, he felt helpless and momentarily unhinged. He could feel Malcom wrenched away suddenly, the possibility of his return dwindling, and the sensation was almost physical. He tempered himself, knowing his emotion would only get in the way now. There would be time enough to feel once he held Malcom within his embrace once more.

"My son for your daughter, FitzSimon," Iain proffered, disposing with ceremony. He flung up the shoe.

FitzSimon didn't bother to catch it, merely eyed it disdainfully as it fell behind the rampart wall, unclaimed at his feet. He laughed suddenly, uproariously, his belly heaving with the effort. "What need have I of that brat?" he asked, and shook his head. "I've sons aplenty and the means to forge myself more." He smacked his belly in a gesture of beneficence. "Take her if it please you, MacKinnon. I shall be keeping the boy, I think. I'm not witless enough to risk Henry's wrath over a bothersome wench—daughter of mine though she may be."

Iain could scarce believe his ears. Stupefied by the hard-hearted pronouncement, he apprised the man, "Refuse me, FitzSimon, and your daughter willna live to see the gloamin'."

FitzSimon grinned down at him. "Really? Well, then..." He turned to leave, unmoved by the threat. "Have yourself a pleasant journey home," he concluded, and chortled once more. Speaking low to his men, he dismissed Iain, once and for all.

Iain's destrier pranced beneath him, snorting in protest to the tensions in his body, and he eased the pressure of his knees, giving the animal respite. The feeling of foreboding was at once resolved, as the lass's words came back to him: I wonder, would you do the same for a daughter? she'd asked.

Christ and bedamned, she had known.

His gut twisted at what was revealed to him.

His jaw clenched. But he refused to concede defeat to the arrogant son of a whore. "FitzSimon!" he called out. The older man halted abruptly and pivoted to face him. "I'm afraid you've little choice in the matter," Iain contended, his tone unyielding. "You'll be sending down the boy now, or you'll be burying a king as well."

FitzSimon's hands fell from his sides, his interest piqued. "What say you, MacKinnon?"

"At this verra moment," Iain lied without compunction, "the rest o' my men have Henry's camp surrounded, awaiting word from me." He didn't care how he achieved his aim, only that he did. "As God is my witness," he swore, "deny me my flesh and blood this day, and I'll smite your bastard king with my verra own hands."

FitzSimon seemed to consider the threat. "You lie,

MacKinnon," he proclaimed after a moment's deliberation.

It was a challenge, Iain thought, and smiled. "D' you think so?" he asked coolly. His mount pranced restively beneath him, tossing its head and sidling backward, reflecting his own agitation. He snapped the reins. "But are you willing to risk it, FitzSimon? Shall I bring the whoreson here and slay him before your verra eyes? Will you believe it then?"

"Bastard," FitzSimon returned. "I think you would not. What, then, would prevent me from delivering your son to you skewered upon my lance?"

Iain's careful control snapped with the threat. He surged from his saddle, standing in the stirrups, his fury evident in every rigid inch of his body. "So help me, FitzSimon! I wouldst lay waste to every inch of this accursed land. I wouldna relent until your black heart rested in my hands. And I swear by Jacob's Stone that I willna rest until your blood salts this land. Return my son to me this moment!"

The older man seemed to recoil a little, but he took a step forward and said, glaring down, "Arrogant Scots bastard! What prevents me from putting an arrow through your bloody skull as we speak?" FitzSimon's men moved into position at the threat, prepared to carry it out, but FitzSimon raised his hand, staying them. "Best you tell me now," he demanded, "afore you tempt me too far."

Iain removed his helm in a defiant gesture, smiling resolutely. He was heartily glad for the lone man he'd left upon the rise in the distance.

"Look to my back, FitzSimon," he suggested, his expression one of utmost confidence. "Do you spy the watchman upon the hill?"

FitzSimon shaded his eyes and peered into the horizon as bade of him. His face, when he gazed down once more, was visibly strained. He'd obviously spied the glitter of mail.

There was no way FitzSimon could know how many men he'd brought with him, or how many lay in wait beyond the hill. He couldn't know that Iain had brought every last man save one to the bargaining table. "You canna reach him in time to prevent my men from carrying out their orders," Iain said. "They lie in wait, even as we speak. And still... the choice is yours. Do you care to try me, FitzSimon?"

FitzSimon's face became a mask of guarded fury. "How is it you learned of Henry's approach?" he asked, stalling shrewdly. He turned to speak harshly to one of the men, and the man hastened away.

Iain settled once more within the saddle, recognizing the first sign of concession. His smile hardened. "You have your daughter to thank for that," he yielded. And then advised, "And dinna be thinking to send a man to warn the king's army. I've anticipated that, as well. He willna make it oot the postern without an arrow through his skull."

FitzSimon lost his composure all at once, stamping his foot and carrying on furiously, shouting obscenities. Iain was taken aback by the callow display. "Damn that worthless bitch," he spat, and then stood, facing down Iain in silence.

Iain sensed his victory in that instant, and demanded, "Send down the boy, FitzSimon, and I'll leave be your king in one piece."

"How can I be certain you speak the truth, MacKinnon? Show me your proof."

"What proof can I offer, save Henry's head, FitzSimon? Nay, I'm afraid you'll have to trust me on this one."

"Trust you?" FitzSimon scoffed. "Only a fool would trust a bloody Scotsman. Even were I to return the boy, what assurance have I that you will not fall upon Henry still?"

"Only my word," Iain countered. "Send down my son and I pledge you my word that I'll no' harm your thieving king. All I wish is Malcom's return, naught more. Gi' him to me, FitzSimon, and I'll take my men and go at once."

FitzSimon yielded to another outburst of temper, cursing the Scots, cursing the fates, cursing David of Scotland for placing him in such an untenable position by calling upon his favor. He conferred with his men and then turned to address Iain. "Very well, I'll send down the boy. Take the witless bugger and be gone." He turned at once, not bothering to await Iain's response, and spoke to one of his men, then vanished from the ramparts. Though it seemed an eternity, it wasn't long before the portcullis was raised. Iain's heart hammered fiercely as he dismounted and began to walk toward the opening gates.

"Wait, laird," Dougal called out. "It could be a ruse."

Iain couldn't have stopped himself had he tried.

He didn't spot Malcom at first, hidden as he was behind the guard who preceded him, but when his little head peeked about the guard's massive frame, Iain thought his heart would burst with joy and relief. Malcom squealed and began to run toward him, and Iain lost all restraint in that instant and began to run as well. His son leapt up into his arms with a joyous cry, and Iain embraced him unashamedly. "Whelp!" he said hoarsely, and buried his face against his son's stout little shoulder. "Malcom, Malcom!"

"I knew you would come, da! I knew you would come!" Malcom snuggled against him. "I didna cry," he declared proudly. "I didna tell them anythin'— I swear, I didna!"

Iain laughed softly. "So I've heard, whelp. So you didna."

He was vaguely aware of the gates being closed against them, and then the portcullis being lowered as Malcom clung to him. "I knew you'd come," Malcom said again, and began to weep a child's tears. Iain braced the boy's head against his shoulder, comforting him, restraining his own raging emotions. "I'm goin' to take you home, son," he swore, his voice breaking.

"How very moving," FitzSimon declared from the ramparts above, his tone full of rancor. "Now take your bastard and go, MacKinnon."

Iain hung his head back, peering up into the ramparts to meet FitzSimon's gaze. "Aye," he agreed. "You've kept your end o' the bargain, FitzSimon, and now I'll keep mine. Your daughter will be returned to you within the hour."

"Nay!" FitzSimon shook his head vehemently. "Keep the bloody bitch."

Iain was struck entirely dumb. Surely he didn't mean that... He was but angry...

"If you return her to me," FitzSimon swore, "I'll rip out her traitorous tongue for her betrayal."

Iain held his son in stunned disbelief. "I have no need of the lass," he returned. "Surely you cannot mean..."

"Keep her, or kill her," FitzSimon declared. "I care not which—only get her the hell out of my sight." And then he withdrew, ending the discourse, once and for all, leaving Iain and his men to stare after him in shock.

CHAPTER 5

T he men seemed unsettled as they rode from the castle.

Iain knew they were both excited and relieved about Malcom's return, but they must have sensed his mood, for they remained reserved, waiting their turn to welcome Malcom back into the fold.

Iain was confused.

It didn't matter that the hostage awaiting them wasn't one of their own clan members, he anticipated her pain and sorrow just the same and found himself angered on her behalf. Uncharacteristically, his son clung to his back, accepting the men's good-natured ribbing and their welcome pats with subdued good cheer. Iain was scarce aware of the men's comings and goings. Try as he might, he couldn't forget the lass's prideful boasts.

She'd seemed so very certain.

Or had she?

Of course he values me... I am his daughter, am I not?

She hadn't appeared so certain, then, and he had wondered...

Have you changed your mind... decided you cannot part with me, after all...

Christ, but she wasn't his concern.

Surely her father would not carry out his threat if he returned her.

She was his daughter, after all, his flesh and blood. He was but angry. And determining so, he reached back to seize Malcom about the waist. He brought his son around to sit before him, inspecting him. His men drifted away, affording them privacy. Malcom giggled softly and latched on to him again, seeming afeared to release him lest he vanish from sight. Iain's heart squeezed within his chest.

"I've missed you, whelp," he said affectionately, tousling Malcom's fine golden hair. He had to restrain himself from beginning an interrogation then and there. More than aught, he wished to discover the name of the traitor, to ask how he'd been treated, to assure him it would never happen again, but now was not the time, he knew. All that mattered at the moment was that Malcom was safe—damned if he'd allow anything to part them ever again. Nay, he would question Malcom later, when his son felt himself secure once more... when FitzSimon's daughter was no longer his bloody concern.

❧

IT HAD BEEN YEARS SINCE PAGE HAD CHEWED HER nails, but she sat gnawing them now, watching the one called Ranald pace the ground before her. To the contrary, Ranald seemed not to notice her at all, and she might have tried to steal away already, save that when she dared to move from her spot by the tree, he turned to growl at her like a mongrel dog protecting his bone.

Page had never kicked a dog before—never even been inclined to—rather had smuggled them within her room, instead, to feed them scraps she'd purloined from the table, but she certainly felt like kicking Ranald right now. Like his laird, he was an overbearing brute.

She wondered whether the MacKinnon had met with her father as yet—worried what her father would say.

Most of all she dreaded facing him.

The MacKinnon, that was, not her father.

She had a suspicion she might never set eyes upon her father again.

But that wasn't what troubled her most.

Unreasonably, the desperation she felt to escape stemmed less from the fact that she longed to go home, and more from the fact that she was wholly and justly humiliated over having to face the MacKinnon. She'd spoken pridefully, and threatened fallaciously, and as soon as he spoke with her father he would know it for what it was.

Why did she care what he thought of her?

Would he laugh in her face? Mock her? Pity her?

She didn't think she could bear it—anything would be better than his pity. Her eyes stung at the merest notion.

Confusing, arrogant Scot.

Why had he shown her any consideration?

It would have been so much easier had he shown her cruelty, instead. That, she might have dealt with. She might have gritted her teeth and borne it. But pity was another matter entirely.

Why did he have to go and call her lass as though he cared?

His tone when he had addressed her made her feel... she wasn't certain how it made her feel. She only knew that the thrill she experienced when he spoke the endearment—it certainly sounded an endearment—didn't begin to eclipse the despair.

Somehow, in the space of a single night, he'd managed to rip open every wound she'd healed throughout the years.

Both she and Ranald heard the approaching hooves at the same time.

Ranald quit his pacing to face his clan as they emerged through the trees into the little copse. Page's heart vaulted into her throat. Hot tears, though she tried to suppress them, burned at her eyes. She didn't dare stand—felt, instead, like burrowing a den deep in the ground and hiding within it for the rest of her given days. She shouldn't care, and told herself she didn't care, but she knew very well it was a bloody lie. Somehow, she cared very much what the MacKinnon thought of her.

The one called Lagan emerged first, waving his hand and speaking his Scots tongue fervidly, and Page had no inkling what he was saying. In truth, she couldn't particularly tell whether he was furious or gleeful, for his expressions were mixed. A few men straggled into the copse behind him; they, too, spoke excitedly.

And then came the MacKinnon, and Page understood at once.

Her emotions rose to choke her, and her tears began to course down her cheeks. She couldn't stop them, for the MacKinnon's son rode before him.

Her father had dealt with them.

He wanted her back.

Her stomach surged and she was so relieved, she thought she might be sick. Swiping the wetness from her cheeks, Page rose to her feet to face the MacKinnon, emotional laughter bubbling up from the depths of her.

Her father wanted her back.

She felt invulnerable with that knowledge, warmed like never before, exhilarated, as if she were soaring to the heights of Heaven with her joy.

Until the MacKinnon's gaze turned upon her.

The look he cast her sent a frisson racing down her spine. His stance was rigid in the saddle, the muscle in his jaw ticked, and his amber-gold eyes pierced her as surely as a Welshman's arrow. God help her, she couldn't have torn her gaze away had she tried.

She'd been weeping.

Inexplicable anger mounted within Iain.

Damn, but she wasn't his concern.

The best he could do was release her and be along his merry way.

So why did he feel like pivoting his mount about, calling her father down, and running his blade through the bastard's black heart?

The moment she'd spied Malcom sitting before him, her eyes lit with joy. Not a trace of avenging pride. And relief, he spied relief there, as well. His heart squeezed painfully, for it occurred to him, then, just what it was she thought. She assumed her father had bargained for her return.

Worthless bastard. He should have bargained for her return.

He didn't have the heart to tell her the truth.

How could he tell her that her whoreson father had given her the greatest insult? That he couldn't have cared one whit what was done to her now—and that he certainly hadn't wished her return? Christ, that he'd sworn, even, to rip out her tongue? What manner of father was that?

Nay, he couldn't do it; he couldn't bring himself to break her heart.

How could her father?

Her hopeful expression was Iain's undoing. Or mayhap 'twas simply the memory of how she'd spoken so heroically of the father who plainly didn't care for her.

It turned his stomach, made him feel things he had no cause to feel.

She came forward, looking more fragile than Iain recalled, and it was all he could do to wipe the disgust from his face. With mere words he thought he might break her in twain. He pictured her lying, weeping at his feet, her spirit broken, and the image both anguished and angered him.

Nay, he couldn't tell her.

"You..." She choked on her words. "You will take me home now?" Her eyes were bright and full of hope, her voice soft and anticipative. "You'll take me home?"

Iain's heart squeezed harder. He wanted in that instant to draw her into his arms, to soothe her, kiss her fears away, smooth the worries from her brow. He wanted to shake her violently and tell her that her father was a poor example of a father and that she didn't need him.

FitzSimon's daughter was the last thing he needed in his life. She was a troublesome wench who was like to turn the rest of his hair gray before his years, but he found himself compelled to save her feelings despite the fact.

Unfortunately, he knew only one way to do so.

Not truly understanding why he was driven to, he said, "Nay, wench. I'll not."

Her brows drew together in confusion, and she straightened. "What do you mean, you will not?"

His jaw clenched, and he said, "Just what I said, wench. I'll not be returning you to your damnable father." His voice lacked the heat of anger, though she didn't seem to notice in her rising temper, and Iain thought she looked stronger armed with fury.

Her eyes were wide with a mixture of shock and outrage. "But he returned your son," she pointed out.

Iain placed his hand upon Malcom's back. "That he did," he agreed, and glanced about at his men, meeting their gazes, one after another. Their astonishment was more than evident in their countenances, but he apprised them silently not to gainsay him. Though in truth, Iain didn't think they would have been capable, even had they wished to. Auld Angus's jaw had slackened near to his belly, and if Iain had not been so bloody angry, he might have found the contrary old bugger's expression comical. His gaze returned to FitzSimon's daughter.

She was becoming infuriated now, and he welcomed it, knowing she would need her rage to sustain her.

"But my father kept his end of the bargain," she said. Iain merely nodded, but his jaw worked. "You would renege upon your word, sir?"

"Apparently so," he lied without compunction.

"But, Papa," Malcom whispered, peering up in surprise. Iain shushed him with a downward glance and a pat upon the back.

"How dare you?" she railed. "Why? Why would you do this?"

"Verra simple," Iain told her, meeting her gaze. "An eye for an eye, lass. Your da conspired in the takin' o' my son. 'Tis only meet I should return the favor in kind."

"You are a madman!"

Iain thought perhaps it was so. "That I may be, lass," he agreed with a frown. "Nonetheless, you'll be coming along wi' us."

"But my father," she exclaimed.

"Your father," he declared, "can go to bloody Hell."

CHAPTER 6

"He'll hunt you down," Page swore.

She couldn't believe it.

She was torn between disbelief that her father would risk the king's wrath to have her back and sheer joy that he'd done so—and she was furious with the man before her, for daring to break his pact with her father when for the first time in her life it seemed her father valued her, wanted her—and this miscreant would dare rob her of that joy.

Not if she could help it!

She glanced about and found his men all staring at their laird, their expressions as shocked as her own must seem. Their stupor gave her the opening she needed. She didn't care how many of his men surrounded her. She had absolutely no intentions of going with them peacefully. Somehow or another, she was returning to her father and they'd have to kill her to stop her.

Without giving them warning of her intent, or time to consider her response, she turned, found an opening behind her, and made a frantic dash into the forest.

She heard the MacKinnon's curse behind her.

Page didn't dare slow her step, even as the sounds of pursuit began in earnest, nor did she look back to see that they were following. She ran with all her might, slipping through the woods with the ease of one who knew them intimately.

And then suddenly her hem snagged upon a gnarled tree root. She muttered an oath, trying to jerk it free, and those precious lost seconds were to her misfortune. Within the instant, she was surrounded by scowling Scotsmen. And then once again she was confronted by the MacKinnon, his son no longer in the saddle before him.

He dismounted, his expression black as he came toward her. Page thought he might strike her, so purposeful was his stride, but he didn't. She didn't cower as he reached out, though he merely seized her hem and jerked it free, then stood staring at her furiously. "You're going to make me sorely regret this."

Page smiled fiercely. "I surely will," she vowed, drawing herself up to her full height. Again it struck her how tall the man was, for she reached only to his chin, and she was not, by any means, diminutive. In truth, her father had always thought her much too long limbed for a woman.

"I should bloody well let you go," he swore, his jaw working angrily.

Page's brows lifted, for he truly seemed to be considering the prospect. "You should?"

"Aye," he said, "and count myself bloody fortunate that you're gone, but I won't."

He wished to let her go? But he wouldn't? Page didn't understand. "Nay?"

"Nay!"

Her heart hammered wildly over the faint suspicion that reared. "Why not?"

"Because my da raised himself a rattlebrained arse," he swore "That's why!" And if his pronouncement hadn't been shocking enough, he lifted her up suddenly, as though she were no more than a sack of grain, and bore her back to his mount, flinging her unceremoniously over his saddle.

Page shrieked in outrage, and then gasped as the air was driven from her lungs. Without preamble, he mounted behind her, holding her fast with an arm, and then lifted her up to scoot forward, pinioning her to his lap with the inescapable strength in his arm. The man must be made of stone, unyielding as he was.

"You will sorely regret this," Page swore. "I will see to it with every waking breath I take." How dare the brute treat her as though she were nothing more than chattel to be absconded with at will. How dare he keep her from her father. She couldn't bear it! All her life she'd waited for this moment, prayed for it, only to lose it by a sordid twist of fate. "I will plague you every day of your miserable life," she vowed.

"I have no doubt of that," he said tightly, and spurred his mount. "I'm merely a man, lass. Keep wiggling that backside so insistently, and I'll be sorely tempted, I assure you."

Page gasped in outrage.

"Gather your belongings," he commanded his men. "We leave at once."

To Page's consternation, it took them little time at all to gather their possessions—barbarians that they were, they traveled with little more than the breacans they wore belted about their bodies. They were off within minutes.

Page refused to allow herself to feel defeat.

For all of her twenty years she had fended for herself. If it was the last thing she did, she was going to find her way home. In the meantime, she fully intended to keep her word. The MacKinnon, indeed, was going to be a miserable man.

SPRING CAME LATE TO THE NORTHERN REACHES.

Biding her time, observing the differences in the landscape as they traveled northward, Page tried not to think of the risk her father had taken on her behalf. What would King Henry do to him when he discovered that her father had given up the boy for her? And then had promptly lost her, as well?

Why hadn't he sent men to see to her return?

How could he have trusted the word of a Scotsman?

Curse the MacKinnon. The ignoble wretch.

The trees now were less abundant with foliage. A few were lush with new green growth; some sprouted new leaves that reminded Page of green feathers. Some trees were as yet bare, still to be touched by God's masterful hand and miraculous paint.

She had always loved the land.

A wildling, her father had called her. It didn't matter; it had never disturbed her in the least that he'd thought her so, for she'd always felt more as though she were Nature's child than his. In truth, it was the only time she ever felt truly whole—when she was at one with God's earth. That was the reason she'd stolen away from the castle all those many nights. It gave her soul great peace.

But it was also the reason she was in this damnable predicament.

Page frowned as she thought of the man seated so intimately at her back. She'd managed to shut him out of her thoughts for most of the morning. Only when he so arrogantly drew her back against him did she deign to acknowledge him, elbowing him and shrugging free to sit forward once more. The more distance she was able to place between them, the more at ease she felt.

Now, again, he drew her back against him and she wrenched forward, turning to glare at him. "Do you mind overmuch?" she asked, exasperated. "Force me to ride well nigh in your lap, if you will, but you cannot force me to abide your touch."

"Suit yourself, vixen." She felt his sigh more than heard it. "You're a sour-mouthed wench, if e'er I knew one."

"Truly?" she asked sweetly, mocking him. "I do wonder why that is."

"'Tis likely you were born that way," he answered uncharitably.

Page felt like turning and slapping his arrogant face. "Nay, but you're a mean brute," she returned. "You must realize my father will come after us," she apprised him. "He does not like to be thwarted, I assure you."

For an instant he didn't respond, and Page could almost feel his tension mounting at her back. "Will he?" he answered, after a moment. She thought he might have been contemplating the possibility. Good. She hoped he was considering the repercussions of his actions, and fearing for his life. Neither her father nor King Henry would stand for his perfidy.

"Sit back, lass," he commanded, though not unkindly, and drew her against him once more, this time pinning her against his chest.

Page struggled against his unwelcome embrace, to no avail. "Arrrghhh!"

"You'll end up lame riding in that unlimber position. Rest yourself. I willna bite."

"I don't believe you," Page said through clenched teeth, sinking her nails into the arm that held her like plaster to his massive frame. "You're a brute," she accused him when he would not budge. Neither did he seem to be affected by the pressure she was inflicting upon his arm. Rather he sat there in stony silence, and it was as though he felt nothing at all. With a disgruntled sigh, she relented and released his arm, allowing herself to slacken against him, though she could not, by any means, rest.

"That's it," he said, bending to whisper his approval into her ear.

Page tried to ignore the shudder that swept down her spine at the solicitous tone of his voice.

"You havena spoken all the morn," he said low, and his voice was like warm silk against her face, soft and soothing. She reminded herself that he was a faithless Scotsman, not some overly attentive beau who cared for her wellbeing. "I dinna mean to aggrieve you, lass."

And still her heart hammered. "Did you not?" she asked, hiding her confusion behind anger.

His chest expanded with another sigh. He released it, and it blew across the pate of her head. The feel of it gave her gooseflesh. He didn't answer.

Page wasn't about to let him lapse into silence so easily now. He'd provoked her well enough. "What, prithee, did you mean to do? And what would you have me do? Laugh hysterically because I've been abducted by a barbarian Scotsman? Converse with you over the wonders of Christendom? I hardly think so."

His chuckle surprised her. Low and rich, it rumbled against her back. "You're a saucy wee wench, for certain."

Page bristled. "I'm no wee wench—and aye, so I've been told. Do not think I mean to apologize for it, either."

"Temper, temper," he reproved, clucking his tongue at her. "Tell me, then, lass... what wonders might we converse over were ye amenable to conversing?"

"Hah!" Page exclaimed. "With you? I should think I would never be amenable—and cease, if you will, to call me lass. It..." Confused her. "Disturbs me," she said petulantly.

He chuckled again, flustering her all the more, and then bent closer to whisper in her ear. "Verra well, lass, then tell me what ye would have me call you instead."

Her nerves were near to shattering. "Naught!" She

shrugged away, moving as far forward as was physically possible. Only then did she realize he hadn't been holding her any longer. How long now since he'd released her? How could she not have noticed? Had she lain against him contentedly all this time? "I would have you call me naught. I would have you cease to speak to me at all."

"Rest, then, and I willna trouble ye any further, lass."

"I've no wish to rest."

"Then you do wish to converse?"

Page thought she could hear a smile in his voice. She jerked her head about to catch his smug expression and said, "I do not."

"Ach, lass, make up your mind," he said, and Page clenched her teeth and tried to convince herself not to slap the arrogant smile from his face.

"I asked you not to—"

"I know, wench. Ye dinna wish for me to call you 'lass,' but you havena said what then I should call—"

"My name is none of your concern," she assured.

He smiled then, flashing perfect white teeth. "Verra well, lass. If you will, then."

"Mary," she lied, trying not to note the boyish dimple that had appeared, as well. "My name is Mary." She turned around, averting her gaze, more than a little rattled by his too easy manner.

Wasn't her abductor supposed to be cruel with his words rather than winning? Why should he care over her comforts, or her preferences, for that matter? "Are you pleased now?" she asked him. "You can bloody well call me Mary."

CHAPTER 7

Of all the names she might have spouted, Mairi was the last one he expected. He'd been unprepared for the sound of it upon her lips.

Bloody hell, nothing else she might have said could have spurred him into silence more swiftly. He'd been determined to melt the icy walls surrounding her, win her over to his people. The last thing they needed was a bitter wench to burden them. They'd already had one of those to contend with.

Mairi.

Even these six years later, they were all still reeling with the legacy she'd left them.

What would he tell Malcom on the day his son should ask of his mother's death?

He didn't know. But Iain wasn't certain he could ever speak of it, for the memory of that morning tormented him more than anything in his life. He could scarce think of that high window without suffering a sweat and his knees turning as soft as boiled meal.

His wife had loathed him so much.

Even Malcom hadn't been enough to keep her.

Sweat beaded upon his forehead. He closed his eyes, warding away the image of her standing before the high

67

window. The vision passed before his eyes in a flash of white-hot pain.

Mairi.

He wasn't certain he could call the lass by that name. He couldn't even bear to think of her as such. The very thought of the name wrenched at his gut.

He opened his eyes and sought out his son, focusing upon the future, not the past. The sight of Malcom, his soft golden hair shining under the sun, laughing and talking with his cousin, comforted Iain at once. He allowed the issue of her name to pass for now, and lapsed into silence along with her, more than aware of the glances he was receiving from his men.

They were trying to understand, he knew. He'd shocked the hell out of them with his lies about her father's intentions, but it couldn't be helped. At the first opportunity he would explain... what? His brows drew together into a frown. God's teeth, but what would he explain? He wasn't even certain he understood it himself. That he'd been driven to the lie? That he couldn't bear to hurt her? That something about the beautiful, contentious, troublesome wench sitting so stiffly before him brought out a fierce protectiveness in him... something apart from the lust she aroused in him?

Christ, but he found himself wondering if, in truth, she'd been championing his son last eve rather than herself. He thought it might have been both, for behind her bluster, Iain feared she masked a lifetime of her father's scorn. A lifetime of trying to please the unpleasable. He sensed in her the same hunger, the same hopes and the same fears that he'd once harbored himself for Mairi's favor.

All for naught.

He could scarce bear to be the one to deal the lass another blow.

She roused in him so many inexplicable emotions, such irrational yearnings. Like the one he felt now to undo the plait in her hair and comb through the soft strands with his fingers until they were silk in his callused hands. He wanted to see the play of sunlight upon her hair—somehow knew it would be splendid. In the noonday light, her brown color turned the shade of firelit henna.

And her scent... sunshine and verdure... the freshness of mountain mist on a day when the heather was in high bloom. Like a wolf scenting his mate, it was all he could do not to bury his face into the crook of her neck and breathe the essence of her into his lungs.

Christ, but he needed to think of other things—needed to get her away from him, somehow. His eyes lifted, scanning the cavalcade for his son once more. He needed to speak with Malcom, needed to hold his son, and yet here he sat, playing nursemaid to a fork-tongued wench instead. He frowned at the thought of her riding with someone else, anyone else, and cursed himself for being an unreasonable arse.

Why should he care whether she affected another man the way she affected him? She wasn't his woman, after all—nor did he desire her to be.

Bedamned, he could be wounded by a wit so cutting as hers.

But he didn't wholly trust his men not to tell her the truth.

Nay, he resolved, until he could speak to them privately, and until he had the opportunity to think of what he would say to them—to her—she would continue to ride with him. Malcom would be well enough riding with Lagan for the time being. It was enough, for now, to know he was safe.

They continued on in silence, and when the lass seemed to waver a little before him, Iain drew her back against him once more, smiling over her indomitable will.

Stubborn wench.

This time she didn't resist him. She went slack against him and blew a spent breath. Iain smiled, for he knew that somehow she'd managed to fall asleep sitting straight in the saddle. She hadn't slept well the night before, and he was surprised she'd lasted so long. He allowed her to nap well into the afternoon, all the while trying not to think about how good it felt to hold the woman in his arms, how right it felt to protect her.

It had been so long.

So bloody long.

&

"WAKE UP, LASS."

Page awoke to an insistent whisper.

"Mary."

A strange woman's name, but whispered in her ear... and she recalled groggily that she'd given the name instead of her own. Her eyes flew open and she peered up into eyes that were the color of the Scots' *uisge beatha*, their renowned water of life. Her father had favored it well. They were the color of sunlit amber, and they were staring down at her intently.

Frowning.

"Mary?" he said, his brow lifting a little, and it seemed somehow a question.

Page sat at once, shaking off her slumber, and snapped a curt "I'm fine." She shrugged free of his unwelcome support, and edged forward until he released her. She noticed, then, that they were the last to remain mounted. It was dusk and the rest of the band was already busy making camp for the night. It seemed she'd only just closed her eyes. Certainly she'd not meant to sleep. "Where are we?" she asked, turning to look at him, a little disoriented.

He was still scowling at her, watching her keenly.

"'Tis where we'll stop for the night," he said only, with narrowed eyes. "Does it suit you... Mary?"

Page thought it seemed he took offense to the name she'd given him, though, for the life of her, she couldn't comprehend why. She thought about the name a moment, and in her drowsy state couldn't account for his reaction. "'Tis a perfectly suitable name," she assured him. One, even, that she might have liked for herself. Her brows knit as she contemplated the source of his displeasure.

"Aye," he agreed, though he was still frowning, and he said nothing more as he dismounted and seized her from the saddle, without even bothering to ask her whether she needed his assistance.

She would have liked to send him flying to perdition.

But she was too exhausted to fight at the moment, and so she merely sat upon a rotting log to watch the lot of them settle in for the evening. It wasn't long before the one called Lagan sauntered toward them, young Malcom tripping at his heels. With a rush and a squeal, the boy flung himself upon his father's back.

Page cringed in anticipation of the MacKinnon's reaction.

Bellowing in surprise, the MacKinnon swung an arm about to catch his son by the waist and drag him around before him. He knelt and hugged the boy fiercely, laughing uproariously as he then ruffled his fine hair.

Page sat, gaping in wonder at the sight of the two of them together.

The boy who would speak naught for so long stood chattering with his father in their incomprehensible tongue, and although Page understood next to nothing of their discourse, she understood the essence of it all. Some part of her sighed with relief that his father did not rebuff him. The greater part of her quailed under an onslaught of emotions: envy, sorrow, a yearning so deep,

71

it made her heart feel like a vast, echoing cavern—and then shame that she would begrudge the boy his father's affection.

Nay, but she was elated for Malcom. She wouldn't wish her misery upon any child, not even her enemy's, and still, inexplicably, it pained her to see the affection between them.

Watching them, it was more than evident that the MacKinnon valued his son. One need only spy the two together to know it was true. The MacKinnon's smile was stunning in its brilliance, and his golden eyes flashed with joy as he listened to his son gibber on—pleading, it seemed.

What might it feel like to be the recipient of such undivided attention? Such undeniable affection?

Page sighed with longing, her heart swelling with tenderness for a father who would love his child so openly.

The MacKinnon peered up at Lagan, offered a clip directive, and Lagan nodded, placing a hand to the MacKinnon's shoulder in assurance. Whatever he said must have pleased Malcom immensely, for the boy threw his arms about his father's neck once again and squealed with glee.

The MacKinnon's gaze met her own over the boy's shoulder, and Page's heart tumbled within her breast.

She averted her gaze at once, uncomfortable with the emotions in peril of being revealed there.

Even once Lagan and Malcom left them, Page didn't dare acknowledge the man who stood before her, watching her still.

And yet, neither could she keep her curiosity quelled. "What is it you said to please him so?" she asked, sounding uninterested, though her very question belied the fact.

He didn't bother to answer until she lifted her face to his. "Malcom?"

Page nodded, mesmerized by the golden hue of his eyes. In the dusky light, burnished by the waning sun, they seemed almost translucent, angelic even. He was beautiful, in truth—a man she could only have dreamt of loving, for no man who looked as he did could ever want her in return.

It was a good thing she loathed him so ... there was little danger in losing her heart to the darksome brute.

"He asked to go hunting."

"And you let him?" Page surmised, somewhat surprised.

"Dinna let his sweet face fool you. My son is a capable hunter." Page couldn't help but hear the note of concern along with the pride in his voice. "Malcom's wi' his clansmen now, lass. No harm will come to him. My cousin Lagan will see to it."

Her brows lifted. "Lagan? Lagan is your cousin?"

"Aye."

Page averted her gaze once more. "I never would have guessed. The two of you seem so little alike."

"Really?" he answered, narrowing his eyes at her. "Curious, that... I never would have taken ye for a Mary, either, but 'tis Mary you are—is that no' right?"

Page furrowed her brow. Did he not believe her?

Or was he simply making the point that she should not judge?

"Often things are no' what they seem," he disclosed.

Page's heartbeat quickened. "And what is it you are trying to say, sir?"

"Merely that you dinna recall me to a Mary. The name doesna suit you."

She released the breath she'd not realized she'd held. "Really," she said, sounding bored, although she wanted more than anything to ask him what name he thought better suited her. But she didn't dare. The last she wished was for him to discover her shame—nor did she care to return to elaborate upon the differences between him and his cousin.

What could she possibly say?

Certainly she wasn't about to admit that he seemed the more kindly of the two. He was her gaoler, after all. How could she think him kind?

"I suggest you address the matter with my father if you do not care for the name. 'Twas his choice, after all," she lied.

"Was it?" he said, and returned to tending his mount, without bothering to await her reply. Though it was as crude a dismissal as Page had ever received, she was silently grateful for the reprieve. At the instant, there was a breach in her armor much too wide to close, and she needed time to mend it.

Anger, she knew, was her refuge, and yet... though she tried... she couldn't even summon a shred of ire for a man who showed such devotion to his son.

CHAPTER 8

H e'd managed to lure the others away, to hunt in some other remote part of these woods.

And Malcom... As expected, the boy had wandered away from them... straight into his waiting hands.

At long last, everything was going as planned. A plan that was far too long coming to fruition. A plan he'd thought to have fully realized six years earlier, when he'd driven Iain's young wife mad with fear of her new husband and had fueled her with so much hatred for him that she'd preferred death to bearing his touch ever again.

It was only too bad she hadn't committed the deed before giving birth to Iain's brat.

And yet, it gave him some measure of satisfaction to know that his father's clan thought Iain her murderer, for Iain had been the last to see her alive. He smiled at that, knowing his half brother would strangle with guilt over the memory until the day he died—well, mayhap that day would come sooner than expected.

Aye, mistakes had been made.

When King David had sought his aid in gaining custody of Iain's son, in response to his own request for David's favor, it had seemed the perfect opportunity to rid himself of Malcom. He'd only too soon realized that it accomplished naught. David's intent had been merely to install the boy as a ward of the English court, far away, and safe even from him. Were anything to happen to Iain, Malcom would then be brought back to take his place as David's poppet.

Nay, better that the boy was dead.

Aye, for it might be only a matter of time before Malcom gave him away, at any rate. The wee brat had awakened from his drugged slumber in the middle of the night, and he'd had to croon him to sleep. Ach, but it had been a sour note he'd sung.

No more mistakes now, for he'd waited far too long.

Keeping sight of Malcom, he withdrew an arrow from his quiver and notched it within his bow. And then he waited for just the right moment...

He wanted Malcom's wee body to fall into the brush, so he wouldn't have to touch him afterward. He wanted this kill to be a clean one, with no blood on his hands to give him away. Nor did he intend for the body to be found until he was far enough from the scene so as to be free from suspicion.

"Malcom! There ye are, lad." Ranald bellowed, coming into view.

The bowman cursed silently, and gently eased the bowstring back into place.

"I was following a rabbit," Malcom declared. "Look, Ranald, look! I think he's in there." He pointed to the bush that separated the bowman from his prey.

Ranald scattered the bush, peering within, over and about, and then he froze, meeting the bowman's gaze through the leafage. "There's naught in the bush, lad," he said stiffly. "Go on wi' ye now."

Malcom's face fell. "I want to make my da proud," he said. "I wanna catch him a rabbit."

"Aye, well, ye willna make him proud by wanderin' aboot all alone and getting yourself lost," Ranald scolded. "Go, now, and find the others—quickly, lest I tell your da ye were a wee rotten scoundrel and strayed away. He willna let ye come again, I think."

"Dinna tell," Malcom pleaded, thrusting out his lower lip.

"Go, then," Ranald instructed.

Malcom turned at once and fled.

Ranald turned again to face the bowman hidden within the bush. "I canna let ye do this," he said once Malcom was gone.

"Ye canna stop me."

"I should never have helped ye to begin wi'," Ranald hissed into the bush. He shook his head. "However did I allow ye to talk me into it?"

"You're my verra best friend," the bowman said simply, quietly.

Ranald's face turned florid with anger. "No' if ye plan to murder an innocent laddie, I am no'! I'll have no part in this treachery. Ye said ye dinna wish to hurt him. Ye said ye only wished to have him gone. I helped ye do that, but I'll no' be helpin' anymore," he swore. "I'm going to tell Iain. He should have known long ago. 'Tis his right to know the truth—all of it."

"Nay!" the bowman snarled. "Ye willna tell him that he is my brother, Ranald. I swore I wouldna, and you willna either. I trusted you. You are the only one who knows, aside from Glenna, and I canna let you tell that tale."

"He deserves to know the truth—and I will tell him, if you willna." And with that, Ranald turned to go.

"Nay, you willna," the bowman said with certainty, and lifted the loaded bow.

Ranald stopped and slowly turned. "You willna use it," he predicted. "You wouldna—"

Without hesitation, the arrow flew, striking true to its aim, straight into Ranald's heart.

Ranald clutched at the shaft as he fell backward. "Bloody bastard," he swore.

When Ranald did not rise, the bowman made his way to where he lay, clutching the arrow still. The trickle of blood from Ranald's lips against the deathlike pallor of his face held the bowman captivated for an instant.

"Ye were... my friend," Ranald choked out, his eyes liquid with tears.

"No longer," the bowman said softly, without remorse, and stamped the arrow deeper with the heel of his boot. He drove it down until it passed into the soft ground. The death rattle came as a strangled gurgle from Ranald's throat. Satisfied, the bowman bent to snap the remainder of the shaft in two, taking with him the feathered fletching. It was his habit to use the downy white feathers of an owl for his shaft end, and he would not have his mark recognized by those who would know.

"You shouldn't have betrayed me, Ranald," he said to the lifeless body. "I would have rewarded ye well. And damn ye, too." For now he would have to wait for a new chance to present itself. It would raise too much suspicion were both Ranald and the boy to turn up missing now, particularly since the three of them had together wandered away from the rest of the hunting party. It wouldn't look so good if only he returned. Malcom was likely back safe in their fold already.

Damn Ranald, the meddling bastard.

&.

IT WASN'T LONG BEFORE PAGE REDISCOVERED HER IRE.

The hunting party returned with quarry in hand, and while they were charitable enough to share a generous portion of their catch with their "hostage," afterward they immediately found a sturdy tree and leashed her to it—like some mongrel they didn't wish to have stray away. Page just sat there, watching them spread their breacans to sleep upon, all the while seething with anger.

How could they expect her to sleep like this each night? All night! Surely they wouldn't yet again?

And the MacKinnon... he hadn't bothered even to acknowledge her since plucking her from his mount. He'd been preoccupied since the hunting party had returned. Lagan had spoken to him briefly, and ever since he'd been in a fit of fury over something—something the boy had done perchance, for he went to Malcom at once and spoke to him sternly, sitting the boy down before him while they supped, and eyeing him reprovingly. Malcom, for his part, appeared suitably repentant. He sat before his father, sulking, until even his papa took pity and patted his head. The boy threw himself into his father's arms then, and squeezed fervently, his little arms scarce able to reach about the MacKinnon's broad chest...

Page found herself staring, unable to keep herself from it.

Judas, but he was a fine specimen—his shoulders broad and well muscled, his body well formed. He appeared to be a man unafraid of strenuous labor, and his body evidenced that fact. She imagined him toiling alongside his kinsmen, with the sweltering sun upon his back. As first she'd thought, his skin was swarthy. His dark hair was striking, and the white hair at his temples was nothing less than startling in contrast to the color of his skin and his youthful features. She wondered again how old he was.

She wished Cora were here. Born in the Lowlands of Scotia, Cora was the daughter of her father's new leman. She'd impressed Page with her command of both the Highland and the English tongues. She was also the first and only friend Page had ever had. Cora would know what they were saying. As it was, Page could only make out that Malcom "wouldn't do it again." But what it was he was promising not to do again, she couldn't begin to decipher.

She watched them together, the way the MacKinnon swept the hair from his son's eyes, and found herself wistful.

It was a glorious sight to behold... father and son.

Would that her father had been so gentle after a reprimanding. She'd have given much for him to look at her just so... if only once. She sighed then, for she might have simply wished he'd been so gentle in his rebuking of her as the MacKinnon had been with his son. But he hadn't been, and she couldn't turn back time.

There was no sense in weeping over it now.

It was only that... now, at last, when her father revealed some glimmer of affection for her—he'd risked Henry's wrath in bartering for her freedom and that had to count for something—MacKinnon stole the chance from her.

"Ach, but ye could set a mon to flames wi' that glower, lass."

Startled, Page's gaze shot upward to find the old man, Angus, standing over her, arms akimbo as he watched her. She turned her glower upon him then. "Would that I could," she remarked. "Do you not have something better to do than to ogle me, sir?"

He further vexed her by simply chuckling at her question.

"Prithee, I see little humor in this," Page hissed at him.

His eyes crinkled at the corners. "Aye, but there's humor to be seen, for certain, lass," he returned cryptically.

Page considered kicking the old man, but doubted she could reach him from where she sat bound. "Why can you not set me free?" she protested, jerking at the ties that bound her wrists. "Why must I remain bound to this accursed tree? What have you to fear of me?"

The old man scratched at his beard and shook his head. "Well, I dunno," he admitted, and proceeded to sit down beside her. He leaned over to whisper, "We've been wondering the same thing ourselves, ye see." He lifted his brows and nodded at her, as though he thought she knew what he was speaking of.

Crazed old fool.

Page narrowed her eyes at him. "Really?" she asked, sounding taxed. "And what, perchance, did you come up with?"

Again he chuckled, and leaned to whisper, "No' a thing, lass."

Page snorted, and rolled her eyes. "Try an eye for an eye," she proposed, mocking his laird's justification. "And make yourself at home, why do you not?" She eyed the ground where he'd plopped himself down, and then turned to smile at him grimly. "In fact, if you would be so kind as to unbind my hands," she suggested in an acidly sweet tone, "I should be verra pleased to run and fetch you a wee dram like a good little lass." She batted her lashes at him for effect.

He didn't laugh this time. Instead, he cocked his head reproachfully. "You dinna see me tryin' to butcher your tongue, now d' you?"

"You dinna have to try," she returned flippantly, smiling fiercely. "I would venture to say you do it quite well naturally." She lifted a brow. "At any rate, I thought it a rather good impersonation."

Angus made to rise, shaking his head. "Ach, but ye are a pawky wench," he swore, grimacing. "'Tis a mystery to me as to why the lad feels so beholden to save—"

"You for myself," the MacKinnon broke in, scowling down at Angus as the old man rose to his feet.

"Ach, you're welcome to her, Iain. 'Tis glad I am to

be leavin' her to ye. I swear that men have died by duller weapons than that vicious tongue o' hers."

Page blinked, her gaze flying upward to meet the MacKinnon's.

Iain.

The old man had called him Iain.

To save her for himself? She opened her mouth to speak, but then closed it again. Surely he hadn't said what she thought he'd said? Or if he had, he couldn't possibly have meant what she thought he meant. Her brows drew together, for he couldn't... possibly... want her?

Nay, she decided. So he must be hiding something. The old man had said that he felt beholden to save—what? Her? But from what?

"Busy makin' friends, are ye, lass?" he asked rudely.

Page blinked, trying to recall every word of the exchange between the two, and nodded her head. "Aye..."

He lifted a brow, and his beautiful lips turned faintly at the corners. "Wool-gathering, are ye?"

Page's brow furrowed. "I—"

She couldn't remember the question. She peered up at him, frowning, for she wasn't about to ask the arrogant wretch what it was he'd said.

He grinned down at her suddenly, flashing white teeth. "'Tis said," he apprised, "that the mind is the first to leave us. Shall we begin the funeral preparations so soon?" He lifted his brows in unison.

Page's cheeks flared. "You're the one with the silver hair," she pointed out baldly, averting her gaze, unable to bear his scrutiny an instant longer.

"So I am, lass." She glanced up to spy the gleam of good humor in his gold-flecked eyes. "So I am."

"How old are you anyway?" Page flung back at him, curiosity getting the better of her. "Two score years?" She cocked her head, and added sweetly, "More?"

He merely chuckled at her impudence, and her ire intensified. Lord, but how dare he be so impervious?

"No' so auld as that, wench," he yielded, his grin turning frankly lascivious. "But auld enough to discern a virgin's blush—and, I warrant, auld enough to know desire when I spy it."

He had the audacity to wink at her.

Page's gasp was audible, and when she could find her tongue to speak again, her words were strangled with fury. "How dare you?"

His grin turned more crooked still. "Well, now, because I'm a barbarous Scotsman, that's how I dare. Have ye no' heard, lass? We're a randy lot, we Scots."

"You're a mighty crude lot," she returned. "And feckless, too."

"Aye, and dinna forget lusty," he added, and winked again.

Sweet Jesu, if it was his intent to distract her, then he was surely succeeding in the endeavor, for she was flustered to her very toes. Page scowled at him. "Bedamned! Is that all you can think of?"

"Aye, wench." His smile turned wicked now, and his voice softened. "When I'm looking at a bonny lass, 'tis all I can think of."

Page was momentarily dumbstruck by his brashness. She averted her face, her heartbeat quickening at his shameless cajolery. He was naught more than a smooth-tongued knave to speak such lies.

And yet...

"Y-you cannot," she stammered, and shook her head. "Y-you cannot possibly think me..." Sweet Mary, but she could scarce even speak the word.

"Bonny?" he supplied.

Page's gaze lifted to his.

He was scowling now, it seemed, staring as though he would see into her very soul, but he said nothing.

He didn't answer.

It was just as she supposed—they were merely false words from a man who cared nothing for her feelings. 'Twas simply his way to be so glib and he couldn't possibly mean it... and yet...

The look in his eyes... the way that he stared...

Could he?

CHAPTER 9

I ain was staggered by the anguish so apparent in those liquid dark eyes.

Christ, did she not realize?

Could she truly not know?

In truth, he'd meant the words as a ploy, a simple flirtation to distract her, and yet it was the truth he spoke. Faced with her pain and her sorrow, he forgot where they stood for the moment, forgot that his men were likely to be watching them, forgot that they were supposed to be enemies—he the accursed foe, who'd dared steal her from her father, she the daughter of the man who'd stolen his son.

He squatted upon his haunches, and reached out to take into his callused hand the disheveled plait of her hair. "Aye, lass," he whispered. His fingers skimmed the length of the braid. "Ye are bonny. Christ, but ye've eyes so dark a mon could lose himself in them. And hair..." He came forward, falling upon one knee, reaching out with his other hand to tug free the ribbon that kept her plait bound. He nudged his thumb into the weave of her hair, working the soft strands loose with his fingers. "'Tis lovely," he murmured as he stroked the unbound locks. "Fine silk against flesh that's ne'er felt the like."

For an instant she seemed unable to respond,

hanging on his every word like a woman starved, and then she blinked, as though regaining her senses, and wrenched her head back, tugging the lock free from his hand.

She glared up at him. 'Twill take more than pretty words to move me, Scot," she swore. She lifted a brow in challenge. "If you mean to woo me, you might better begin by unbinding my wrists. They hurt."

Iain considered her request, thinking it a well founded grievance. And yet... he didn't intend to stay awake all night guarding the troublesome wench. Her chin lifted and she held his gaze, her eyes burning with indignation and ire.

"I'm no animal to be kept fettered," she persisted.

"Nay," Iain agreed, "you are not, lass." He sighed. "Verra well." He leaned forward and reached about her, stretching his body across hers as he groped blindly around the tree for the ropes at her wrists.

It was a mistake, he realized. He should have gone around her. Certainly it would have been the sensible thing to do.

As it was, he found himself embracing her, his chin resting upon her shoulder and his lips too near the warmth of her neck. Her gasp was almost inaudible. He felt it more than heard it, and then she went wholly still beneath him.

Iain, too, froze, utterly aware of the woman within his arms.

Christ, but it had been much too long since he'd been this close to any female... He could feel the peaks of her breasts rise with her breath, teasing his chest and his physical reaction was immediate. It was all he could do not to lean into her, inhale the essence of her—that glorious scent that was purely female and wholly intoxicating.

He had to remind himself who she was—who he was—that they were not alone.

And still he couldn't help himself; he lowered his body in an effort to reach the bindings and leaned into her. Trying for a lighthearted tone, he asked, "You're no' busy planning your escape, are ye, lass?"

She said nothing, and he persisted, though he hadn't the least notion why he should care. "Promise me you'll no' try to escape." His hands arrested at her back, awaiting her response.

For an instant longer, she said nothing, and then she asked, "If I cannot promise? Will you still release me?"

So she was a woman of her word, was she?

Iain smiled.

He didn't know why he felt driven to protect her, but he knew with a certainty that he'd not let her go. "Nay, lass," he whispered against her hair, nudging it away from his face with his chin. A few strands stuck to his lips, and he tasted them, closing his eyes as he imagined the silky curtain unbound and cascading into his face as she rode him. The scent of her taunted him, aroused him to the point of pain. The image made him shudder. She was an innocent not to know how she could affect a man... how she affected him. "I'll not," he murmured, clearing his throat. "I'll not release you if you cannot promise."

Though he knew it was impossible, she seemed to shrink away from him, into the ground beneath him. "In such case," she answered, somewhat breathlessly, and more than a little flippantly, "I promise not to try."

He smiled at her cunning. "You promise not to try?" he repeated, disbelieving her audacity.

"I believe 'tis what I said, Scot."

He couldn't see her face, but imagined her saucy expression and chuckled. He nudged aside her hair with his lips and whispered against her ear, "Swear you'll not escape."

She made some keening sound as he brushed her

neck with his mouth and wrenched herself away. "Very well, Scot. I'll not steal away. Untie me now."

He chuckled.

"Get yourself off me," she demanded. "I cannot bear for you to touch me."

Iain smiled, for her quiver gave lie to her avowal. She was affected by him no less than he was by her. He'd wager his eyeteeth over it.

Still she sounded quite desperate, and he didn't wish to upset her any more than she was already. "You'll keep your word?" he persisted.

He imagined that she rolled her eyes, and his smile deepened, as she said more than a little acerbically, "To the man who broke faith with my father? Certainly! Now get off."

He chuckled at her quick wit. "Ye've a point," he ceded, and began at once to untie the bindings at her wrists. "Never mind, I believe I know the perfect solution."

"You do?"

He couldn't help but grin, for she sounded so ill at ease with the prospect. "Somethin' that should please the both o' us," he revealed mischievously. God only knew, he was certainly looking forward to it himself.

Page stiffened at his assurance.

Something that would please them both?

She certainly didn't think so.

She tried not to panic as she considered every conceivable solution—tried not to consider them at all. But it was all she could do not to think of the man poised so intimately above her. Nay, he wasn't lying, precisely, on top of her, but he might as well have been. Though he shielded her from his weight, she could feel every inch of his body as though it were melded to her own. And Judas, never in her life had she been more acutely aware of her own body—the places it brushed against his, the wicked, wonderful sensations that made her feel so very much a woman.

A lump rose in her throat.

He'd said she was bonny.

Could he truly have meant it?

The possibility made her tremble with... something she shouldn't be feeling for her enemy. Her brows drew together.

How could she possibly allow herself to be distracted so easily? Aye, 'twas his intent to distract her, of a certainty, but did she have to be so blessed accommodating? Nay, he couldn't possibly have meant it, she convinced herself.

She knew what she looked like—had seen her reflection oft enough to know that she was no enchanting faerie creature, able to steal a man's heart and soul with a single glance. She was rather unremarkable. Her hair was not the spun gold of the troubadour's favor, it was dirt colored; her face not fair and unblemished, but darkened by the sun and freckled across her nose. Her eyes were not the lucid blue of a summer sky, or the green of a new leaf in spring, just common brown.

Page felt her heart squeeze at the cruelty of his glib words and then berated herself for her foolishness. What more could she have expected from a devious, faithless, oath-breaking Scot?

She bucked beneath him.

He groaned. "I'd not do that if I were you," he advised.

"What is taking you so bloody long?" she demanded. "Have you not even the sense to untie a simple knot?"

"Ach, wench, but I'm trying. I didna tie this accursed thing—and bloody hell, 'tis no simple knot." He muttered an unintelligible oath beneath his breath.

Feeling a little desperate, Page lifted her knee, jabbing him in the thigh. "You'll need do more than try," she hissed.

He made some strangled sound and fell atop her just as the binds were undone at last. Page twisted beneath him, eager to be free. With hardly an effort and before she could stop him, he had her pinned, her arms spread at her sides and clasped to the ground.

"That wasna verra nice," he told her, his jaw set firm, and his eyes burning with fury.

"I did not mean to be nice," Page told him angrily, her eyes stinging with tears she refused to shed. Her nerves were near to shattering, but she could not bear another moment of his presence. His eyes continued to bore into her, demanding—what?

"How could you expect me to be?" she asked him. "You've abducted me from my home, kept me bound to a tree like an animal—and you think I should tender thanks? Please!" she appealed. "Can you not just set me free?" She couldn't help herself; tears welled. They spilled from her eyes, down the side of her face, onto the ground. She felt the wetness upon her neck, and blinked. Could he not see how very much it meant to her to return to her father? "You have your son," she beseeched him. Another tear slipped past her guard, and she shook her head, losing composure entirely. "I could find my way still," she pleaded. "Let me go... please?"

He shook his head, lowering his eyes. "I canna, lass," he said softly, regretfully. He met her gaze once more, and she spied the determination in his eyes. "I'm sorry, but I canna."

"You mean you will not," Page snarled at him.

He nodded once. "If you will, then, aye, I willna."

She swallowed her pride. "But my father," she entreated, her voice breaking. "He—"

"Your father is a bastard," he said impassionedly, though the blaze in his eyes had extinguished somewhat.

"He bargained with you in good faith!"

His jaw clenched, and he averted his gaze. For an

instant he said nothing, and then he turned to face her once more, resolute. "Your father conspired wi' David to take my son."

Page shook her head. "Nay," she argued. "He did not. Your King conspired with Henry. My father simply provided your son safe harbor at David's urging and King Henry's command. Naught more."

He seemed to be considering, and Page sensed his hesitation and added hastily, "He told my father you abused the boy. That he was so ill treated he would not speak for fear of chastening."

Still he seemed to be considering, but he said nothing; instead he seemed to be waiting for her to continue.

Page swallowed, afraid to hope, her heart racing. "So you see," she urged him desperately, "he thought he was helping your son. Let me go. You have your son, now let me go!"

"Nay, lass."

In the space of an instant, her hopes were dashed. And so easily. "You are vile," she spat, and twisted away from him. "Get off me!"

He complied at once, but didn't go far. He sat beside her, leaning an arm upon his lifted knee, his face screwed with some emotion she couldn't quite decipher. She hoped he was suddenly conscience-stricken over his faithlessness, but knew better than to hope for such a human emotion from a wretch such as he.

Page sat, too, glaring at him. "I swore I would make your life miserable, and I will. I'll not go willingly."

"But you will go," he avowed.

It was getting dark now, shadows descending. Page felt them seep into her heart. The numbness in her wrists was fading now, and her hands and fingers were beginning to hurt. She massaged them, embracing the pain. It was a welcome distraction.

He reached out suddenly and grasped her wrist, not

injuriously. Page started to jerk away, but he held her fast.

"I'm going to bind your wrist to mine," he explained.

Page opened her mouth to object, but he stopped her with a curt gesture.

"'Tis the only way I'll allow ye to remain unfettered."

"Unfettered," Page contended, incredulous. She tried to jerk her arm free, but his grip was unyielding. "What do you call binding my wrist to yours?"

"A safety measure," he relented.

Page glared at him.

"The choice is yours, lass..."

She let her arm go slack in his grasp, and snorted inelegantly. "What a choice! Bind me, then."

He did at once, binding her right hand to his left hand, securing the bonds, and then with his other hand, he removed the scarlet and black checkered blanket from his shoulders. He muttered an oath as he floundered over its removal, and then he glanced at her as though asking for her assistance.

Page screwed her face at him and drew back a little, thinking him mad. "You cannot possibly think I would help?"

His lips curved into a crooked grin. "I dinna suppose you would, at that." He eyed her discerningly and resolved to use both hands. He drew off his breacan and spread it between them, lifting himself up to draw half of the blanket beneath himself. Page considered a moment, and then did the same, knowing she'd only spite herself if she resisted. He offered her a little lopsided grin for her effort, but she refused to acknowledge it. She didn't wait for him to lie down, but did so at once herself, taking up as much of the blanket as she dared, and a little bit more.

To her surprise, he didn't complain when there was

only a sliver of blanket left for him. He simply lay upon his apportioned share, half on the blanket, half off.

So he meant to be chivalrous, did he?

Well, she fully intended to be anything but courtly.

"Iain," Lagan said, appearing above them. His face twisted into a frown as he stared down at them. "How verra cozy," he remarked with a curve to his lips. Page averted her gaze, wholly uncomfortable with the glare he cast her.

"What is it, Lagan?"

"Ranald," Lagan said, and his look softened to one of concern. He spoke to the MacKinnon in his own tongue.

"Go and look for him, then," Iain answered so that she understood. "But dinna fret overmuch... Remember 'tis Ranald the scavenger we're speaking of. He'll be back on his own... as always."

"Aye," Lagan agreed. "You're like to be right. He'll come back when it suits him... He always does. G'nite, then, Iain."

"G'nite," Iain replied. "Get yourself some rest, Lagan."

"Aye," Lagan said, turning from them, his lips curving into a leer. "You too, Iain."

He walked away, leaving them alone once more—as alone as they might be with a horde of barbarians surrounding them.

Without the sun to warm them, the northern spring night was wintry, but peaceful. Page lay there, staring past the budding leaves on the treetops, until the leaves were no more than shadows against the night sky. She stared up at the frosty points of light, trying not to notice the rising chill. Curious, that... last eve, on her way to her swim, she'd gazed up at those very same stars... they had seemed more like brilliant winking fires then... promising the gentle warmth of a summer night's breeze.

She shivered and curled upon the blanket as she heard little Malcom come and make his bed on the other side of his father. The two of them whispered together in their tongue, and the MacKinnon chuckled. Envy pricked at her, but she ignored it, wholly shamed by the uncharacteristic reaction.

What was wrong with her that she would begrudge a child his father's affections?

He was what was wrong with her, Page assured herself, bristling.

He'd come into her life and had made her feel again —all these accursed emotions she'd tucked so neatly away.

Well, she was going to have the last word tonight— or rather the last song—and she hoped she kept them awake all night long. She hoped they would be so blessed weary come first light that they would need put twigs in their eyes to keep them open.

She waited patiently until the darkness descended more fully, until it seemed everyone had settled for the night, and then she began to sing at the top of her lungs.

CHAPTER 10

Iain had only begun to doze.

He came fully awake with a start, his eyes crossing at the resounding shrillness of her voice. Bloody hell, but he should have known her compliance was too good to be true. He frowned as Malcom's little body jerked awake.

One by one, his men came awake, as well—some with a snort of surprise, others with mumbled "Huhs?" and still others with muttered curses.

And still she sang on, some English ballad about some man whose truest love had spurned him.

"Softly the west wind blows; gaily the warm sun goes; The earth her bosom showeth, and with all sweetness floweth. I see it with mine eyes, I hear it with mine ears, But in my heart of sighs, yet am I full of tears. Alone with thought I sit, and blench, remembering it; Sometimes I lift my head, I neither see nor hear..."

And so she continued, her song blaring, her melody true, but grating in its untimeliness and its volume. Iain waited impatiently, teeth clenched until he thought they might shatter. He stared into the darkness, while his men continued to grumble complaints, refusing to allow himself to be baited. He knew what she was trying to do, and it was working. But he'd be damned if he'd let her know it.

She'd grow tired soon enough and quit, he assured himself, and was rewarded when at the end of the verse, she suddenly quieted.

Sighing with vexed relief, Iain closed his eyes, only to snap them open when she began the verse over again.

This time louder.

Muttering silent curses, he said nothing, keeping reign upon his temper. Neither did his men speak but to themselves, until she began the verse yet a third time.

"Ach, now, Iain," Angus complained loudly. "Canna ye make her leave the lays until the morrow?"

His complaint was reinforced by a number of groans and muttered curses as the lass sang louder still. Iain closed his eyes and gritted his teeth, praying to God to give him strength.

"Bloody willful English," muttered Lagan.

He'd taken the words right out of Iain's mouth.

When Malcom lifted his little head and peered at her through the shadows, he decided enough was enough. Before his son could voice his own complaint, Iain inhaled a bellow—and strangled on his words as an enormous bug flew down his throat, silencing him.

Choking and coughing, Iain dragged his son from atop him and turned to slap a hand over the wench's mouth, trying to save her from herself. Christ, he could have sworn she smiled at his attempt to hush her. Pre-occupied with strangling as he was, his muzzle stopped her all of two seconds and then she began the verse yet another time, though this time the words were muffled through his fingers.

"Bloody hell, doesna she know another song, at least?" Dougal asked.

Iain might have asked the very same thing, were he not struggling for his next breath. Damn the vexsome wench. Still choking, he sat, dragging her with him as he leaned to hawk the bug from his mouth. Nothing came, and he was mightily afraid he'd swallowed the creature. Damn.

She sang louder, and Iain peered at her from the corner of his eyes, considering thrusting the whole of his arm down her throat. "Stubborn," he rasped, and choked again, giving in to another coughing fit. "Stubborn, fashious wench," he finished when he could.

"Da... will ye leave her to sing," Malcom whispered.

Shocked by the request, Iain stared down at his son through the shadows, thinking that surely the bug had addled his brains, or he must have imagined the soft plea. Malcom had never favored coddling. Ever. He'd been a wee man from the first day he could walk and talk.

"I dinna want her to stop," his son said somewhat desperately.

Though nothing else had managed to accomplish the feat, Malcom's uncertain request hushed the lass abruptly.

The glade turned silent, his men mute.

"'Tis a verra pretty song," Malcom said. "Will ye sing me another, Page?"

Shocked by his son's entreaty, Iain felt her swallow and he dropped his hand to allow her to reply, his heart twisting at the innocent request. The glade seemed to become quieter still as everyone awaited her reply.

For a long instant, she didn't answer, and Iain held his breath as his son added, a little aggrievedly, "My mammy never sung to me. She went to be wi' God when I was born. Will ye sing to me, please?"

Iain's heart twisted and his eyes burned with tears he'd never shed for a wife who had never loved him. "Malcom," he began, anticipating her refusal.

"Iain, ye heartless cur," Angus's gruff voice interjected. "Let the lass—" The old man's voice broke with emotion, and Iain knew that his eyes stung, as did his own. "Let the lass sing to the wee laddie, will ye?" he finished, his voice sounding more tender than the old coot would surely have liked.

"Aye," added Dougal. "Let her sing to the wee lad! Malcom never had him someone to sing him a lullai bye."

Iain swallowed his grief for his son and felt a leaden weight in his heart. "'Tis a fickle lot, ye are," he groused.

"Can she, da?" Malcom begged. "Can she sing to me?"

"Will she?" Iain amended, frowning. Bloody hell, but he couldn't make the lass sing if she didn't wish to— no more than he could have made her stop when she would not.

"Aye," she answered abruptly, surprising him. Iain's gaze tried to reach her through the shadows, but she was staring down at his son. "I'll sing," she said softly, and there were murmurs of approval from his men.

"What is it you wish me to sing?" she asked Malcom after a moment.

"Ach, ye can sing anythin'," his son declared excitedly, and then crawled over Iain to lie between them, as though it were a perfectly natural thing for him to do.

Iain sat speechless.

For an instant there was no movement from her side of the breacan, and then she lay down next to his son, jerking Iain's arm out from under him and tugging him down to lie beside them. Iain thought she might have done it on purpose—her way of letting him know that while she'd given in to the son's request, she didn't like the father any better for it. He would have grinned over her pique, save that he was too stunned by the turn of events even to think clearly.

"D' ye know anythin' Scots?" Malcom asked hopefully, facing her.

"I know one," she answered, "but not the words."

"Oh," Malcom answered, sounding a little disappointed. As he watched the two of them together, Iain's heart ached for all the things Mairi had deprived him of. Six years old and his son still craved a gentle voice to lull him to sleep. He couldn't help but wonder what else Malcom craved.

What had he missed? And had he done things right? No one had been there to tell him otherwise, and he'd just done what he could—what he knew to do. What if he'd not been a good father to Malcom all these years?

He coughed lightly, telling himself it was the bug that still scratched his throat, and not grief that strangled him.

"I-I can hum it," the lass said, and began, a little hesitantly.

For an instant Iain was too benumbed to make out the voice, and less the melody. And then it became clearer, and the ballad penetrated the fog of his brain.

His heartbeat quickened.

From where did he know that song?

Hauntingly familiar, and yet so strange coming from the lass's English lips, he couldn't make it out, though he tried.

As she continued to hum, the memory tried to surface from the blackness of his mind, achingly dulcet, and yet so hazy and indistinct, he couldn't bring it fully to light; a woman's voice... so familiar and soothing...

Not Mairi's voice, for he'd never heard her sing a note in her life.

Not Glenna either.

Whose voice?

His heartbeat thundered in his ears, as the words of a forgotten verse came to him.

Hush ye, my bairnie, my bonny wee laddie... when you're a man, ye shall follow your daddy...

He felt the jolt physically, as though his body had been stricken by an invisible bolt of lightning.

Bewildered, Iain laid his head down upon the breacan and stared into the darkness, at the almost indistinguishable silhouette of the two lying beside him, trying to remember.

Hush ye, my bairnie, my bonny wee laddie, when ye're a man, ye shall follow your daddy...

"Lift me a coo, and a goat and a wether," he murmured, trying desperately to recall the words. He joined her hum without realizing. "Bring them home to your minnie together..."

Christ, he couldn't recall the rest. His chest hammered. Whose voice was it he recalled?

His mother's?

Nay. He shook his head, for it couldn't be. His mother had died giving him birth. It couldn't be. He couldn't be remembering a woman who'd taken her last breath the very instant he'd sucked in his first. 'Twas said that she had never even heard his first wail.

Whose voice, then?

His heart beat frantically, and his palms began to sweat. "Hush ye, my bairnie, my bonny wee laddie," he sang softly, puzzling over the memory, unaware that he sang off tune and out of place—or that his men all were listening to him croon like a half-wit and a fool.

"Lammie," auld Angus broke in suddenly, sounding weary and unusually heavy hearted.

Iain blinked, and asked, "What did ye say?"

"My bonny wee lammie. The next verse is lammie," Angus revealed, and then sang, "Hush ye, my bairnie, my bonny wee lammie; Plenty o' guid things ye shall bring to your mammy..."

Auld Angus waited until the lass reached the proper place in the ballad and then joined her hum with his rich baritone. "Hush ye, my bairnie, my bonny wee lammie; Plenty o' guid things ye shall bring to your mammy..."

Some of the other men were humming now, and Iain

couldn't stifle his grin over the lass's plan gone awry. He was suddenly aware that Dougal had taken to his reed and was playing the tune, as well.

The haunting strains floated upon the night with his memory...

"... *Hare from the meadow, and deer from the mountain, Grouse from the muir'lan, and trout from the fountain.*"

In unison his men all began to hum, and in his mind, the woman's soft voice continued...

"Hush ye, my bairnie, my bonny wee dearie," auld Angus crooned. "Sleep, come and close eyes so heavy and weary; Closed are ye eyes, an' rest ye are takin'; Sound be your sleepin', and bright be your waking."

By the time they finished the last verse, Malcom's little body was curled so close to the lass that Iain could scarce make out who was who. His son's soft snore revealed he'd fallen asleep. Iain lay there a long moment, enjoying the haunting beauty of the reed's song, wondering of the woman's voice from his memory.

"However did ye come by the tune, lass?" he asked after a moment, hoping she wasn't asleep as yet.

CHAPTER 11

"Cora," Page answered softly.

"Cora?"

She sighed, uncertain how to explain about Cora. Certainly she wasn't going to reveal to this stranger that her father kept a leman. Her face flamed at the very thought. "She's... my... friend."

Jesu! She wasn't certain what she'd expected from her ploy tonight—certainly not a chorus of fool Scotsmen to sing along with her.

They'd done it for the boy, she knew. As had she. Her heart ached for the child lying so intimately within her arms. He'd called her by name. She'd been so afraid that the MacKinnon would hear it, and that she'd be shamed. But he hadn't, and then Malcom had asked her so sweetly—how could she have refused him, when grown men could no more do so?

"Thank you," the MacKinnon whispered at her side, and Page's throat closed with emotion. Lying so intimately as they were, with his son nestled between them, she could no more hold on to her ire than she could have refused the boy.

"Ye didna have to do it," he murmured, "but you've my gratitude, lass."

For an instant Page couldn't find her voice to

speak, and then she dared ask, "Thankful enough to return me to my father?" She was desperate to be away from these people—desperate, because some crazy part of her wanted to hold fast to them and never let go.

All because of a simple song they'd shared together, at the request of a little boy.

Foolish, foolish heart.

For her own sake, she needed to get away. Before she might be tempted to stay. And that would never, never do because they didn't really want her—aye, they did for revenge, but as soon as that was satisfied, she'd be worth less than nothing to them.

He hadn't answered as yet, and some traitorous part of Page was afraid that he might agree to her request. Ludicrous, she realized, but nevertheless true. "Will you take me back?" she persisted.

His answer was a sigh and a whisper in the darkness. "Nay, lass."

Page released the breath she'd not realized she'd held. Was that disappointment she felt? Relief? She didn't know, and she didn't argue with him, couldn't find her voice to do so.

The reed's music faded, the haunting strains coming softer now.

"When I heard him speak to you, and realized he was not mute, I assumed Malcom could not understand the English tongue," she remarked with some annoyance.

"Of course he understands," he said. "I intend to teach him Latin, as well."

Her surprise was evident in her tone. "You speak Latin?"

"D' ye think it only an Englishman's right to know God's tongue?" he asked her.

Page bit into her lip to keep from revealing the lowering fact that she'd never been taught. That he, a savage Scot, would know these things, and she not, made her feel like the wretched waif she must appear.

Then again, when had she ever felt like anything more than a poor relation?

She sensed, more than saw, him turn to face her. His movement tugged at her arm just a little, but not enough to wake Malcom, who was lying so peacefully upon it. Her arm was growing numb, but she didn't care. There was something so sweet about having him sleep there.

Something so right... and so breathtaking about lying beside his father.

Iain. Angus had called him Iain. Page savored the name privately.

Sheer foolishness, and still she stared, trying to spy the MacKinnon's face through the shadows, her heart tripping against her breast. "He would not speak to me in my father's house," she yielded.

For an instant he didn't respond, and her breath quickened painfully as she waited to hear his voice again.

"What would you have done in his place?" he asked her, after a moment.

"If I were a child alone in the hands of strangers?" she asked softly. Her gaze shifted to the shadow of the child lying so quietly beside her. "I... I don't know."

"He was afeared, is all."

"I... I might have been, too," she admitted.

"Are ye now, lass?"

Page swallowed.

"Afeared?"

"Should I be?"

"That I might hurt you?" he answered. "Nay. Ye dinna have to fear for that."

Something about the way that his voice fluctuated, softened to a gruff whisper, sent her heart skidding against her ribs. It mesmerized her, seduced her, drugged her senses. He might have done anything to her in that instant and she wouldn't have been the least prepared.

"What is it I should fear?" she asked him boldly, her heart beating faster.

The silence between them was deafening as Page awaited his response.

"That I might want ye," he whispered, his voice deep and dark and silky.

Page choked. "M-me?" she stammered. "Y- you? Nay," she said breathlessly. "You couldn't possibly."

He chuckled and reached out unerringly to seize her hand, drawing it toward him. It seemed to Page that her blood roared through her ears as he tugged her gently toward him, to place her hand upon his tunic, over that most private part of him. She was shocked unto death to find him full and hard, and in her astonishment, forgot to wrench her hand away. She couldn't speak, so stunned was she.

"Dinna seem so surprised, lass," he murmured softly, leaning closer.

Page's body convulsed secretly as she felt his presence move toward her in the darkness, closing the space between them, until his son's body was all that kept them separated.

Unreasonably, in that instant Page wished his son were not sleeping so peacefully between them, for she craved his father's arms more than she'd ever craved anything in her life. "I—" She stammered and forgot what it was she'd meant to say.

"Aye, lass," he swore, and his body pulsed beneath her hand, giving evidence to his words. "If my son wasna lying between us... you'd have much to fear."

Page's breath caught.

Had he read her mind? Had she spoken aloud? The blood quickened through her veins, but she was too shocked by his bold words to be afraid. She felt his gaze pierce her through the darkness, and dared to ask, her heart hammering fiercely, "What... what is it... you would do?"

"'Tis a dangerous question ye ask."

Page's heart lurched. "You... you swore you would not hurt me," she reminded him.

"Aye, lass, but I might be tempted to show you."

He pressed her hand more fully against him, and Page felt him pulse again beneath her palm. She blinked, as though coming aware suddenly of where her hand lay, and then jerked it away, flushing with embarrassment. How could she possibly have been so brazen?

He chuckled softly, and she laid back upon the breacan to stare with mortification into the feathery darkness, her breathing labored and her blush high—thank God for the shadows that concealed it.

"G'nite, lass," he whispered, a smile in his voice.

Page couldn't find her own voice to respond. She lay there, trying to determine what in creation had happened—how things had gone so awry.

She'd gone into this night expecting to goad the MacKinnon into anger, to make him sorely regret her presence, and had ended trying to goad him into taking her into his arms.

What else could she have intended by asking him questions of such a nature?

She'd also intended that his men should be so weary after a night of her relentless singing that they could scarce ride on the morrow. As it turned out, Page could hardly close her eyes. Every moment, she was acutely aware of the man and child lying beside her—of the ties at her wrist that kept her bound to him. She might have attempted to reposition Malcom's head and work the bindings free, but she couldn't bear to move the boy from where he lay. And then, when the MacKinnon turned abruptly in his sleep and drew her into an embrace that encompassed the three of them, she couldn't bear to end the sweet sense of belonging. She closed her eyes, and vowed to savor every last second of this euphoria in her heart. Shielding herself from the cold, she dared to nestle deeper within the embrace.

Tomorrow she could devote herself to escape.

Tonight she needed this more than she did her next breath—if only for the night, she could pretend. Only sometime, deep in the night, sleep cruelly deprived her, and she slept.

CHAPTER 12

Somehow morning dawned colder than the night before.

Page awoke, shivering. Her sense of emptiness returned. Misty sunlight shone into the glade, but that meager light was not enough to warm her stiff bones, and the overcast day promised a freezing rain that was certain to make the stiffness eternal.

She had to find a way to escape today.

There must be some way to evade them... somehow...

The MacKinnon had risen. So, too, had his son, leaving her to sleep alone upon the breacan.

Well, she berated herself. What had she expected? A morning kiss from the mighty MacKinnon? A waking hug from his son? Hardly! They weren't her family, she reminded herself. They were her gaolers, naught more —no matter that they'd shared a sweet moment the night before. It meant naught. Less than naught.

Save to her, it seemed.

It had filled her with a sense of belonging so keen and so beautiful that this morning she could only mourn its loss.

She closed her eyes and shielded her face from the

morning light with an arm thrown across her eyes. If she willed herself back... she could still feel the tendrils of warmth and affection squeezing at her heart.

Certainly the warmth that sidled through her this morn had naught to do with his bawdy promise. Her cheeks burned at the mere memory of where her hand had been.

He'd said that he wanted her—for what, she had no need to guess by the fullness of his loins. God have mercy upon her soul, for some part of her had been ready to cast herself into his arms, for merely the promise of affection, when she should have recoiled at the insinuation.

Was she so hungry for affection that she was willing to seek it, even at the risk of her own ruination?

It seemed so.

She sighed then, and sat, nettled by the turn of her thoughts, for she knew what a futile gesture it would be. She wasn't part of this family. She wasn't part of any family. Offering her body as a sacrifice for his pleasure wasn't going to change anything at all.

And her father wanted her back, she reminded herself, hope surging again. At any cost, she must find a way to return to her father.

Leaning back against a tree, she hugged her knees to her breast, watching the MacKinnon huddle together with his men. They spoke urgently in their own tongue, and she wondered what it was they discussed. She didn't ponder it long, however, for she spied Malcom then, standing next to a tree, with his back to her, rocking from foot to foot.

Poor wretched child, she thought. He seemed sad somehow this morn, his shoulders drooping, his head down, and she couldn't help but wonder if he was thinking of his mother after last night. Page couldn't forget the wistful way he'd spoken of her. There'd been no complaint in his voice, merely truth, and yet the sadness with which he'd spoken of the mother he'd never known had wrenched at Page's heart. She knew firsthand how difficult it could be to grow up without a mother—or a father, but that was another story entirely.

Her mother hadn't wanted her, had ensconced herself within a nunnery after her birth—shamed by the sight of her, her father had said. Page sighed. To this day she suffered guilt over it. 'Twas no wonder her father scorned her so, for 'twas said that he'd loved her mother more than life itself.

And Page had driven her away.

What had she done? Wailed too much? Had she been too demanding? She must have been a difficult child—certainly her father had said so often enough.

And still it plagued her.

What might she have done differently?

Her brows drew together at the self-defeating vein of thought. What was done was done, she knew, and she couldn't alter the course of her life now. Her mother was dead—had perished in the nunnery long ago of some fever of the lungs.

The best she could do now was make peace with her father, and the sooner she returned to Aldergh, the sooner she could begin.

A fresh wash of anger flooded her.

Stealing a glance at the one to whom it was directed, she wondered if the tales were true, that he'd murdered his wife. Somehow, she didn't think so. For as little as she knew of the man, he didn't strike her as a murderer of innocent women. But then... Her brows drew together. Mayhap his wife had not been innocent.

In any case, 'twas certain the MacKinnon had had plenty of opportunity to harm Page already if he'd so wished, and yet he had not so much as lifted a finger against her in anger.

Although he may have wished to last night.

Page couldn't suppress a vengeful smile at the thought of her rebelliousness. Sweet Mary, but she would have given much to have spied the MacKinnon's face when she'd first screamed her song into his ear— and then his glower when he couldn't get her to stop. Unable to keep herself from it, she indulged in a private giggle, and then bit her lip to sober herself.

He was a dangerous man, she knew.

So why didn't she feel herself more afeared?

She frowned at that and then contemplated his reaction to her defiance. Though she had feared his reaction beforehand, she couldn't help but think his frustration rather humorous this morning—curious too, for a man such as the MacKinnon, whose legendary prowess upon the field of battle preceded him. As did his cruel reputation. There weren't many in the northlands—nay, in all of England—who had not heard the tale of his poor wife's demise. 'Twas said that he'd tossed her out from the tower window the very morning of his son's birth, that he'd had no more use for her. She'd borne him his son, and that was all he'd required from her.

'Twas also said that his influence in the Highlands rivaled that of King David—that in truth, the Highlanders looked to the MacKinnon for their leadership, and that it sat sorely with David of Scotland.

Perhaps that was why David had stolen Malcom and had awarded the boy to the English court—to control the father?

Pondering the thought, Page rose and determined to lift little Malcom's spirits—he'd allowed her to soothe him last eve; mayhap he would again. Later in the day, she would be gone from their presence, she hoped, but for now, mayhap she could make a difference in the little boy's mood. Mayhap she could make him see that he could and would endure. She certainly had.

As she neared the boy, she realized he was singing to himself, and her heart twisted painfully as a vague memory came back to her, a dizzying whirlwind vision of herself lying within a golden field of grain, staring up as great tufts of white puffy clouds floated across a pale blue sky. She was singing herself a lullaby.

"Hush ye, my bairnie, my bonny wee laddie," he sang, in his lilting Scots brogue, bringing Page back. "When ye're a man, ye shall follow your daddy..."

Page smiled at his song, and the way that he swayed to the time.

"Lift me a coo, and a goat and a wether," he continued, and just then Page reached him, and put her hand upon his back, letting him know that she was there with comfort if he would only accept it. He stopped singing abruptly, and peered up at her over his shoulder, his little face screwing into a frown.

Page noticed he was holding something beneath his tunic, though she was unable to see it for the bulk of his breacan. She thought he might be hiding something from her, and wondered what it might possibly be. Her father had said they were a thieving lot, the Scots. Frowning, she reached back to seize the end of her plait and brought it about to be certain she still owned the only valuable thing she had to her name—the braided gold cord she'd pilfered from her father's cloak and now used to bind her hair. She breathed a sigh of relief when she saw that it was still there, adorning her gnarled tresses, like a strand of gold in a bird's nest. Again she frowned, and cast another glance at the MacKinnon, assuring herself that she didn't care whether he found her wanting.

She returned her attention to Malcom, her curiosity piqued. "What are you doing?" she asked.

He was still peering up at her, his little brows drawn together in an adorable little frown. He seemed to be considering how best to answer, and then yielded, "Paintin'."

Page's brows lifted. "Painting?" she asked with some surprise. "Oh, I see." The rascal, he was too shy to show his artwork. She smiled, and knelt at his back, hoping to coax him into bringing the art piece out from under his tunic. His gaze followed her down, and his little face remained screwed in a wary frown. "Might I see your painting?" she asked softly, coaxing him as she would a shy pup. "I very, very much like to paint myself," she told him truthfully, and then waited patiently for him to decide.

"Weel," he said, twisting his little lips as he considered. "I suppose ye can," he yielded, and started to fiddle with something beneath his tunic. Page smiled in triumph, and then to her horror, watched as he began to pee upon the ground. "See," he said, with some pride, lifting a finger to point at the wet dirt before him. It was then Page noticed that part of the ground was damp already.

"There's horns," he pointed out delightedly, "and there's eyes. I'm doin' a nose just now." And then he groaned in complaint, when his stream ended abruptly, "but I ne'er can finish 'cause I always run out." He turned to her then, wrinkling his forehead in childish disgust.

Page knelt there behind him in openmouthed shock, her face flaming. She didn't know what to say.

"'Tis... quite... lovely," she stammered, and then screeched in fright when the MacKinnon came and placed a hand upon her shoulder. She shrugged free of his touch, leaping to her feet.

Malcom peered up at his father, his smile suddenly beatific once more. "Halloo, Da," he said, beaming. "I was showin' Page my goat."

"Were ye now?" the MacKinnon asked, frowning, and then he turned to look at her, his scowl deepening.

Page took a defensive step backward. "I... I... I didn't realize," she said at once, stammering over her words. She shook her head in horror. "I... I would never have interrupted—I-I never imagined."

The MacKinnon peered over his son's shoulder at the ground before his son's feet, his brows drawn together.

Malcom shrugged. "She asked to see my goat, da, but it wasna finished," his son explained, eyeing Page as though she'd suddenly gone daft.

The MacKinnon's stern face broke into a grin then. He turned to Page and said, looking much as though he would break into hoots and howls of laughter, "He's a boy, lass, what can I say?"

Malcom was still staring up at his father, frowning. "But, da," he complained, "I didna get to finish again!" And then he turned to Page and declared, "Sometimes me and my da match to see who can piss the farthest."

The MacKinnon was quick to place a hand to his son's lips, shushing him. "Malcom!"

Forsooth! Page didn't think her face could grow any hotter than it was already.

"Me da always wins," Malcom's little voice announced, undeterred, his words muffled through his father's fingers. It was obvious he was very proud of his father's accomplishment. He tugged his father's hands away from his face and boasted, "On 'count of he's bigger, ye see. Right, da?" he asked, peering up at his father for witness.

Page lowered her gaze, blinking.

"Taller, lass, taller," the MacKinnon proclaimed, reaching out and lifting her face to his. "Because I'm taller," he explained quickly.

It was only then Page realized where she'd been staring, and her eyes widened in comprehension. She felt like swooning. Her face burned hot with embarrassment, and her only comfort was that the MacKinnon's blush was nigh as deep as her own must be. His cheeks were high with color.

She turned abruptly, feeling like a peagoose, and walked away, wishing to heaven she'd never woken up this morn at all. Mercy, but she didn't think she'd ever be able to face him again—father or son.

The MacKinnon came after her, and then his footsteps halted abruptly. "Page," he barked, his voice like a clap of thunder.

Page froze, blinking at the sharpness of his voice.

And then she realized what it was he'd said, and her knees went weak beneath her.

Mother of Christ.

He knew.

Her mind raced, trying to discern how he could possibly, and then she realized belatedly that Malcom had used her name yet again. Squeezing her eyes shut, she willed the world away. Lord help her, but she'd never felt more like crawling into a hole and remaining there the whole of her life. Now, in truth, she couldn't bear to face him.

What would she say?

How could she explain?

Her heart raced painfully.

Iain could scarce believe it, though the proof was there before him. She'd frozen in her step when he'd called her by name, and she stood there still, looking like a beautiful carving of stone in her utter stillness.

He'd heard Malcom speak the word last eve, but had assumed his son had misnamed the verse a page. He'd thought nothing more of it. Until Malcom had spoken it again.

Iain had been momentarily distracted over his son's artwork, but no more.

He had to know the truth.

And sweet Christ, but he did. He could tell by the way she stood, so stiffly, refusing to face him. She knew precisely what it was he wished to know, and she gave him his answer with her silence.

As he watched her tilt her head back and peer into the sky, as though in supplication, Iain shook with a rage so potent, it was manifest. He could taste it bitterly. He could feel it—from the fury that burned him, to the heart that squeezed him. He could smell it, and the stench was putrid. If FitzSimon, the bastard, stood before him this instant, Iain thought he might tear out his bloody heart and shove it down his throat—provided he had a heart at all. Damn the ill-begotten whoreson!

What sort of man went so far as not to name his own daughter? Page was no name at all, but a mere role to be played.

How could a man—how could anybody—have so little concern over a human being? His own flesh and blood?

His jaw clenched so tightly that he thought he could taste his own blood.

He muttered an oath beneath his breath, and swore that if ever again he faced the man who called himself her father, he would strangle the fool with his bare hands.

Uncertain what else to do, Iain merely stared at her back—she'd been unable to turn and face him as yet—and he saw that she quaked, as well.

Nothing he had done to her, nothing he had said, had caused such a reaction in her, and he swore another bitter oath as he turned abruptly, unable to face her as yet, unable to force her to face him.

Turning, he nearly plowed into Lagan in his blind rage.

"'Tis Ranald," Lagan announced. "Iain... he hasna returned."

Iain muttered an oath. "Gather a search party," he commanded Lagan. "Damn, but I'm gain' to strangle the wandering whoreson when we find him."

CHAPTER 13

They combed the woodlands more furiously now, hacking away at the flowering vines and foliage in their paths.

Lagan and Ranald had been companions since childhood, and Iain could tell his cousin was growing more distressed with every inch of ground they covered in search of his friend.

Iain hadn't been overly concerned the night before, only because he'd thought Ranald needed time to calm himself—that perhaps his disappearance had been a gesture of defiance. He was well aware the men had been displeased with his decision to bring Page along with them.

Ach, but if he thought he despised the name she gave him before, he loathed this one all the more. Nay, but 'twas no name at all.

As the party continued to search, Iain considered others that might better suit her—and decided that every last one of them suited her better than Page. The very thought of her father's insult made his ire rise tenfold. He hacked at a thick vine with the flat of his sword, cutting it in twain with the blunt force of his blow.

Christ and bedamned! Where was Ranald?

Angry as he may have been, Iain knew Ranald would never have deserted them. His brow furrowed. Most assuredly not without his mount.

His thoughts skittered back to Page, and he shook his head in disgust. Damn, but how could any man allow—nay, demand—that his own flesh and blood be borne away by the enemy? Iain clenched his teeth at the unpalatable thought. Try as he might, he couldn't comprehend the workings of FitzSimon's mind. Even had Mairi been unfaithful and borne him another man's bairn, Iain knew he would have loved that child as if it were his own. It was never the bairn's fault, was it? He couldn't comprehend such blatant lack of regard in a father who shared the same blood with his daughter.

Surely 'twas an abomination before God's eyes? Although God might reap his own justice, Iain found he wished to show the whoreson a more earthly sort of hell—and he damned well would if he ever set eyes upon the man again.

"Begin searching the brush," he commanded. A sense of unease lifted the hairs of his nape. Until now, they'd been scouring the ground for some evidence of struggle—some clue to Ranald's disappearance—tracks through the soft earth of the forest, leaves disturbed. There was nothing.

"He canna have gone far withoot his mount," he reminded his men, thinking aloud, and still his brooding thoughts returned to Page.

Maggie was a good sounding Scots name.

Anger surged through him once more.

At his wits' end with the search, he cursed and hacked off the crown of a bush, then bellowed for Dougal. "Take Broc and Kerwyn," Iain directed the lad. "Search to the right; circle about. Lagan," he commanded, turning to address his dour-faced cousin. "Take Kerr and Kermichil and sweep to the left."

Lagan nodded and did as he was directed without

question. Iain took the remaining two men with him. The greater number of his forces, he'd assigned to remain with Page and Malcom. The last thing he intended was to lose his son again to FitzSimon.

As far as Iain was aware, they'd not been followed, but he didn't intend to take unnecessary risks where Malcom was concerned—for all he knew, FitzSimon had pursued them, but at a discreet distance, with the intent of luring them away upon this fruitless search, so that he might in the meantime reclaim Malcom.

While Iain was certain the bastard was unwilling to stir himself for his daughter's sake, Malcom was another matter entirely. Doubtless FitzSimon would be facing Henry's wrath over losing his ward. In truth, 'twas why Iain had forsaken the old road, opting for the shorter, more arduous route across the border and into the Highlands—just in case the fool thought to follow. Aye, for there was a reason Scotia had resisted outlanders so well and so long; the land was their ally.

Nor did he wish for Page to have access to the old road to facilitate her escape. Though why he should care whether she fled them, he didn't know. He only knew that he could scarce stomach the thought of her facing her father and the despicable truth—that he didn't want her.

The look he'd spied upon her face when, with Malcom in tow, he'd returned from dealing with her father haunted him still.

It was Broc who discovered the body, not long after their divergence. The lad's hue and cry seemed more a woman's squawk in its unrestrained hysteria.

Iain spun and raced through the woods, batting at limbs and leaping over low shrubbery to find Broc doubled over and spewing out his guts.

"Wolves," Broc declared with a strangled gasp.

Iain followed his gaze to where Kerwyn and Dougal

were dragging the body out from under bracken and brush, their faces ashen as they heaved out their friend by his arms. At the sight of them, Broc doubled over to retch yet again. Were Iain not suddenly so sick at heart himself, he might have been amused by the sight of the strapping young lad doubled over before him. Easily the tallest of them all, Broc, for all his bluster, bore a woman's heart, along with his much too bonny face.

"Looks like something made a feast of him during the night," Dougal said grimly.

"And buried him for another meal," Kerwyn added, his jaw clenching.

"Ach," Dougal said, shaking his head and grimacing, "but ye canna even tell 'tis Ranald, save for the breacan he wears."

Iain walked to where they had dropped the body, and stood looking down upon the lifeless carcass at their feet. Both Kerwyn and Dougal averted their gazes, unable to peer down into the mangled face and body of their kinsman.

"What'll we do?" Kerwyn asked. "What'll we tell his minnie?"

"The truth," Iain answered, his gaze fixing upon the wooden shaft that protruded from Ranald's chest. He bent to examine the broken arrow, running a finger over the jagged end. "Whatever that may be. Wolves may have feasted here," he declared, "but be damned if someone else didn't get to him first." The wolves' attack had been so ravenous, they'd obviously broken the arrow in their frenzy. Iain considered the broken arrow another moment, something about it niggling at him, until Lagan, Kermichil, and Kerr broke into the copse where they had gathered.

Eyeing Broc with lifted brows, Kermichil then turned his gaze to the body, his lips twisting into a grimace. "Christ!" he exclaimed.

With a keening cry of grief, Lagan came to his knees at Ranald's side. "Stupid bastard," he lamented, letting out another low, tortured moan. "Stupid, stupid bastard."

Iain placed a hand to his cousin's shoulder and squeezed, comforting him, urging him to his feet. "There's naught we can do for him now, Lagan," he said. Lagan came to his feet, nodding, battling grief—a grief that was reflected in each and every man's eyes, though none spoke it openly. Each had understood the risks they would face in coming to this place.

Iain removed his breacan and tossed it at Dougal, his heart heavy with the task ahead. "Wrap him," he commanded, his voice hoarse. "He deserves a proper burial." His jaw clenched. "We'll be takin' him home to see that he gets it."

"Nay! Use mine," Lagan offered, his voice breaking and his eyes suspiciously aglaze. He removed his breacan and tossed it at Dougal. Dougal tossed Iain's back to him. Iain clutched it within his fist, nodding his assent when Dougal looked at him for approval.

Dougal nodded, and averted his face, scarce able to meet Lagan's eyes—all knew that the two had shared a friendship that bordered on the familial. In truth, Lagan and Ranald were more family than even Iain and Lagan were. Though he didn't begrudge it, the knowledge aggrieved Iain, for he was alone in so many ways.

He had his clan, aye. And he'd had his father, and he had Malcom, too, but never a sister to tease, nor a brother to spar with. As a boy, he had, in truth, envied their friendship. As a man, he'd held it in high regard. As chieftain, he mourned the death of his kinsman.

Without a word they set to the task of wrapping Ranald's bloody body within the unsullied red, black, and white folds of the MacKinnon colors.

PAGE WAS DETERMINED TO MAKE THE BOY REALIZE how much his silence in her father's house had plagued her. Until now, he'd quietly listened to her rebuke, his brows knit, his little face growing more and more markedly resentful. She didn't allow it to dissuade her. After all, she'd spent weeks trying to ease his fears and befriend him—and all the while he'd understood every word she'd spoken to him. Somehow, it wounded her still that he would simply distrust her out of hand. She'd tried so hard. "Why did you not speak to make me aware you understood me, Malcom? I wouldn't have hurt you."

He merely shrugged, though his expression was one of irritation.

"Did I not stand in defense of you against my father?" Page asked him, making herself more comfortable upon the ground beside him. She lifted her knees, hugging them to her breast, and peered up to see what Angus and the rest were doing. She found them all pacing still, and her brows knit, for she hadn't as yet discovered what it was that had them so agitated.

She'd half expected they would be off and away as soon as they'd gathered their belongings together this morn, but here they sat still, waiting—though for what, she had no notion.

"Malcom... why did you not trust me?" she persisted, glancing down at the small pile of dirt he had raked into a heap between them. Reaching out, she swept her palm over the ground, helping him to arrange the soil. "I understand why you might have been afeared of my father. Your father explained. But..."

He glanced up at her then, the indignation in his eyes robbing her of words. "Because you said awful things about my da," he answered grudgingly. "You lied to me and said he was bad."

Page blinked, too taken aback to reply for an instant.

"You tried to make me not like him," he accused her. "And my da is guid! Ye dunno my da."

Judas, but it hadn't occurred to her that she might have offended him. It hadn't occurred to her because she'd been more than prepared to believe the worst of his father.

Her face heated. She didn't know what to say in her defense. "I... I'm sorry," she offered. "I suppose that I did, but I—" But she didn't get the chance to explain, for they returned then, the MacKinnon and his men, like grim specters marching from the woods, their faces leaden and their eyes ablaze.

Page's gaze focused upon the MacKinnon in their lead. His gaze met hers, and for an instant, for the space of a heartbeat, Page felt the incredible urge to flee. Her heart thudded within her breast, and although she knew instinctively that the anger within the depths of his amber gaze was not meant for her, it made her tremble, nonetheless. She tried to look away, but couldn't, and in the blink of an eye, his gaze passed to his son. The rigidness in his incredible frame seemed to ease at once.

It was only after she was freed from the MacKinnon's piercing gaze that she spied the man-sized bundle borne upon the shoulders of his men.

Page knew instinctively that it would be one of their own, for she noted, too, that the body was wrapped within the MacKinnon colors. Yet who it might be, she couldn't begin to conceive. Her gaze raced from man to man as she tried to recall an absent face, but her mind drew a blank. These were not her people, and she knew them not at all.

She stood at once, watching in horror as they bore the body to their mounts. Both she and Malcom stared as they hitched the unwieldy bundle to a horse. Only when they were finished did she find herself able to peer down at Malcom.

His gaze lifted to hers, and in his glistening eyes she saw that he knew without being told.

"Ranald," he said, blinking away a lone tear.

CHAPTER 14

They rode without speaking, their mood somber and their faces grim.

Page felt as though she were part of a funeral procession—a brooding stranger amongst grieving kin.

Ranald's body had been strapped to the back of Lagan's mount, and though they'd taken great care to wrap him tightly, the length of his body made it impossible for the blanket to cover him completely. A leaden foot peeked out, waving at her with every jouncing movement of the horse's stride.

The sight of it turned Page's stomach. Had she chanced to eat anything this morn, she might have lost the contents of her belly. As it was, she was in danger of no such thing, because she hadn't eaten anything at all. They'd begun the search almost at once upon waking, and after the discovery of the body they hadn't seemed inclined to take the time to fill their stomachs. Page could scarce blame them for their lack of appetite. Though her own belly churned in protest, she doubted she could have kept anything down for long.

She'd never seen a dead body before—in truth, hadn't as yet, for they hadn't unveiled him. But she knew he was there. Even had she been able to pretend the bundle was no more than hefty baggage, the waving foot remained a grim reminder.

Though she tried to ignore the body, and the foot, it was nigh impossible—particularly as they'd allowed her the use of poor Ranald's mount. Like dogs herding sheep, they kept her girdled between them, making any sudden flight for freedom she might undertake all but impossible.

Nevertheless, when the time was right, she fully intended to try.

She couldn't believe their arrogance in giving her a mount—not that she wasn't grateful, mind you. She was more than pleased not to have to ride with the MacKinnon again. His presence disturbed her. But she doubted they'd simply have handed her the reins had she been a man. Did they believe just because she was a woman she would not possess the wherewithal to attempt an escape? Well! She loathed to disappoint, but she would escape them, the very instant an opportunity presented itself.

For her sake, she hoped it came sooner rather than later.

Having had so little sleep the previous two nights, she struggled to keep alert. Every moment carried them farther from Aldergh, she knew, and lessened her chances for escape. Out of sheer desperation, she had taken to tearing snippets from her undershift and dropping them furtively upon the ground to mark their path.

Ridiculous as it might seem, she had to do something. She couldn't simply sit here upon poor Ranald's horse and ride into oblivion. As of yet, no one had noticed, and she praised God for that small stroke of good fortune.

By late afternoon she began to worry that she wasn't going to be afforded the opportunity to use the snippets to find her way back. It was becoming more and more difficult to tear at her shift without gaining notice, as the hem had long since whittled to her knees. When the sun began to fade at last, she resisted the urge to peer back to see how visible the tiny scraps were. She couldn't afford to have them suspect her.

While the MacKinnon hadn't spared her more than a glance in the hours they'd been traveling, the old man Angus and the one they called Broc kept her, without fail, within their sights.

Angus, for his part, seemed disinclined to forgive her for her surly temper of the previous eve. The old man frowned at her every time he chanced to peer her way. Well, she didn't care. She didn't need the old fool to like her. Forsooth! But she'd lived a lifetime without his favor. Why should she care that some old goose she'd only just met, and wouldn't know long—her enemy at that—disapproved of her? She certainly did not.

Broc, on the other hand... She couldn't quite figure him out. Hours ago, she could have sworn he'd spied her tearing her shift and casting the fragment upon the ground, and yet he'd said nothing at all. He'd kept his silence, casting her dubious glances now and again, but naught more.

Mayhap he'd not spied her, she wondered, nibbling the inside of her lip.

Well, she'd soon enough have her answer, because it was time to tear another. She didn't wish the scraps planted too far apart—nor too close, lest she run out of shift to rend. Though judging by the position of the sun, she thought they might be stopping soon for the night. Running out of material didn't seem to be her greatest concern—locating the scraps in the dark would be. And yet there was no help for it.

Each time she dropped a scrap, Page tried her best to note the surrounding landscape. She only hoped she would be able to recognize the way come nightfall. In her favor, the moon would be almost full again tonight. Its light should help to guide her—if she found a way to escape, she reminded herself. She wasn't free as yet.

Mayhap she could talk the MacKinnon into leaving her unfettered.

Trying to be as inconspicuous as possible, Page gathered her bliaut into her fist, raising her skirt. She glanced about, as nonchalantly as possible, to be certain no one was watching. No one was, and she quickly ripped another fragment from her shift, then released her skirts, letting the hem fall once more. Clutching the scrap within her fist, she tried to gather the nerve once more to drop it.

She made the mistake of peering about then, for she met the MacKinnon's gaze, and her heart leapt into her throat.

He was watching her over his shoulder...

Had he spied her?

But nay... she didn't think so, for his face was a mask without expression. He held her gaze imprisoned for an eternity, holding her as surely as though in physical bonds, but his expression remained unreadable.

Page's heart began to pound as she gripped the cloth within her fist.

Drop it, she told herself. He wouldn't see it, for his gaze was riveted upon her face. With the flurry of movement about them, the rise and fall of so many hooves, there was no way he would spy it.

She couldn't do it. His gaze held her riveted and paralyzed, while her heart beat like thunder in her ears.

And then he suddenly released her, glancing away, back toward his son. Page felt the withdrawal acutely, and to her shock, found she didn't want him to go back to ignoring her.

She stared at his back, feeling bereft in a way she didn't quite comprehend.

He'd ridden the entire day with his son, the two of

them talking, laughing, sharing in a way that made Page ache deep down. She didn't wish to feel this... this... envy. It was deep and black and ugly, but she could scarce help herself. Seeing the MacKinnon smooth the back of his son's hair with his open palm, the gesture such a loving one, filled her heart with grief like she'd never known. It left her with an emptiness she'd only suspected was there before now.

The undiscovered void.

All her life she'd filled it with indifference and resentment, and in the space of a day these people, the MacKinnon and his son, had revealed it.

Watching the way that he squeezed the boy's shoulder, the way that he leaned forward to almost embrace him, as though he didn't wish to embarrass the child, or himself before his men, but couldn't quite help himself, made her eyes sting with tears.

She'd never known the feel of a hand upon her shoulder, or the tender brush of a palm upon her face...

Her eyes closed and she remembered against her will... the gentle way he'd held her face... the whisper-soft way he'd spoken to her... It made her quiver still... made her yearn for that moment once more.

How piteous, she thought, that she would be reduced to such a shameful longing.

Like some Jezebel who cared not a whit who her lover was, nor even whether she knew his name, only that he was there when the lights were doused, she craved her enemy's touch.

Even knowing it was contemptible.

Even knowing he had betrayed her father.

Even knowing her father wanted her back.

Long after he'd turned away, Page clutched the cloth within her hand, unaware that she did so.

She was startled from her thoughts by an unfamiliar voice, and turned to find that Broc had somehow maneuvered his way alongside her. He sat his mount beside her, staring as though awaiting a response.

To what? What had he said? And where had he come from so quickly? She'd not heard, nor spied his approach. Her heart hammered guiltily as she recalled the cloth in her hand. She tried to conceal the evidence within the folds of her skirt.

Broc glanced about, and then turned narrowed eyes upon her. The spite in his expression gave lie to the sweetness of his youthful face. "I said... 'twill take more than a siren's voice and a pretty song to woo the rest o' us, wench."

For an instant Page didn't understand what it was that he was speaking of, and then it occurred to her that he must be referring to the lullai bye she'd sung to Malcom the night before. She stiffened in the saddle, offended by the conclusions he'd drawn. "I was trying to woo no one," she assured him. Nothing could have been further from the truth.

"Guid, then," he said, leering at her, "because 'tis no one ye wooed."

Page resisted the urge to throw the scrap she held into his face. She wanted to throw something at him, but the cloth wouldn't hurt him, she knew—would likely make him laugh with glee, and then she would be left to explain its existence.

"I dinna ken why the laird doesna simply leave ye," he said nastily, "nor why he seems compelled to save ye from your bastard da—but I've no such compunction. 'Tis your fault poor Ranald is strapped t' the back o' Lagan's mount. Your fault, and no other, d' ye hear me, wench?"

For an instant Page was too stunned by his accusation to do any more than stare up at the fair-haired giant. Sweet Mary, but these Scots were each one taller than the other. And their tempers, one more surly than the next.

How dare he place the blame for Ranald's death at her feet.

Refusing to cow to his charge, Page narrowed her eyes at him. "How dare you accuse me, sir? I have absolutely no idea what poor Ranald wandered into, but whatever it was, was of his own doing—not mine. I assure you."

He scratched idly behind his head.

"So ye say."

He couldn't possibly think her responsible. Could he? Her breath snagged at the sudden hope that spiraled to life within her. Unless... If her father had come after her... "My father?" she asked, and couldn't conceal the note of hope in her voice.

"Nay," the behemoth answered, with unmistakable disgust, and then surprised her by adding, "No such luck, wench. But he willna be rid o' ye so easily—I swear by the stone!"

"So easily?" Page blinked in confusion. "But... I don't understand..." Her brows collided. "What is it you are trying to tell me?"

He glowered at her. "Never mind, wench," he said, shaking his head, as though he thought she was too obtuse to understand, and didn't care to waste more words. He leaned closer to speak in a whisper. "I didna come to speak o' your whoreson da," he revealed, reaching back and scratching at his scalp. "But to tell ye to drop the bloody piece o' cloth, already."

Momentarily shocked, Page crushed the cloth fragment within her fist and instinctively buried her hand deeper within her skirts.

His lips twisted with unconcealed contempt and his gaze shifted to the hand she'd shielded. "Drop the bloody cloth," he charged her.

Page stiffened in the saddle, her gaze flying about in alarm.

"Ach, wench, I'll no' be exposin' ye," he assured her.

Her gaze snapped back to his face. "You... you'll not?"

He shook his head, eyes gleaming. "I want ye gone, e'en more than you wish to go," he swore. "But if ye willna drop the accursed thing, wi' our luck, ye'll wander in circles and end up right back in our bloody camp."

Page frowned, growing more and more confused. "But... I... I don't understand." She shook her head. "What of your laird?" She cast a nervous glance at the MacKinnon's back. "I... I thought he..."

"Wanted ye?" The behemoth snorted and then turned to glance at his chieftain. "A mon says many things in a moment of... weakness."

His gaze returned to Page, and her face heated as she remembered the moment she and the MacKinnon had shared the night before.

His moment of weakness.

What is it I have to fear? she recalled asking him.

That I might want ye, he'd whispered.

Judas! Had everyone else overheard, as well? If Page had cared one whit what these people thought of her, then she would have been riddled with shame. But she didn't care, she told herself. And she was not.

He scratched at his forehead. "I tell ye true... the MacKinnon doesna want ye any more than the rest o' us do," he told her.

Page said nothing in response, merely glared at him. Somehow, his words wounded, though she told herself she didn't care. After all, wanting a woman in a moment of physical weakness was certainly not the same as wanting for a lifetime. She knew that.

"I'd be doin' Iain a favor," he persisted. "He simply doesna wish to have your death upon his conscience, is all. And he doesna have to if you'll but drop the bloody cloth."

Deny it all she wished, but the truth pained her. Her

confusion intensified with the ache in her heart. Something niggled at her... something... He didn't wish to have her death upon his conscience? And yet why should he have her death upon his conscience unless he meant to kill her? And he didn't want her... but he'd taken her, nevertheless?

Something was not right.

He'd said he'd taken her out of revenge... an eye for an eye, she reminded herself. And then, too, he had said he'd wanted her. Last night. Or that he might want her —Lord, but she was growing confused.

"But..." Page averted her gaze, unwilling to show him her pain, or the upheaval of her thoughts. "He said—"

"Never mind what he said. Drop the cloth," he commanded her quietly. "Drop it now, and then keep them droppin' till ye're sittin' bare arsed upon poor Ranald's mount. I'll shield ye... and then I'll help ye to escape when the time comes. Do it," he hounded her.

Page stared a long moment at the MacKinnon's back.

He was preoccupied with his son, never the least aware of her presence. He didn't want her—couldn't possibly—and why should he?

She peered at the rest of the men, watching them a moment longer. Not a one of them seemed to be the least concerned with the discussion she and Broc were having together.

For truth, it seemed she was unwanted.

It seemed to be her destiny.

The ache in her heart intensified. Why? Her brows drew together. Why should she care one whit what these people felt for her? She couldn't possibly have thought they'd want her, after all? That they would take her as one of their own into their fold? She couldn't have possibly hoped?

How disgustingly foolish she was, for she suspected

that some silent aching part of her had longed for just those things.

"Drop it," Broc demanded again, and Page moved her hand out from her skirts. She held her fist clenched at her side, concealed between them.

He eyed her closed hand expectantly, and she was uncertain whether to drop the fragment or nay. It could be a trap, she realized. In truth, he might well be trying to coax the evidence from her hand...

And then again, nay, for all he would need do was utter a single word to his laird, and then her ploy would be finished... and he'd not done so.

"Unless ye dinna wish to go," he taunted her. Page met his mocking blue gaze. "Are ye so smitten wi' the MacKinnon already, English? D' ye want him to want you?" He lifted a pale brow in challenge. "Is that it?"

Glaring at him, Page opened her hand, releasing the piece of cloth. It fluttered down between cantering hooves.

He merely smiled. "There now," he said. "That wasna so difficult, was it?"

"Scot!" She spat the word as though it were a blasphemy, but he seemed impervious to her anger. "I can scarce wait to be free of the lot of you."

"Guid," the giant said, grinning. "Because the feeling is mutual."

"Bloody behemoth," she hissed at him. "Do you oft make it a practice to tyrannize those weaker than you?"

His grin suddenly turned into a frown, and he seemed genuinely insulted by her question. Good! Let him be.

"I'd rather be a bloody behemoth," he grumbled, "than an impertinent little dwarf."

Page straightened her spine, utterly insulted. "I am not a dwarf, you despotic oaf." She stared at him, wondering if he was blind. "I am tall for a woman, I'll have you know—or mayhap Scots women all are bloody behemoths, too?" He didn't react enough to Page's liking and she added spitefully, "Or mayhap you wouldn't know? Perchance all women run in fear of you?"

Scarlet color crept up Broc's fair neck and into his pretty face, and Page was wholly shocked to find that her words had unerringly hit the mark. With a face like the one he possessed, she'd never have guessed. His blue eyes were clear and bright, and his features well defined. He had not the stark, masculine beauty of the MacKinnon's face, but he was comely nonetheless. Guilt stung her, though she told herself he deserved every word.

"Do you not have a woman, Broc?" she asked, trying to soothe his bruised feelings, though she knew not why she should.

The giant straightened his spine, his disposition surly as he revealed, "I have a dog. What need have I for a woman?"

He turned away, his face bright red, and Page nipped at her lip to keep from grinning at his innocent question—his even more callow reply. Sweet Mary, but even she knew what a man needed with a woman. She'd certainly spied enough lovers in the shadows of Aldergh.

"She's a verra smart dog," he added defensively, though he didn't bother to look at her. "The smartest dog I've ever known."

Page didn't reply.

"Loyal, too," he added, and she nearly burst into hysterical laughter at his plaintive tone.

Good Lord. She continued to stare, and had to resist the urge to breach the barrier between them, to put her hand upon his arm and soothe his injured pride.

He scratched rather earnestly at his groin area, and then the back of his ear, and Page grimaced, wondering if he'd gotten fleas from sleeping with his dog.

"What are ye looking at?" he snapped, when he turned and found her staring.

She cringed at the harsh tone of his voice and averted her gaze, determined not to banter words with the surly giant any longer. Damnation, though she'd never admit it to him, she'd certainly run in fear of him too.

Shielded by his towering form, she continued to tear snippets from her shift and then drop them at intervals, and though she cursed Broc's arrogant presence beside her, he didn't break his word.

He didn't give her away.

CHAPTER 15

Of all Page wasn't certain which was worse to bear: the presence of the irksome giant beside her... the gruesome foot waving at her from under the blanket on the horse before her... or the sight of the MacKinnon riding at their lead.

Like some heathen idol he sat his mount, tall and magnificent in the saddle, his dark, wavy hair blowing softly at his back. In the afternoon sunlight, the streaks of silver at his temples seemed almost a pagan ornament, for the metallic gleam of his braid was almost startling against his youthful features. The sinewy strength evident in the wide set of his shoulders and solid breadth of his back only served to emphasize the fact that he might have killed her any time he'd wished, with no more than a swat of his hand—that same hand that caressed his son so tenderly now.

In truth, he'd not even spoken to her harshly. He'd been naught but gentle, and it mightily confused her.

In fact, he might have done anything he'd wished to her, and no one could have stopped him. Scarce a handful of men present were even as big as the MacKinnon, and only two were taller—the man at her side being one of them. She cast him an irritated glance. And yet she knew Broc would no more prevail against his laird than he would consider rising up against him in the first place.

None of them would.

Her gaze swept the lot of them. It was evident that each and every man wholly embraced the MacKinnon as their leader. It was almost comical the way they allowed him the lead of their party. Like dogs, they followed wherever he went—and if one man chanced to pass him by, Page was struck with wonder that that man would unconsciously look to his laird, and then slow his gait to allow Iain to pass once more.

The MacKinnon, on the other hand, seemed oblivious to this ritual. He forged onward, his attention fixed only upon his son, who sat before him in the saddle.

There was an undeniable air of authority about him, one he wore with unaffected ease, and an air of total acceptance from his men.

And yet, he obviously did not oppress them, else the giant beside her would never be aiding her as he was. 'Twas evident by the way that he looked at his laird that he did so only because he meant to do him a favor. He seemed to think he was protecting the MacKinnon—and did so rather vehemently, Page thought.

Well, who would protect her from the MacKinnon? she wondered irritably.

Aye, she'd already determined that he'd not harm her, but what of her heart, and her soul, and her body?

She was drawn to him in a way she couldn't comprehend, though she knew it was a dangerous longing. And still she couldn't stop herself from yearning.

For what? The sweet promise of his whisper? The gentle touch of his hand?

His love? she thought with self-disdain.

It was growing more and more difficult to keep her eyes from wandering in his direction.

Particularly so given his meager state of dress.

The short tunic and wayward breacan exposed a sinfully bare thigh as he rode. And he seemed completely oblivious to the fact that the wind every so oft lifted his blanket for a tantalizing glimpse of the man beneath. She tried not to look—she truly did—but she could scarce keep herself from it, for the beauty of the man seduced her, stole her breath away.

Her heart quickened, for she was once again accosted by the image of them lying together upon his breacan... the way he'd taken her hand...

She swallowed at the memory, her throat feeling suddenly too raw.

Lord! She was a woman, was she not? No child. Why did every need have to be emotional? Mayhap it wasn't love that drew her, after all. Why couldn't it simply be that she wanted the things she knew instinctively he could give her as a man? Though she was innocent in the ways of men and women, she was no halfwit! She was wholly aware of the way he made her feel... bold and breathless... achy.

It was a physical thing, for certain.

Aye, she wanted his arms about her. What was so wrong with that? Certainly she wasn't the only woman who had been so inclined? Why was it that a man could want these things but a woman could not?

Why was it that a woman's needs were to be masked by such a thing called love? Love was certainly overrated, she thought, and she wasn't even sure it existed.

So then, if there was no such thing as love... wasn't the mask a lie? Wasn't it truly a weakness to fall back upon this myth? Wasn't it better to be honest with oneself and admit the truth of the matter—that it was lust, instead?

Aye, she truly thought so... and though the MacKinnon might be her enemy, she was drawn to him in the way a man attracts a woman. Nothing more. Lust was uncontrollable, was it not? It was a primal thing that lured and seized one's senses. And every waking thought. That's what men claimed, at any rate. She'd heard more than a few faithless husbands tell their wives just so.

She stole a glance at the MacKinnon, just as the wind whipped, lifting his breacan and tunic. Her breath caught, and her body betrayed her then. Her heart began to thump against her ribs.

Like warm spiced mead, heat slid through her, burning her flesh, and making her mouth go drier than sun-dried leather. The movement of the horse between her thighs quickened her breath, even as the sight of the MacKinnon awakened her body to life. Her hand fluttered to her throat, and then slid down the front of her gown; she paused at her breast, marveling at the sensations that stirred there.

He was the only man who had ever made her feel...

She closed her eyes and lifted her hand, caressing the bared flesh at her throat, imagining his hand there instead...

He was the first man ever to have awakened her body to life... the first whose touch she'd ever craved... the first man who'd ever wanted her...

Aye, and she wanted him to want her, but it wasn't his love she yearned for, she told herself. She was no dog to go begging for affection, but a woman whose body was not made of cold steel.

She wanted him, she admitted wantonly.

And she wanted him to want her.

Her enemy.

Her eyes flew open, and her breath caught as she looked about anxiously, praying no one had spied her at her wicked musings. Her cheeks flamed with mortification.

Her gaze settled upon the man who had so easily and without trying invaded her every thought.

He was wholly unaware of her.

He rode with his son, oblivious to the reactions of

Page's treacherous body. Her brows drew together, and she nibbled the inside of her lip. What a fool she was!

He didn't want her, she berated herself.

Whatever had possessed her to believe him when he'd said he did? The man riding before her could have any woman he so chose. And Page was no man's choice.

Not even her own father's.

Which brought her to wonder ... whatever had Broc meant when he'd said that the MacKinnon felt compelled to save her from her da? She stole a glance at the behemoth riding beside her. *But he willna be rid o' ye so easily, I swear by the stone,* she heard him say to her again, and she blinked. Her father? Her father wouldn't be rid of her so easily? A feeling of unease sidled through her.

The one thing she knew for certain was that somehow, she needed to find a way back home.

She was desperate to find a way to escape.

❦

IAIN PLACED A HAND TO HIS SON'S SHOULDER, squeezing gently, with a desperation that belied the reassurance of his touch. "Try to remember, Malcom..."

For a long instant there was silence between them, as Malcom tried desperately to do as was bade of him. "I canna, da," he answered unhappily. "I only remember wakin' up." His son peered up at him, and his little brows were drawn together in a frown.

"Wi' David?"

His answer was a soft child's murmur.

"Weel, then, son, dinna fash yourself. 'Tis no failing o' yours that you canna remember."

Malcom nodded, and Iain asked, "They didna hurt you, did they?"

Malcom shook his head.

"Guid," Iain said. If he discovered elsewise, he'd have to turn his mount about and strangle the first

Sassenach neck he encountered. "Tell me one more time, son... and I willna trouble you with it for a while more... Tell me exactly what you remember about that night."

"I only remember eating... and then I was sleepy," he said.

"Who was there eating wi' ye, d' ye remember that much?"

"Ummm... auld Angus?"

He sounded so uncertain that Iain had to wonder how much of the sleeping drog they'd given him. Christ, but 'twas a wonder they'd not killed him. His anger mounted once again, though no one could have suspected by the ease of his posture. Only the muscle ticking at his jaw, as he listened to his son, gave testament to his incredible fury. "I know aboot Angus... Anyone else, son?"

"Maggie," Malcom declared. "And Glenna—and Broc."

Most every man had been with Iain, save for Angus and Broc, he reflected. And Lagan.

But Lagan had been brawling again with auld man MacLean over his youngest daughter. His cousin had long ago taken a liking to the dun-haired lass, but Mac-Lean had sworn he'd never trust another of his lasses to MacKinnon men. Iain couldn't say as he blamed the man.

Mairi's death had not been by his own hands, but the fault lay still upon his shoulders. He should have known. He should have stopped her somehow. And he might have, had he not been holding their son.

Malcom. He'd long grieved for Malcom, for she'd abandoned him as surely as though she'd slapped his face and then walked away. Christ, but he loathed her for that.

And for leaving him with her blood upon his hands.

As far as MacLean was concerned, Iain was her murderer, for he had been the last to see her alive and he had been the one at the window, while his daughter's body lay sprawled upon the jagged rocks below. Any chance for peace had been crushed along with her that day.

In truth, looking at it through MacLean's eyes, it didn't matter much whether Iain had pushed her from that window, or whether he'd merely driven her to it. He was responsible either way, and were Iain in MacLean's shoes, he didn't think he'd give another daughter to settle any feud.

God help him, even to his own mind, he was guilty. Somehow, he'd failed Mairi. He didn't know what it was he'd done to drive her out from that tower window, but he must have done something.

Something.

He hadn't loved her precisely. She'd been much too reserved with her own affections for that, but he'd cared for her nonetheless. And he'd wanted to love her. There just hadn't been enough time.

What had he done to drive her from that window?

In the beginning, the need to know had driven him near mad. It tormented him still. He must have done something, but he couldn't recall ever treating her unkindly. He'd set out to woo her, but he'd failed miserably. To this day, the image of her standing before the tower window haunted him—hair mussed, eyes wild, and that slight smile that made the hairs upon his nape stand on end even after all this time.

He shuddered, willing away the graven image, and asked his son, "And you dinna recall going to bed? Or waking in the night?"

"Nay, da," Malcom answered dejectedly. "I dinna recall."

Iain ruffled his hair. "Dinna worry yourself aboot it then."

From what Maggie had told him, Malcom had fallen

asleep at table, over his haggis—not surprising when the boy would and did do anything to keep from having to eat his pudding. Maggie had tried to wake him, and upon finding him truly asleep, had carried him to his bed. Feeling drowsed herself, she'd never made it out of the room. She'd dozed while recounting him a story, and had slept sitting beside the bed, her head pillowed within her arms. It was only in the morn, after she'd passed auld Angus still asleep at table, slumped over his plate, that she'd begun to suspect. Glenna had fallen asleep in the kitchen, Malcom was nowhere to be found, and no one had witnessed a bloody thing. What Iain wanted to know... almost as much as who... was how they'd managed to *drogue* the entire household with no one the wiser.

He damned well intended to find out.

It occurred to him suddenly that he couldn't call Page Maggie. Ach, but two Maggies in one household would be one too many. He'd have to think of another name. He was certain she couldn't be enamored of Page, but how to broach the issue without offending her... Or mayhap he wouldn't broach it at all, he'd simply call her by whatever new name he decided upon. If she objected, he would simply have to set about finding her another, until he found one she preferred.

When had he made the decision to keep her? he wondered.

Christ only knew, he didn't need the battle of wills —nor was she a beast of burden for her fate to be decided upon so easily, and yet those were precisely the reasons he wasn't about to let her go. Somehow, it had become crucial to him that she not be hurt any more than he was certain she was hurt already. And if she discovered her father didn't want her...

He frowned. She still harbored hope that he would come after her—bastard! He spied it upon her face, and in the way she turned so often to peer behind. As though looking for him. Iain almost wished the whoreson would pursue them, so she wouldn't be disappointed.

So that he might cast his blade into the bastard's stone-cold heart.

He'd thought to have the opportunity when they'd found Ranald's body, but Iain had seen no sign of FitzSimon's party since then. In truth, he hadn't even then, save for the evidence of Ranald's body.

If not FitzSimon, who had gotten to Ranald?

Who would have motive?

The possibility that one of his own might be responsible made his gut turn. He squeezed his eyes shut, trying to think. Something lay at the edge of his thoughts, something, though he could not capture it. Every time he came close, he heard the ghost of the lass' song in his ears.

Hush ye, my bairnie, my bonny wee lammie...

Christ, where had he heard the lay before? Whose voice was it that haunted him?

The memory escaped him.

On the other hand, he was intensely aware of the woman riding at his flank—of every glance she gave him, every move she made. And aye, he was aware, too, that she was dropping the scraps. He'd spied her at her mischief just about the time Broc had. Iain hadn't confronted her because the matter he'd been discussing with Malcom had been more important. And just in case she managed an escape, he fully intended to go back after them tonight—gather just enough to thwart her. Her scheme wasn't going to help her any at all.

And he intended to discover what Broc was up to. The lad was the last person Iain might have suspected of recreancy, but the evidence was there before him. Iain had thought at first that Broc meant to confront her, but even after their heated discourse, the lass continued to drop her scraps. Whatever his reason, Broc was aiding her. That much was plain to see.

Conspicuous as well were her continued glances toward him. The yearning reflected within the depths of those overwise brown eyes squeezed at his heart. It wasn't Iain she coveted, he thought, but the affection between Malcom and himself. He sensed that even as he sensed the heat of her gaze upon him, and he felt the overwhelming desire to take her into his arms, soothe away her pain.

Emotions warred within him.

Bloody hell, but if she didn't cease to look at him with such obvious longing, he wasn't certain he was going to be able to restrain himself. He was only a man, after all, a man too long without a woman. It was becoming more and more difficult to recall himself to the fact that it wasn't him she desired, but something else he couldn't give her. He didn't have it in him to give. Once he had thought to open his heart; now it was sealed tighter than a tomb.

And still she drew him.

She was lovely, aye, but there was something more.

It'd been a long time since he'd felt so utterly distracted by a woman. Not even Mairi had affected him so. His wife had been beautiful, but her heart had been poisoned against him. Loving her had been a duty. Wanting her had been unthinkable.

But he wanted FitzSimon's daughter.

His warning to her last night had not solely been to distract her, and the effect her glances were having upon him was painfully physical. His body craved the things she silently asked of him. Christ, but he might have been blind and still sensed her presence.

Like a man thirsting for water, and maddened by its scent upon the air.

He was on edge.

He turned to find her staring, and his blood began

to simmer. Brazen thing that she was, she held his gaze, her dark eyes smoldering, reflecting a carnal knowledge he knew she couldn't possibly possess... or could she?

The possibility aroused him, evoked new images. His heartbeat quickened.

Or was it his own reflection he saw mirrored there in the fathomless depths of her eyes, his own dark yearnings?

Suddenly her eyes sparkled with challenge, or mayhap defiance, and she snapped the reins, urging Ranald's mount toward him. Iain turned away, recognizing the battle to come, knowing it would be near impossible to watch her approach, anticipate her, and still keep his reason when she confronted him.

For someone who was supposed to be a hapless hostage, she acted more like a haughty queen, snapping rebukes to Broc, and sending daggers with those lovely eyes. Mostly in his direction and Iain could scarce keep from grinning at the thought.

And then he sighed, for those beautiful, wide brown eyes of hers were too expressive for her own good.

CHAPTER 16

I t was the look upon his face that provoked Page—that arrogant twist of his lips that made her feel as though he mocked her somehow.

What could he possibly know? The cur! Certainly not that she was dropping the scraps of cloth—else he would have put an end to it long ere now.

And lest he be a sorcerer, nor could he possibly have divined her wicked thoughts. They were hers, and hers alone to contend with, and if her cheeks were high with color, 'twas simply because the wretched man had driven them forward, ever forward, never stopping, never resting. She was weary. And she had to do the necessary, besides—since after noon.

Page hadn't complained even the first time, determined as she was not to speak to a one of them. She'd long determined that Broc was a flea-bitten moron. Scarce had he spoken a kind word to her all day, and his only saving grace was that he fiercely loved his little Merry Bells. She'd be willing to wager he even slept with the beast—wouldn't doubt that it was where he'd managed to catch his fleas. And she was nearly certain he had them now.

Just to be certain she didn't fall heir to a few, she edged her mount away from him, and tried not to be

149

overly amused when he bragged to Kerwyn about the animal's keen intellect. Kerwyn, for his part, ignored her. He listened to Broc's boasts with half an ear, and an enduring smile that suggested he'd heard the tales before.

Then there was Angus. Angus was an addle-pated old fool, staring at her as he did so oft—as though she were some confounded riddle to be deciphered. He was unsettling her—nigh as much as his laird. Her only comfort lay in the fact that he obviously thought the MacKinnon all the more daft, for the looks he cast in Iain's direction were decidedly bemused.

And the MacKinnon... She'd already determined how he made her feel.

Confused.

Hopeful.

Titillated.

And she'd be hanged before she'd let him know it.

Her patience at an end, she snapped the reins, spurring poor Ranald's mount toward the lead rider. She headed straight toward the MacKinnon, cursing the circle of mounts that enclosed her. Be damned if they were going to keep her from speaking her mind. Determined to have words with her tormentor, she forced her way through the band of Scotsmen, ignoring the scores of curses and warnings that flew at her back.

No one stopped her, and in less than a moment, she found herself face-to-face with the man who had managed to plague most every second of every waking thought.

Iain MacKinnon.

Even his name made gooseflesh erupt.

"I demand you stop this instant," she insisted of him.

He lifted a brow, and his sensuous lips curved with humor at her expense. "D' you now?" he asked her. "And what is it precisely you wish me to stop, lass?" When

Malcom, too, peered up at her, a little anxiously, he placed a hand gently to his son's shoulder, reassuring him. Page tried not to note the simple fatherly gesture, and chose instead to focus upon her anger.

She chafed over his arrogant tone of voice. "I mean halt," she said, indicating the cavalcade with an impatient wave of her hand. She eyed his son prudently, imagining the boy must think her a madwoman. She could scarce blame him; certainly she felt like one. Truly, she'd felt discomposed from the instant he had first set eyes upon her. Befuddled. And then her gaze returned to the MacKinnon's glittering amber eyes, and she suddenly couldn't think at all.

Her heart leapt at what she saw in the depths of his gaze.

Desire.

No mistaking it.

Like golden flames flickering at her, his eyes sent molten heat through her body, making her skin prickle in a way that was both agonizing and breathtakingly sweet.

Those eyes mesmerized her, invited her to bask in their warmth.

An unwanted shiver coursed down her spine.

She tried to ignore it, and failed miserably. The assault upon her senses was too keen. Her gaze lowered to his mouth, and she stared, unable to look away.

"What is it ye would be wantin' me to stop, lass?" he asked, his voice husky and low.

Her heart did a little somersault as she met his gaze.

He blinked, waiting, and Page swallowed. "I need to rest," she clarified, slightly dazed, and more than a little breathless. The thickened sound of her voice embarrassed her.

He seemed to realize the effect his gaze had upon her, for his lips curved a fraction more, and she stammered, "W-we've b-been..."

He smiled suddenly, a devastating smile, and the breath left her completely. Her stomach floated, and her heart took wing, like the wind before a storm, flying into her throat—like dry leaves swept helplessly upward by a merciless gust only to choke within the gnarled limbs of trees.

"R-riding all the morn," she finished lamely, swallowing.

He said nothing, merely deepened the smile, and Page felt suddenly like a wretched waif whose tongue had been cut out for merely stealing a taste of forbidden fruit. She felt suddenly so meritless beneath his scrutiny. Judas, but he was beautiful... everything about him. Everything. From the curve of his lips, to the contours of his face, the long lean length of his body, and the muscled strength in his mostly bare limbs.

And she... she was so... plain.

He couldn't possibly desire her for anything but revenge.

Truly, he must have been toying with her, playing some cruel, cruel game, for a man such as he could never want a woman such as she.

Not even for the space of a heartbeat.

His kindness only served to confuse her. It made her heart wrench painfully.

The lilting brogue and the soft tone of his voice tormented her, for it made her wish for things that could never be... a lover's embrace... a whisper at her ear... his breath upon her lips.

All the things she'd heard whispered about in the dark corners of her father's home.

"What is it, lass?" he asked softly.

Page turned abruptly away, unsettled by the wicked turn of her thoughts. She felt the flush creep into her face. "W-we've ridden all day without the least chance to rest," she complained. "Nor to—" She gazed at him quickly, and then her glance skittered away. She was both annoyed and disconcerted that she should have to broach such a tender subject—hurt and disappointed, though she had no right to be, that he would play such games with her tattered soul. "You know…"

How could he? she asked herself.

He couldn't know that the shreds of her heart were welded so delicately together. That a single whisper from his beautiful lips could melt her piteous heart like the first tender snowflakes upon the sun-blistered ground.

Nay, as far as the MacKinnon was concerned, she was her father's beloved daughter. And she… She was his vengeance against the man who had stolen his precious son.

She started suddenly when he bellowed a command to his men in his Scots tongue. At the fierce sound, Page startled where she sat. Anger was her first thought —he was angry with her—and she shuddered.

What had she done?

Mercy, she couldn't even remember what she'd said.

His men at once changed course, away from the valley they'd been following, up the rise of a gently rolling hill. The MacKinnon spoke to his son briefly, the boy nodded, and he then bellowed for his cousin Lagan to come and attend him. He handed his son to Lagan, sparing a quick glance toward Page, and then snapped an indecipherable command to his cousin. He reached the distance between them suddenly, seizing her reins, and then veered onto a path that led into a sparse woodland, away from the party.

"Where are we going?"

"To gi' ye the privacy ye need," Iain snapped, angry with himself, not so much for neglecting her needs, but for what he spied in the depths of her eyes. His men didn't stand on ceremony where bodily demands were concerned, they simply did what they must. He'd forgotten to consider hers, and was irritated by the fact, but what angered him most was that wounded look she'd given him.

Damn her father for an uncaring ass.

Though her bearing was proud and unbroken still, her eyes revealed everything. He'd recognized the attraction at once, in the impassioned depths of her dewy-eyed gaze, and his body had reacted tenfold. As if he were a beardless youth, the sweat from his palms had begun to salt the leather reins he held. His arousal had been immediate and painful. He'd sat there, listening to her ramblings, and had been hard put to keep his thoughts on any single word she spoke.

Even the sound of her voice seduced him.

Lulled him.

Husky and breathless.

The way she might sound after being thoroughly loved.

The thought set his heart to pounding.

And then just as quickly as her passion had unfolded, it had vanished, and was replaced with that same wounded gaze he now recognized from the first time he'd set eyes upon her—the look of a woman scorned.

Christ, man, didn't she realize what her presence did to him? Had he not made it clear enough last eve? He had half a notion to find the most secluded spot here in these woods, yank her down from that mount, and show her just how much he was affected by her.

Bloody hell, how could she not know?

"What of the rest?" she asked a little anxiously. "Where do they go?"

Iain's jaw remained taut, though he tried to rid himself of his anger. For her sake. "To find a place to settle for the eve."

"Without us?" She sounded distressed, and a little breathless, and Iain turned to appraise her. She was staring again, those beautiful soulful eyes wide and fraught with anxiety. She nibbled at her lip nervously, and he lapped at his own gone dry.

Afeared to be alone with him, was she?

Somehow, the thought both tormented and pleased him immensely.

"We'll catch them," he assured, turning away. "As soon as we're through."

"Where will they go?"

"Just beyond the rise. 'Tis a secluded enough place, we'll not be troubled."

"I see," she said, but didn't sound so very reassured.

"There lies a loch, as well," Iain added. "I thought perchance ye would wish to refresh yourself." He peered over at her, watching her expression as she rode, gauging her mood, and then added, "Suisan." Christ forgive him, he hadn't meant to test the name so soon, hadn't even thought about what to call her, but the name came to his lips even so, and he thought it suited her perfectly.

Delicate and beautiful, like the lily she was, but sturdy, too, coming back each spring after weathering the bitterest of snows.

Her gaze flew to his, and she blinked, then turned abruptly away. "I am no beast to be named at your pleasure," she hissed.

Iain didn't know what to say. It was true. Leading the rest of the way in silence, he drew her into the thickest part of the forest, and then reined in and dismounted.

"No, you're no'," he acknowledged finally.

Page remained stiff in the saddle. Iain went to her side, intending to help her dismount, but he made the mistake of peering up at her in that instant.

There were tears in her eyes.

He could see them though she wouldn't meet his gaze, and his heart wrenched. Had he acted wrongly? he wondered, and then knew he had, for when she turned to look down at him again, there was anger in her eyes, an anger so filled with pain that Iain's heart bled at the sight of it.

Damn, but why should he care what she felt? He didn't know this woman. Didn't owe her a bloody damned thing. Hadn't wanted to bring her...

And yet he had.

It occurred to him suddenly that if he truly hadn't wished to bring her, he simply wouldn't have. He cared what she felt, because she'd reached some part of his soul that had lain untouched for too many years. Somehow, she'd pierced that shadowy realm with that first heart-stirring glance.

Mounted before him, towering above him as she did, her long plait unraveling down her back, her dark eyes flashing and luminous, and her stance proud, she seemed almost a wild thing in that instant. Wild and unapproachable, like the deer of the forests, those wide brown eyes both forbidding and heedful at once.

For an instant Iain was wholly mesmerized by those fathomless dark pools, some part of him yearning to leap into their misty depths, discover the hidden mysteries... and pleasures.

He knew she thought he pitied her, that much was apparent. He could spy it in her eyes, but it was so far from the truth. If anything, he admired her. Not many men could have taken the abuse he sensed she'd received at her father's hands, and still come through unscathed as she had.

Though wounded she might be, she was far from conquered.

He envied her, too, he realized. Envied her for the freedom she was unafraid to embrace.

He thought about the moment he'd first spied her, soaked from a midnight swim no true lady would have dared even fancy. Her eyes had flashed with defiance, though she'd been cast at his feet.

Christ, he wanted, in that moment, not to conquer, but to join her.

Too many years he'd lived in this dark room that was his life—always doing what was right, what was just, never pursuing the candlelight that beckoned just beyond his chamber threshold.

He'd been his father's only son, and for all intents and purposes had been born into the world a man. His father, though Iain was certain had loved him well, had never truly been a father at all, but a teacher, instead, always fearful that his only heir would somehow depart this life before him and that his sovereign bloodline would end. He had both protected Iain interminably and trained him fiercely so that he might fend for himself and his clan when at last the old laird closed his eyes. And Christ, he'd closed them all too soon, his final time during Iain's seventeenth winter.

His father would have been proud of him, he thought, for he had given everything to his clan. Every moment of every waking hour of his life.

He'd spared them naught.

And still some part of him was not his own to give, for it eluded even him.

And then he'd been alone.

He'd never known his mother, had never ceased to mourn that fact. Though sometimes... sometimes... he thought he spied her kindly face shrouded amidst his deeper memories.

Nothing more than fancy, he knew, for she'd never even held him within her arms. He'd never had the chance to look into soothing eyes—didn't even know what color they were, though he had the vaguest impression of blue—to suckle as a babe at her breast, to spy her watching him as he played with other children.

Mairi, too, had been his duty to his clan.

He'd wanted so much from her, so much—mayhap too much. He was willing to take that much responsibility for her death. Hell, he'd taken it all—as ever was his duty. Her rejection of him, and the infernal ends to which she had gone to escape him, had finally extinguished the lone guttering taper he had tended so zealously all of his life. In the space of a heartbeat, in the wake of her flight from his high tower window, the candle had flickered and died.

The woman sitting so proudly before him was like that light shining just beyond his threshold, beckoning him out from the darkness he knew so well.

He wanted to follow it.

Those brief moments of reflection were Iain's undoing, for she seemed to recover herself from the stupor they had shared, and reacted suddenly with all the vengeance her eyes foreboded.

Too late, he seized the reins from her hands. She spurred Ranald's mount furiously. The horse reared, surging forward. Iain lost hold of the reins with all but one finger, and with that tentative hold, he tried to force her to stop.

Ranald's mount, addled now, seemed to hesitate, and Iain at once tried to regain his hold upon the reins, but she spurred the horse again, more furiously this time, and he was flung forward. The leather sliced the flesh of his hand, searing it with the force of its pull. His arm twisted within the rein, and he was dragged with her.

He howled in pain, trying to find a foothold, but the horse tore away too swiftly. Realizing in that moment that she was bloody well going to kill him, that she wasn't going to stop, that he would need pursue her with his own mount, he tried to free himself at once. He succeeded, though not before managing to drag himself under the horse's hooves. His answering curse was a cry of pain.

His arm untangled and he was flung to the ground.

His head impacted with a crack that reverberated clear into his unconscious mind.

It took Page an instant too long to free herself from the angry fog that had enveloped her. Realizing suddenly what she'd done, she whirled her mount about, and sat, horseflesh rippling impatiently beneath her as she stared at the body lying so still upon the ground.

Sweet Mary, what had she done to him?

Some part of her wanted to go to him.

Her heart twisted painfully.

She turned to stare in horror and panic at the path that led to freedom, and for an instant was anguished and torn.

There would never be a greater opportunity for escape.

And some part of her wanted to go—to her father— some part of her truly did, but the greater part of her could not leave with him lying there as he was.

So still.

Her father's enemy, she reminded herself.

A liar and a faithless cheat.

The man who had treated her with nothing less than kindness. The man whose worst crime against her had been to give her a name her father had never stirred himself to bestow.

Suisan.

Her heart wrenched. She wondered what it meant.

The sound of it upon his lips, like a lover's whisper, had made her heart leap, had filled her eyes with tears she'd never dared to shed.

Aye, and she'd dared in that moment to love him, this fierce stranger, whom she dared not even like.

Her heart hammered as she stared at the body lying so still before her.

The realization that he pitied her had turned her heart to stone, her thoughts to fury.

She came aware of tears streaming down her cheeks.

Sobs rang in her ears—her own?

Why should she weep for this man?

How could she not go? She'd waited all her life for her father to want her, and now that he did, she must go to him. She must!

This man had betrayed him, had broken faith. Why should she care that he lay there?

Possibly dying.

Possibly dead.

Her stomach twisted.

He didn't so much as move as she watched. He lay there upon the forest floor, his big body crushing the bracken beneath. She gauged the light frantically through the sparse-limbed trees; it was fast growing dark.

What if they couldn't find him before the sun made its final descent? She recalled what Broc had told her about Ranald—in what condition his body had been found—and fear squeezed her heart.

She couldn't bear for that fate to be Iain MacKinnon's, no matter that she wanted to loathe him still.

She couldn't go, God save her, but she couldn't.

Spurring her mount back, she reined in beside him, dismounting quickly, kneeling at once at his side.

He lay so still, so still that Page's heart thumped and fear deluged her.

Desperate to hear his breath, some evidence that he yet lived, she placed her cheek against his lips, warm still with the sweet elixir of life. Her eyes closed with relief when she felt his breath, so light and airy against her face.

Thank God!

She couldn't have borne it.

Thank God, thank God, thank God.

For the longest instant she couldn't move, so benumbed was she with giddy relief.

Of a sudden, a hand caught her at her nape, and then his eyes flew open. She felt his lashes flutter against her cheek but couldn't move for the clasp he had upon her neck. She filled her lungs with a gulping breath as his grip held her more firmly against him. His nostrils flared, as though scenting her, and then he groaned and clenched his jaw.

Her heart began to hammer fiercely. It pounded erratically, the sound of it echoing like savage drums in her ears. She tried to draw away, alarmed by the currents that jolted through her at the intimate position of their bodies.

"Nay," he rasped.

The single word was a plea, a tormented whisper that bore more desperation, even, than did the depths of her very soul. That more than the force of his grip held her quiescent against him.

For an instant, neither of them spoke; he simply held her to his face, his lips pressed against her cheek, with a desperation that Page had thought only she knew.

She stirred, and his grasp tightened.

"Don't go," he pleaded, and she could feel his heartbeat quicken against the palm she had braced at his chest.

"I..." Page swallowed convulsively. Unreasonable as it seemed, she took fierce pleasure in the simple request. It choked the breath from her lungs. "I... I feared to have killed you," she confessed softly, and closed her eyes, allowing him to move his lips against her face.

Sweet Mary... soft, warm, and sweet... his lips were... making her daft. She trembled with keen pleasure.

His breath came labored, as did her own, and his whisper was hot and sweet against her face, and still he did not release her. Page tried to writhe away, before her body could betray her, but somehow, his lips found their way to her ear, and he murmured, "Stay, lass..."

Sweet Christ... Page thought she would die from the sensations that swept through her at his plea, at the warmth of his breath against her lobe... the way that he seemed to be savoring her face... like a blind lover seeking knowledge of the one he loved... though Iain's fingers were his lips... and he was making her insane.

"Are... are you hurt?" she found the wits to ask. Her fingers slid into his hair, searching, secretly reveling in the thick healthy texture of his hair.

"Nay."

She breathed a sigh of relief at his answer, and then he whispered in her ear. "Why did you come back?"

"I... I don't know," she answered, and truly she didn't.

"I'm verra glad you did, lass."

"I shouldn't have," she acknowledged softly.

"But you did."

"Aye." Page swallowed convulsively, for his lips began to move tentatively against her cheek once more. She didn't stop him. Couldn't. She closed her eyes to savor the feel of them caressing her face. Sweet Heaven above, she had never known a heart could feel so taxed and still continue to beat.

That her flesh could feel so sensitive to the touch.

That her body could yearn so... desperately.

Her body, not her heart, she reminded herself, for her heart was entombed in stone—stone walls she had erected herself with blood and mortar, and painful precision. Only her father had the power to bring them down, and instead he had helped to build them, handing her the bricks, one by one, that she might lay them firmly upon the foundation that was her life.

Ah, but her soul... her soul had yearned and soared, flying from its confines within the prison of her heart, like a specter walking through solid walls.

Her body yearned now, too, and she had not the will to deny it.

Her fingers unknowingly tangled within his hair, and she was unaware that he eased his grip.

"I'm sorry," he whispered. "Forgive me, lass." He kissed her cheek while his arms urged her down upon him. "I didna mean to hurt you..."

"I know," Page cried, and somehow knew that it was so. And then she couldn't think at all, for his hands had somehow found their way to her face. He cupped her cheek as he had that first night... with a tenderness that stole her breath and heart away, and tears sprang to her eyes.

CHAPTER 17

T he desire she revealed to him so unabashedly
made Iain's heart trip painfully. It sluiced through
his soul like a hallowed stream of light, banishing
shadows from the darkest cobwebbed reaches.

"I shouldn't," she whispered. "Shouldn't want..."
And the desperation he heard in her voice tore at his
soul. He shouldn't want her either, but he did. God help
him, but he did.

He turned her face to meet his gaze. "But you do?"

She closed her eyes and rested her forehead upon
his. "Nay."

He drew away a fraction, staring into her eyes.
Deeper shadows descended upon the forest, bathing
them in gloaming light, but still he could see the bewil-
derment in her eyes.

The truth.

"I spy it in your gaze, lass," he said.

She denied it once more, a quick jerk of her head
that convinced him not at all.

"I shouldn't," she persisted.

He cupped her chin, drawing it up so that he might
better see her lips when she spoke. "That look tells me
otherwise. It speaks to my lips..."

He drew himself up and placed his lips to her beau-

164

tiful chin. "It begs for this..." Instinctively she tilted her head low, of her own accord, and he covered her mouth with his own, tasting her lips, tentatively at first.

Page felt every sweet caress deep into her soul. Every soft foray across her lips sent her heart into a wild skitter.

Sweet Mary, how she wanted this...

How she wanted him.

Never in her life had she craved anything more...

What could possibly be wrong with taking what little he would give her? What did it matter that she would leave him? It wasn't... and didn't, she told herself.

What if this one instant in time were to be her fleeting moment of happiness? Her one chance at this sense... of belonging... of feeling... wanted...

Would she regret never taking it?

She knew he couldn't possibly love her, nor could she love him, for they were strangers. And yet... he did want her. She knew it by the way he touched her... so gently, and yet with so much ardor that it made her heart cry out with joy.

His tongue swept across her lips with a relish that made her heart squeeze painfully. Page opened her mouth to his gentle prodding, his erotic, demanding caresses, and her body quivered as his tongue swept inside, boldly, plundering her mouth... teasing her tongue, until she moaned with delight and joined him in the gentle play.

It was the sweetest taste of bliss.

Everything she had ever dreamed.

"Tell me now ye dinna want me, lass," he challenged her, tearing his lips away from her mouth.

He left her with her eyes closed, unable to open them to the tangible world. Lord, she wanted to go back... experience every delicious shudder all over again.

"Aye," she whispered breathlessly, never opening her eyes. If she didn't open them, it didn't have to be real...

She could pretend...

"I do..."

At her honest admission, pleasure so keen it was almost pain shot through Iain. And then he groaned as an entirely different sort of pain dizzied him. It burst through his limbs when he tried to lift himself from the ground to better kiss her senseless. "Ah... Christ..." He closed his eyes against it.

He heard her gasp of alarm. "Are you hurt?" she asked once more, and he could see the concern in her eyes, hear it in her voice. It was like a balm for his soul.

Christ, he bloody well didn't know if he was hurt. He grimaced, for he'd come to, surprised to find her warm, soft face nestled so intimately against his own, and was at once ensorcelled by her scent, her nearness, so much so that he'd somehow forgotten why the bloody hell he was sprawled in the middle of the soggy forest floor to begin with.

He lay back down for an instant, and then tried to move his legs. They moved well enough, he thought, though they ached like the devil. He met her worried gaze, and felt the need to reassure her, "Naught broken so far." He smiled, not wholly convinced himself.

Neither did she seem overly assured, and her lovely brows drew together into a barely discernible frown.

"Truly?"

Iain moved his legs again to show her, grimacing, and then tried to rise. He fell back upon his rear, his brows drawing together in discomfiture. "No' broken mayhap, but a wee unsteady." He winked at her. "Ach, ye weave a wicked spell, lass." He grinned then, to be certain she understood he was jesting with her. "I'll be fine," he assured, when she failed to smile.

He sat there upon his rump a long instant, watching her as the sun continued its descent, and wished to bloody hell that the moment's spell hadn't broken. In the dimming light, her blush faded to shadows, but the delicate contours of her face remained to bewitch him.

Ach, she was lovely. She might have been wearing that infernal meal sack she'd rolled out of so indignantly and Iain would have still thought her exquisite.

They stared at each other for what seemed an eternity, neither speaking.

"I'm sorry if I hurt you," he said at last. "Dinna mean to." He leaned against one hand and propped up a knee, watching her. She averted her gaze; the silhouette of her face nodded against the twilight shadows of the forest. Iain reached out, lifting her gaze to meet his eyes in the darkness. "I dinna mean to," he swore.

She tried to turn away, but he wouldn't allow it. Forced to hold his gaze, she glared, making some choked sound that revealed both her anger and her pain.

He'd meant well. Christ, but he had. It was all he could do not to avert his gaze from her accusing look, so much self-disgust did he feel.

She began to weep then, right there before him upon the forest floor. Damn the pain; he drew her into his arms and held her, her body trembling softly within his embrace.

Page clung to him, unable to refuse the comfort of his strong arms.

How many times had she yearned to be held thus? How many times had she wept alone?

Too many to recount.

It felt so good to be embraced... so good to be held as though she were loved. For the space of an instant, she could almost believe...

She buried her face into the crook of his neck and was heartily grateful he could not see the tears she shed. It was enough he could hear them. She couldn't stop the tremors. Heaven help her, she tried, but couldn't.

"What does it mean?" she asked on a sob.

"What, lass?" he whispered.

"Suisan."

He peered down at her. She could feel his gaze, and the sweet warmth of his breath, and dared to lift her face to his.

"It means lily."

"Lily?"

"Bonny and sweet," he whispered.

"Nay," Page denied.

"Aye, lass," he murmured, and continued to stare down at her. "Lovely..." He lowered his face and touched his mouth softly to hers. "Sweet," he whispered, and then pecked her lips with another gentle kiss.

Page's arms tightened about his neck, her heart hammering like a ram, and near to bursting with gratitude. "Thank you," she relented softly, and prayed with all her heart that he would deepen the kiss once more.

She wanted to give him everything. And her body was all she had.

Hope, like weak candlelight, flickered within her heart.

For an instant she thought he might, for he stared down at her as though he would, his heart beating as fiercely as her own, his breathing as labored. She almost drew him down to her, so much did she wish for it, craving the gentle reassurance of his warm lips, the hunger in his kiss.

He came so close...

She could almost sense the heat of his mouth so near her own that her stomach fluttered wildly. His embrace tightened, his fingers digging into her flesh. In that intimate position they remained for what seemed an eternity—a heartbeat too long, for she lost the chance to lift her mouth to his lips and ask for what he would give her in that wordless language that lovers shared.

"We should go now," he said, and Page's heart knotted with regret.

"Yes," Page replied softly, sullenly. "Afore it gets dark."

He chuckled and squeezed her playfully. "Ach, lass, but it is dark," he pointed out jovially.

His laughter and his waggish tone brought a reluctant smile to Page's lips. She found herself teasing in return. "I hadn't noticed."

He laughed softly. "Didn't ye now?" And then his mood turned serious. "Page," he whispered.

For an instant Page could scarce breathe, so much pain did the single word evoke. It wasn't a name she'd been given; she'd simply grown into it, having carried out a page's duties for her father. It spoke of loneliness and sorrow and disdain.

Suisan was beautiful. Lilies. A wistful smile came to her lips. He'd said he thought her lovely and sweet, but she thought him wonderful and beautiful and kind, and her heart threatened to steal away with him.

Without considering the significance of her request, she said, "Call me Suisan... if it please you..."

He didn't reply at once, and then after a moment whispered, "Aye, lass... it would please me verra much."

&

THAT NIGHT PAGE COULDN'T SLEEP.

Her heart raced and her body thrilled with awareness of the man who lay sleeping beside her. It was impossible to forget the way it had felt to lie within his arms—as though it were the very place she'd always longed to be, and she never wanted to leave.

But she had to go.

She was more determined now than ever.

For her own sake, if not for her father's—she didn't want Iain coming after her, didn't want to lose her father now that there was, at long last, a chance to know him.

She didn't want him to regret his decision.

Then, too, she was heartily afraid she was wrong about the attraction she was feeling toward Iain MacKinnon—that it wasn't one of the body, but one of the heart and mind.

Aye, for she was tempted to love him.

When she thought of him, her heart seemed to swell with emotions—both bitter and sweet. Lying next to him now, she felt alive as never before.

Suisan.

The memory of his whisper sent a quiver down her spine.

When he spoke the name, it was so easy to dream... to imagine him loving her... to envision the children she would bear him... to remember his kiss...

She closed her eyes, battling her wayward emotions and her private fancies. But she couldn't allow it—couldn't give her heart to this man. He would crush it beneath his feet, with no more effort than it took for him to conjure that devastating smile.

She shifted upon the pallet, inadvertently tugging at the wrist he had bound to his own, and her throat tightened.

Tomorrow.

She had to find a way to leave on the morrow.

CHAPTER 18

S he was planning escape.

He was no fool. He could see it in her eyes, the devious little brain churning behind them.

Good.

Let her. He hoped she stumbled into a gullet and wolves dragged her out and feasted upon her body as they had Ranald's—the bloody damned Judas.

'Twould be for the best, he thought, for then he could save the sawed girdings for Malcom...

He'd determined to be rid of the both of them, no matter what it took, and it would be better to do it before they arrived again at *Chreagach Mhor*, where Malcom was like to be watched closely.

Damn, but he'd waited far too long to see vengeance carried out. He'd as lief be gutted than wait any longer.

No Sassenach wench was going to stop him. Damn Iain. She'd bewitched the fool for certain. And he didn't see how. She was a foulmouthed wench who would have turned his own blood to ice long before she chanced to heat it.

Christ, but he could spy it in their eyes... the way they watched each other when either thought the other could not see. It had been revolting enough to watch Iain draw her into his protection, when she no more deserved it than her bastard father did. But to know that he'd gone back after the scraps of her clothing, in order to prevent her escape? He could scarce stomach the thought.

Aye, Iain was a fool, but that was well and good, for a fool smitten by a woman was a fool of the greatest sort.

He planned to make short work of this requital. Iain would never know what befell him... until the moment ere he closed his whoreson eyes... and then he would tell him...

Everything.

Aye, he'd watch the bastard suffer the truth as he finally closed his eyes—just as he'd envisioned doing to Iain's father.

In the meanwhile, he watched the scene before him with an inward smile, waiting for just the proper moment to step into the fray.

"WHAT HARM CAN COME OF MY WASHING IN THE lake?" Page asked, her tone fraught with challenge.

She'd nigh had them convinced, and then Angus had been quick to remind them of her midnight swim, and the fact that she'd attempted to use the lake to make her escape, nearly succeeding in the endeavor. It seemed the majority of them could not swim, after all. She gave the old man a withering look, and informed him resolutely, "Well, the MacKinnon promised me a wash, and a wash I'll be getting." And she turned about to make her way down to the water's edge, daring them to stop her.

Angus placed himself within her path, and Page swore beneath her breath. Rot and curse these stubborn Scots. "Ye'll be takin' one when the MacKinnon returns, and no' a minute sooner."

Page didn't dare wait for his return. "And when might that be?" she asked. "Where has he gone?"

"To clean up ye're bloody mess," the old man said cryptically, standing stubbornly before her, arms akimbo.

"You are a mulish, bearish old man," she told him angrily. "Why is it you persist in plaguing me so? Isn't it enough that you steal me away from my home, keep me in fetters and abuse me with your mouths? You would have me live in filth, as well? I am not accustomed to sleeping upon the dirty ground and I need a bath."

"Ach! I dinna wish to even trouble myself, ye saucy Sassenach wench! Though for some reason, the MacKinnon is thinkin' to keep ye." He thumped his chest with a hand. "I'll be seein' that he does."

Canny old man. Though they trembled, Page's hands went to her hips in challenge. "Aye? And where might I go, prithee?"

He didn't reply, and Page stood there staring, inviting him to answer. By God, she was going to escape this morning if it killed her.

Last eve she'd thought to never have another opportunity, but this morning one had presented itself like a miracle from Heaven. She'd been only half-awake when the MacKinnon had risen and unfettered himself from her, but in enough of a weary stupor that she'd not bothered to open her eyes. Nor had she dared to face him. And then he had gone—to Christ knew where, for there yet no sign of him and she felt desperate to leave before he returned.

Before he could look at her with that knee- weakening, soul-stirring gaze.

And leave, she would—if ever she could convince the old fool standing before her that a bath was a perfectly harmless pursuit.

"Certainly you cannot be afeared of me?" she taunted him.

Still he didn't respond, merely continued to eye her as though she were some evil sorceress about to perform her witchery and vanish before his eyes. Page might have laughed at his vigilant expression and ready stance, save that she was too angry to indulge in even a shred of good humor.

"Really!" she persisted. "You cannot be afeared of me! Wherever would I go?" she asked a little hysterically. Her eyes scanned the immediate horizon, once again surveying her greatest vantage spot—where the forest trees hung like curious old men over the lake. Their foliaged limbs brushed the water's edge, as though stretching downward for a cool drink. It offered a temporary hideaway.

If she could ever get herself into the lake.

The horses were also tethered near the far bank.

It was perfect.

It was time to play upon their vanity, Page decided, and her brow lifted in challenge. "Certainly the lot of you... how many?" She peered about, counting, and then turned to Angus. "I count at least a score of you," she told him. "Certainly you can manage a single weakly woman?"

"Fie," Angus exclaimed.

"Aye, Angus," Dougal piped in. "Surely we can manage a single weakly woman?"

Page nearly laughed aloud at the question in his tone.

"Fie," Angus exclaimed once more.

"I dinna see anything amiss wi' allowin' the lass to wash," Broc interjected, stepping into their midst, and eyeing her knowingly. Page was almost thankful to the great behemoth. Almost, for then he added, "Ach, but I would be verra pleased if she would bathe herself, dirty as she is. Can no' ye smell that Sassenach stench?" he asked, and laughed uproariously.

Page narrowed her eyes at him, thinking he should

say a prayer of thanks come nightfall that she'd not be present to box his ears into oblivion. She'd like to stomp him into the ground with booted feet. Arrogant Scotsmen. She'd certainly had more than her fill of the lot of them. She cast Broc a furious glance and said, turning to address a mottle-faced Angus, "Follow me into the water, if you please... if you do not trust me..."

"Verra well, let her bathe herself," Lagan decreed, and then he waved a hand at the lot of them standing idly about. "But follow her in. Dinna let her oot o' your sight."

Page met his gaze and shuddered, for she could tell he did not like her, nor did he trust her. Were he to have it his own way, he'd not afford her any opportunities.

"Lagan," Dougal protested. "I dinna need a bloody bath! I dinna want to follow her in. She can bathe herself, and we can watch from the bank."

"I'll bathe wi' her," Kerwyn exclaimed, his tone fraught with innuendo. He laughed, amused by himself.

"And I," agreed Kermichil, sharing a private smile with Kerwyn.

Page shuddered at the lecherous looks that suddenly appeared in their eyes, the knowing glances they exchanged between them.

And then suddenly they were all peering at each other just so, mumbling in their Scots tongue and laughing, racing to strip down to their bare buttocks.

Page's eyes went wide.

This, she hadn't bargained for.

All at once they began to stampede toward her, and it no longer mattered that Angus stood between her and safety. She gave a little shriek of alarm and ran toward the lake, wading in quickly. The frigid water struck her like ice palms, snatching her breath away, but she ignored the sting of her flesh and rushed headlong into the deepest water.

Judas, but neither had she expected it to be so cold.

When she was far enough out that she could no longer stand, and was certain no one had followed, she turned, treading water, trying to stay afloat despite her billowing gown, and watched, stupefied, as the entire lot of naked Scotsmen frolicked like babes in the water. They had all of them discarded their meager clothing and now stood in the shallow water, their male anatomy bared to the breeze, splashing water at each other and laughing uproariously. Though she'd definitely not mistaken the lecherous glances they'd given her, they'd somehow forgotten even her presence now, preoccupied as they were with their own revelry.

Only Angus, Broc, and Lagan stood upon the bank.

Grinning at the lot of them, Lagan walked away without sparing Page a glance, shaking his head and laughing as he went.

Broc, for his part, stood laughing—laughing and scratching at his groin, the gesture too earnest to be precisely obscene, and the thought struck Page suddenly that he was the one man here who was in sore need of a bath. There was no other way to rid himself of those fleas. In a momentary lapse, she thought to tell him so, and then decided against it, reminding herself that she didn't care whether he ever rid himself of the accursed contagion. The sour-tempered behemoth was no concern of hers at all. Let him suffer the vermin, for all she cared. She hoped he scored his skin raw.

Angus, on the other hand, stood glaring at her—as though to blame her for the loss of good sense in the grown men surrounding her. Well, she was certainly not to blame.

Her gaze traveled the lot of them. None of them were paying her any mind. Kerwyn stood in shallow water, bending over to dunk his gnarled head into the frigid lake. He brought it up, shaking water like a wet beast, and making horrendous noises that sounded to

Page's ears like a wounded animal. To her amazement, she watched as Kermichil did the same, and then stood waiting for Kerwyn to try again, as though they were having some curious contest of sorts. Page could scarce imagine what they might be competing over.

Whose head would turn blue first from the cold?

Her teeth were chattering as her gaze returned to the bank. Angus was waving for her to come nearer. Though she was tempted to try to make her escape now, while the lot of them were preoccupied, she did as he bade her, knowing that Angus would foil her plan long before she set it into motion. The old man was wily as a fox, and he was watching her too closely for her to even attempt an escape as yet. The last thing she needed was for him to begin shouting at her now and draw attention.

Resisting the urge to cast a longing glance at the spot where the horses were tethered, Page waded back toward shore, though not all the way. She stopped when Angus gave her leave to, remaining at a safe distance from the others. And then she began to wash herself, pretending an interest in a nonexistent stain in her gown. She scrubbed at it incessantly, taking quick peeks at the old man watching from the shore. When she'd taken long enough with that self-imposed task, she dared her first duck beneath the water to wet her hair, coming up quickly, watching Angus and the others as she unplaited her hair. Still, no one but Angus watched her. Even Broc wandered away. But she knew it was merely a matter of time before they tired of their child's play and decided to plague her once more, so she didn't linger once her hair was unbound. She plunged into the water once more, this time taking her time about resurfacing.

Knowing Angus would be watching, she took great pains to remain in the same spot, and didn't dare wait too long before resurfacing. She didn't intend for Angus to call the guards after her. On the contrary, her intent was to stay under longer and longer, until he lost interest.

Until she deemed it long enough a time to make that mad swim toward freedom.

He was staring anxiously when she resurfaced for the second time, but Page continued on, pretending to bathe, until at last it seemed he was not quite so suspicious. She dunked herself a few more times for good measure, and on the final time found him busy speaking with Kerwyn and Kermichil.

Knowing her time was limited, Page made her final dunk beneath the water's surface. This time, she dove deep and propelled herself in the direction of the horses, praying to God that her direction was not wrong. She knew instinctively this would be her only opportunity.

She swam with her eyes open, despite the sting of the cold, and swam with all her might, hoping her path wasn't visible from the water's surface.

When she reached the bank, she surfaced slowly, praying for the cover of foliage, and nearly died with relief and joy when she found herself in the very heart of the leafy enclosure and heard the soft nickering and chewing of horses at their leisure.

Thank the lord! She'd made it.

Thus far.

She knew her time was short, and she still needed to steal a mount without their noticing—else she'd not get very far. She wasted little time worrying about the probability of being caught, for she had precious little time to spare. Any moment Angus would sound the alarm. Even as she slipped from the water, she kept expecting to hear his cranky old bellow.

She made her way quickly through the trees and bushes, not daring even to risk a glance in Angus's direction.

She wasn't particular about her mount, simply seized one and untethered it. Only when she was about to mount did she realize it was the one upon which poor Ranald was bound—not very well, at that, she realized almost at once. Rather than take the time to choose another horse, and then more time to untether it, and thus risk gaining notice, Page drew up her courage and mounted before poor Ranald, but the horse seemed not to appreciate the fact that she was dripping wet, and protested, snorting and prancing.

And then suddenly she heard the warning shout, and knew her time was ended. Panicking, she spurred the horse with the heel of her foot. It reared, and Page held on for dear life. To her dismay and horror, it danced backward, trying to unseat her. Nickering furiously, it retreated into the water. And then startled, it reared once again. Page clung to its withers as though to save her very soul. Poor Ranald slid off and dove into the water as the horse surged from the lake and broke into a furious run. She heard the shouts and curses behind her, more splashes as men dove in frantically after poor Ranald, but dared not turn to look, fearing they would still be too close at her heels. When at last she dared to peer back, it was to find a mob of shouting, cursing, naked Scotsmen chasing far behind her.

Even as she watched, a few turned and raced for their mounts, but it was too late.

Far too late.

Page breathed a sigh of relief and turned back toward freedom. She fully intended to flee them, even if she had to run morning till eventide.

She dared another glance backward, and couldn't help herself; she burst into hysterical laughter at the hilarious sight they presented.

Naked and furious, they ran, chasing her still.

CHAPTER 19

I t was the last thing Iain expected to find upon his
return.

His first thought as he reined in to watch the spec-
tacle was, how the devil had she managed to undress
some thirty Scotsmen?

He'd wholly expected to find she'd half driven them
mad, and was afeared to discover they'd murdered her
before his return, but this... this, he'd certainly not anticipated—to find her riding away upon a stolen horse,
and his men panting and bellowing like idiots while
they chased her, their male anatomies swinging free to
the breeze. Some ran clutching their groins with both
hands, some with one, waving furiously with the other
for her to return. A mere handful had evidently gone
back after their mounts, for they came racing after her,
riding naked as bairns from their mothers' wombs.

"What are they doin', da?" his son asked, sounding
as bewildered as Iain felt.

"Damned if I know, son," Iain answered after a
moment.

He didn't know whether to be angry or amused, so
he sat there bemused instead, watching the scene unfold and wondering how one measly woman could cause
so much bloody trouble.

He didn't have the chance to ponder it long, for his son reminded him of the obvious. "I dunno either, but I think she's gettin' away, da."

"I'll be damned if she isna, son," he agreed, and urged Kerr to come forward. He handed Malcom to him, directed them to return to camp and await him there, and then he spurred his mount after her.

"Bloody obstinate wench," he muttered to himself.

So why the hell didn't he simply let her go?

He could easily sacrifice a mount for the sake of her safety, and appease any guilt he might feel over leaving her to fend for herself. If she had any sense of direction at all, she'd soon enough be ensconced within her father's walls. Nor had he retrieved all the scraps she'd discarded. She'd come upon them soon enough, and they would serve to guide her...

If he let her go...

So why didn't he?

Because he bloody well didn't want to, that's why. It wasn't only because he feared for her safety at the hands of her father. He just didn't want to.

Something within him snapped as he watched her race away—some twist of emotion that felt like fear.

She was slipping away, shadows creeping in. A heavy door clanging shut. Darkness.

He leaned purposefully over his steed, urging his mount faster, closing the distance between them, coming at her from the left flank, and drawing alongside her. Preoccupied as she was with the naked mob pursuing her, he took her by surprise. He didn't think in that moment, merely acted, reaching out with an angry bellow to pluck her from her saddle. She shrieked in alarm, and for the instant was too startled to fight him. He drew her against him, holding her imprisoned.

"Let me go," she demanded, regaining her wits at once. "Let me go! Let me go!" Realizing who had captured her, she squirmed against him furiously, soaking his tunic and breacan.

"Nay, lass," he growled. "I told ye I wouldna! And I willna!"

"You lunatic Scotsman," she railed at him. "Do you not realize you might have killed me?"

He didn't respond. In truth, he didn't know what to say to that bit of logic, for he'd not thought about anything at all, save stopping her. Some dark fog had enveloped him, some undeniable sweep of emotion that left him trembling still. Empty in a way that was painful. The same way he'd felt after Mairi had flung herself from his window.

Only, that he understood.

This, he did not.

"You might have warned me," she added furiously.

Aye, he might have, if he'd been brainless enough to do so. "So ye might lead me upon a merry chase? I dinna think so."

He didn't bother to return as yet, instead rode on, trying to determine what the hell had come over him. A backward glance told him that her mount had slowed enough for his men to overtake. At any rate, he sure as Christ wasn't going to allow her to remain in her wet gown and catch her death, and neither did he intend to have her undress before his men.

She needed privacy.

He wanted to hold her.

"Why can you not let me go?" she asked him furiously.

Would that he had the answers to her questions.

Christ, but he didn't know. It somehow went far beyond the simple fact that he wished to save her from her father. In truth, that had been the last thing on his mind as she'd been flying away from him. The one thought that had spurred him more swiftly than any other was that she was slipping away... this woman who somehow banished shadows with her sultry sidelong glances.

Like a lad with his coveted prize, Iain held her securely against him, letting the black fog lift, relishing the feel of her warm flesh beneath the cold, wet gown she wore. His hand splayed at her belly and he could scarce keep himself from noticing the tiny waistline, the delicate outline of her ribs. His fingers traced them higher, until he could feel the weight of her breasts rest upon his hand. His loins quickened.

"Let me go," she pleaded.

"I canna, lass," he answered her. "I canna." And he shuddered at the desire that gripped him so fiercely of a sudden. Just so easily she aroused him to the point of madness. Without even trying. This woman who vexed him unto death. She plagued him by day, and tormented him by night. And God help him, it was such pleasurable torture.

"Aye, but you can," she argued desperately. "You can," she reasoned with him. "If only you wished to." She began to sob as his fingers continued to explore, but she didn't stop him.

If she asked... he would.

But she didn't.

Instead, her breath caught on one last sob and she whimpered softly, arching backward, thrusting her head against his shoulder.

At her innocent response, Iain's body convulsed with a hunger so keen, it cast all thoughts from his head, save for those of the woman within his arms. Sucking the sweet scent of her into his lungs, he dared to lift a hand, skimming her breast, going to her throat, caressing gently, reverently. Unable to resist, he bent to bury his face against the curve of her neck, once again inhaling the beguiling scent of her.

"There ye have it then, lass," he whispered against

the flesh of her throat, nibbling gently. "It seems I dinna wish to."

He heard her intake of breath as his fingers gripped her shoulder, and her delicate shudder as his hand slid down her arm, and knew she was not unaffected.

The simple knowledge aroused him fully.

"I want you, lass," he whispered against her ear, before he could stop himself, and meant it fiercely. "Want ye... so verra much..."

She stopped weeping suddenly and sat before him still as stone.

Page could scarce breathe suddenly, less weep.

Mere words. But words so powerful and compelling, they sent shock pummeling through her.

Her body convulsed. Her heart skipped its natural beat, and her thoughts scattered to the winds.

She closed her eyes and could feel every rise and fall of his chest at her back. His hand continued to explore, his caresses wresting delicious shivers from her body. She wanted to let his fingers roam forever. Wanted to let him do anything he would with her.

Anything.

Aye, she was wanton... and wicked, but she didn't care.

Her heart felt near to bursting with joy over his avowal.

He wanted her.

It didn't matter that it was merely for the moment, she wanted him too—and thought she'd die if she couldn't take a piece of him with her. A single bittersweet moment would suffice to bring a wistful tear to her eye when she was old and gray and had nothing left to sustain her but memories.

When his thumb caressed the underside of her breast, and then his hand dared to cup her so gently, she clasped trembling fingers over his and turned her face up to meet his gaze.

His eyes were like molten gold, glittering with promise, seducing her with the hunger so apparent behind them.

She willed him to know... willed him to see her own desire... willed him to hold her... kiss her.

His voice was hoarse when he spoke again. "Tell me now... if ye wish me to stop, lass."

Page's throat closed, the words wouldn't come, but she managed to shake her head, hoping he would comprehend her silent plea.

He kissed her throat then, nibbled it gently, lapped it hungrily, and she knew he'd understood.

"Ach, lass," he whispered, his breath hot against her neck, "are ye sure?" His hand slid up to cup her breast, squeezing gently, as though to make clear his intentions.

For answer, Page followed his hand, willing him to continue, reveling in the way that his fingers cherished her body, wringing delightful quivers from her. She pressed his hand to her breast in blatant invitation, and watched the expression upon his face.

Like a man tormented, he closed his eyes and groaned deep in his throat, lifting his face to the blue sky as he kneaded the tender flesh cradled within his palm. Page watched the knob in his throat bob, mesmerized by the intensity of the expression upon his face, the taut lines of his jaw. It was as though he had lived all his life for this moment, and she... she had never in all her days known such joy in simply being.

And then his gaze lowered, and he bent his head once more. His lips covered her mouth, and Page thought she would die with the pleasure it brought her. Her body melted, convulsed in the most private of places. He might have done anything at all to her in that instant, and she'd have welcomed it joyfully.

He wanted her truly.

She could spy it upon his face.

Could feel it in the way he touched her.

And she wanted him.

His tongue traced the seam of her lips, and then slid within her mouth to taste her. Page moaned with pleasure. And when he groaned with his own satisfaction, Page thought her heart would shatter and her body would ignite to flame.

He tore his lips away abruptly, and it wasn't until then, in that instant, Page realized the horse had stopped—or even that they were mounted still.

Somehow, when he kissed her, all the world ceased to exist. He made her feel as though there were only her. He filled her heart.

Made her soul unafraid to yearn.

When he dismounted before her, she knew what he intended, and when he lifted his arms out to her, Page slid into them without taking the time to consider the consequences, her heart hammering fiercely. She didn't want to consider anything at all. She wanted only to feel.

Carrying her far enough that she would be safe from being trampled, but no farther than he had to, Iain laid her down upon a bed of yellow crocuses, taking immense pleasure in the desire so evident in her gaze, in the haze of her eyes.

Some part of him cautioned him to stop, now before it was truly too late—that she couldn't possibly understand what it was he was about to do to her. All the things he wanted to do to her. He wanted this too much, was no longer rational.

For the longest instant, Iain merely stared into her eyes, not daring even to blink, fearful of closing his eyes and opening them only to find that her desire was no more than some cruel invention of his fevered imagination.

Could she possibly understand? Could she know what it was she was asking for with that love-me-now gaze?

She couldn't possibly, he decided, though he couldn't seem to muster himself to give a bloody damn. He fell to his knees beside her, and bent over her, entrapping her between his arms, and then he lowered his head to kiss her, anticipating the sweet, welcoming taste of her mouth upon his lips. "Sweet," he murmured against her mouth. "So beautiful."

"Nay," she murmured with a sigh, closing her eyes.

"Aye, lass," he asserted. "Ye are." And he deepened the kiss.

With all her heart, Page welcomed the gentle invasion of her mouth, delighting in the way he seemed to savor her with every liquid stroke of his tongue... the way his mouth seemed to revere her own. Never in her life had she felt so cherished.

Never in her life had she loved someone more.

But this was not love, she reminded herself.

To expect love would bring her only heartache. Nay... this was something else entirely... and if she didn't want for something more... something she could never have, then she'd not be crushed by sorrow when it never came.

Aye, this was something else, not love.

This was a possession of her body, sweet and wicked.

Nothing more.

That's what she told herself. And she wanted it more desperately than she'd ever wanted anything in her life.

Iain was a man consumed.

It was his greatest desire to pleasure her.

Aye, but he wanted even more than that to make her stay. He withdrew and gazed down into her passion-flushed face. He wanted her to look at him just so always... to bask in his kisses like a blossom opening to the heat of the sun. But then he knew the way to bind her to him was not to make love to her. He'd attempted

that with Mairi, and while in the dark of the night she'd
relented to his skillful persuasion, in the morning light
she'd despised him for it, too.

And then she'd borne him a child, and he'd lost her
forever.

He'd be damned if he'd travel that road again.

Before Mairi, there had been lasses aplenty. Since
her, there had been nary a one.

Because he couldn't forget.

This loving would be for her, he decided.

For sweet, lovely Page.

For himself he would claim only the pleasure of
seeing the passion played out upon her face.

Nothing more.

That's what he commanded himself.

When he reached out and lifted her arm, placing
tiny, delicate kisses along the sensitive inner flesh, Page
shuddered and squeezed her eyes closed, abandoning
herself wholly to his will. Arriving at her hand, he
kissed her palm, lapped it with his tongue, suckled her
fingers, and nibbled the heel of her palm, until Page
shuddered with rapture, and then he guided that hand
above her head, moving to the other and doing the
same. With one hand he held both her wrists, pinioning
her arms above her head as he shifted over her, his body
shielding her from the sun, bathing her in cool shadows.

But she was far from cool. She was hot. Burning hot,
her skin afire.

Page sensed the heat of his gaze upon her, though
she wasn't bold enough to meet his knowing eyes. As he
hovered above her, she was aware of everything in that
moment. Every nuance. The subtle shifting of the
breeze, the warmth of the sun against her skin where it
touched her, the birds twittering somewhere high
above. The sound of the grass as it succumbed beneath
their bodies. The elusive scent of the crocus. And the
musky male scent of the man hovering above her.

When he lowered his face to her neck, she shuddered, and dared to bare it fully, arching with complete abandon, moaning with delight as he suckled her flesh, lapped it with his tongue once more. Like a painter in love with his labors, he left no part of her untouched by his divining brush. He cherished her body, showered her with kisses until it seemed her very soul would rise out of her body and meld with his.

"Yesssss," she whispered, and felt him shudder above her.

His kisses became more fervent then, straying to her breasts. He suckled through her wet gown, and Page's heart thundered, for she wanted in that insane instant for him to rip the offending gown from her body, to feel the heat of his lips upon her bare flesh. To feel his body lie upon her.

Instead, he moved lower still... leaving her hands free, and sliding his arm beneath her waist to raise her body for his fervent kisses. She moaned with exhilaration, nearly mindless with the pleasure he was giving her, impatient with his caresses. She clutched at her gown, drawing it up desperately, inviting him without words.

Still she dared not open her eyes, dared not speak to break the sorcerer's spell, but cried out exultantly when his lips kissed her bare belly. And sweet Jesu... those lips remained for the longest instant, unmoving, frozen in place, liquid flame against her bare flesh. Page reached out to hold him to her, wanting him never to go.

And then he wandered down to her thighs, nipping and kissing.

She gasped aloud, her heart pummeling against her ribs, as he dared to kiss her in the most private of places. Her body convulsed with a pleasure so incredible, it was almost like a glimpse into Heaven itself. And then when his tongue slipped within her body to explore so boldly, she thought she would dissolve into a liquid pool beneath him.

"Oh, yes," she whispered. "Oh... my... yessss..."

"Sweet," he murmured, and pushed his tongue within her body, tasting with abandon, until Page thought her heart would shatter into a thousand brilliant pieces.

She could scarce bear any more.

"Please," she murmured, and whimpered, writhing beneath him, not truly understanding what it was she was needing, but knowing instinctively it was something more.

His hands moved over her body more insistently now, while his lips continued to worship her, and then he slid both hands beneath her bottom, cupping her, lifting her for his pleasure, and Page felt her eyes cross behind her lids, so much gratification did it bring her. Her body felt on the verge of some undiscovered glory, and she wanted so desperately to reach for it, cling to it, hold it forever.

And then suddenly he moaned, a tormented sound, and stopped, lowering her, releasing her to the ground.

Page's lashes flew wide, and she stared into his fevered eyes, her heart hammering fiercely.

He knelt before her, his expression sober, his eyes pleading. "I want you, lass," he whispered once more.

CHAPTER 20

C hrist, but he couldn't do it.

He'd thought he could, but he couldn't.

Wanting her was driving him to a madness beyond bearing.

His body ached, he needed her so desperately. She blinked, her face prettily flushed, and nodded. He didn't think she could possibly understand, though he wanted so badly to believe that she did.

"Are ye sure, lass?" he asked once more, and his voice was thick with need.

For answer, she rose up, reaching forward to catch trembling fingers within his belt, her wide, beautiful eyes never leaving his. His heart hammering, he undid the belt at once, and tossed it quickly away, holding her gaze, afeared she'd change her mind, afeared she'd not.

Christ, but he wanted this. More than he could re-call wanting anything at all.

Every muscle in his body tensed as she once again reached forward to touch his breacan, just a delicate brush of her fingers, nothing bolder, but he understood as though she'd spoken the request aloud and he drew it off at once, discarding the blanket upon the grass. He knelt before her, wearing only his short tunic, and he reached down to draw it off, as well, needing her to see the full measure of his desire.

Needing her to understand before it was too late. If she would flee him, it must be now. Before he lost what will remained.

Before he dared to touch her once more.

One more kiss would seal her fate.

And bind her to him eternally.

She stared up at him, her eyes wide, her face flushed.

Page's throat tightened at the sight of the man kneeling before her, gloriously naked, his skin bronzed from the sun, and his body tumescent with desire. She tried not to look so well, but could scarce keep herself from it. She swallowed her fear.

How could a man such as this... want her?

She wanted to weep with joy, for the evidence was there before her, undeniable in its magnificence. She wanted to strip herself too, be together with him as God had made them both, but was afeared he would find her lacking, and so she lay, marveling at the beauty of the man before her.

"D' ye wish to stop, lass?" he asked her, his voice husky.

Page shook her head at once, meeting his gaze, her face burning with chagrin as she realized he'd caught her staring. "Nay," she said softly, and then asked, "D-do you?" She watched as his beautiful lips broke into a disarming smile.

He chuckled lightly. "Nay, lass, I dinna." He shook his head and reached out. She stared at his hand a bewildered instant, dumbfounded. "Give me your hand," he commanded her, smiling still.

Page blinked, and yielded to him, her heart beating fiercely. She let him draw her to her knees before him, unable to keep her gaze from lowering once again to that very male part of him.

"Ach, lass, but do I look like I wish to stop?" he teased.

Her gaze flew to his. Page couldn't speak to answer, and he didn't give her the opportunity. His hands reached out, grasping her waist, squeezing gently, and he closed his eyes, as though savoring the feel of her body beneath his hands.

Page, too, savored the moment, her head falling slightly backward, though still she watched him, for she wished to miss nothing.

When he opened his eyes again, it was to meet her gaze, his golden eyes gleaming, and he whispered, "I wish to see all o' ye, lass..."

Page managed a nod, but no more, and he slid his hands down to clutch the hem of her gown, drawing it slowly up, and peering up at her as though he thought she might any moment refuse him.

She didn't intend to. She was dizzy with desire, eager for whatever he would give her.

He drew the gown up and over her head, along with her rent undergown, and tossed the damp fabric aside upon the grass. And then he simply stared. Page waited anxiously for his response, and was mesmerized by the dazzling smile that appeared upon his face.

"Beautiful," he whispered fervently, and Page wanted to cast herself into his arms and weep. When he leaned forward at last, she welcomed him wholly, closing her eyes, and lifting her arms in a gesture of total and joyful submission.

And then she could think no longer, for his lips closed over the peak of one breast, and he began to suckle. She thought she would die with the pleasure he wrought from her body. His kisses lifted to her face, while his hand caressed the flesh he'd abandoned with his lips. When his mouth touched upon her own, she thought the world might suddenly spin away. She clung to him desperately, wrapping her arms about his neck, and he kissed her deeply, his tongue sparring first gently with her own, and then more urgently.

She was scarce aware that he laid her down upon the grass once more. His body covered hers, his weight both welcome and cherished, while his lips and hands continued to explore and seduce her. Her torso, her breasts, her thighs.

And then his fingers were suddenly there between her legs, and she opened for him instinctively, feeling again that incredible bliss. He settled between her thighs, and she felt that rigid part of him nudge her. Welcoming him, Page lifted her legs, wrapping them instinctively about him.

The first thrust came without warning. Bracing her hips with his hands, he entered her swiftly, muffling her cry of pain with his mouth and his kisses. Her heart felt as though it would be thrust into her throat, so deep did he drive himself within her. Casting her head backward, she cried out.

"Tell me to stop," he murmured against her mouth, raining tiny feverish kisses upon her chin and her throat. "It's no' too late. If ye will it... I'll stop, lass... Just say the words..."

A cold sheen of perspiration broke upon her fevered body, but Page shook her head frantically, embracing even the pain. She wanted everything he would give her —everything—knowing somewhere in her heart that her first time with him would be her last.

And then the pain dissipated and she felt again the sweetest ache within. He lay still upon her, filling her completely, waiting, it seemed, for her to respond. Page began to move, trying to rediscover that elusive sensation.

Iain groaned with a pleasure so keen, it was almost pain.

He didn't intend to move so soon, but she was too insistent, too passionate, moving beneath him as though she would milk him of every last drop of his will.

And Christ... he wanted her to... want this...

He couldn't keep himself from it.

He thrust again, and again, driving himself mindlessly, until the fog in his brain cleared enough for him to consider the consequences of his actions. He tried to withdraw, for her sake, but she lifted her legs, entwining them about his. He cried out, shuddered, and held on to his will like never before, refusing to spill himself within her. Though his heart felt near to strangling, he drew upon every last shred of will and thrust again, and again, never stopping until he felt her succumb beneath him.

When her body trembled with her own release, and she gave a soft keening cry that ended in a blissful sigh, he knew he'd pleased her well, and he withdrew swiftly, spilling himself without her instead. Sated and depleted, he collapsed atop her, savoring the musky scent of their loving that surrounded them... the cool sheen of sweat upon their bodies, and the breeze across his back.

He was grateful to her in a fashion he could never repay, and connected now in a manner he would never forswear.

Like a besotted youth, he reached out and plucked a bright yellow crocus from the grass beside her and handed it to her. She accepted the blossom, and he buried his face within the crook of her neck, embracing her.

She was his now.

He'd made it so.

And he vowed, upon his life, that he'd never let her rue this day.

WHILE THE REST OF THEM HAD WAITED ABOUT LIKE idiots, fiddling their fingers, the two of them had been rutting.

Damn but it galled.

If he'd not witnessed the sight of them together with his own eyes, he'd never have believed it.

When Iain should have beaten the impertinent bitch, he returns, instead, cradling her within his arms while she sleeps like a wee bairn. After the trouble she'd stirred, he'd half expected, half hoped, his brother would send her flying back to her father. At the very minimum, that their long absence meant he'd taken it upon himself to return her to Aldergh, dumping her like so much offal into the castle ditch.

It was no more than she deserved.

Instead, Iain had been picking crocus blossoms for the Sassenach slut. She clutched one still within her fist whilst she slept.

Damn, but naught was going as planned—naught at all. By this time, he'd hoped to be rid of Iain's whelp once and for all. And the wench—she never should have become a problem to begin with—rot Iain and his bleeding heart.

He sat, watching Kerwyn and Dougal load Ranald's still-soaked body upon the horse he'd intended for Malcom, and could feel his face burn with impotent rage. They'd had to fish the poor bastard out of the loch and then rewrap him, and only now were strapping him on again. It seemed the lass was to go with Iain, Malcom with auld Angus, and he was helpless to do anything but stand and watch and seethe. He'd hoped Page and Malcom might ride together.

He loathed feeling this way—helpless—despised Iain's bloody guts for it, too. Bastard! Just like his father, he was. Thinking himself so noble for the sacrifices he made.

Iain's da, the damn bastard, had sacrificed even him
—without so much as a backward thought.

Well... he intended to right the wrong soon enough
—rid himself first of Malcom, then of Iain, and then
lead the clan himself.

It was his right after having suffered in silence all
these years.

Damn Iain's sire for a selfish old fool. Had the old man
truly expected that his deceit would never be discovered?
Had he anticipated that Lagan would simply accept the
lie so glibly when the truth was at last made known? That
he'd forget he'd been left, as a result of his father's murder
and the ultimate deception, without a mother, or a father?

Foolhardy old man. In trying to save his son from
the repulsive truth—that his wife had dared to love another man, a MacLean at that—he'd managed to strip
Lagan of every birthright.

Aye, for while Iain lamented never having known
the mother who had once suckled him at her breast,
Lagan had truly never known her at all. Christ, but he
had not even the right to grieve for her openly. He had
only snatches of her memory from Glenna, for not even
Glenna would speak of the sister she'd lost so shamefully—not even to the son she'd died giving birth to.

Iain, at least, had known her for those two years—
two years Lagan might have plucked out his eyes to
have had the same luxury—and his brother had not the
right to grieve.

Whether he recalled her or nay.

Poor wretched Iain... his father's revered son...
While Iain had been assiduously trained to take the
lead of his clan... Lagan had been naught more than a
discarded kinsman.

How he'd envied the old laird's attentions to his son.
How he'd craved it. Never knowing...

Christ, but he'd not even been told of his father

until he'd been too old to feel anything more than bitterness. That was all he'd ever been told—that his father had been a deceiving MacLean, no more—and never once had the MacLeans acknowledged him.

Never once.

It had been Glenna, the aunt he'd once called mother, who had revealed the connivance after all. Her own guilt had been great—and rightly so. She should never have contrived to deprive him of his rightful life.

Damn them all, for he'd been robbed by clansmen he'd loved—clansmen who'd favored the old laird more than they had the lonely child he had been. Every last MacKinnon had conspired to keep the dirty secret of his birth. None of them had come forth, not a one.

And now those who would recall were mostly dead, but for Glenna and a scarce few others. They too would pay. And then... when the guilty were gone from his sight, he could learn at last to live—never forgive, but to put the past behind him once and for all.

The jest was upon old MacKinnon—might he turn in his grave—for in trying to spare his son, Iain, he'd burdened him with a lifetime of guilt over his mother's death. Stupid bastard, for it had been his own birth that had killed her, not his half brother's. And yet Iain had lived every day of his miserable life thinking he'd been the one to rob their mother of her last breath of life. Let him think so—bloody bastard—he could take his bloody guilt to the grave, for all he cared—that, along with the guilt he suffered over Mairi's death. Damn, but he'd hoped she would die at her childbed. He'd wanted her to so badly—had tried so hard to make it come to pass.

Instead, she'd tossed herself from the accursed window, and had stolen his chance with her youngest sister. Stupid bitch. His dire warnings against Iain had been meant to frighten her, make her life miserable, not send her out upon a window ledge.

And yet... he had to admit... she'd succeeded in wounding the whoreson in a way that might never have been possible elsewhere, for Iain had not once, since Mairi's death, taken a woman to his bed.

Until now.

He smiled, for this was one more way to see the bastard bleed before he died.

His one dilemma now... to decide who should depart the world sooner... the son... or the lover.

Mayhap both.

Together.

&

LONG AFTER PAGE AWOKE FROM HER SATED SLUMBER, she clung to the pretense of sleep, not quite able to face Iain.

Nor could she deal with the accusations from his men as Iain returned with her in his arms. She overheard their grievances, their voiced indignation over her foul treatment of poor Ranald, and felt more than a twinge of guilt over the havoc she'd wreaked once more. Certainly she'd not meant to dump the cadaver in the lake. It had been an accident, no more. But her heart had filled with joy to hear Iain MacKinnon become her champion. He'd commanded them all to silence, and with his unsolicited defense, a gladness had flowered in her heart.

If the truth be known, more than aught else, she didn't wish to leave the refuge of his arms as yet. He held her like a babe, his strong arms enfolding her within an embrace that felt more like Heaven than even those puffy white clouds could possibly.

Nay... she didn't want to wake... wanted to cling to him always.

To this illusion of love.

She felt cherished by the way he held her, the way

he stroked the hair from her face. But it was an illusion, no more. She understood that well enough—just as she understood that once she opened her eyes, she would no more be his lover, but his hostage once again.

Oh, but how wonderful it had been for the time.

She would cherish the memory of their loving deep in her heart, remember every wonderful instant... and on those evenings when she stared out from her chamber window... no more would she wish for things that had never been, could never be... She would carefully unwrap the crocus she held in her hand. Though it might be faded and brittle with age, she would see it bright and yellow and kissed by the dew. She would see his face—would feel the great sweep of emotion that had twisted her heart and made a mockery of her avowal that she felt mere lust for him. Aye, for in that moment, she had loved him fiercely. In that magical instant she had wanted to stay with him always.

Aye, and she'd wanted him to love her.

Her throat thickened with overwhelming emotion when she recalled the way he'd plucked the bloom and placed it within her hand. It was a simple gesture, one he might have performed a thousand times, for a thousand different lovers... but this one had been for her and her alone.

She wanted to weep, but didn't dare, lest he discover her awake.

The trail they were following veered upward, a steeper incline than any they'd traveled as yet, and Page sighed contentedly as she was forced closer to the man who would ever after haunt her dreams.

As far as she could tell, it was late afternoon.

Through the haze of her lashes, she could spy ribbons of rose-red stretching across a faded blue sky. The sun bathed the heathered hills in a buttery light, like a gentle mother kissing all it touched before snuffing its light.

When the path turned steeper yet, Page dared to cling to her dubious savior, taking comfort in his strength to keep her safe. Her hand at his back took great pleasure in exploring the sinew of his flesh, the broadness of his back, her pretense of slumber affording her a boldness she would never have dared elsewise.

He was a marvelous exemplar of a man, every part of him well formed. She sighed at the memory of him kneeling unclothed before her, magnificent and primeval.

The way he'd gazed at her; no one had ever looked at her just so.

His eyes... they were the sort to make a woman weak when they fell upon her in full measure. Something flittered down deep within her belly with scarce the memory of his smoldering gaze. Arrogantly confident, they appraised like one who knew what he wanted and knew instinctively how to get it. They probed for secrets, used them to ravage the heart... and the body.

She shivered at the thought.

Of his hands upon her...

And his lips... lips that promised unspeakable things... promises kept with such great relish. Mercy, but he'd taken immense pleasure, judging by the mischievous turn of his lips, in all that he'd done to her. He'd made love to her again with that exquisite mouth, taking more pleasure in the endeavor than it seemed possible a man could take in such a thing.

Unable to contain it, she gave a sleepy little moan, and turned to bury her face against his chest. But it was a mistake, she realized at once, for she breathed in the scent of him, and was wholly undone by it.

She wanted to stay this way forever.

But forever was an impossibility, and the moment would be over too soon. Hot tears slipped from her lashes, though she told herself they were absurd.

How could she love a man she scarcely knew? But she thought she did.

How could she have given herself so freely? Loved him back without compunction?

Not love. Anything but love.

Lust, she tried to convince herself. It was lust, simple and true.

So, then, why did the sting of tears persist?

And why did her heart feel suddenly so heavy as though it were weighted with stone?

Stiffening at the delicate brush of fingers across his back, Iain peered down, trying to determine whether Page slept or nay.

It was a lover's caress. A sleepy lover's caress that stirred his senses and started his pulse to pounding. He thought she might have awakened, but she didn't open her eyes.

No matter, he took pleasure in holding her so. She was so light, delicate within his arms, fragile even—despite the invulnerable facade she put forth. She appeared at first sight to be as sturdy as the stone walls her father had erected about his keep, but remove a single brick, and her walls came toppling down.

She'd been exhausted after he'd loved her so thoroughly, so much so that she'd fallen asleep within his arms as he'd stroked the damp wisps of hair back from her face. Ach, but this he relished more than he should... the trust she'd placed in him to so easily fall asleep within his embrace.

It was a simple show of faith, one that endeared her to him more readily than even her enduring nature. It was something he'd never had from Mairi. Trust. Something he would never have dared even hope for.

Instead, his wife had withdrawn from their bed to that infernal window, where she'd stood staring into the night. He'd listened to her weeping, and watched her quiet revulsion for the act of love they had committed, and his heart had wept pure blood.

Once she'd conceived, he'd never touched her again —nor had she desired him to by the way she so studiously avoided him. She'd carried his bairn without sharing a single whisper of him, had mourned every moment she'd nurtured his babe within her womb, as though it were an abomination of her being.

His son had been magnificent.

Aye, Malcom was everything he'd ever hoped for in a son; free of spirit and unafraid to love. It was something Iain envied of him.

Page... he smiled at the memory of her halting acceptance of the name he'd chosen for her: Suisan. It gave him pleasure to think of her so. Her response to him... her openhearted acceptance of his loving—not mere acquiescence—was like a balm for his soul.

It made him dream again, opened doors in his heart he'd never known were closed.

She wiggled away from him slightly and he reached out, never touching, but tracing the outline of her belly with his palm, imagining his babe growing there. It gave him a fierce pleasure. He'd withdrawn each time before planting his seed within her body, but couldn't keep himself from imagining her belly swollen with his bairn.

He wanted to do it again... so badly—love her, aye, but more than that, to give her his child. He'd thought his chances were all gone. All the things he'd wanted to do with Mairi and never could... place his hand to her belly, feel the first stirring of life from their bairn... touch his cheek and lips to her body where it nurtured their babe... lay her naked upon his bed each morn and every night to study the glorious changes in her body.

All those things he suddenly found himself wanting with the woman lying so serenely within his arms.

It made his heart full with joy and alight with anticipation merely to think of it.

Damn, but he had to chuckle at the look auld Angus had given him when he'd come bearing her back to camp—a mixture of outright indignation and reluctant approval. The old man had been after him long enough to get himself a woman, but Iain thought he might have favored one a little less vexing. He chuckled softly, for in truth, he might have preferred one a little less troublesome, as well.

The little termagant.

Ach, but the truth was, he loved her spirit, including her tempers, for they were evidence that her soul burned with life. No quiet, seething, mourning woman was she. Nay, she was passion incarnate, feeling everything, be it anger, or lust—and love?—to its fullest degree.

His cousin, on the contrary, had been wholly disapproving, if the look upon his face was any indication. Too bad. Iain had long since abided by his own decisions, and it was a lifetime too late for Lagan to insinuate himself upon them. His cousin would simply have to learn to live with the Sassenach spitfire in their midst —as would the rest of them, for he intended to keep her.

As for himself, becoming used to her presence was an undertaking he suspected he was going to wholly enjoy.

Thoughts of his cousin brought a pensive wrinkle to his brow.

Lagan had been acting strangely of late, brooding incessantly. Ever since his quarrel with auld man MacLean over his youngest daughter. Mayhap he should talk to the MacLean himself—much as he was loath to—for Lagan's sake. Mayhap there was something he could do, as yet?

And mayhap not; auld MacLean loathed the hell out of him, for certain. His mediation was more like to drive the wedge more firmly betwixt them.

"Da! Da!"

Malcom's shrill cry of alarm pierced his thoughts like the blow of an ax. He pivoted about, heart lurching, to find his son unharmed, but pointing wildly.

"Ranald's gettin' away," Malcom shouted. "Ranald's gettin' away!"

Iain's brows drew together at his son's hue and cry. How the hell could Ranald possibly do that, dead as the bastard was. Following the direction of Malcom's pointed finger, he caught sight of the crisis that held his son's concern. Ranald's body had somehow snapped free of its bindings—not the bindings, he realized, upon closer inspection. The harness had snapped, and while Ranald was tethered still, the saddle was slipping free. Even as he fully absorbed Ranald's predicament, Ranald broke free suddenly, and began tumbling down the steep hillside, losing the saddle after the first violent turns. The tartan about him unraveled with every subsequent roll.

"Christ," he muttered. Damn, but Ranald must have earned himself one hell of a curse during his lifetime. Iain doubted a dead man had ever had such bloody misfortune.

A few of his men vaulted from their saddles at once, and for the second time in the space of a day, went in pursuit of Ranald's errant body.

Iain cursed roundly as he peered down, frowning, into Page's blinking eyes.

She was awake, staring up at him. "I didn't do it," she swore at once.

CHAPTER 21

There wasn't a grimace-free expression amongst the faces staring down at Ranald's body. Between the wolves, the plunge into the lake, his wet blankets, and the roll down the hill, Ranald was, without a doubt, the worse for his wear.

Page stood silently amongst the gathered, her face screwing in revulsion at the sight of the body lying so twisted before them. Her guilt was tremendous, for she knew she shared some measure of blame for the poor man's misfortune. Lord, but her father had always said she could tax a dead man's soul, and it seemed he was certainly correct, for this particular dead man was about as taxed as a soul could be.

Even so, she simply wasn't about to take all the blame. She certainly hadn't killed the man to begin with —neither had she set the wolves against him. She had, however, dumped him into the lake during her escape. Of a certainty his wet blankets hadn't done his appearance any service. He'd not been the most comely fellow she'd ever set eyes upon to begin with, but now he was fairly grotesque. She wrinkled her nose and turned away. It was a good thing she had such a strong fortitude.

"I'll no' be puttin' him on my horse," Dougal interjected suddenly, his tone fraught with disgust, his expression revealing as much.

"Neither mine," announced Kerwyn. "Turns my belly sour just to look at him."

Broc's too, apparently, Page noted, a little bemused by the behemoth's reaction to the dead man. In truth, he hadn't even come nigh to the body, and still he knelt away from the gathered crowd, retching and making the most ungodly sounds Page had ever heard in her entire life.

Although she was loath to intrude, she wandered near to him. "Might I help?"

Broc seemed momentarily bewildered by her question. "Help me spill my guts?" he answered, peering up at her, frowning a little. "Why should ye wish to help me, wench?"

Page shrugged and gave him a slight smile. "Because you're not so very rotten as you think."

"Aye?" he asked. "Says who?"

Page's smile deepened despite his glare. "Says me," she replied pertly. "My thanks to you for trying to help me this morn... Broc."

"Sassenach wench," he replied without heat.

"Behemoth," she answered, grinning.

He ceded the tiniest hint of a smile.

"Aye, well... for all the guid it did me," he quipped. "Ye dinna get verra far, now did ye."

"Nay," Page replied, her cheeks heating at the memory of her capture at his laird's hands. She felt in that instant as though every guilty pleasure was written there upon her face. What must he think of her? What must they all think of her? She really didn't wish to know. "I-I did not," she lamented, and then ventured once more, "May I... that is to say... are you feeling better now?" Somehow, it suddenly seemed important to her that they not think of her unkindly—not even the surly behemoth kneeling so pitifully before her.

His brows collided into a fierce frown. Dinna fash yourself' o'er me," he snapped. His gaze skidded away. "Go away now, and leave me be."

Moody wretch. Page glowered at him, but didn't persist. She moved again toward the gathered crowd, thinking that 'twas no wonder these Scots were forever at war. Churlish beasts.

"Christ, but he stinks to Heaven," Kermichil swore, grimacing. But he didn't look away, Page noted. He stared, seeming fascinated by the body before them. It seemed morbid curiosity kept them all rooted to the spot.

"He doesna e'en look like Ranald anymore," Lagan lamented, shaking his head in a gesture of regret. And yet his eyes revealed nothing of the sentiment as they shifted to Page. Only the depths of his anger lingered then. He not only blamed her, she realized, he loathed her.

She didn't know why, but he disturbed her somehow —for more reason than that he simply didn't like her. It was something more. She shuddered, unnerved by the look he gave her, and turned away.

"Poor damned Ranald," Angus answered gruffly.

"Damn but he's no' riding wi' me either," Kermichil interjected.

"Poor bastard," someone chimed in.

"Aye, poor damned bastard," came the echo.

There was a long interval of weighted silence as they all stared, nodding in agreement.

"Ach, Iain... mayhap we should leave him," suggested Dougal.

Iain's brows drew together. "Nay," he declared at once. "He's deservin' of a proper funeral. We'll no' be leaving him here to rot."

"Weel..." Dougal put forth, a little fretfully. He scratched his head. "I'll no' be ridin' wi' him, that's for certain." He peered nervously up at Iain. "I dinna think I could stand it," he added quickly.

Page didn't particularly blame him, as she didn't think she could either. Her brows knit. Someone would have to take him. Iain intended to ride with his son, and he'd given her Ranald's mount to use for herself—against his men's wishes, it seemed. Nor did they appear overly appreciative of the fact that he'd given her his saddle and harness after Ranald's had been rendered unusable in the fall. They said nothing over the fact, but she knew by the looks upon their faces that the decision curdled in their bellies.

"Nor I," Kerwyn joined them in saying.

"Nor me," Kerr said, grimacing.

"Nor Broc either," Angus announced with no small measure of disgust. "Ach, but look at him over there, pukin' his guts like a wee bairn. For a muckle lad he has the weakest damned belly this auld man's e'er seen."

"Ranald's coming wi' us," Iain maintained.

Lagan remained silent, staring at Page.

"Ach, Iain," Dougal began, and stamped his foot like a petulant child. "I dinna want to ride wi' him."

"What would ye have me tell his minnie, Dougal?" Iain asked. His jaw tautened in anger—the muscle working there the only evidence of his carefully controlled temper. "Mayhap ye would like t' have the pleasure of explaining how we forsook her only son to the wolves and the bloody vultures?"

Dougal's face reddened. He shook his head, hanging it shamefully, and stared disconcertedly at the foot he stabbed into a trampled patch of muir grass.

Page could see in their faces the aversion they felt over riding with a dead man—she couldn't blame them. It was a loathsome prospect, one she wasn't particularly keen upon herself, but she certainly didn't wish to see Iain angry. Years of trying to avoid her father's tempers made her yearn to speak up. One look at the putrid body kept her tongue stilled.

"Ach, but we're a miserable lot," Angus began, the tone of his voice making Page cringe where she stood. "A miserable lot o'—"

"I-I'll ride with him," Page suddenly blurted, startling even herself with the offer. She regretted the outburst at once.

Every gaze snapped up and trained upon her.

His state was partially her responsibility, she reasoned frantically. And mayhap she would please Iain by keeping the peace for him? Perchance even gain his men's acceptance by saving them Ranald's undesired company?

Though these were not her people, she rationalized, she would need endure their company only until her father showed himself to claim her. And he would come, she told herself. He had to come.

Mayhap he was rallying his men even now?

"I... I... do not... mind," she lied with difficulty. But the disgust was surely there to be seen upon her face.

Like that first night, they all stared at her, mouths slightly agape, saying nothing, only this time Page refrained from adding her acid wit. As she watched, their faces reddened, some of their expressions grew incredulous, some doubtful, and she backed away a pace. She cast a dubious glance at Iain and found him scowling fiercely. Lord, what had she done? Committed some cardinal Scots sin with her offer?

She met his eyes, searching.

Iain stared, blinking, scarcely able to believe his ears.

He'd been about to speak up and resign himself to carry Ranald when she'd beaten him to it. That she would be willing to subject herself to such an unpleasant task for her own kindred's sake would have stunned him well enough already—particularly as his own men, Ranald's friends, were all loath to bear up to the responsibility. Christ, but that she would be willing for Ranald's sake was inconceivable.

Judging by the expression upon his men's faces, they were every one as stupefied by her unanticipated offer as was he. If he weren't so bloody provoked by the lot of them, he would have laughed at the response she'd managed to elicit from them. Damn, but she was priceless. In that instant he admired her immensely—wanted to draw her into his arms and kiss her soundly upon those delightful lips of hers.

And that's not all he wanted to do to her. God, but she was endearing standing there, looking so beautifully anxious, her wide brown eyes so wary and yet forewarning. Her dress had, without doubt, seen better days, and yet it didn't matter. Upon her it might have been made of spun gold. She filled it exquisitely, her breasts high and firm. He remembered the supple feel of them within his hands, beneath his fingertips, and felt himself harden, his blood pulse, at the mere thought. Worn as it was, the dress clung to her every curve like gossamer webs to bare flesh. Her hair. He suddenly wished he'd taken the time to unplait it and thread his fingers through the sunlit length. There would be another time, he decided. Damn, but he suddenly felt grateful to her bastard father. Aye, for she was a gift, not a burden. He gave her a wink, and her tension visibly eased.

"Weel," Angus began, his face screwing thoughtfully.

"I'll take him, da," Malcom offered eagerly, tugging at his father's breacan. "I'm a big boy. I can take him. Aren't I, Angus?" He turned to look at the surly old Scot.

Angus's brows lifted. "Ye're a muckle lad, all right, but ye're no—"

"Bloody hell. Let her carry Ranald," Dougal broke in

furiously. "Why should we give up a horse for her? 'Tisna our fault her da didna want her."

Page froze at the declaration, her gaze flying to Dougal. For an instant she wasn't certain she'd heard correctly. The suddenly wary expressions upon the faces staring at her told her differently. Her heart twisted as she turned to meet Iain's gaze. "What... what did he mean... that my father did not want me?"

"Dinna listen to Dougal, lass." She saw the truth in his eyes, though he denied it.

"Did my father not want me?" she persisted, her body tense, her breath bated while she awaited his response.

He stood silent, staring, refusing to answer, and Page saw in his expression the one thing she could not bear. Pity. She saw his pity, and her heart filled with sudden fury—fury at her father for discarding her so easily, fury at Iain MacKinnon for lying to her—fury at herself for wanting something that could never be.

"I'll take the poor bastard," Broc announced, elbowing his way into the gathering. "I'll take him. It isna right to let her bear the burden. What's wrong wi' the lot o' ye anyhoo?" He glared at Dougal particularly, and pointed out, "We're his friends."

The silence that fell between them might have lasted an instant, or an eternity, Page didn't know. She felt benumbed.

"I'll take him," Kerwyn relented, shoving Dougal angrily.

"Nay... I should," Kermichil suggested, casting a glower in Dougal's direction.

"Mayhap I should," Kerr yielded, and he, too, gave Dougal a fierce glare. "Look what ye've gone and done," he said, casting a glance in Page's direction.

Shamed into it, Dougal relented. "Verra well! I'll carry the stinkin' whoreson."

"Nay, I said I would take him," Broc argued. "Ach,

but you've gone and done enough already, ye bloody mewling bastard."

Page was scarcely aware of the glance Broc cast in her direction, but she felt his pity like a mountain of ash, blackening her mood just as surely as had she wallowed in it. She didn't fool herself into believing the behemoth cared for her. Nay, but he felt sorry for her. And that was the very last thing she wished from any of them.

If she hadn't been so staggered by Dougal's disclosure, she might have been amused by the fact that they were all fighting now over who would carry Ranald. Brawling Scots. She moved away from the dispute, wanting to weep, but refusing to shed a single tear.

Her father didn't want her.

Had he refused outright? Or simply refused to deal with Iain? Or wasn't it really the same?

Iain pitied her. He must. Surely they all did.

"Lass," Iain began, coming up behind her and placing a hand gently to her shoulder.

Page shrugged away from him, infused with anger. "Don't touch me," she spat, and whirled to face him. "How dare you lie to me? How dare you!"

He was silent in the face of her accusation, his expression pensive as he stood staring.

"Why did you lie to me?" she asked him, and then regretted the question at once. She knew why, of course. He pitied her. She was the wretched, unwanted daughter of his enemy—and he pitied her. "What did he say—my father?" she demanded to know. "How did he refuse me?"

"Ach, lass, does it matter?"

Her fury mounted with the reminder that he could not even say her name. "Aye, it matters. Aye! Did you not believe I had a right to know?"

She suddenly recalled the moment he'd come riding into the clearing with his son, the way he'd looked at

TANYA ANNE CROSBY

her, and so much made sense. The looks upon all their
faces—the shock when the MacKinnon had declared
his intent to carry her home. The resentment they all
seemed to feel for her. Broc aiding her in her escape...

She could scarce bear the thought of it all.

He seemed to consider her question, opened his
mouth to speak, and then closed it. He shook his head.
"It matters not, lass... You've a home wi' us."

Page made a woeful keening sound, and her throat
closed with a tide of emotion. She swallowed. "Like
some stray animal brought in out of the storm?" She
swallowed again, and let her anger become a balm for
her pain. "I think not. What if I've no wish to make my
home with you? Judas! Why would I care to live
amongst a rude band of Scots who cannot even seem to
get along among themselves!" She didn't care if she was
being cruel. She wanted to be—wanted to lash out and
wound. That he had the audacity to stand there and
seem unfazed by her churlish remark only made her all
the angrier.

All this time he'd known how her father had felt. All
this time he must have pitied her. Somehow, it blas-
phemed even their lovemaking, for how could he have
wanted her? Not even her father wanted her. She
couldn't bear it.

"I have a right to know," Page persisted.

He stood silent, his stance unyielding, his lips tight
with displeasure.

"Did he refuse you outright?"

He didn't answer. Didn't even blink, merely stared.

"Did my father refuse you?"

He turned away, his jaw taut, and shook his head
with what Page perceived to be disgust. "Aye," he said.
"He did, lass."

Page felt the very life leave her suddenly, all her
hopes, everything. Her legs would have given beneath
her, but there was nowhere to lean, save her own two

feet. As ever. Her voice sounded frail even to her own ears. "What did he say?"

He turned to look at her, seeming to study her, and then said, "He simply refused, is all. He said naught." And then he turned away abruptly, as though he could scarce bear to look at her.

"I see," she said, and somehow knew he was keeping the worst from her. Her father's cruelty? Hah! She knew it already, didn't he realize? She understood better than he did how brutal her father's words could be. How many times had he taunted her that she was no man's daughter? Certainly not his own? That she couldn't possibly be his own flesh and blood? How many times had he told her she was unlovable? Despicable?

More times than Page could recount.

She wanted in that moment to tell Iain to fly to the devil—that she didn't need him, or his charity, but it would be a ridiculous thing to claim.

She did need him.

What were her choices, after all? To live here in the woods with the beasts of the forest? To go crawling upon her knees to a king who would as likely spit in her face as not? Nay, she had no options, save for the one Iain MacKinnon offered her. But rather than feel grateful to him, she loathed him for it, and she wasn't even certain why. Because he'd witnessed her shame? Because he'd made her feel wanted? Only to turn about and discover that he didn't truly want her at all? That no one did. The knowledge filled her with a grief she'd never allowed herself before to feel.

Somewhere, in the dusty, cobwebbed recesses of her heart, she had dared to believe that he'd been enticed by her—that he'd taken her because he'd wanted her. Not so. He'd pitied her—had been forced to bring her along solely because he had a conscience. Simple as that.

And their afternoon? A simple tryst. No more. He

was a man, and she a woman, after all, and he had needs that she could satisfy. And, God save her soul, she had done so readily, wantonly.

Remembering the bloom in her hand, she opened her fist, only now realizing she'd held it so tightly closed, and stared at the crushed crocus. She was too disgusted with herself to even feel chagrined that she'd held on to it for so long. It was faded now, its petals worn and veined. Pursing her lips in self-disgust, she tossed the blossom to the ground, turned, and walked away, not daring a glance backward at Iain MacKinnon lest he spy her shame upon her face.

The entire lot of them were coming near to blows now, still squabbling over who would carry Ranald. Page heard them, and yet heard nothing at all. Sweet Mary, but they were fickle souls, these Scots. Well, let them kill themselves over the dubious honor. She no longer had intentions of carrying poor damned Ranald. Poor damned Ranald could carry himself for all she cared. She had half an inclination to go find the nearest rock and sit down upon it until she withered away.

CHAPTER 22

Iain had to restrain himself from going after her.

Keeping him from it was the knowledge that any words he might think to utter would be wholly inadequate to ease the incredible sorrow he saw reflected there in her eyes.

His gaze was drawn downward to the crumpled crocus blossom she had discarded. It was beaten beyond repair, its petals folded and distorted, but the fact that she had kept the memento told him it was somehow important to her, and just as he had felt compelled to pluck the blossom in the first place, he felt bound now to retrieve it to save for her. He bent, lifting it as gingerly as his big, unwieldy hands could manage, and then placed it within the folds of his breacan.

"I really like her, da," his son said in a whisper, appearing suddenly at his side.

Iain glanced down at the smaller, begrimed image of himself and smiled. "Me too," he said, and patted a hand over the crown of Malcom's head.

"But she has a mean da," Malcom proclaimed. "I didna like him."

Iain's gaze returned to Page. "Aye, son, that she does." He stared pensively, thinking of her bastard da, only half listening to his son. "I didna like him either."

"He howled like a banshee and was verra mean."

Iain's gaze snapped down to his son. "To you?"

Malcom shook his head, and his little brows drew together into a frown. "Nay... to her. I was gain' to beat him up," he revealed with no small measure of pride.

Iain chuckled and ruffled his son's hair. "Were ye now?" He didn't see any reason to point out the unlikely outcome of such a venture. "And what stopped ye, Malcom?"

His brows lifted and he nodded. "I was verra scared," he confessed.

Iain's grin widened at his son's innate honesty.

And then his little brows drew together once more. "Da," he ventured. "Were ye afeared o' her da, too?"

Iain came to his haunches to face his son, sensing his question was not one to be taken lightly. In it he heard all the confusion of childhood—the irresolutions carried into manhood. It was an echo of his own childhood—the self-doubt never voiced for fear that his da would disparage him for it. He placed his hand to his son's shoulder and confessed, "Verra much, Malcom." Certainly not in the sense his son was speaking of, but he had been terrified unto death for Malcom's sake. In truth, he'd been too damned furious, too afeared for Malcom's safety to consider his own. Nor, he was ashamed to concede, did he consider the safety of his men. Nonetheless, Malcom was too young to understand the difference between the two, and Iain sensed his son needed to know his fear was only natural. "In truth, I was verra scared," he confided in a whisper.

Malcom nodded, and returned the embrace, placing his little hand upon Iain's shoulder. "Dinna worry, da," he said. "I willna tell, all right?"

Iain smiled.

Malcom returned the smile and drew himself up to his full height, straightening his back. His gaze slid to Page and then back to his da, and then he said, patting

Iain's shoulder, "She's a right bonny lass, Da. Dinna ye think so?"

Iain choked on a chuckle. He managed a sober nod. "Aye, son, I do."

Malcom nodded, as well. "And she sings verra pretty, too."

Iain's gaze was drawn to where she sat upon a small stone. "That she does," he agreed. "That she does." He stood, staring pensively.

"So d' ye think we can keep her?" Malcom ventured.

Iain found himself grinning down at his son, and soon to be coconspirator. "D' ye wish to keep her, Malcom?"

"Aye, da," Malcom answered at once. "Sometimes..." he imparted, "dinna tell anybody, now... I wish for a mammy to sing me to sleep."

Iain's heart squeezed a little at his son's admission. There was no need to stretch the truth this time as he confessed, "I used to wish for the same, Malcom, when I was your age."

"Did ye truly, da?"

"Aye." More often than he could ever count, he had wished for that very thing. Mayhap, even, 'twas why he heard the echo in his mind of a voice that could never have existed. His mother's voice. A haunting lilt that tugged at his heart and plagued his very soul.

"Guid, then. Let us both woo her together. You work on her heart," he charged his son.

"And what part o' her will you work to woo?" Malcom asked innocently. "Her brain, da? Will ye work to woo her brain?"

Again Iain's gaze was drawn to her. She sat, hugging a knee to her breast. The other leg stretched out, long, lean, and luscious, from beneath the tattered hem of her skirt. The very sight of it caused his blood to simmer and stir. He could almost feel the soft, supple flesh of her calf slide beneath the touch of his hand. He watched an instant longer, shuddering, and then relented, turning back to his son. "Aye," he said, his throat thick with a longing he could not suppress. "That, too." He winked at his son conspiratorially.

"Iain," shouted Angus.

Iain's attention was drawn to the group of men who had gathered about Ranald's body.

Angus was holding the harness in his hands. He held it up for Iain to see. "I think ye'd better take a look at this," he urged.

Iain nodded, and turned back to his son. He ruffled a hand through Malcom's hair. "Go on wi' ye now, son, and woo her guid, ye hear?"

Malcom beamed. "Aye, da," he said, winking back in an exaggerated version of his father's wink. "I will!" And then he turned and raced away.

Iain watched Malcom scurry to where Page sat, knowing his son would succeed with her in ways he could never. No one could resist that dirty, plump little face. Certainly Iain couldn't. Sure enough, she peered up from her melancholy thoughts to spy him, and even as Iain watched, Malcom managed to coax a smile from her lush lips.

Satisfied that his son's endeavors were going well enough, he went to see what it was that seemed to have Angus in a stir. All eyes remained upon him as he approached. The hairs at his nape stood at end. "What is it?"

"Take a look for yourself," Angus directed.

Iain did, accepting the harness into his hands. At first glance, he saw nothing awry. He turned the harness, searching, and then his eyes fell upon the cleanly sliced cinch. He stiffened, knowing instinctively what it meant. He lifted the leather strap at once, inspecting it closer, ran a finger across the cut edge, and his body tensed.

"Someone cut it."

"Aye," agreed Angus. "Someone did."

"But who?" Iain's gaze searched the lot of them.

Angus shrugged. Broc stared at the mutilated harness, his brows drawn together into a frown. Kerwyn, Dougal, and Kermichil shook their heads and shrugged.

Lagan held out his hand, asking without words to see the damage. Iain handed the harness to him, and he inspected it thoroughly. "Without doubt, 'twas cut," he yielded after a moment's deliberation. "But I saw no one among us do such a thing," he avowed, casting a meaningful glance in Page's direction. "Only the Sassenach wench was near the mounts alone," he proclaimed.

"'Tis the truth," Dougal attested. "Only she was near the horses alone when she made her escape."

"Nay," Broc argued. "She dinna do it. I watched her every moment, and she dinna do it."

Iain was too damned furious to consider Broc's sudden change of heart toward Page. And if the truth be known, too damned relieved. He had no doubts over Page's innocence, but he was glad she had a champion aside from himself, one who'd been present, while he had not been.

Page was certainly no genteel princess, but she would never have stooped to this, even to gain her freedom, he was certain. One look into her eyes while she'd defended her bastard da, or even his own son, told him as much. If she could defend a man who deserved to be drawn and quartered for his sins against her, there was no way she would harm another human being. Aye, and if she could defend a child she scarce knew, against a man such as he was reputed to be, he knew her heart was pure.

But somebody had cut the cinch.

The question was...

Who?

And was it intended for Ranald... or someone else?

Never had such unease and mistrust run rampant

through his clan. It seemed in the short time since Malcom's abduction, the glue that held them bound was beginning to weaken. Mayhap David of Scotland would have his way, after all. He intended that the Highlands would fall behind him, and those who would not should fall by the wayside.

Iain refused to comply. Be damned if he was going to stand about and watch while David handed all of Scotland to his Sassenach minions. And be damned if he was going to allow the English bastards to lay the yoke upon his people. He wasn't about to hand over his son's birthright to be trampled upon by English rule. The Highlands were their lands, no matter that they were bitter and cold in the winters, or too rugged and wild in the summers. It was their land, and if Iain had any say over the matter, it would be their land until the last MacKinnon chieftain knelt before Heaven's throne.

"Aye?" Lagan challenged Broc. "Ye watched her every moment? So, then, tell us... is that why she was able to swim away from us and steal our horses?"

"One horse," Broc argued with a frown for Dougal, and one for Lagan.

Iain met Broc's gaze, his own eyes narrowed in question. Broc's gaze skidded away, his face reddening under so much scrutiny.

"Answer to it, Broc," Iain directed. "Did you, or did you not, watch her as you claim?"

"Aye, laird," Broc confessed. "I did. I watched her every moment as I said."

"Then he must be scheming wi' her," Lagan declared furiously. "Why would he watch her and let her go unless he was?"

Iain had a suspicion as to why, but he wanted to hear it from Broc's own lips. His gaze upon Broc was unrelenting, and the youth seemed to sense it, for he didn't dare to meet Iain's eyes. "Broc? What say you to that?"

"I didna think ye really wanted her, laird," he confessed, peering up from the ground at long last.

"Neither did she seem to wish to stay. And I dinna like her for the way she seemed to mock us." His mouth twisted into an embarrassed grimace. "I didna believe she should come wi' us, and I thought ye just didna hae the heart to send her away."

"So ye thought to do me a service and help her on her way?"

Broc nodded.

"D' ye no' think I could make such a decision on my own, lad?" Iain asked him.

"Aye," Broc answered.

"Christ and bedamned, what ails the lot o' ye?" Iain asked them angrily. "You bring to mind a company of old maids, bickering like ye do amongst yourselves."

"Somethin's been amiss since we came into this Sassenach land, Iain," Angus proposed. "First poor Ranald, now this."

"And I wager 'tis all her doin'," Dougal asserted, casting a menacing glance in Page's direction.

Iain shook his head. "Something's been amiss since the verra beginning," he countered. "Ye dinna remember the reason we came into this Sassenach land to begin wi'. It wasna reivin' or wenchin' that brought us here. Someone took my bloody son, remember?" His hands went to his hips. "Nay." He cast a glance in Page's direction, and then returned it to the small group of men standing before him.

Not all of his men were aware of the situation: some were idling away the time, waiting for the cavalcade to begin once again. Iain's gaze scanned the area, watching the small groups at their discourse and respite. "I dinna think she had anythin' to do wi' Ranald's death," he asserted.

"And ye dinna think 'twas her da?" Kermichil asked, his lips pursing in deliberation.

"Nay. We've no' been followed," Iain answered with certainty. "I thought so at first, but nay. I've no notion who got to Ranald, but 'twas no' her da, and she dinna do it," he assured them. "Someone did. But Ranald, ye recall, was slain by an arrow through the breast. Even were she skilled with the bow, she's had no access to such a weapon, and she was watched besides—by me," he interjected, lest there be any doubt. "Nay, 'twas someone else."

Both Broc and Angus nodded agreement.

"What d'ye think, then, Iain?" asked Lagan. "If 'twas no' her da..."

"Then it must be brigands," Kerwyn interposed.

"Or one o' us," Broc suggested, though he seemed loath to put forth such a notion. His gaze scanned the men present, waiting, it seemed, for them to point the finger at him once more.

"Aye, Broc," Iain agreed, nodding, his expression grave. "Or one o' us..." Iain, too, scrutinized them, taking in their sober expressions, their rigid stances. All of them had been closely knit too long to suspect a single one of them. Some, he'd seen their naked arses spanked by their mammies as laddies; a few others had been there to see his own walloped by his da. Their lives and their legacies were intermingled and belonged to the clan MacKinnon, their heritage handed down by the mighty sons of MacAlpin. It pained his heart to think of any one of them as guilty.

And yet one of them was.

"I say 'tis Broc!" Dougal exploded, turning and shoving the titan youth with all his might.

Broc barely budged over the effort, and Iain nearly laughed out loud despite the gravity of their situation.

"You whoreson Sassenach abettor," Dougal snarled.

To his credit, though, Broc's eyes reflected his fury, he didn't bother to return Dougal's callow shove. He stood, frowning down at his peer. Broc and Dougal had long shared a friendly rivalry, one that seemed now to have become heartfelt.

"Enough, Dougal," Iain reproved, his tone unyielding, lest they mistake his reasoning for lack of intent. "Fighting amidst ourselves gains us naught," he told them.

Dougal, red faced over the lack of impact he'd had upon Broc's massive form, and Iain's rebuke, nodded his agreement as he stared, brooding now, at the ground before him.

"My charge to all o' ye is this," Iain told them, his eyes narrowing and alighting upon each and every one separately. "Watch your backs, all o' ye. Guard each other well. Dougal and Broc," he directed, "put your differences aside for now." He cast them each a foreboding glance and said, "It seems there is a traitor amongst us."

Each and every man nodded, looking as glum as Iain had ever seen them. There was no denying the truth.

The evidence was indisputable.

"A message o' warning to whoever that mon might be," Iain concluded. "When I discover who ye are... and I will unmask the bloody whoreson... I'll hold your heart in my hands and watch ye greet your maker as the heartless bastard ye are."

Every man present shook his head, denying responsibility.

"I didna do it," Dougal muttered, shaking his head adamantly.

"Nor I," muttered another.

"Or me," came the echo.

"Weel," Iain answered, "ye can bloody damned well pass it on, anyhoo."

"The whoreson knows who he is," Angus agreed somberly. "And I'd wager he dinna have in mind for that tumble down the mount to be poor Ranald's either."

"That he does," Iain granted. "And nay... that tumble

down the hillside was meant to put more than scrapes on a bloody corpse. Mayhap 'twas meant for her..." He cast a nod in Page's direction. "And mayhap 'twas meant for my son." His jaw went taut. His hands clenched at his sides. "Either way... may God forgive his cold heart, because I mean to carve it from his verra body with my own hands and feed it to the raving wolves. Tell him that for me, will ye now," Iain charged them, and left them to mull over his counsel.

CHAPTER 23

The MacKinnon was in a foul mood.

Page didn't need to hear the whispered warnings to know she should endeavor to stay out of his way. She'd learned her lessons well in her father's home. She wasn't precisely certain what it was that had turned his mood so foul, but she knew it had something to do with the discourse he'd shared with his men earlier in the day. She'd known by the way he'd stood talking with them, and then by the way he'd pivoted and left them. The scowl upon his face had been daunting enough to make her cower where she'd sat upon her little stone.

Without a word he'd saddled her mount with his own harness and trappings, and then had decreed she would ride with Malcom. And then without a word he'd ridden beside them, making only an occasional swoop over his cavalcade, speaking sharply to those he stopped to address.

Only Malcom seemed unaffected by his mood, and Page thought it either very foolish, or very telling. She was beginning to believe the latter, as she'd never heard Iain speak a single unkind word to his son, but she was beyond the point of feeling envious over that fact. On the contrary, she was glad for Malcom. He was a bright

227

child, with a wit almost as sharp as his father's. And no child deserved ill treatment—not from anyone.

She and Malcom whiled away the hours talking about everything. He told her of his home, *Chreagach Mhor*—that the stone walls of his father's donjon had been built long before the first MacKinnon had set foot upon God's earth. He told her all about his da, about things she wasn't certain Iain would wish her to know— that his da sometimes had nightmares, and that he called out his mother's name.

Mairi.

Of all names to choose, it was the first false name she'd given him, she realized. He'd fallen silent. She wondered if he found her lacking compared to his wife.

Likely so.

He plainly loved her still.

The fact bothered Page more than it should have. She didn't understand it, but somehow, knowing that Iain could never have harmed his wife, she'd rather have thought he might than to think he yet loved her, and dreamt of her so oft. She didn't understand it, didn't even try to, for it seemed a ludicrous notion, and she rather thought that if he were capable of such a horror as murdering a wife, she couldn't even like him. Tangled emotions. Even more tangled thoughts.

The only one thing that she did know was that, like it or nay, she would have to make the best of this situation God had cast her within. Her father wasn't coming after her. She could stop peering over her shoulder now, and dropping scraps of cloth for him to follow. She could stop hoping, and start living as best she could.

She refused to stop loathing him. Somehow, with the knowledge that he had so easily and so completely repudiated her—to strangers—she found that every last shred of kindly emotion she'd once harbored for him fled. And in truth, it had never been easy to love him, she acknowledged. She had loved him only because she'd felt she must. Because he was the only kin she'd ever known. Well, no more! The knowledge had freed her of whatever obligatory love she'd once had for him.

For better or for worse, these were to be her people now.

Sitting there alone upon that stone, she'd felt so far removed from everything and everyone she'd ever known.

And then Malcom had come to speak with her, and he'd brightened her heart with his smiles and his words. This dirty little Scots boy, with the green eyes, golden hair, and a face that was an almost perfect replica of his father's.

Aye, these were her people now, she resolved.

Mayhap she would never have chosen them—nor they her—but God had seen fit to cast them together, and she was determined to feel grateful, despite the anger and hurt she felt. And she was even more determined to earn her keep, however possible.

They continued the northward ride mostly in silence, but for Malcom's occasional familiar illumination. When the winds lifted, Malcom turned and buried his little face against her bosom, and she sheltered him as best she could, singing to him to pass the time. Amazing, she'd never thought a body could withstand such frigid temperatures, though while Malcom seemed ready enough to snuggle against her, she was the only one left shivering.

Mayhap it was the emptiness within her that made her feel so chilled. Absurdly, the thought that Iain MacKinnon pitied her made her feel more depleted even than her father's betrayal.

Foolish girl, she berated herself.

How could you have possibly believed he could love you?

She hadn't expected love, she told herself, and

TANYA ANNE CROSBY

hadn't gotten it. So why should she feel so disheartened?

She didn't know, but she did.

The weather became more insane the farther north they traveled.

They awakened the next morning to a fine, cold mist that no sooner settled upon the flesh than it began seeping down into the bones. And still she was the only one shivering. These Scotsmen surrounding her seemed wholly immune to the savage weather they faced.

It seemed remarkable to Page that it could be so cold when the sun shone brightly down upon them. But it was. And it was a cold that benumbed the flesh and paralyzed the body. They gained an early start, covering more ground than it seemed conceivable for the horses to cover, when her own fragile bones seemed frozen and incapable of motion.

When it ceased to rain at last she had no chance to rejoice in the fact, for within mere instants of the rain's departure came the snow. Stunned, she put out her hand to be certain she wasn't imagining it, and was stupefied to find white feathery flakes alighting upon her sun-pinkened flesh—such fine flakes, they melted upon contact, but flakes, they were.

It was in that moment, as she scrutinized the MacKinnon men, that she realized what remarkable fortitudes they each possessed. Not a one of them complained even the least, though more than half wore not even shoes. Bare legged and bare of feet, with only their breacans to buffer them from the piercing wind and cold, they rode with their spines rigid and their heads held high and proud.

Not Page. She, on the other hand, while she dared not voice her discomfort, was huddled over Malcom, trying desperately to warm her body. Her feet were bare as well, but she did not endure it so nobly. Her distress must have been evident, for Iain removed his breacan and approached her, throwing the thick woolen blanket as a mantle over her shoulders. She was loath to take his charity, but didn't dare refuse it. As it was, were it not for Malcom's little body seated before her, she thought she would have perished long before now. Whatever the rain left untouched, the chill wind permeated.

Broc, too, came and offered his blanket, unsettling Page, and making her eyes burn with tears. She tried to refuse him, but he held his hand out resolutely.

"For the lad," he said low, nodding and urging her to take it.

Swallowing her pride, for Malcom lay sleeping against her bosom with nary a single shiver—she knew the gesture was for her—she accepted the blanket, her eyes stinging horribly.

Broc remained at her side a moment longer, making idle talk about his dog, Merry Bells, and reminding her belatedly of his unfortunate affliction. She stared down at the blanket she'd placed over Malcom and herself, and endeavored to hide her grimace of disgust. She fought the urge to fling the blanket back at the fair-faced behemoth, but was reluctant to offend him. Poor child would likely end up with fleas—and herself, as well. She cast a glance at Broc to find him scratching his head, and determined to help rid him once and for all of his infestation.

Broc remained by her side, regaling her with tales of the world's most clever dog, until Iain returned to ride beside her. A single glance from his laird sent Broc on his way. And then once again Page rode in silence, for Iain didn't deign to speak to her.

He wouldn't even look at her.

Though she knew it was ludicrous, she was still angry with him—couldn't help herself. In withholding the truth, he had, after all, merely had the audacity to consider her feelings. She should have been grateful, but somehow couldn't gather the sentiment. She wanted to cut out his tongue for lying to her—for keeping the truth from her. It was the same as a lie, wasn't it? She wanted to slap his mouth for daring to kiss her—for having the gall to make her feel cherished, when she dared not feel anything at all.

More than aught else, she wanted to fling herself into his arms and weep until the last tear was shed. She wanted him to hold her, kiss her, love her. She wanted to forget herself within his arms, let him carry her again to that sweet place where only the body mattered, the heart did not—and she wanted to stay there for all of eternity, never to return.

She wanted to force him to acknowledge her, to look at her again as he had—not with that piteous expression that made her heart ache and made her want to gouge out his eyes.

As ever, it seemed, she wanted too much, for Iain MacKinnon continued to ride beside her deep in silence, casting her only the occasional brooding glance.

HE WAS RUNNING OUT OF TIME.

It wouldn't be long now before Iain began to unravel the tangled thread of clues.

And where would that leave him? With nothing once again—damned if he'd allow it to happen.

Nay, he'd have to accelerate his plans, make the most of every opportunity. Bloody troublesome wench had managed to set them all to rights without even lifting her voice in censure. Christ, but she'd had them all scurrying with shame o'er the honor of carrying Ranald's stinkin' body.

He hadn't offered, and he wondered now if Iain had noticed. He cast a furtive glance at the laird of the Mac-Kinnons, and found him brooding still, his expression black as his da's heart had been. He hadn't said much since Ranald's tumble. Not to anyone—not even to his Sassenach whore, though he watched her every second he thought she would not spy him at his lovelorn glances.

For her part, she sat there, her expressions too easy to read: a mixture of longing, fury, and pain. Aye, well, he'd put the bitch out of her misery afore long.

Merely the thought of it brought an anticipatory smile to his lips.

CHAPTER 24

Soaring upon a gently sloping, heathered hill,
Chreagach Mhor seemed an enchanted place. Not
even Malcom's tales, pride filled though they were,
could have prepared her for the rustic, fantastical
beauty of the stone sentinel upon the hilltop. The very
sight of it stole Page's breath away.

As cool as the weather remained high in these hills,
the heather bloomed a brilliant violet against a vivid
carpet of green. Scattered across the lush landscape,
rugged stones stood like proud sentries to guard the
mammoth tower. Small thatch-roofed buildings spat-
tered the hillside. The rounded donjon itself was like no
other donjon Page had ever set eyes upon. The struc-
ture rose against the twilight sky, a sleek, tapering
grayish silhouette against the darkening horizon.

Page held her breath as they climbed the hill toward
it, her expression one of awe. It was a dream vision of
incomparable beauty, nothing at all like the ugly stone
fortress that was Aldergh.

Built solely for defense, Aldergh was a monstrosity,
a scabrous creation that sullied the beauty of the English meadow upon which it was seated.

This place, this rugged fortress settled high upon a

violet mantle, with its single visible high window, was like a majestic suzerain reigning over the landscape.

As she watched in awe, kith and kin appeared from the thatch-roofed dwellings, and gathered anxiously along the single worn path that led to the donjon itself. With craned necks and murmured voices they awaited the cavalcade.

Malcom's animated voice and Iain's ensuing laughter drew Page's attention to father and son riding beside her. His brooding countenance vanished, replaced with an expression of supreme pleasure. Father and son seemed to forget her in their moment of homecoming. Page didn't care. Their joy was infectious.

Understanding what it was his people sought to know, Iain suddenly lifted his son from before him upon the saddle and seated him high upon his shoulders. Arms flailing, Malcom shouted to his kinfolk, a gleeful Gaelic greeting, and Page found herself smiling over his exuberant display.

Caught up within their exhilaration, Page blinked away the sting of tears. Iain's laughter at his son's excitement made her heart swell. What must it feel like to be so loved? To love so much in return?

So constricted was her chest suddenly, Page could scarce take a breath. In profile, Iain MacKinnon's smile was stunning, but when he suddenly turned to look at her and winked, she thought her heart would leap from her breast.

"What d' ye think, lass?" he asked her.

Page swallowed, and shook her head, unable to respond with her heart so firmly entrenched within her throat.

"Ach, lass," he said, and maneuvered his mount nearer. Gripping Malcom's legs, he leaned as far toward her as he was able with his wriggling son seated high atop his shoulders. "Dinna look so glum," he bade her, smiling. "They'll no' bite, *mo chridhe*."

Page wasn't so certain. She lifted a brow, telling him so without words.

He chuckled and turned to Angus, "Stay wi' her, Angus," he commanded.

The two shared an indecipherable look, making Page feel as though she'd missed something of import. She tried to recall what Iain had said, and couldn't. Auld Angus nodded, and Page watched, still contemplating their silent exchange, as Iain rode to the fore of his men.

Angus watched him as well, she noted, his expression one of astonished bemusement. "My heart, you say?" the old man said to Iain, and shook his head. He cast her a meaningful glance, his lips curving softly as he turned away.

His heart, what? Did it ail him? Page wondered.

Though she could scarce share Angus's mirth, she couldn't suppress her own smile at the obvious clamor father and son elicited merely with their presence. She never would have guessed by the casual ease with which they all treated each other on the journey home, nor by the way they seemed so inclined to quarrel amongst themselves. While it was apparent they respected the MacKinnon and yielded to him always, they were unafraid to voice their convictions and stand apart. Seeing the furor over his return, it was more than evident these people truly valued their laird, and she couldn't help but consider the differences between Iain and her father.

Her father's men walked behind him always, skulking shadows ready to snatch his mantle lest it fall to the ground. But when they thought there were no ears about to hear them, they disparaged him to one another. Page had never blamed them. So oft they voiced the very sentiments she wished she had nerve enough to express.

"Wait until you see her," Broc said, drawing up beside her.

"Who?" Page asked with a wistful sigh, her eyes still drinking in the sight of Iain riding with his son perched high upon his shoulders. She had the deepest yearning suddenly to be at his side, to see the smile of pleasure he wore upon his face, to know what it felt like to be cherished as he seemed to be.

Judas, but she did know. He'd given her the briefest taste of it while she was in his arms, and she wanted to be there again.

"Merry Bells," Broc clarified, and Page blinked, trying to determine what in God's creation he was speaking of.

"She's a verra smart dog," he said, and Page choked upon a giggle. She concealed her amusement with a discreet clearing of her throat. She turned and found Angus smiling to himself and she thought she knew precisely what brought such a devilish turn to the old man's lips. Broc was relentless in the telling of his dog tales. In truth, if she hadn't begun to like the behemoth so blessed much, she might have choked him long ere now for his incessant rambling over the beast.

He sat there, scratching his head, and searching the crowd.

"There she is," he said suddenly, spying the dog, and then decreed, "Watch this!"

Page watched as he bade her. Following his gaze, she located the black and white spotted dog standing beside a young child who was busily scratching her back. Broc gave a whistle, and the dog's ears perked at once. And then she suddenly came flying.

"Watch this," Broc demanded of her, turning to be sure she was watching. She gave him a smile and nod, and he turned again to watch his dog. Only, Merry Bells had been quicker than Broc had obviously anticipated. Just as he turned to await the animal, Merry Bells leapt high into the air. Behemoth and beast met face-to-face, and Page heard the sickening crack as Broc's nose was broken by the impact of his dog's snout against his face. She gasped in alarm as both Broc and his animal fell yelping backward.

She reined in at once to the sound of startled curses, and Angus's great peal of laughter. Slipping from her mount, she hurried to inspect the fallen pair. Merry Bells, for her part, seemed startled but unharmed. The dog rolled at once from atop Broc and scurried away, tail between her legs. Broc, his face flush with embarrassment, and his nose bleeding, simply lay upon the ground, stupefied.

Page took pity upon him and kept her mirth bridled. Without hesitation, she lifted her gown and ripped a strip from her already tattered hem and then pressed it to Broc's bleeding nostril. She was scarce aware of the crowd that gathered, some laughing, most suddenly too curious over her presence amongst them to do anything more than stare at the pair of them, Broc sprawled before her upon the ground, and her ministering to his wounds.

"Well, now, damn me to hell," someone shouted. "Broc's got himself a woman."

"Broc's got himself a woman?" another echoed, and the crowd suddenly began to close in about them.

"I'll be hanged," someone decreed, laughter in his voice. "No wonder puir Merry Bells just aboot took your nose off, ye cheatin' whoreson. Ho! But damned if I can blame ye. She's a damn sight bonnier than Merry Bells."

Merry Bells sidled into the circle at that moment, shimmying under legs to reach her master. She came wagging her tail behind her, casting a black-eyed glance in Page's direction, before scurrying over to Broc. The dog lapped his face hesitantly at first, and then eagerly, whining. Tail perking and wagging, she seemed to forget everything but her precious master in that moment.

"Looks to me like Broc'll be sharing his bed wi' two bitches tonight."

Another round of bawdy laughter followed that remark, and Page's cheeks flamed.

All of a sudden the gathering parted as Iain MacKinnon came toward her, his look dark and his stride purposeful.

Without a word, he bent low. Casting angry glances at his men, he snatched her up by the waist and tossed her unceremoniously over his shoulders. "She'll damn well no' be sharing Broc's bed," he declared to one and all, and then marched away, with Page clinging to his shoulders for dear life.

A hush fell over them all.

Openmouthed stares followed them.

Page's cheeks burned hotter. "While I certainly am grateful for the deliverance," she remarked rather flippantly, pounding him once on the back for emphasis, "you might have gone about this with a little more civility."

Aye, he might have, Iain acknowledged, but he'd lost his composure watching her with Broc. Ach, but it wasn't so much that she'd tended him so solicitously— aye, but it was. And still he might have dealt with it had the talk not turned toward bedding Broc. The image had wholly unsettled him, and he'd found himself handing Malcom into Glenna's capable arms and marching toward them. He'd be damned if he'd let them mistake who she was.

She was his.

He wasn't certain, precisely, at which moment he'd decided such a thing—whether it was in the instant after their loving, or after seeing her ride companionably beside Broc all afternoon, speaking low and laughing softly as would two lovers together. Never in his life had he felt such a stab of covetousness. Like some jealous beau, he'd had a difficult time keeping himself from maneuvering his mount betwixt the two, and commanding Broc away from her. Amazing, in such short time she'd managed to win Broc's favor—the others, as well, with the exception of a few. He could tell by the way they looked upon her, and in the small ways they tried to shield her. He couldn't believe how vehemently Broc had come to her defense.

Damn, but mayhap it was simply in watching her ride with his son that he came to the decision. He'd watched her smooth the hair back from Malcom's face as she listened to him speak... like a mother with her beloved child, and his heart had thundered within his breast to see it. In that instant he'd wanted to snatch her up into his arms and love her madly.

Damned if he understood why he felt so.

He only knew that he wanted her.

And this moment, he wanted her badly enough not to care what anyone thought of his manners. Damn propriety. Damn everyone.

Malcom was home. Aye, and it was his son they wished to see this moment, not him. He knew Glenna would watch him well; she loved Malcom as though he were her own. And Glenna was the closest thing to a grandparent Malcom would ever know. They needed time to reacquaint themselves. He, on the other hand, needed something else entirely.

Something only Page could give him.

Ignoring her protests and her threats, he bore her without a word into his home, and up the stairwell to his chamber.

"Put me down," she demanded. "I am perfectly capable of making my way upon my own two feet, thank you!"

"Of a certainty, ye can, lass."

But he didn't stop, and she shrieked in outrage. "Put me down," she demanded. "Everyone is watching!"

"Are they really?" he asked with little concern.

She actually growled at that, and Iain had to suppress a hearty chuckle at her fierce expression of frustration.

"Put me down, I tell you! Now! You overbearing brute!"

"Of a certainty, I shall," Iain said amenably, though he continued to carry her up the steps, disregarding her request until he was within his chamber, and managed to kick the door closed. Only then did he put her down and release her.

CHAPTER 25

The instant her feet touched the wooden floor, Page scurried across the room, too outraged to care that she might stumble over some misplaced object within the gloomy confines of the room. She went as far as she dared, and then whirled upon him, her hands going to her hips as she glared at him through the shadows. She tried to focus upon his imposing form standing so forbiddingly before the only door.

"Sweet Jesu," she exclaimed, when she still could not see him clearly enough. "Have you no tapers?"

Lord, but she couldn't recall when she'd been so humiliated. And then at once she reconsidered. Of course she could. No other moment in her life would ever pain her more than the instant she'd discovered her father's treachery. Be that as it may, Iain MacKinnon's rude conduct came mightily close.

"We dinna keep servants to anticipate our every whim," he answered calmly. "We do for ourselves, lass. If the room is dark and cold, I beg your pardon."

Page had to clamp her lips together to keep from lashing out a response to his unjust insinuation—that she would have had servants to coddle her. Indeed! If her father could scarce trouble himself to name her, he certainly hadn't been any more inclined to see to her comforts.

On the contrary, he'd worked her tirelessly, and the common coarseness of her hands bespoke as much. She clenched her fists at her sides, and gritted her teeth in renewed anger at the reminder of her father and his heartless disowning.

"No servants?" she answered flippantly. "What a pity. Ah, well, I shall find myself quite at home anyway," she answered truthfully.

"I shall see to it," he promised, his words a seething whisper.

There was a moment of taut silence as he pushed away from the door and moved through the shadows. Page followed him with her eyes.

When at last her vision adjusted to the gloom, she watched as he finally lit a taper. Its flame thrust immediately upward and remained steady and true, brightening the chamber. It was a large room by most any standard —large enough to make it appear utterly barren despite the massive bed that occupied its space. The bed itself was strewn with furs, but the rest of the room was completely devoid of anything that would give it warmth. Nothing upon the walls, nothing upon the floors.

In the center of the room stood a small brazier, its pith blackened and unused. It, along with the bed, remained the only evidence the room was in use at all, for the chamber was impeccable and uncluttered—appeared abandoned even. A hasty glance about revealed a single window at her back, curiously barred. Through the rashly placed wooden slats, thin rays of sunlight sluiced into the musty confines of the stone-walled chamber.

At once her gaze was drawn back toward the soft flicker of the taper within Iain's hands. Its glow illuminated his hard masculine features fully, and she shuddered at the way his gold-flecked eyes watched her so intently.

Was he awaiting her reaction to this place he'd brought her? Did he intend to imprison her here? But why should he? She had no place to run to, she thought morosely.

"What is this place?" she asked him.

"My chamber."

"You sleep here?" Page asked with no small measure of surprise. Mentally she compared the sparse room to her father's lavish bedchamber—his so filled with richly colored tapestries and manifold extravagances.

"Aye."

Page cast another glance about, her eyes trying to perceive the room in a different light, but there was nothing present to give her even the slightest clue of him. "It... appears so... very... desolate," she remarked, frowning.

"It serves its purpose well enough," Iain said. "What need have I for finery when my eyes willna see it whilst I sleep?"

Page's own bedchamber had been as chaste as a monk's cell, but not by choice. To make it appear less so, she had usurped forsaken baubles from her father's home, stealing them into her own chamber in order to enliven it. Her frown deepened at the piteous thought.

Iain hadn't moved from where he stood, holding the burning taper. He was watching her curiously while she studied the room, waiting, it seemed, for some response from her. Curse him, too, for it seemed he was always watching. Scrutinizing. Waiting.

The very sight of him elicited such conflicting emotions, for while he was the one person in her life who'd made her feel cherished, he was also the one person who compelled her to see herself as she was.

And she didn't like what she saw... save when she looked into his eyes.

And even then, she recalled all of which she'd been deprived.

He gazed at her as though she were precious... and therein lay the heart of the matter, for she knew herself as unworthy.

All those years she'd pretended she didn't care... he'd made them all a terrible lie. Aye, for she cared with every fiber of her being—hurt with every last drop of blood that was wrung from her heart.

And it was Iain MacKinnon's fault, because before him, she had been blissfully numb.

She narrowed her eyes at him. "Tell me," she said irascibly, "did your mother never teach you better than to fling unwilling women over your shoulder?"

His brows collided, and his jaw went taut. He peered away. Good, let him suffer it, if he would. She might have slapped him, in truth, for she was still blenching over the looks his people were giving her as he'd carried her into his home. How dare he treat her so commonly?

And then he turned to face her, and though he deserved considerably more than her anger for treating her so coarsely, Page regretted her outburst the instant she saw the look upon his face. It was obvious she'd managed to wound him, and she couldn't help but wonder what it was that made his eyes seem so melancholy of a sudden.

"Ach, lass," he answered, his expression sober, if not entirely contrite, "the burden o' my manners doesna fall to my minnie at all." He cast a glance at the floor, and then met her gaze once more, his golden eyes shadowed. "I knew her not, y' see." The candlelight glinted upon his eyes. The glimmer mesmerized her as much as his admission moved her.

"Oh," Page said softly. She felt a keen stab of guilt.

"She died giving me birth."

Their gazes held, locked.

Embraced.

"I... I did not know." More than she had, she sensed he'd suffered the loss of his mother. It was wholly discomposing the way his simple revelation affected her. With nary more than a few words, he'd managed not only to defuse her anger, but to make her long to cast herself into his arms and share his misery.

"Dinna fash yourself o'er it," he said softly, nodding, his eyes fixed upon her still. "How could ye have known?"

"I never would have—"

"Hush, lass," he broke in, carrying a finger to his lips. "I'm no wee bairn to need suckling at her breast. 'Tis all right." His eyes narrowed then, slitted, lowered from her eyes, to her mouth, and then to her breast, lingering there.

She knew at once what he was thinking, and her heart skipped its normal beat. Her breath caught as she followed his gaze to find that her body had somehow betrayed her. A guilty flush crept into her cheeks, through her body, warming her.

"Nay?" she asked, gulping in a breath as she lifted her face to meet his heavy-lidded gaze once more. He was still staring at her bosom. And then suddenly realizing what it must sound as though she were asking, she said much more firmly, "Nay! Oh, nay, you are not."

His lips curved ever so slightly and he blinked, lifting his gaze once more to her face.

In the depths of his smoldering eyes Page saw the stark intensity of his desire for her, and shamelessly rejoiced in it. Her breath accelerated, and her heartbeat quickened with the knowledge that he wanted her still.

Warmth flared through her. "Neither... neither did I," she revealed, swallowing convulsively. Her thoughts scattered.

He moved toward her, and Page felt her legs go suddenly weak. Heat suffused her. He stopped to set the candle upon the brazier. "Neither did you what?" he asked softly.

"Neither did I what?" Page repeated dumbly. He turned to face her, lifted a brow, and she recalled herself at once. "Oh! My mother! Neither did I know my mother!"

"I know, lass," he said.

Page's brows knit. "How could you possibly?"

His jaws clenched. As she watched, he closed his eyes and sucked in a breath, and by those gestures Page surmised he was trying to temper himself and his answer.

"Because," he answered tautly. Anger swirled in the depths of his golden eyes. "No mother—no mother worthy of being called so—would have allowed her daughter to grow to womanhood without something so simple as a name."

Page felt the sting of tears come to her eyes at the slap of truth, but she didn't turn away. She refused to feel shamed by it. Nay, instead she would take refuge in the outrage he seemed to feel on her behalf.

"Nay," she agreed. And for the first time, acknowledged, "No mother would have." She unclenched the fist at her side, and then squeezed it closed once more. "Nor a father," she yielded, her voice shaky with indignity.

"Nay, lass," he agreed, closing the distance between them in a few easy strides. He reached out with a finger to lift her chin. "Nor a father."

Page felt herself begin to quake, though she wasn't afeared, she told herself. On the contrary, she was titillated by the warm, gentle touch of his finger upon her face. "Nay," she agreed, her voice thick with emotion. A shiver coursed through her.

"I always blamed myself," she admitted to him, "for driving her away. My mother..."

His brows drew together. "How could ye? Were ye'

no' but a babe? How could ye have possibly had anythin' to do with her leaving?"

Page shrugged and tried to look away. "I used to dream of her face," she said softly.

He lifted her chin, urging her gaze upward. "I, too, once blamed myself for things I shouldna... but we canna take the world upon our shoulders, lass."

"But my father blamed me, as well," Page yielded. "Impossible not to feel culpable when his words and heart accused me every time he set his eyes upon me."

"Ye deserved better... Only tell me your heart's desire," he murmured, "and I shall give it, if I can. I want to make it all up to you."

Her breath caught on a strangled moan.

"Anything," he whispered. "Anything at all."

Her brows flinched. She reached out to place tentative fingers upon his arm. Another shiver bolted through her as she touched him, and he responded with a shudder of his own.

"I want you to be happy here," he urged her. "I want you to make this your home."

Page swallowed. "I... I wish..." She forced in a breath. "Only... to be known as Suisan... to you... to your people. I... I don't want them to know."

"Ach, then Suisan ye are," he murmured low. "Bonny and sweet." Another quiver swept over her at the earnestness of his vow. "What else... Suisan... what else would please ye? Merely ask and 'tis yours."

Page closed her eyes and swallowed with difficulty. When she opened her eyes once more, she knew they revealed her heart to him wholly. She couldn't help it. Never in her life had anyone spoken so sweetly to her.

Never in her life had she yearned for someone's love more.

And yet, she couldn't ask for it. Dared not.

"Naught," she lied, swallowing once more. "Naught more." She stared at his mouth, her body betraying her. Even as she stood there, heat suffused her. Her breasts began to ache with the sweet memory of his touch. Lord save her wicked soul... mayhap the words would not come, but her Jezebel body knew how to respond.

Try though she did, she couldn't wrench her gaze away from the sensual curve of his lips. Couldn't stop herself from yearning for the touch of his mouth upon her own.

The feel of his hands, warm and tender, upon her breasts.

He lifted his thumb to her lips, caressing gently, and her breath caught. Her head lolled back. Eyes closed.

He moved to kiss her, but hesitated.

In a fit of fury, Iain had carried her up here, to his bedchamber... with only one thing in mind. That, he could scarce deny. And yet now that he had her here, he found he could not.

Damn, but he'd destroyed the lives of the only two women he'd had in his life—his mother and his wife—and he couldn't bring himself to ravage yet another.

Christ, but he wanted her.

"Ach, lass," he whispered, his heart racing. "If ye dinna cease to look that way..."

She lifted her face higher, he thought, opening her eyes, and blinking much too innocently. He lapped at his lips gone dry.

"What way?" she asked quietly, her soft pink tongue darting out to moisten her lips.

"Waiting," he whispered. "As though ye were waiting..." He reached out with his free hand, hooked it about her waist, and drew her closer.

"And if I do not... what will you do?"

It was a challenge, he thought. Damned if she wasn't making this more difficult for him. His heart leapt at the look of acquiescence in her wide, beautiful eyes. So be it. He wasn't noble enough to refuse her invitation.

He drew her against himself, letting her feel him, letting her know.

He wanted her too damned much—for far too long.

His heart began to pound as he bent his head forward a fraction, restraining himself still, for he wanted her to be the one to dictate, beyond doubt, all that came to pass between them. He wanted this, aye, but more than that, even, he wanted her to want him.

Christ, but he'd wanted her long before he'd ever set eyes upon her, he realized in that instant. Aye, for he'd never realized how much he'd needed to see himself in the eyes of an eager lover... until now... this very moment... while she looked upon him with those yearning eyes... and tempted him with lips that trembled so sweetly in anticipation of his kiss.

Ach, he wanted to kiss those lips, wanted to devour them... wanted to love every inch of her delectable body, then spill himself deep within her body as he'd craved to do the first time. He'd wanted it so badly. Wanted it now... though he knew he would not.

Never again could he bear to see the hatred that had been so vivid upon Mairi's face that fearsome morn. And less could he endure it were it to come from Page, for Mairi had never once gazed at him the way Page was gazing at him now.

He felt the air between them grow thick with his need, and his nostrils flared with the luscious scent of the woman standing so boldly before him.

"What will you do?" she dared whisper once more.

Iain's body reacted with a violence that nearly unmanned him, hardening him fully. He swallowed, hard, trying to keep his reason.

One more time, he thought to caution her. "If ye dinna walk away, lass... now... I shall be forced to show you." His heart quickened, his breath, as well, as she leaned into him instead of drawing away. She lifted a hand toward his face, and Iain caught her wrist, fearing her touch.

Once she set the warmth of her fingers upon his flesh, he would be lost. She would be doomed.

Aye, for he didn't know whether he could find the will again to keep from planting his seed deep within her womb. Visions of her bearing his babe came swiftly to mind, and he was at once torn. Torn between wanting fiercely to see her body swell with his bairn, and dread of her revulsion.

"Suisan," she whispered breathlessly. "Call me Suisan."

"Aye," he murmured, his voice sounding strange even to his own ears. "Suisan..." He released her hand, letting her touch his face with the delicate tips of her fingers. He closed his eyes as she caressed his whiskered jaw, and a shudder shook him at the gentleness of her touch.

"Show me," she whispered boldly, and lifted herself upon the tips of her toes. "Show me..."

CHAPTER 26

P age could scarce help herself.

God have mercy upon her wicked soul. She knew what it was she was asking—knew, too, where it would lead.

But she wanted the touch of his lips upon her own with a hunger that was madness. She tilted her head back, inviting without words. Holy Mary...

She closed her eyes and prayed with all her might that he might want her too.

He groaned, and the guttural, tormented sound was like heavenly song to her ears, an echo of her own longing... proof of his own. The hand at her chin moved to cup her face so gently that she had to fight the sudden overwhelming urge to weep, and then his fingers slid to her nape... sweet merciful Jesu... causing gooseflesh to erupt. A blissful sigh escaped her as she stood there, her body suddenly awash with delicious sensation. It was as though she were standing bare within a warm misty shower—like nothing she had ever known—and more glorious, even, than it had been before.

She wanted this...

Her hands slid up and wound about his neck, clinging shamelessly, tugging him down... She didn't care. How could she care? In his arms, she became everything she'd ever longed to be.

And more.

The first tentative touch of his lips upon her own sent her pulse skittering and her heart leaping from her breast. Soft... stirring, it caused her knees to weaken and her breath to catch. All the more desperately, she clung to him. Sweet Mary, but she couldn't help herself. He responded by clutching her more firmly against himself.

She felt him then, unmistakably male, and her breath caught. Though she trembled at the proof of his desire, she exulted in it as well. For no matter what else he might feel for her, this, Page knew, could scarce be denied.

He did want her.

As a man wanted a woman.

The knowledge thrilled her.

Once again his mouth covered hers, achingly tender, tasting, caressing, suckling, coaxing, and it was all Page could do to cling to him while he savored her lips in that slow, erotic way that snatched her breath and whetted her senses. She felt the passion he held in restraint in the shuddering of his body, in the way that he gripped her arm and urged her backward into the room while he kissed her, and was wholly undone by it.

"I need you," he whispered, removing his breacan and jerking it free, casting it to the floor. "So much..."

Page couldn't reply, too overcome was she by the power of his words.

His hand splayed across her back, lowered to her bottom, pressing her more solidly against his arousal. He held her there, and his lips slid to her cheek, to her temple. "D' ye feel how much?" he whispered at her ear.

"Aye," Page answered, swallowing.

"Ach, lass..." She felt his jaw tauten against her face,

heard him swallow, and felt her throat convulse with overwhelming emotion.

"Judas," Page croaked, her eyes closing, her heart pounding madly. She wanted him to want her.

Wanted him to make love to her. So very much.

"I need you to tell me what it is you wish me to do..."

Page shook her head, unable to voice her single coherent thought.

"D' ye wish me to stop?" he asked her.

"Nay," she answered at once.

Never did she wish him to.

He growled, a sound of immense satisfaction, and bent to sweep her up into his arms suddenly. Page gasped, clinging to him. Her heart hammered fiercely as he bore her to the fur-strewn bed and laid her down upon it.

Standing before her, he drew his tunic up and over his head, and the sight of him, magnificent in his nakedness, filled her with awe. She swallowed.

"Now, lass... I'm gain' to show you how 'tis really done," he promised, straddling her and trapping her beneath him. His smile was utterly wicked.

Without another word, he bent to kiss her, and Page thought she would draw her final breath, so profoundly did the touch of his lips affect her.

For the briefest instant, she forgot even how to respond.

"Open for me," he demanded. "I want to taste you," he whispered seductively against her lips. Page obeyed, shivering at his whispered words. "That's it," he murmured, coaxing her lips and her heart. He dipped his tongue gently within her mouth. "Mmmnnnnnn," he whispered.

Page's heart jolted. Tentatively, her heart hammering fiercely, she gave him her own tongue to spar with, taking his example, wanting to give back equal measure. She wanted to please him. Lifting her hands to his chest, she allowed her fingers to roam his shoulders and tangle within his hair.

"Ah, Christ," he hissed, and groaned, wrapping his arms about her and rolling with her unexpectedly. "I believe I've changed my mind," he revealed. He grinned engagingly as he settled her atop him. "Make love to me," he urged her. She froze, as though unsure she'd heard correctly, and he tossed his hands playfully. "I'm yours," he declared with a wink. "Do wi' me what you will."

Iain thought she looked terrified, and he suppressed a chuckle. His grin widened, and he lifted a brow in challenge. "You might even torture me if it please you."

At once her beautiful lips broke into an impish smile, and she asked, "I can do anything?"

"Anything' at all," he assured. What better way to be certain she dictated their lovemaking?

Her brown eyes flickered with mischief. "And what if I should, indeed, decide to torture you?"

Iain's heart lurched. His eyes narrowed with infinite pleasure over the wicked possibilities that flashed through his thoughts. "Then I should die a contented man," he disclosed. And God help him, he thought he just might.

His hands slid beneath the hem of her gown, guiding it up her bare calves. His body quickened painfully at the delicious feel of the warm, soft flesh beneath his fingertips.

Still, she hadn't moved, merely watched him, her breasts rising and falling with her every breath, her expressive eyes wide and anticipating. When he reached her thigh, she suddenly reached out, stilling his hand.

For the space of a heartbeat, Iain thought she meant to refuse him, and then she slid his hand away, smiling softly as she did.

His heart stilled as she lifted herself enough to tug

the gown from beneath her. It snatched free of their
bodies and she drew the gown up, slowly, teasing him.
The wench. His heart hammered fiercely. He dared not
look away, wanting to miss nothing as she tugged the
gown up and over her head. She flung it aside, and with
it came free the gold braided binding from her hair.
Like strands of silken thread, her beautiful tresses cas-
caded down to cover her exquisite breasts. It was all he
could do not to reach out and brush it aside, expose her
to his hungry eyes once more.

Ah, but Christ, it was the look in her eyes that
made his heart quicken painfully. Pleasure. There was
no mistaking it. She took immense pleasure in revealing
her body to him—though no more than he did in
watching her do so.

She was beautiful.

Exquisite.

He wanted her... now... this moment... madly.

Reaching out, he grasped her by the waist and lifted
her from his body, eager to take her. She gasped softly,
and then again when he settled her over his shaft. His
body trembling, he guided her down over him. "Ride,"
he bade her, his jaw taut with savage pleasure as he
watched the rapturous expression come over her face
while she sheathed him fully.

Her head fell slightly back, her eyes closed.

The sight of her drunkened him.

"*Marchaich mo ghradh*," he murmured, lapsing into
the old tongue as he cast his head back against the bed
to savor the feel of her body enclosing him. "Ride, my
love," he whispered.

For an instant Page was too overwhelmed by the
feel of him filling her body so completely to hear, much
less understand, his behest, and then he spoke so pas-
sionately in his guttural tongue—some strange endearment that prickled her senses and made her bold.

Warmth flooded her from within, flowing there from that region where they were joined.

And then he repeated his wicked demand, and a shudder shook her. Scandalized though she might be by his bawdy request, followed by those words... *my love*... she knew she would do anything at all... if only he asked.

She wanted to please him—that was all that she wished. Nothing more.

His hands gripped her hips, guiding her movements, gently at first, and tentatively Page began to move with him. She was rewarded with a deep moan of satisfaction from Iain MacKinnon's sensual lips.

"Aye, lass," he whispered. "That's it."

Page continued to move atop him, marveling at the power of her woman's body. Her breathing belabored and her heart pounding madly at the sight of him lying so powerless beneath her, she took immense satisfaction in every groan of pleasure she elicited from his lips. Every sigh.

And then he suddenly abandoned her to her own pace. His head cast to one side, his jaw taut, he allowed her to move at her own will, while his hands slid upward, exploring her breasts, her sides, her shoulders... her face. He drew her down and kissed her deeply, and wanton though she might feel, she closed her eyes and abandoned herself wholly to carnality.

His hands left her face. Like flittering butterflies they explored her shoulders once more, moved down to cup her breasts, kneading them gently, his fingers masterful in their stroking, and Page thought she would die from so much pleasure.

And all the while, he kissed her deeply, the most exquisite, heartrending, tender kiss...

She was passion incarnate.

Iain marveled at the way she embraced loving him. She moved with complete abandon, gave him everything unabashedly, kissing him back with the slow, erotic cadence they shared together in other regions.

He wanted... craved... madly... to turn her about and bury himself deep within her body, spend himself violently and furiously within her. Wholly. Completely. Irrevocably.

Ending the kiss, he let her rise, one hand still upon her breast as he lifted his hips, following her movement, undulating beneath her.

Withholding his own release was the most painful pleasure he'd ever experienced, but he did so, wanting to feel her, intending to withdraw. Clenching his jaw, he lifted his head from the bed, watching her, mesmerized by the artless beauty of the woman loving him.

When she opened her beautiful eyes, glassy with passion, and gazed down upon him, he thought he would lose his resolve completely, so disarmed was he by what he saw within them.

There, in the fathomless depths of her eyes, he spied everything he'd ever yearned for.

Everything.

Christ, and she was right here within his arms—all he needed to do in order to know she was real... was to feel. And Christ, did he feel.

A shudder shook him as he slid his hand back down, his fingers skimming her belly. Like a mistress of the loch calling out to him, her body's sinuous movement was like a siren's lay, coaxing his seed from his body.

And he wanted to give it... craved the release she could give him. But he didn't dare.

Still she seduced him... nearer to the edge, closer to his release, wooing his body with too little effort. When she closed her eyes, he closed his own, summoning every last shred of will he possessed.

Damn, but he wasn't going to allow himself this. Wanted her to experience it—but she cajoled him so sweetly with her soft moans and her uninhibited responses. He knew by her rhythm she was nearing completion, and the very thought nearly lost him his control. He opened his eyes to watch her face, wanting to see her at her moment of release, and the intensity of her expression nearly unmanned him.

She struggled to capture it, he knew.

His heart hammered fiercely. "D' ye feel it?" he whispered softly. The muscles flexed in his legs and arms as he vied for control of his body. "D' ye feel it?" he asked her urgently.

Her answering moan sent his pulses leaping and his body into carnal oblivion. He bucked beneath her, groaning in torment, losing himself, losing restraint.

He was losing control.

Iain squeezed his eyes shut and thought of his horse. Damn, but a vision of mating animals suddenly came to mind. Mentally eradicating the image, his mind searched for a safer device—bloody hell, but he couldn't do it.

Couldn't hold back.

His hands grasped her hips. "Seize it," he demanded, groaning, his body moving against his will, convulsing. "Seize it," he urged her. "Now before I canna... ahhh!" he cried, when her body tightened about him. "Bloody hell!" It was almost too late for him, he felt himself begin, and tried to lift her at once from atop him.

"Nay," she cried out, resisting him.

His hands trembling, his body stilling at once, Iain told her, his breath labored and his voice harsh, "Ye dinna understand." He could scarce focus upon her, his eyes were so glazed.

"I do," she whispered fiercely, shuddering and moving once more atop him, stubbornly disobeying. "I do."

Iain's climax was immediate and violent. "Ah, Christ," he cried out, and bucked against her, driving his seed within her womb. He clutched her to him with quivering hands, and still she moved atop him, milking every last drop from his body.

Gratitude washed over him first, a fierce satisfaction that he'd never in his life experienced—and close upon its heels an overwhelming, blinding emotion he'd never known could possibly exist within his long-jaded heart.

In his instant of gratification, he loved intensely and without restraint.

She fell forward, crying out softly, and he clutched her against his thundering heart. Stroking her hair, he vowed with all his soul and his might that he'd please her always and keep her safe. That, he vowed with his life.

God have mercy upon his wretched soul if she ever looked upon him with such loathing as Mairi had that last morn.

Needing her embrace even more than he had her loving, he held her fast against him, not allowing her to rise when she tried.

They drifted to sleep just so.

CHAPTER 27

Always the room precipitated the dream.

It began in that half-conscious state, once the room fell to darkness—in that surreal moment when, after he'd eluded sleep so long, the candle at last guttered. With the final hiss of the extinguishing flame came the disorienting glow from the hall. First, merely a flicker, one that urged him to crawl from beneath his covers and spy into the corridor.

He didn't go.

Then came the wails, the woman's shrieks and entreaties for mercy.

He clung to the blankets as a procession of voices passed his room. A flurry of torchlight. Rushing feet.

And he was a bairn once more... a child of no more than two... though he couldn't be certain... whether it was a dream... or a long-buried memory.

In his dream, the pleas were his mother's.

Beyond the doorway, the light shone brightly, a beacon in the darkness of the corridor, and he lay beneath the blankets, sweating and afeared to move.

The screaming intensified.

At the end of the hall, the door slammed shut, casting the hall, along with his chamber, in total darkness. The boy he was squeezed his eyes shut and wished the screams to end. He wished with all his might. Wished. Wished.

Silence descended.

Irrevocable silence.

And suddenly he was a babe in arms, cooing as he peered up into blue eyes.

Hush ye, my bairnie, my bonny wee dearie, the voice crooned, sleep, come and close eyes so heavy and weary... Closed are ye eyes, an' rest ye are takin'... Sound be your sleepin', and bright be your wakin'...

Iain shuddered awake, his eyes flying open, his lashes damp. Though the room was cool, sweat drenched his brow.

This time, he wasn't alone in the room, he told himself. He wasn't alone in the entombing darkness.

Nor was the silence so deafening or impenetrable.

Though his heart pounded fiercely still, the warmth of the body lying within his arms assured him that it had merely been a dream.

Willing his breath to ease and his heart to calm, he analyzed the dream.

There had been a new element this time. The lay. The eyes. Familiar eyes.

But whose?

And whose voice?

Always before he had awakened with the impact of silence. A silence that was damning and irrevocable. A silence that fell like the dread of the thunder.

Not this time. This time there was light—faint though the candle's afterglow might be. And sound. The sound of a woman's sighing breath as she slept. His woman. The very thought made his lips turn with pleasure. And when his senses cleared enough, he made out yet another sound. He heard and understood the faint wail of a pipe coming from deep in the night, and without hesitation rolled free of the tangled, sleeping form beside him to seek it.

Page was uncertain what prompted her from slumber, but the closing of the door brought her full awake.

Though she awoke disoriented within the darkened chamber, her eyes were drawn at once to the door. And though she knew instinctively she would find the bed empty beside her, she rolled into the space where Iain had lain, sighing contentedly. It was still warm from his body, and she caressed the sheets adoringly with her palms, her fingers... as though to drink in the intoxicating heat of the man who had rested there mere moments before.

Had she ever thought herself immune to him? How could she have thought it possible? She was both terrified and exhilarated at once—terrified because she knew instinctively that this was the last time she could dare lay her heart so bare.

And it was bare... No matter that she would deny it... she could scarce deceive herself.

Somehow, without even trying, he'd found his way beyond the carefully tended barriers that had long since kept her safe... and so alone.

Once upon a time she'd sworn never to care about love, or even the respect of others—she couldn't control those things—had even ceased to vie for them, choosing instead to go her own way. That frame of mind had gotten her into so much difficulty with her father. She knew that, and yet had provoked him nevertheless—not because she'd so desperately craved his affection, but because she was furious with him. She knew that now because Iain had forced her to acknowledge the truth of the matter. That she was furious with her father—enraged with a strength and depth of emotion that could never have waxed so full overnight.

Dare she open her heart completely? Dare she hope he could love her in return, when no one else had?

Page nipped at her lip, biting until she felt pain, for she wanted to so very desperately.

Swallowing the knot that rose to choke her, she lay there and contemplated the sparseness of the room. Even in the darkness she could sense its nagging emptiness. There was nothing here to give even the slightest insight into the man with whom she'd lain with so freely.

The man she dared to love.

She knew Iain MacKinnon loved his clan fiercely—knew he loved his son even more. But who was he?

There was a brooding sadness about him—a sadness he hid behind that mask of unrelenting good humor. She sensed that. She knew, too, that he suffered nightmares... but of what?

As she lay there, contemplating the possibilities, she came aware of the distant wail of a pipe. Melancholy and haunting, the melody drifted through the night like a shuddering cry.

Driven with curiosity, she rolled from the bed and searched out her clothing, intending to follow the piper's haunting song.

§

"DA!" MALCOM SHOUTED AT SEEING HIM. HE CAME running, leaping into Iain's arms, his smile brilliant, his eyes shining.

Iain laughed as he caught his son. He squeezed him tightly, embracing him unabashedly.

"Glenna told me no' to pester ye," Malcom complained. "She said I couldna go an' wake ye."

Iain's grin widened at hearing his son's grievance. "Did she now?"

"Aye," Malcom declared, squeezing him back with all the strength his stout little arms possessed. "I wanna ride your shoulders, da," he declared.

"Verra well, y' wee auld man."

Malcom giggled a mischievous little giggle and

nearly strangled Iain with his glee. When, at last, he released the hold upon his throat, Iain hoisted his son atop his shoulders and waited until he was settled before making his way toward the gathering of kinsmen. "Well, now," he remarked, more to himself than to Malcom. "I see everyone is ready at hand."

"Aye, da, but dinna worry. We didna begin withoot ye."

"I see ye didna," Iain remarked blithely, and thanked his son for standing in for him while he'd been else-wise occupied.

"Aw... dinna fash yourself, da. I told 'em ye couldna help yourself."

"Ho!" Iain choked in surprise. "Did ye now?"

"Aye, and Angus said I had the right o' it, too."

"Did he now?"

"Aye! He said ye been without a woman too long."

Iain strangled on a chuckle. He made a mental note to speak with Angus about Malcom's premature education. Ach, but he thought his son understood far too much for his tender age.

Then again, he reconsidered, mayhap 'twas for the best. He knew better than any that one could not control fate. Were he to cock up his toes this very night, or tomorrow, or the next, Malcom would need every wisp of knowledge he might possess in order to survive. Aye, for he could shelter his son only so far. MacKinnon men had not the luxury of languishing in boyhood. Damn, but they were pulled from the womb as men, with the weight of the clan upon their shoulders, and the shadows of their predecessors pecking at their backs. In truth, though Iain had vowed to allow Malcom as ordinary a boyhood as was conceivable, he was sworn by birthright, and by duty, to prepare his son to lead.

"Well, now," Iain began.

"Awwww, dinna worry, da," Malcom broke in as he wrapped his chubby little hands around Iain's chin and laid his own chin atop the pate of Iain's head. Iain savored the feel of his son's wee pointy chin needling the crown of his head. Ach, but it wouldn't be long before this was naught more than a pleasant memory. The thought made him sigh wistfully. "I understand," Malcom said, his tone conspiratorial.

Iain's brow furrowed. "D' ye now, son?"

"Aye, da," his son declared with a certainty. "I been without a woman too long, too," he revealed somewhat dejectedly.

Iain choked, but not solely because of the little hands that were now tightening their grip upon his throat. Bones o' the bloody saints, he wasn't certain whether to be amused or disconcerted by his son's revelation. "You've been without a woman too long?" he repeated with no small measure of surprise.

"Aw, yeah, da," Malcom answered resolutely. "Ach, but I been thinkin' it would be a guid thing to have a lassie aboot to croon me to sleep now and again."

Iain chuckled at his son's waggish admission. Struggling to contain his mirth, he whacked his son's leg affectionately, and smiled as he walked.

"Oh, da," Malcom ventured once more.

"Aye, Malcom?"

"Di' she sing ye a guid lay, I was wonderin'?"

Iain blinked at the innocent question.

"I heard cousin Lagan say she was gonna gi' ye one."

It took Iain a full moment to realize what it was his son was asking. Damn, but he asked the question with such childish innocence that it made his heart squeeze. No matter that Malcom had no notion what it was he was asking, Iain's heartbeat sped at the memory. His face and neck heated. Had she ever—with her sweet, passionate whimpers and her pleas. Her open desire for him had been like a balm for his soul. But God's teeth, he wasn't about to tell his son that it was the finest lay he'd ever had in his life.

"Aye, Malcom," Iain confessed, clearing his throat. "She sings sweeter than any woman I e'er did hear."

"I thought so, Da," Malcom avowed. "She croons better than cousin Lagan, of a certain."

Iain's brows lifted in surprise. "Lagan?" He stopped walking, surprised by the disclosure. Damn, but though Lagan had always been good enough to Malcom, Iain could scarce imagine his dour-faced cousin croonin' to anyone. "Lagan sang ye to sleep, Malcom?"

"Aye, da," his son assured him. "He surely did."

"I'll be damned," Iain declared. "Now, when did he go and do a thing like that?"

"Hmmmm..."

Iain imagined his son's scrunched nose as he concentrated, and couldn't keep from smiling once more.

"I dunno, da," Malcom yielded after a moment's deliberation. "But he surely did. I canna remember when, but I know he surely did."

"Well, I'll be damned," Iain said again, and started once more toward the gathering. He decided there was much about his cousin that he had yet to learn.

"Oh, da?"

"Aye, son?"

"I was wonderin' too... does she sing a finer lilt than did me minnie?"

Once again Iain halted in his step, his heart squeezing within his chest. His brows drew together at the simple question, and he swallowed the knob that appeared in his throat, answering honestly. "I dunno, Malcom. I never did hear your minnie sing, at all."

"Oh."

There was keen disappointment in the single word. Iain heard it and his heart twisted.

"Da, you're hurtin' me leg," Malcom said, a frown in his voice.

Starting at the complaint, Iain eased his grip upon Malcom's little legs at once. He sucked in a breath and said, "Forgive me, son." He swallowed the grief that rose to choke him, though it was no longer grief for himself. "You know what, though, son," he lied with ease, for Malcom's sake. "She woulda sung to ye... if she could have..."

"D' y' think so, da?"

The note of hope in his voice was like *vin aigre* spilled into a freshly healing wound. Iain's eyes stung, though not from the smoke of the raging bonfire. The image of Mairi standing before the window, her eyes burning with hatred, rose up to mock him. There was no doubt in his mind that she had left them both, for she'd left him standing there with their brand-new bairn cradled within his arms. Still, he forced the lie from his lips. Again for Malcom's sake. "I know so, son," he swore vehemently. "I know so. Had she been able to see your wee li'l face, she would have sung to you. I know it."

"I would have liked that, da," Malcom exclaimed, and Iain could hear the smile in his son's voice. His jaw clenched, and he closed his eyes, swallowing the curse that rose to his lips.

Damn Mairi's soul to hell.

"What about you? Did your mammie e'er sing to you, da?"

Iain opened his eyes, watching the gathering at the bonfire as he considered the question, uncertain as to why he hesitated, for the answer could only be no. He closed his eyes once more and contemplated the woman's voice from his dream—the song, the eyes—and was filled with keen frustration. "Nay," he answered, confused. He opened his eyes to stare at the bonfire, frowning.

And it occurred to him suddenly that his own mother's death had gone undiscussed much too long. It was something he and his son shared in common, the lack of a mother from birth, and yet he'd grown so accustomed to it being an unspeakable matter between himself and his own da that he'd never even thought to broach it with his son.

As a boy, Iain had asked questions interminably, only to be turned away at every occasion. And not merely by his father, but by every last clansman who might have known his ma. *If your da wants ye to know,* they had all persistently told him, *he'll tell ye himself.* Ach, but his da had never told him a damned thing, and after a while, Iain had quit asking altogether. All he knew of his mother, he'd learned from his aunt Glenna, and even that was precious little.

If Iain hadn't known better, that his da had loved his mother fiercely, that he'd mourned her death till the day he'd died, he'd have thought her name a blasphemy in his house, for it had surely been unspeakable within his presence... and without.

"Da?" Malcom ventured once more, breaking into his gloom-filled thoughts.

"Aye, Malcom?"

"D' ye think she would mind if I called her mammy?"

"Who, Malcom?"

"Page."

Iain went perfectly still at the question.

"I think ye would do better to call her Suisan," Page heard him tell his son.

She'd overheard enough of their conversation to feel the sting of tears prick her eyes. She hadn't meant to, but had nevertheless, and now she didn't know whether to make her presence known, or to turn about and flee.

Drawn by the firelight and the melancholy sound of the reed, she had come upon father and son standing there together in the shadows of the night, speaking softly with each other. A private conversation such as that Page might have longed for as a child. Lord, but she might have... had she known it possible to share such confidences. She stemmed the flood of envy that rose to nag her.

Ahead of them, the fire's glow was a beacon in the dark of night.

A lone piper stood before it, playing his instrument with such funereal intensity that it seduced her feet to move forward. Curiosity along with the piper's song drew her to Iain's side to watch the strange gathering.

It seemed every last clan member was present for the occasion, their silhouettes congregated before the fire like moths before torchlight.

Both father and son turned to peer down at her.

For a long instant, Page couldn't find her voice to speak, so moved was she by Malcom's sweet question. Still they stared down at her.

"He can call me anything he likes," she yielded softly. "Page is fine."

A moment of silence passed between them while Iain stared down at her with unblinking eyes. "I thought you preferred Suisan," he said at long last.

Page drew in a breath. "I thought I would," she replied, holding his gaze, unblinking, as well. "Till just this instant I thought I would." It occurred to her suddenly that her name was simply that, a name. In a sense, it was a badge of honor for all she'd suffered at her father's hands. But no more did she feel shamed by it. To the contrary, she felt pride—because she had endured. Because she was unbroken still. What greater revenge could she have over her misbegotten father than to live, and to live well, to walk with pride? Who could dare pity her when her heart was filled with gladness?

"I've decided," she told them both, a slight smile crooking her lips, "that I like my name, after all."

Iain's beautiful lips curved at her declaration. "D' ye now?"

"Aye," Page answered flippantly, lifting a brow. "I believe I rather do." Her heart swelled with a strange elation that she couldn't quite fathom... and yet it was there... a keen, overwhelming sense of joy that was both unfamiliar and titillating.

Iain's grin widened, and even in the darkness, Page could see the glimmer of his smile and the amused twinkle in his eyes.

She turned away, feeling strangely elated. "What are they doing?" she asked father and son together.

She watched the clansmen from the corners of her eyes.

"'Tis for Ranald," Iain told her, still scrutinizing her. Page turned to peer up at him. Illuminated by the distant firelight, his face was startlingly beautiful with its hard masculine lines. And his youthful features were striking in contrast with the bold silver at his temples. Her heart fluttered within her breast. "Our way of saying goodbye," he revealed.

Page turned to regard the bonfire with new eyes, and at once focused upon the crudely constructed scaffold near it. Understanding dawned, and her smile at once twisted into a grimace. "You plan to burn him?"

"Aye, lass," Iain answered.

"Sweet heaven above! Why? 'Tis barbaric!"

He merely chuckled. "Mayhap so."

"No mayhap about it! Poor Ranald!"

"It canna be helped, Page."

It was the first time he'd spoken her name so gently, and Page lifted her face to meet his gaze, her heart leaping at the sound of it upon his lips.

"Ye canna bury a man in stone," he yielded, his tone soft and matter-of-fact. The firelight flickered within his eyes, and the glimmer was both sad and amused at once. "*ChreagachMhor* is built upon solid rock. No spade can turn soil so unyielding as this."

"Oh," Page replied. He turned again to watch the mourners before the fire. So, too, did Page.

"The stone walls of my home," he revealed, "were carved from these cliffs so long ago that not even my forefathers could recall whose hands first hewed them. And still they stand."

He turned to peer over his shoulder at the strange tapered donjon that loomed behind them. Page followed his gaze. "Every last stone remains in place."

She thought of her father's endless repairs, and conceded, "'Tis remarkable."

She was remarkable.

Iain found himself staring, admiring the proud tilt of her head, the stubborn lift of her chin, and the soft curve of her lips. He could scarce conceive that the woman he was seeing was the same woman he had thought to pity. There was naught about her bearing that elicited such a response from him this moment. Naught at all. She seemed taller even—something he'd never quite noticed about her—and he frowned, for she was perchance taller than any woman he'd e'er known.

She found she liked the name, did she? The vixen.

Oddly enough, he found he suddenly liked the name, too.

Her face, illumined by the distant firelight, was aglow with something new... something he couldn't quite place. Something delightful and heartening.

And his heart... it, too, was filled with something new... something deep and warm and yearning.

Something he dared not fully embrace lest he wake one unspeakable morn to find her expression rife with repulsion. He'd sworn to protect and care for her, aye, but love was an entanglement best eschewed.

CHAPTER 28

The funeral extended well into the night.

In his own manner, every last kinsman present paid last respects to poor Ranald, and then Iain lit a torch from the bonfire and set the pyre to flame. Ranald's mother stood by, wailing. A few others wept softly. Most stood silent, their faces somber and their eyes melancholy. Among them, a lone piper played his reed, the melody both hypnotic and forlorn—and still a few others danced curiously to his strangely buoyant song.

Page watched in both revulsion and awe as the fire licked its way up the scaffold toward the body wrapped in new blankets. And even once the flames reached the platform she couldn't make herself look away.

As she watched the flames consume, she felt curiously removed. For an instant, the piper's sound drifted away, and only the roar of the fire reached her ears. From the corners of her eyes she saw the writhing dancers, and yet her focus remained upon the ashes that rose from the pyre—feathery shadows that floated up and disappeared beyond the rosy light of the bonfire into freedom. Free to roam the earth and settle at will, or not at all. Page imagined herself one of those floating ashes, and felt her soul lift along with it, into the cool black night. She lifted her gaze to peer into the moonless sky and found herself floating, floating... free...

Freedom. It was what she'd always wanted... what she'd sorely craved...

Or was it in truth?

Had she instead only longed that her father would reach out and snatch her far-wandering soul, and hold her fast against his heart?

Her gaze fastened upon a dark fluttering ash... Were she free to go... free to fly... where would she alight?

The soft sound of children's voices drew her out of her reverie, and she peered down to spy Malcom and his friends working at catching ashes in their palms.

She watched them an eternity, feeling never more the stranger in their midst.

As she watched them, they gathered what remained of Ranald's body into their tiny hands, along with those charred wood flakes. They ran, scurrying to catch all that they could, gathering black rain into their little fists. They blackened their faces with the soot, blackened their eager little fingers.

And then as Page watched, they brought the fruits of their labors to Ranald's mother... handed her the smothered ashes. One by one, they turned over their hands and sprinkled black dust into her cupped hands.

A smile touched her lips as Malcom turned over his own and nothing came forth. He scrunched his little nose as he peered down at his soot-blackened hand, and then he shrugged and wiped his fingers across her upturned hand. She smiled, and after speaking low to the lot of them, stood and lifted up her palms to the sky and let the ashes fly once more. What soot remained, she smeared across her breast—the part of him she would keep—and once again began to weep.

Page's eyes stung with tears, and the thought struck her that true love was as ungrudging as a mother's simple but unselfish gesture of releasing her beloved son's ashes into the wind.

THE KITCHEN REEKED OF LYE SOAP.

Steam from boiling kettles curled upward to mix with acid fumes, the combination of heat and lye strong enough to burn the lungs from any breathing creature who should merely think to pass by the small stone building. And yet they all remained cheerful within, working diligently at her every command. She didn't fool herself for an instant; these people were clearly desperate to rid themselves of their fleas and seemed eternally grateful and even eager to comply in any manner conceivable.

Page had awakened to a dark, empty room—Iain nowhere to be found—but she hadn't been afforded time to lament the fact. Glenna had entered almost at once, her voice a cheerful admonition to be up and about.

Page might have loathed the woman at once, save that she was much too agreeable to be despised. Glenna had brought with her a tunic for Page to wear—one she'd claimed had never belonged to Iain's wife at all. Page had found herself smiling as Glenna had assured her, blushing, that it was one of her own—from her younger, thinner days, of course.

It was a grand gesture, Page thought. She had never concerned herself overmuch with her manner of dress, and was only mildly embarrassed that Glenna should think she needed a new gown. She was entirely dismayed, however, to find that even the tunic had fleas.

Page had, at once, taken it upon herself to rid the MacKinnon clan of their fleas. Recalling how they'd managed Aldergh's infestation a few years past, she set about the tasks with zeal. With Glenna's help, she man-

275

aged to gather the infested men and women together and was in the process of boiling garments within the massive iron kettles.

The kitchen was pervaded with perspiring bodies; some merely observing the strange ritual, others participating. When she dared to bathe Broc's dog, the flea-breeding culprit, stunned murmurs accosted her ears. Some whispered in Gaelic. Others in plain English.

"Ach, but I think she's gain' to wash the bloody dog," exclaimed someone.

"I'll be damned, she is gain' to wash the bloody dog," said another.

"Must be a Sassenach curse to ward away fleas," whispered another.

Page didn't hesitate at her task, nor did she linger to explain. She thought it rather an obvious solution, and marveled that no one had ever thought of it before now. Smiling, she cast the animal into a lye-soaped tub, and scrubbed her matted fur until she thought she might go bald from the scouring. The beast never protested, for all that, it merely arched its back like a blessed cat, and luxuriated in the bath. Poor Merry Bells. Likely the dog was so bitten and abused by the horrid little creatures that even Page's scrubbing was a favor.

When she was done with Merry Bells, she granted Malcom and one of his friends the dubious honor of hunting whatever fleas remained. She showed them how to search, found a few for them, and then set them to work. She left the two snickering, pretending to hunt down "dirty MacLeans hiding within MacKinnon territory."

That done, she emptied the tub, and then began to refill it with clean water to bathe the Behemoth and his friends. Without a doubt, she knew they wouldn't like it, but somehow she would need to convince them that it was for their own good.

She didn't notice the crowd gathered before the

wash kettle until it was too late and they were all divested of their clothing. Starting when she turned to spy their bare bottoms and nude bodies congregated about the steaming cauldron, she gasped aloud and slapped a hand over her eyes to hide the shocking view. These Scotsmen had no shame at all, she decided. Never in her life had she known men so eager to undress—or mayhap she had, but certainly none without some ulterior motive. Peeking between fingers, she spied the last of them dropping tunic and breacan into the wash kettle, and her face heated from more than just the heat of the steam-filled kitchen.

Never mind that she'd thought herself perfectly capable of carrying out this task—she was mortified.

Certainly she'd seen men unclothed. Her father and brothers had had little regard for small courtesies where she had been concerned—and she had fully intended to wash Broc, after all—but this was ludicrous. She peered about to find that the other women present were perfectly at ease. While they were—thank God—somewhat more modest, they seemed to take little heed of the rampant nudity accosting them.

Groaning in dismay, Page snapped her fingers together and contemplated her options. She could go screaming from the room, and look like a fool. Or she could uncover her eyes and finish the task she'd begun. She rubbed at her temples, pretending a headache.

Iain wasn't certain whether to kiss her senseless, or paddle her delightful derriere.

He'd missed her—missed her like he'd never thought it possible to miss the sight of a bonny face in the few hours since he'd seen her last, lying so cozy within his bed.

He stood in the doorway to the kitchen now, his hands braced upon either side of the frame, and simply stared within.

At his end of the room stood his witless men, chattering idly about a steaming cauldron like a huddle of old women—all of them naked as the day they'd been spewed from their mammies' wombs. He certainly didn't believe in false modesties, and his men had never been overly discreet, but this was ridiculous. Leave her alone with them for five bloody minutes, and he returns to find them undressed every damned time. Damn, but if she didn't look so bloody abashed by the lot of them, he might have thought it deliberate upon her part, for he couldn't recall a time when his men had been so eager to strut about unclothed.

It took him a few befuddled minutes to even make out the purpose of this boiler room. His first clue had been a very wet Merry Bells—with his son and young Keith diligently searching her shaggy coat. His next was the stench of lye, and the boiling cauldron of bleeding wool. And lastly, his son's excited shout of "A flea! A flea! I got one!" as he held out his pinched fingers for Keith's eager inspection.

"I see no flea," Keith argued.

Iain didn't know whether to be proud that she was concerned for the welfare of his kinfolk, or furious that she would so unwisely place herself in a room full of naked, lust-ridden men. Christ, but it was all he could do not to dunk them all into that boiling cauldron along with their clothes.

His gaze remained upon Page as he waited to see what she would do.

Until he happened to spy Broc's bare arse headed in her direction, and in that moment, any warm thoughts over her charitable gesture fled entirely. With a snarl of displeasure, he shoved away from the doorframe and stalked into the room. Spying him, Broc halted in his step, and the room fell to a hush. Page, however, was unaware of his presence, for her eyes were still dutifully covered, until he snatched her by the arm.

She shrieked in startle when he jerked her after him, dragging her out of the room.

"Wait," she protested. "I'm not yet done!"

"Aye ye are," Iain asserted.

"But I have to give Broc a bath," she announced, though she didn't struggle.

"Oh, no ye don'," he argued.

"The fleas," Page protested, stumbling after him.

"What about them?" Iain answered, no hesitation in his stride. "Ach, but the lad has been bathin' himself for four and twenty years—I think he'll do well enough withoot ye."

He led her out of the kitchen, leaving those within to stare, grinning, after them.

Lagan's smile faded the instant they walked out from the door. "Besotted fools," he whispered to Glenna.

Glenna's smile faded, as well, as she turned to contemplate the boy she'd raised from birth. "Lagan," she reasoned, her voice aggrieved. "Can ye no' be happy for him just once? Can ye no' see that he's suffered enough?"

Lagan's eyes glittered with resentment. "And what of me?" he asked. "Have I no' suffered enough, as well?"

"Lagan," she objected. "He is your—"

"We both know what he is to me, Mother," he scoffed.

"Ach, Lagan, but have I not loved ye well?" He stared, unmoved by her question, and she lowered her eyes. "Then at least remember that he is your laird, and do not speak of him so."

"My brother, my laird," he whispered into her ear, mocking her. "Damn but it galls. What have I ever had of him?" he asked her, his lips curling into a snarl.

"Everything that he could give," she answered him.

"The only thing I have ever wanted was the right to grieve for my own mother."

"Ye canna, Lagan. He does not know."

"And, o' course, as ever, 'tis him we should be concerned o'er, right?"

"It was the old laird's wish," Glenna reminded him.

"And what o' my da's wishes? What o' them? The bastard killed him because my mother dared to love him."

"It was an accident, Lagan."

"How can you defend him?" Lagan returned angrily.

Glenna shook her head. "He was as much aggrieved by Dougal MacLean's death as any. The old laird's anger drove him to it. How can you not forgive?"

"Ach, but 'tis your own sister's bairn, your flesh and blood, he denied. Me."

Glenna hung her head. "I gave you everything, Lagan. You wanted for naught."

"I wanted for plenty. You were just too blind to see."

She shook her head, lamenting. "I should ne'er have told ye, Lagan."

"Aye, but you did," he returned acidly, his eyes narrowing wrathfully. "As God is my witness, it shall be made right."

Her gaze flew to his, searching. "What will you do, Lagan? Dinna do anythin' foolish," she admonished, worry etched in her eyes.

"I intend to see that justice is done," he hissed at her, and walked away, grumbling after.

CHAPTER 29

I t seemed no matter where she went, trouble pursued her.

Vowing to keep herself free from provocation, Page decided to remain within Iain's chamber the next day.

The notion came to her in the middle of the night to refurbish his tower room, and she awoke the next morn with a mission, hoping to complete the task before his return. She waited until he left her, and then enlisted Glenna's help once more—Broc's, as well. She began by hauling up buckets with which to clean. That done, she scoured the floors with a vengeance, scrubbing until there was nary a speck of dust or dirt to be found. And when she finished the floors, she moved to the walls, scrubbing until the stone was free of soot and grime.

Glenna set herself to laundering the bedding.

There was little enough Page could do to add cheer to the bedchamber, for Iain seemed to have few indulgences. Search though she did, there was nothing she could find to place upon the floors or walls; no tapestries to add color, no rugs to ward away the chill that seemed to permeate the room and remain forever present—despite that the sun shone brightly outside.

There was, however, one thing she determined

would aid immensely, and she started at once for the boarded window, resolving to let in the sunlight. The sun, she was certain, would do wonders to transform the room's gaol-like quality into something somewhat more gay.

The wooden slats barring the window were heavy and crude, clearly not meant to be ornate. Placed at odd angles to each other, they gave the impression they were hurriedly placed, and perhaps not meant to be permanent. Well, it was long past time they should come down, she resolved, as she wrestled with the bottommost slat. She struggled with the board only an instant before determining she would need help.

"Broc," she called out. No answer. "Broc?" She turned to find he'd vanished from the room. Bewildered by his sudden disappearance, she turned and found Glenna frozen at the far side of the room, staring, a look akin to horror registered upon her face, a bundle of clean bedding visibly clenched within her arms.

"Where did he go?" Page asked. "I need his help to unbar the window."

"Oh, hinnie," Glenna whispered a little frantically. "I dinna think ye should." She turned to peer out from the open doorway, as though suddenly afeared someone would spy them.

Page blinked. "Why? I do not understand," she said, confused by the grave expression upon the older woman's face. "Is there a reason this window should remain barred?"

"Aye... well—aye!" Glenna stammered, shifting her weight from foot to foot, and looking ill at ease.

Page raised a brow at the much too hesitant and then exuberant reply. "Why?"

"Ach, but 'tis a long ways down," Glenna disclosed.

The explanation sounded lame to Page, and she screwed her face as she contemplated the strange reasoning.

"For Malcom's sake," she added, tossing down the bedsheets upon the bed. "It was boarded to keep him safe."

Page nodded in comprehension. "Oh, I see. When he was younger?"

"Aye," Glenna exclaimed, looking relieved now.

Page drew her brows together. "But he's older," she reasoned, turning her attention back to the window, eyeing it speculatively. "I can see no harm in removing the bars now. It looks like a gaol in here." She tested the slats once more—every last one of them, though she had to climb upon the sill to reach the uppermost boards. The top slat cracked free, only a bit, but enough that she was able to pry her fingers beneath and seize hold of it. Using her weight for leverage, she tugged it free. Rather than lose her footing, Page released the board. It landed upon the floor with a resounding clatter.

A brilliant stream of sunlight pierced the room.

"Splendid," she exclaimed. "The floors and walls will dry so much better with the sun." She turned to appraise Glenna's reaction and found the older woman had vanished, as well. Her brows knit, for she hadn't even been the least aware of Glenna's departure. Page shrugged, thinking Glenna's reaction to the window curious, but she wasn't going to let it stop her. She was certain that once they saw the improvement in the room, they would wholeheartedly agree it was the right thing to do. Without delay, she began to work at unbarring the window, removing the gloomy barrier board by board.

❦

IAIN HAD BEEN REPAIRING THE STONE ENCLOSURE that kept their fold penned when Broc found him. Sputtering some babble about clean floors and unshuttering the tower window, he'd urged Iain to make haste. Dread over whatever dire circumstance had reduced Broc to spouting nonsensical drivel kept him from lingering to decipher the cryptic message. But it wasn't until Glenna accosted him on his way into the tower that he fully understood what it was that Broc had been trying to say, and he took the tower steps two at a time in his haste to reach her.

Too late.

He burst through the doorway of his chamber and froze at the sight that greeted him.

The room was aglow with light. Brilliant white sunlight flooded every corner and washed over the wooden floors like a mantle of gold.

In the space of an instant, he was propelled backward in time.

She stood looking out from the window, sunlight streaming in around her. It touched her hair and brushed it with copper. Iain took a step into the room and felt suddenly as though he'd walked into an inferno... the nightmare real once more.

Sweat beaded upon his brow and prickled his upper lip.

She didn't turn and he couldn't find his voice to speak.

Like some beautiful specter from his past, she stood there, peering down at the cliffs below the tower, the wind blowing and lifting her unbound hair. It fluttered at her back and she leaned forward to catch the breeze.

Iain's breath caught and his heart began to hammer. In his mind's eye he saw Mairi, not Page, standing there. Though he stood there empty-handed, he felt again the weight of their newborn bairn in his arms and the sting of tears in his eyes.

That morning... it had begun just so.

It couldn't be happening again.

He wouldn't let it.

Page had never seen such a glorious sight as the one she now beheld.

In all her life she had never known a view could be so breathtaking. With the advantage of height, one could see clearly out to the loch below the jutting cliffs. From the ground, all that was visible was an up-ward- sloping hill. She would have guessed that the hill continued to a gentle slope beyond the summit, as well.

And she would have been wrong.

The wind was a roar within her ears, and the sun shining down upon her face was like the hand of God warming her wind-chilled brow. She stood in amaze-ment, marveling over the glitter of blue that stretched forth between one cliffside and the next. Mercy, but she could feel every sensation acutely here—the crispness of the air, the warmth of the sun's rays, the caress of the wind.

She couldn't imagine why the window would have been boarded—it seemed a shame to take for granted something so incredibly beautiful as this view. Glenna's explanation had been reasonable enough... when one stopped to think of the dangers to a small child, al-though Page doubted she would ever have considered such a thing. But then, she was neither a mother nor a father, and was like never to be protecting one of her own.

Lord, but even the breeze was sweet with the scent of wild heather.

Instinctively she leaned out to seek the elusive scent, to inhale it more deeply into her greedy lungs.

"Nay!"

The thunderous command startled her.

Page spun about, her hand flying to her breast, to find Iain standing in the room. She'd not even heard him approach. "You startled me," she accused him.

"Get away from that window!" He came toward her, his eyes narrowed wrathfully. "Now!"

Page took a step backward, alarmed by the purposeful look in his eyes, the glassy sheen to them. He looked at her as though he did not quite recognize her.

"I said get away from the bloody window!" He lunged after her suddenly, before she could take another evasive step, and seized her ruthlessly by the arm. He spun her about, dragging her within the chamber.

Alarmed, Page struggled against him. Never had she seen him so enraged, so crazed. The flickering gold of his eyes shimmered with the intensity of angry, burning flames. The transformation in him was frightening. "You're hurting me," she protested, grimacing.

But he didn't seem to hear her.

He jerked her after him, hurled her heedlessly across his bed. Page landed, disoriented, but didn't dare wait to catch her breath. She scurried to the far side of the bed and turned to face him there, watching him warily.

"Who the bloody hell said you could open that damned window?" he demanded.

Page shook her head, unable to speak. She didn't know this side of him. Never once had he looked at her so cruelly, or spoken so harshly. She couldn't even begin to comprehend what she could have done to provoke him to such an extreme—not when she'd worked so incessantly at it before and had never even managed to prick his temper at all. She'd been more in danger of inspiring his laughter than she ever had his fury.

Reasoning that he was not lucid this instant, she yielded, "I'm sorry. I... I didn't know... I didn't realize... Iain?"

Strange how, though she knew the lengths to which her father would go, she'd always stood her ground with him. With Iain, she was certain he'd never harm her—ever—and yet she felt the need to conciliate.

Still, she wasn't about to come anywhere near him until the cloud of rage cleared from his eyes.

It was the look upon her face that recalled Iain to himself.

She crouched upon his bed, her eyes watching him with that same intensely guarded look she'd given him that first night he'd met her. It was wariness, not hatred he saw there.

Not revulsion.

He blinked, focusing.

Christ, it was not Mairi at the window... not Mairi shrinking from him at the far end of the bed.

And still he couldn't help but shudder at the look in her eyes. At the black rage in his heart. So many years he'd kept the emotions buried. Damn, but he wasn't simply angry with Mairi for leaving their son—he despised her for it. Unwilling to betray his emotions, Iain turned his back to Page and sat upon the bed, his body tense and trembling with restraint.

He sat for what seemed an eternity, staring at the open window.

Blue skies for as far as the eye could behold.

Malcom would have his seventh winter soon.

He looked about him, seeing his chamber for the first time in so many years... He'd always loathed this room. Even before Mairi... he had suffered the dreams. Her death had only intensified them.

Only, this moment... there was something different about it, he thought... something bright and cheery. He'd seen it this way before... but the difference this instant... was the presence of the woman at his back.

He started when he felt her delicate tap upon his shoulder. His breath caught, but he didn't turn to face her.

Christ, but he didn't know what to say.

She likely thought him a madman.

And he could scarce blame her for it.

Page approached him warily, laying her hand upon his shoulder, and gasped when he started. He didn't turn to look at her, seemed discomposed, and she wanted so much to ease his burdens... as he had done so often for her.

They were true, she realized, as she watched him stare so intently at the window—the rumors she'd heard about his wife.

And yet it was evident from his expression, from his reaction to the open window, that the memory pained him still. The connection had never occurred to her— the barred window and the death of his wife.

She swallowed, gathered her courage, and lifted her hand to his clenched jaw.

Her heart lurched when he leaned into it, allowing her to comfort him, and her breath caught when he turned to look at her suddenly.

His golden eyes were full of grief.

"'Tis true, then? Your wife..."

For a long instant he didn't reply. He removed his face from her hand, sitting rigid before her. "What?" he asked her, his whisper sounding pained. "Is it true that I murdered her? That I pushed her from the window?"

"Nay," Page said with a rush of breath. She shook her head vehemently. "I never did think so."

He closed his eyes and clenched his jaw. "She killed herself." His voice broke. "Leapt... from that window." He turned again to the wide, unobstructed opening, nodding.

Page experienced the most overwhelming desire to embrace him in that instant. She let herself, her heart quickening...

For the first time in her life, she didn't worry about rejection... or her own tattered soul. She wrapped her arms about the man she loved. Though he stiffened at the unexpected show of compassion, he allowed it.

For a long instant they remained just so.

"It seemed she preferred death... to me," he admitted softly, brokenly. "Her final words were... I want ye to know... the thought o' ye ever touchin' me again did this... You killed me, Iain."

Page's eyes stung with tears for the pain he'd endured at her hands.

"I hear those words still in my dreams."

He shuddered at the confession, and her heart swelled with emotion. "I understand," she said softly. "I do." All this time she had never guessed he could be suffering the same as she—he with his good humor and his easy manner. She knew what it felt like to be unloved, to be cast aside.

They were the same.

He turned to look at her, and his eyes crinkled at the corners. "Aye," he said, "I know ye do, lass."

Not this time. She wasn't going to allow him to divert her attention—for once, it wasn't about her. "I'm stubborn and canny," she told him. "Don't worry about me." And she smiled softly—for the first time in her life knowing of a certainty it was so.

He gave her a halfhearted smile, a slight turn of his lips.

She wanted to love him, wanted to nurture him—wanted him to know that not only would she gladly bear his touch, but she craved it fiercely. And in that instant she knew that she loved him truly. It had to be love, for she was unafraid to offer him all that she had to give—no matter that he had the power to wound her as did no other. Were he to rebuff her, she knew she would never recover.

Even so... not caring what his reaction to her brazenness might be... she bent to brush her lips against his whiskered jaw.

She kissed him softly, but with all the emotion she possessed in her heart.

She wanted him to cherish her, wanted him to make love to her, wanted to embrace him just so for the rest of her days.

He groaned, the guttural sound low and tormented, and Page felt her body quicken in response.

"*Ach, mo cridhe... nighean mo ruin,*" he whispered fiercely, turning and cupping her face within his callused hands. He closed his eyes and kissed her lips with a heart-jolting tenderness that stole her breath away.

Shuddering as he drew her down upon the bed and covered her body with his own, Page dared to pretend that his strangely muttered words were I love you.

CHAPTER 30

It had been a long time since Iain had watched the sun set from his chamber window.

Even longer since he'd made love by the blush of its waning light. He'd forgotten how sweet it could be. Even more, he had never known the contentment that was possible in the sharing of two bodies.

Aye, he'd experienced those moments of gratification after a thorough loving... the physical sense of serenity. He'd wallowed in those pleasures like a lazy hound in the heat of a noonday sun. But he'd never imagined such a plane existed within the soul itself.

Exhausted from her day's labor within his chamber, and their lovemaking, Page slept deeply beside him. Iain could scarce keep his hands to himself. He stroked her hair reverently, marveling that she slept so peacefully. He traced the outline of her body with his hands, afeared to touch her that she might wake, and yet unable to keep himself from appreciating the beauty of her form. Her long, lean limbs were tangled within the bedsheets. Her copper hair flowed down her back.

Like a wild woodland nymph, she lay bare beside him, naked and wholly revealed to his eyes—even her heart exposed to him this instant. Ach, but he sensed her soul, and it was beauteous beyond imagination. Like a wary sculptor disrobing his long-guarded creation, she'd dared unveil herself to him with this loving, and his heart was filled near to brimming with emotion.

Emotions he couldn't quite disentangle, so jumbled were they together in this twisted mass that was his heart.

And yet he knew they were significant, for never in his life had he felt such a buoyant sense of bonding. Christ, but if he could remain with her together... the way they were this instant... for the rest of their lives... Iain thought he might.

And so when the knock sounded upon the door, he was loath to respond. He lay there, muttering silent curses and willing the intruder to go away. The summons came once more, and he growled in disgust. Drawing the sheets up to cover Page from greedy eyes, he lifted himself from the bed as quietly as he was able, leaving her to sleep while he answered the door.

"Broc," he said, frowning as he opened the door to find the youth standing there. Naked though he was, he stood barring the view within.

"Laird!" Broc began, looking suddenly sheepish. "Pardon, but ach! Seems 'tis my duty today to be the bearer of bad tidings."

Iain peered back over his shoulder at the sleeping form within his bed, and sighed. "What now?" he asked, returning his attention to a red-faced Broc.

"Well," Broc began. "'Tis Glenna..."

"What about her?" Iain snapped.

"Well," he began again, fidgeting under Iain's impatient stare. "She didna see to the evenin' meal... We went to find oot why... but she willna come oot o' her croft."

Iain's face screwed. "Sweet lord, mon!" It wasn't like Glenna, but she was certainly entitled to a moment's peace. He needed only see how weary Page was to know that Glenna was like to be the same. "Ye're grown men," he admonished. "Dinna ye think she—"

"She's weepin'," Broc interjected before Iain could reprimand him further.

"Weepin'?"

Broc nodded. "Loudly. Ye can hear her clearly from outside the door. She says she doesna wish to talk to anybody, and willna open the door."

"Where is Lagan?"

Broc shrugged. "We've looked everywhere, but it doesna really matter as she says she doesna wish to see him either."

Iain was certain his surprise was manifest in his face. "She willna see her son?"

Broc shook his head. "It isna her way, I know."

Iain's brow furrowed. "Nay," he agreed, deliberating over the facts. And it truly was not. Glenna had never been one to indulge in tempers. Not in all the years he'd known her. "Go on, then. I'll be there anon."

"Aye," Broc said, and turned to go.

"But do not tell her I am coming," Iain charged him.

The last thing he wished was for his stalwart aunt to prepare herself to face him—to put away her sorrows and her worries. If there was aught plaguing her, he would know it. After all that she'd been there for him, it was the least he could do for her.

He only wondered why it was that she would not see her son. When he thought on it, Lagan had been acting strange of late, as well, although Iain attributed the fact to his quarrel with auld mon MacLean, and then to Ranald's death. And yet his cousin had been conspicuously absent at Ranald's wake—neither had he offered to carry his longtime friend on the voyage home.

Had Iain not been so preoccupied with finding the traitor in their midst, he might have taken notice sooner. But something was amiss between them, and he would set it to rights at once.

Better late than not at all.

&

TIME WAS HIS ENEMY NOW.

His final chance had presented itself, and he knew he must hie to take advantage.

Nightfall would come soon enough, and knowing Malcom would never disobey his da by wandering out to the Lover's Bluff alone after twilight, he'd been forced to lie to the lad, telling him Iain awaited him upon the cliff top. The little whelp had gone without question.

But Malcom wouldn't remain there long once he discovered his father was not there, and once the light began to fade he would come scurrying back as fast as his wee legs could take him.

Aye, he would need plan carefully now... in order for all to go as it should.

He hadn't intended to do a bloody thing this eve, but he'd been watching... and waiting.

'Twas a good thing, too, for Broc had, at long last, managed to draw Iain away from his Sassenach whore.

The tale he would tell was clear in his mind: As this was the first time Iain had left her completely unattended, she would naturally choose it to make her escape. And certainly she would wish to take the boy with her to appease her father.

Such a shame she'd not realized how abruptly the bluffs ended.

And of course, it would be much too dark for her to realize until she and Malcom had already plummeted over the cliff to the rocks below.

Such a bloody rotten shame...

Of course, he knew the reality would scarce be so

simple. He was fully aware he'd need use some... persuasion... to get the wench o'er the cliff.

Malcom would be another matter entirely. The brat would give him little enough trouble. He would simply lift him up by his stout little-boy arms and toss him o'er the ledge.

The very thought made him smile—not that he particularly cared to hear the lad's screams, o' course, or to hear him suffer and plead—but he was tired of looking at his bratty li'l face.

Ach! And only imagine what a misfortune it would become... were Iain to find their bodies broken together upon the rocks below... the woman he loved—once more—and his beloved son...

Certainly it would be conceivable that he might find himself unable to cope. That was his hope. After all... what man wouldn't find it unbearable to lose two women—both having flown to escape him—and then his only son?

In the end, wouldn't it seem perfectly comprehensible that the three would tragically meet the same fate?

Such poetic justice.

Damn, but if Iain didn't think of ending it so himself, Lagan would surely find a way to prescribe it.

And with that thought he quickened his pace, feeling a rush of excitement o'er the confrontation at hand. He had no notion how long Iain would be gone from his chamber, or to where he had gone—nor did he intend to linger for anyone to spy him stealing up the tower steps. He climbed them swiftly, his footsteps lithe and full of purpose. The light within the tower had faded with the gloaming, and though he noted the absence of lit torches, he didn't take the time to consider why Glenna would be so slow to light them tonight.

Whatever the reason, it worked to his favor.

At long last, the waiting was over, and Lagan would finally see justice done—for the father he'd never known, the mother he'd never claimed, and the brother who had never even once looked into his eyes and spied the truth between them.

PAGE WAS UNCERTAIN WHAT IT WAS THAT WOKE HER —some sound, something—but she opened her eyes to a room filled with the gray shades of twilight. Sated from the afternoon's exertions, she stretched lazily, and turned, only to find a scream caught in her throat. Startled, she lurched up in the bed, jerking up the sheets to conceal herself.

The shadow came forward, revealing himself. "I wasna certain whether to wake ye, or nay."

"What are you doing here?" Page demanded of him.

"'Tis the lad," Lagan told her. "Malcom. I wouldna trouble ye, lass, were he no' so distressed."

"Malcom?" Her brow furrowed with worry. Whatever ill will she felt for Lagan, she set aside for Malcom's sake. "What is it? What's happened?"

Lagan was silent a moment, his expression grave, and Page's heart began to hammer with fear. "What is it?" Her gaze swept the room. "Where is Iain?"

"Well, you see..." Lagan knelt beside the bed, peering quickly at the door as he did so. And then his gaze returned to Page, and it seemed fraught with worry. "I canna tell his da... 'Tis his da he's afeared for."

Page's brows knit. "I do not understand."

"Ye see..." He glanced up at the window and then back. In the fading light his face was ashen with despair. "He overheard his da shouting at ye, lass... an' he's afeared 'tis happened again."

"What has happened again?" Page asked, following his gaze to the window once more. Her brows lifted in comprehension, and her gaze returned to Lagan. "Surely he cannot think his da would—"

"Ach, lass, but he does."

"Nay!" Page exclaimed in dismay. "However could he think such a thing."

Lagan's mouth twisted into a grimace. He peered down at the floor between them. "Secrets have their way o' revealin' themselves," he told her.

Something about the tone of his voice sent a quiver racing down her spine. "Aye," she agreed, and clutched the covers more firmly to her breast.

"If he could but see ye... then he would know he fears for naught. Will ye come?"

"Of course," Page assured him. "Where is he?"

"He ran oot upon the bluff."

Her gaze returned to the window. The rosy sky was fast turning to violet-gray shadows.

"I'll go," Page agreed. "Only give me a moment to dress."

"Certainly," he said, and stood. But he didn't leave, nor did he turn away.

He stared a long instant at the sheet she had clutched to her bosom, and her face burned under his scrutiny. "Alone, please," she urged him.

"Ye dinna mind Iain watching, do ye, though?" he snapped at her, and then seemed to snake himself free of his anger. "Verra well, I'll be just beyond the door— come quickly," he urged. "The hour grows late, and I wouldna have Malcom come to any harm."

"Nor I," Page assured him, shuddering at the sharp sway of his mood. She waited until he'd left her, closing the door in his wake, and then she scrambled out of the bed to dress.

It was evident Lagan did not like her—less did he seem to relish finding her in Iain's bed. But then it was a mutual disgust, for neither did she care for him. Though it mattered not at all, for only Malcom mattered at this moment. She would have done anything for Iain's son, and bearing Lagan's company seemed a small enough price to repay Iain for all he'd done for her.

It was certainly the least she could do in return.

🙚

UPON ENTERING THE SMALL CROFT, IAIN FOUND THE room dark with descending shadows, no candles lit at all.

Glenna sat hunched over a table, weeping disconsolately into her hands. It wrenched at his gut to see the woman who had raised him feeling so aggrieved. She was still a bonny lass, though time and toil had carved their marks upon her face, and he never once looked upon her without wondering if his own mother's face had been so fair.

"Glenna," he called out softly.

Startled, she lifted her tear-streaked face at once, and then quickly swiped the telltale wetness from her cheeks. "What is it, Iain, love?" she asked. "What's happened?"

It was so like her to put aside her own cares for those of the kinsmen she loved. It had never mattered to Glenna whether she herself was sick, or tired, or simply downcast, if she was needed by any of her kin, she was always there. He'd not quite spoken true when he'd told Page that here all fended for themselves, for Glenna looked diligently after them all. Malcom particularly. Ever eager, she performed her duties with nary a complaint.

The night Malcom had been born, she'd been sick with her lungs, yet she'd stayed all the night long with Mairi, brushing the hair from Mairi's face, dampening her lips when she'd thirsted. Ach, but she'd always found room in her heart for a little boy who'd craved his mother's skirts as desperately as a leper for human touch—so hungry for notice and human compassion that he would cherish the passing smile from a stranger's lips. His own need for her affection had been great. Malcom's too. And she had loved them both as she had her own.

Christ, but he'd envied Lagan.

Iain would have given all just to know his mother's voice, while Lagan had never treated his own with a modicum of respect—not even as a child had he allowed her to succor him. He had shunned her motherly touch, as though ashamed of the woman whose hands had mopped his brow and whose breasts had suckled him as a babe.

"In truth," he told his aunt, as he came into the room, closing the door behind him, "I came to see to you."

"Naught is wrong," she answered much too quickly, shaking her head, stubbornly denying him the truth.

"So I see," Iain replied.

She suddenly burst once more into tears, concealing her face within her hands. "Oh, Iain!"

Iain went to her at once. Kneeling beside her, he placed an arm about her sturdy shoulders. "Glenna," he whispered. "Naught could be so bad as all that. Tell me what's happened. I shall help to make it right."

"Nay," she wailed unhappily. "Ye canna." She turned and thrust herself into his arms. "'Tis done! Ach, but naught will bring back the years."

Confusion clouded his thoughts, robbed him of response. He couldn't begin to comprehend what it was she was speaking of, for she was speaking in riddles. "What is it that canna be undone?" he persisted. For the first time in his life, it seemed his wise aunt was making about as much sense as a tenet-spouting prelate. He patted her back, consoling her. "Tell me, Glenna," he urged her. "Let me help you. What is it?"

"Lagan," she cried, weeping all the more earnestly

against his shoulder, soaking his breacan. "He was here and we fought."

"O'er what?" Iain asked. "Whatever it is, it canna possibly be so terrible that we canna mend it together. Is that no' what you always told me, Glenna?"

He felt her nod against his shoulder.

"What has he done?"

"Naught," she cried softly, rising to her feet and wiping her face with her sleeve. "Naught as yet," she clarified. "But I dunno what he's going to do. He's so angry, Iain... and he loathes ye," she disclosed.

Iain's brows lifted in stunned surprise. He rocked backward upon his heels. "Me?"

Her expression was filled with sorrow. "Aye, Iain, but he does."

"I dinna understand."

"Oh, Iain," she whispered brokenly. "Iain, my love..." She shook her head and placed a hand upon his shoulder. Her next words left him dumb. "Lagan isna your cousin, ye see... he isna me son."

"Nay?" he asked, reeling from the weight of her words. "Surely you jest?"

She shook her head. Fat tears rolled down her cheeks.

His mind grasped her words, and his heart believed her, for he knew well enough that she would never speak but in truth. "But who then? Who is he?"

She reached out to touch his jaw, cradle his chin. "Your brother," she whispered.

The blow of her words to his mind was not near as staggering as that to his heart. "Impossible," he exclaimed at once, his face screwing with disbelief.

"Nay, but 'tis true," she countered, her brows lifting. "Ach, but, Iain, dinna ye see?"

This moment he saw nothing. Nothing was clear.

Nor could he think to speak.

"'Twas no' your birth that took your dear mother's

life," she told him, "but Lagan's, instead, love." She nodded sadly, her eyes pooling once more with tears. "Lagan is my sister's son," she avowed, her hand trembling upon his face. "God forgive me, Iain, but I swear it on my soul. He is your brother, in truth."

CHAPTER 31

The gathering darkness obscured his vision, but Lagan scarce slowed his pace, even when the silhouette of a small child darted out before them.

"Lagan," Malcom cried. "I couldna find him. I couldna! I looked but I couldna."

"Hush, Malcom," Lagan commanded him, reining in much too recklessly before the frantic child.

It was obvious to Page that he was afeared, and she suddenly didn't feel any more at ease than he sounded. Her heart leapt as the horse snorted and kicked in protest, nearly striking Malcom's little shoulder, and she held her breath until the animal came to a full halt—held her tongue as well, for she didn't wholly trust Lagan. She would have risked anything for Malcom's sake, but she was beginning to sense that something was very wrong.

Lagan dismounted quickly, and Page's sense of unease only intensified as she watched him immediately lift his crossbow from its carrier. But she scarce had time to consider his actions, for he made them clear enough at once.

"I dinna believe in wastin' time," he said, and aimed the weapon at Malcom. "Get yourself on the horse, Malcom," he commanded the child.

The answering look upon Malcom's face twisted Page's heart. In the dusky twilight, his face seemed to turn ashen before her eyes. His innocent green eyes widened in grown-up comprehension and then slanted sadly like those of an old man. "Lagan," he cried woefully. His little-boy eyes welled with tears.

Page started to dismount at once, to go to him, but Lagan turned to her and commanded, "Stay!"

She froze when he turned the weapon upon her—a momentary lapse, for she was no fearless warrior. It took her an instant to recover herself, and then she was heartily grateful the weapon was no longer trained upon Malcom.

Bolstering her courage, she straightened her spine and lifted her chin. "What is it you hope to gain from this?" she asked him contemptuously. "What could possibly be worth harming your own cousin? He's naught but a child."

"Cousin?" he asked her, his words fraught with bitterness. "Nay, he is my nephew. But I wasna given a choice o'er what he should call me. Well, I dinna want him now. He can go to the devil, where I'm gain' to send his da, as well."

"I... I do not understand," Page said.

"I dinna have the time to explain it to ye." He turned the weapon upon Malcom once more, dismissing her. "Get yourself on the horse, brat."

With the canopy of darkness descended almost fully now, Malcom stood deeper within shadow, unmoving. Though she could no longer see his face clearly, she felt her heart wrench for the grief she knew he must be feeling. She knew he must be terrified. Knew he must feel confused.

She knew, too, that she must divert Lagan's attention from him, for he was like to be no more capable of responding to Lagan's dictates than she had been all those times her father had shattered her own illusions of him. She remembered only the numbness—a cold, gray numbness that had filtered into every corner of her soul, washing the colors from her life—a numbness she'd carried within her very heart—until Iain MacKinnon had taught her to feel again.

And here was his son.

She'd be damned to hell before she allowed Lagan to destroy his childish dreams and trust, his innocence and his zeal for life.

Anger filled her, a deep cleansing anger.

"What can you possibly hope to gain from this?" she asked Lagan once more, knowing instinctively that she could not prevail against him without understanding the battle he waged—she knew his reasons, and now she would know his intent. "Surely everyone will learn what you've done... should any harm come to Malcom by your hand?"

"No' by my hand," he assured her, snorting disdainfully. "By yours."

"Nay," Page countered, "for I'll not raise a finger against him. You will never force me to. Place your arrow where you please, but I'll not lift my hand against this child—nor any other. Bloody your own hands!"

"I dinna think so." Chortling nastily, he turned to Malcom. "Get on the horse, Malcom," he persisted.

Malcom moved forward uncertainly this time, and Page's gaze scanned the shadowed horizon in panic, trying to discern his intentions. He wanted Malcom upon the horse. Why? Nothing was immediately discernible. The hillside sloped upward sharply so that she could not see what lay beyond the summit—

Her breath caught, and her heart jolted, for suddenly she understood.

His gaze followed hers. "Canny lass," he commended her. "'Tis a pity ye didna realize sooner... or ye ne'er would have chosen this route for escape."

Her mind raced for a way to stall him. Anything to

give them precious time. "And what of Malcom? Why would I bring him?"

"To appease your da, o' course," he said sweetly, and then turned and shouted at Malcom. "I said to get on the horse, and do it now."

"Nay, Malcom," Page asserted. "Do not come any nearer."

She sensed, more than saw, Malcom's compliance.

Though Lagan had the crossbow trained once more upon her, Page slid down from the horse, daring to defy him. Her father had always said she was unmindful, but she was glad for it this moment, because she knew instinctively that meekness would find the two of them lying at the bottom of a cliff come morn.

Page could scarce see his features, but for the eyes, and they were openly malicious. Night descended more deeply in the long moments that they stared at one another. Her heart pounded so fiercely that she feared the intensity of its beating.

"Get yourself back upon that horse," Lagan snarled at her.

Though she knew he could not see her, she stood her place and lifted her chin. "Nay," she refused, swallowing convulsively. "I'll not!"

He turned the weapon upon Malcom and faced her as he demanded, "Get back on that horse!"

Page took a deep breath. Her heart hammered fiercely, but she said again, "Nay, if you would murder us, then you'll do it your bloody self. I'll not aid you in the endeavor." She turned to Malcom, and cursed the darkness that she could no longer see his face, nor even the obscure silhouette of his body, for he stood too far from her. And Lagan stood between them.

"Malcom?" she called out.

His response was a barely discernible murmur. He was afeared, she knew. But he was a brave child. She knew that, too, for he'd endured her father's tirades without the first tear or single fearful whimper. Despite her father's endless interrogations—the likes of which had brought wretched tears to her eyes as a child—he'd held his tongue. He'd remained his father's son, through and through. Not broken and beaten as she'd first thought, for his silence had not been in weakness, but in strength.

"Malcom," she asked, her heart sounding like thunder in her ears, "do you trust me?"

"A-Aye," came his soft, quavering response.

"Lie down upon the ground," she directed him. "Lie down upon the ground, and do not get up. Do you understand?"

"Aye," he answered, and Page struggled to see him through the darkness.

She prayed to God that he did as she bade him.

Lagan turned to her. "I dinna see what ye hope to gain wi' that," he told her. "Ach! Twill be a simple matter to toss him o'er once I'm finished wi' you."

"Aye?" Page taunted him. Boldness had gained her much in her life. She sensed this was one time she needed the advantage it would give her. Even knowing where it would lead her, she turned her back toward the ledge. She knew it was there, knew he knew it was there. She only hoped it wasn't obvious to him that she was aware of it, hoped he would think it his own bright notion to walk her to the cliff. Praying with all her might that she was doing the right thing—at least for Malcom's sake—she took a step backward, hoping he would subconsciously take the hint. If he followed, then it would place much-needed distance between him and Malcom. And that, ultimately, was her first goal—to see Malcom safely away.

She wasn't certain whether to cry out in fear or sigh in relief when he responded by taking a step toward her. She crossed herself, and began to pray aloud. "Holy Mary, Mother of Christ," she whispered beneath her breath. "Pray for us sinners..." She took another step backward, and did cry out when he responded with another step forward. "Now and at the hour of our death," she intoned.

Her heart pounded against her ribs.

He merely chuckled, and continued to urge her backward toward the cliff. "'Tis just like a Sassenach," he scorned her. "Turn to God when ye canna fight your battles like a man!"

Despite her predicament, Page's brows knit in outrage. "Aye, well, I am a woman," she reminded him caustically, and wondered if she would ever learn to curb her tongue. But what did it matter what she was, man or woman, when she was going to be a dead one soon enough.

Well, she vowed, at least she would die knowing Malcom was safe, because if she went over that cliff, she fully intended to take Lagan down with her—villain that he was.

She continued to retreat while he followed, until she neared the edge of the cliff and could scarce move back any farther without tumbling downward. She pretended surprise at the place of her arrival, but her gasp of fear was not at all feigned.

Though she could barely discern Lagan's features now, his smile was evident by the moon's reflection. She stilled at the cliff edge, her heart tripping painfully as he continued forward, stalking her... closer until his features were once again discernible and he was within arm's reach, and then she screamed at the top of her lungs, "Run, Malcom! Run!"

Lagan turned at once to stop him. He lifted his bow, and Page hurled herself against him. Cursing fiercely, he shoved her backward, and attempted once more to aim for the distant fleeing shadow. Page tried once more to stop him, but she stumbled and lost her footing. She reached out to grasp something of substance and found only Lagan's hair, seizing a handful as she toppled backward. With a yelp of pain and a cry of surprise, Lagan dropped the bow and pitched after her.

For an instant and an eternity they tottered together upon the bluff's edge.

Page gasped, her grip tightening desperately upon his hair. He struggled to free himself, but he was all that was solid and real, and then there was nothingness behind her as she fell backward.

"AND SO THE DREAM..."

"Was no dream a'tall, Iain," Glenna revealed. "What ye describe to me is exactly the way it was the night your mother died."

"Ach God..." It was Iain's turn to bury his face within his hands. His jaw tautened against the new tide of emotions. The voice in his dreams. The eyes. They had all been memories... not fanciful wisps of his imagination. His mother's beautiful lilt.

And the dream... the scared little boy awakened within his darkened bedchamber by a suffering mother's screams. While he'd lain within his bed clutching the bedsheets, afeared to move, and yet wanting to run to her as much as he wanted to hide beneath the sheets, it was Lagan she had been bearing into the world... Lagan and not himself.

How could it be? How was it possible that everyone could keep such a secret—so brilliantly that he had never once perceived it?

And yet he somehow knew it for truth, for with Glenna's shocking revelation, the memory seemed to grow in clarity.

He clenched his jaw. "Bloody damn you all!"

"Iain..."

"Why did no one e'er tell me?" he asked her,

without lifting his face to look at her. He wasn't certain he could—not without betraying his incredible fury.

"It was your da's wish that ye not be told," Glenna revealed. "He didna wish for you to know."

"Evidently. Who else knew of this, Glenna?"

"'Twas for your own guid, Iain."

He lifted his gaze to her face. "Who else knew of this, Glenna?"

"The MacLeans, o'course."

He sat abruptly, slamming a fist atop the table. "Nay! I mean to say... amongst my own kinsmen... who else knew of this?"

"Angus, o' course. He was your da's closest fellow."

"Who else?" he demanded of her.

"Ach, Iain, many. But we didna tell our children because your da forbade us."

Iain shook his head, disbelieving his ears. "So everyone knows?"

"Nay... only those of us who were of an age... Most do not. Your da never meant to hurt ye, Iain, love..."

"Nay? So tell me... how did Lagan learn?"

Glenna lowered her eyes. "I told him." She shook her head lamentably. "When he returned so aggrieved after tryin' to woo MacLean's youngest daughter, he wanted to know why auld mon MacLean wouldna listen to reason, why he seemed to condemn him e'en before he listened to a single bloody word."

"And why would that be?" Iain asked her, his tone controlled, his body restrained, lest he destroy all that he saw within sight in his temper. This very moment, he felt near as violent in his anger as he had the day when he'd returned to find Malcom gone.

"Because... Iain... it had been his brother your mother loved... his brother your father killed. It was an accident, o'course. The two had long been friends... but they fought... and there was too much rage between them to stop it." Her voice softened. "And ye dinna re-

TANYA ANNE CROSBY

alize, Iain, lad, but Lagan is the verra image o' your minnie... while ye are the likeness o' your da."

Iain closed his eyes and tried to hear his father's reason. He imagined the anger his brother... Christ... his
brother... must feel.

"Lagan never had a chance with MacLean's daughter, Iain. I thought he should know why. It was surprising enough that auld MacLean had been willin' to
entrust his eldest daughter into your hands. I wish I
hadna told him."

"Why did he do it for me, I wonder?"

"MacLean?" Glenna shook her head. "I dunno, but I
wish he had not. Were the choice between you and Lagan, I wish it had been Lagan," she told him honestly,
"and ye know I dinna mean to wish ye ill. 'Tis merely
that for ye and for Mairi there was ne'er any love.
While Lagan loved Mairi's sister, of a certain—and he's
envied ye all his life, besides. He never wanted me,
Iain," she lamented. "It was you and your da he always
envied."

Iain shook his head, benumbed. "I cannot believe ye
didna tell me, Glenna."

"It was your da's wish... to protect ye, love."

"Nay, Glenna," Iain countered with conviction, his
tone clipped with pain and fury. For the first time in his
life, he understood so much. "It was my da's wish to
hide from the truth," he disputed her. "He didna wish
to face the fact that his wife was in love wi' another
man. Just as it was his wish to raise a perfect son—a son
without weaknesses—a legacy for himself. Bastard. 'Tis
no wonder Lagan resents me so. Who could blame
him?"

There was an instant of silence between them.
Glenna hung her head, unable to respond.

"And why should ye choose now... this instant to unburden yourself to me, Glenna?"

310

Her chin lifted. Her eyes welled again with tears. "Ach! 'Tis Lagan," she began. "I dinna—"

The door burst open.

"Iain!" Broc bellowed. "I think ye'd better come."

Iain's nerves were near to snapping. He doubted there was one more incident he could deal with this day. "What now, Broc?" he asked without turning, his fist clenching upon the table before him.

"'Tis David," Broc revealed.

Iain stiffened. "David?"

"Aye... he rides wi' FitzSimon to reclaim FitzSimon's daughter."

CHAPTER 32

To his credit, David, King of Scotia—so he claimed —sat his mount in thoughtful silence, listening. Iain was aware of him, his easy demeanor, though his own thoughts were racing with the possible reasons for Page's disappearance. He'd summoned her at once upon her father's arrival, only to learn she'd vanished.

She couldn't possibly have known of her father's approach, and it didn't make much sense to Iain that she would wander away so late. Nor had it been so long since he'd left her. She couldn't have gone far.

Her da, however, had long since dismounted and paced before him now like a maddened beast.

"I cannot believe you would lose her," FitzSimon shouted at him, and it was all Iain could do not to murder the man where he stood.

"I entrust my daughter to your hands," he spat. "And this is how you care for her?"

Iain restrained his temper, telling himself that there would be plenty of time to kill him once he resolved the situation at hand. He couldn't keep his tongue stilled, however, as FitzSimon was a lying bastard. "Entrust? Is that what ye call it when ye Sassenachs cast your own kin away?"

FitzSimon had the decency to stutter at the question. "I—I was angry," he reasoned. "I did not realize what I was saying—what I was doing."

"Bloody lyin' bastard. Ye seemed to know just fine," Angus interjected.

Iain cast Angus a quelling glance, and then returned his attention to FitzSimon. "You sounded to me like a mon who knew his mind well enough," Iain proposed. "I gave you plenty o' opportunity to change your mind and ye didna. Ye wouldna."

"I was angry," FitzSimon reasoned once more.

"And do ye think I'm no' angry?" Iain returned. "Just because I'm standin' here listenin' to you doesna mean to say I dinna take pleasure in the thought o' carvin' the heart from your feckless body."

FitzSimon stared warily.

"A mon is no' a mon, but a beast, if he canna use his reason," Iain said.

FitzSimon said nothing, and Iain decided he hadn't spoken clearly enough.

"You are worse than any beast I know, for e'en a beast doesna sacrifice his young."

"I did not know she was my daughter," FitzSimon admitted, shocking Iain with the disclosure. Of all the things he might have spoken, it was the one thing to which Iain could not respond. His own revelations were too freshly revealed.

He opened his mouth to speak, but before he could, Dougal came running from the tower, breathless. "I canna find Malcom, either," he said, between pants. "I looked everywhere, and I canna. Nor Lagan either!"

Murmurs filled the air. Iain's heart began to pound all the more fiercely. "Neither Malcom, Lagan, nor Page?" The hairs of his nape stood upon end.

"Nary a one!"

Iain tried not to give in to panic. Panic would gain him naught, he knew. "Did no one see them go?"

It seemed a thousand murmurs responded, none of them yes.

And then he heard his son's shouts, distant, but unmistakable, and his heart jolted. He tore through the crowd at once, shoving his way through to follow the sound. "Malcom," he called out.

"Da!" his son cried, running through the night toward them, his voice full of fear. "Da!"

Iain began to run.

"Da," Malcom wailed.

Iain reached him and swept him up into his arms, embracing him desperately. "What, Malcom?"

"Lagan," Malcom sobbed. "Page!" And then he began to cry hysterically, uncontrollably.

Iain's heart tripped. He shook his son in a moment of desperation. "Malcom, tell me!"

"Lagan was g-gain' t-to k-kill me, da," he cried, choking on his sobs. "P-Page p-pushed him." He sobbed, clutching Iain's neck, and Iain felt his legs go weak beneath him. His mind raced.

"Pushed him? Where?"

He gripped his son beneath the arms, pulling him away, his arms trembling.

Malcom held on all the tighter. "I didna want to leave her, Da, but she told me to run."

"Where is she now?" Iain choked out, and his heartbeat stilled for the answer.

"O'er the bluff side," Malcom cried. "She went o'er the bluff, Da!"

Praying to God he wasn't too late, he thrust Malcom away and into waiting arms. Christ in Heaven above, he thought. Do not let it be too late.

❧

PAGE HAD FALLEN, HER BODY SCRAPING OVER ROCK and brush, onto a ledge in the cliffside where the rock jutted outward. Somehow, though the impact had driven the air from her lungs, she'd managed to hold on to the small platform.

Groping blindly with her feet for a better hold than the tentative one she had, she found a place in the craggy cliffside where she could snuggle her toes. And then she held on for her life.

It seemed an eternity passed before she heard the first voices above.

She didn't wait to be called upon; she shouted at the top of her lungs. And still it was another eternity before they followed her voice to where she hung so precariously along the cliffside.

"Are ye hurt, lass?" Page heard Iain ask.

It was about time. "Well, if I am," she returned somewhat caustically, "I certainly have no wish to know this minute. Rather ask me when I'm safe above!"

His answering chuckle, uneasy though it sounded, reassured her somehow. "Verra well," he told her, his tone clearly filled with relief. "Hold fast now," he said, "I'm comin' down after ye, lass."

"Ach!" Page mocked him. "But ye dinna have to tell me so, I think. I'm holding! I'm holding!"

Once again his laughter drifted down from above, and Page tried to ignore the fact that her fingers were growing weary and raw from gripping the jagged rock. She was not going to die. Not now! She refused.

"Hurry," she urged him, and knew she sounded afeared.

"Keep talking to me, dearlin'," he directed her, his voice calm, though she could scarce mistake the urgency in his command. "I'll be coming for ye anon."

Keep talking? By the bloody saints! What in creation was she supposed to talk about?

She asked him as much, and he said, "Anything, lass... just so I know where to find ye."

"Let me talk to her," she heard a familiar voice say, and her heart leapt. Nay! But it could not be!

"Bloody hell if you will," she heard Iain deny him. "Ye've done enough harm as it is. Get oot o' my way, and leave her be."

Page was so staggered by the discovery that he'd come, after all, that she nearly lost her tenuous grip upon the rock.

She screeched as she slipped a little. "Father?" she called out. Her heart began to pound all the faster, and her vision threatened to turn black. "Is it you?"

"Aye, Page," he answered. "'Tis me."

She heard Iain's curse, but was too dazed to comprehend its cause.

"You've come!" she cried, and squealed as her fingers slipped a little. In desperation, she released one hand and grasped out, thanking God for the bush he'd placed within her reach. She used it to support her weight while her other hand searched and found a more tangible hold. She found it just in time, for the bush began to uproot.

"Sweet Mary," she exclaimed.

"Aye, Page," he shouted down to her. "I've much to tell you, daughter mine."

Fine time, Page thought.

"No' now, ye willna," she heard Iain argue with him. "Now isna the time to unburden yourself. Now get the bloody hell oota my way!"

"In the meantime," Page shouted a little frantically, "whilst you two argue, my hands are aching, and my feet are slipping, and I do not wish to end like Lagan, if you please!"

There was a long interval of silence, too long, Page thought, and then Iain said, "Dinna worry, love. I'll be comin' down now." And sure enough, she heard him making his way down the cliffside. "Page?" he called out once more.

Page squeezed her eyes shut and prayed that he would reach her soon. The pebbles at her toes were beginning to loosen and roll free.

"Are ye certain Lagan went down, lass?"

Page swallowed at the memory of his screams as he'd fallen. He'd fallen so far and so long, and his bellow had continued for what had seemed an eternity.

"Aye," she answered. "He's gone."

She heard the scuffing of his boots as he came nearer.

"We fell together," she told him, groaning, and opened her eyes to search for his descending shadow against the cliffside. "Only I somehow ended here, and he down there." And she added silently, thank God.

"Thank God," he said, and his voice was nearer now. "Malcom told me what ye did. I thought we'd lost ye too, lass."

"Aye, well..." She whimpered as her toe lost its footing. She heard the loose rocks cascade downward, dragging the cliffside, until they descended into stony silence, and swallowed convulsively as she searched out another toehold. "I... I did tell you I was stubborn and canny," she warned him, trying to make merry.

"That ye did, lass," he told her, chuckling softly, much closer now. "That ye did."

And then suddenly she could see him, and her heart leapt with joy. When his face came into view, the moonlight reflecting within his wonderful golden eyes, she thought she would weep with delight.

And then suddenly he was there at her side. Page might have cast herself into his arms, but she was so afeared to move that he had to pry her free from the rock.

"I canna save ye if ye willna let go," he advised her.

"And I will not let go until you save me," she returned.

"Ach, but ye've a saucy tongue."

"Aye, well, my father's here to take me off your hands at last. You'll not have to endure it much longer, it seems."

He made some sound, like a snarl, and jerked her away from the rock. When at last she was in his arms, her tears began to flow at once. She clung to him, weeping, babbling nonsensically, and all the while he stroked her head and held her close. And she didn't know which she was more aggrieved over: the fact that she'd come so close to cracking her head upon the rocks below, or that her father had finally come to collect her.

"Wrap yourself about me, Page," he whispered. "And dinna let go."

Page did as she was told, burying her face against his throat, her lips against the warmth of his flesh. She wrapped her legs about his waist and held to him for dear life.

"Ach," he whispered, holding her close. Page thought he would squeeze her until she broke, but she couldn't truly care this moment. She wanted him to hold her so, never wanted him to let her go.

"Malcom told me everything. You're a stouthearted lass," he told her with pride. "I believe we'll make a fine Scotswoman oota ye yet."

"I'm sorry about Lagan," she whispered.

"'Tis no fault o' your own," he said, kissing the pate of her head.

"Malcom?"

"His heart is bruised, but he'll live," Iain assured her.

"And my father?"

"Aye, Page," he answered. "He's come for ye... as ye always said he would."

Page squeezed her eyes closed against his breacan, reveling in the scent of the man who held her. She wasn't certain what it was she was feeling this moment, whether joy or something else entirely—regret?—but she knew without a doubt who it was who held her. Not her father.

"By the blessed stone, Iain MacKinnon... dinna be keepin' us waitin'," came a voice from above. "D' ye have the lassie, or nay?"

"Are ye ready to face him?" Iain whispered.

Page laughed softly and held him all the more tightly. "Do I have a choice?" she asked him morosely. When she left this embrace... would it be their last? "If I say nay, can we stay here forever?"

He chuckled softly. "Ach, but, lass, I believe Angus may have somethin' to say aboot that."

"Iain," Angus shouted down at them. "Come on now, lad! These auld arms canna hold ye burly arse down there forever."

"See?" Iain asked her, and he lifted his head from the embrace to shout his reply. "Aye, Angus! Draw us up now, will ye?"

Page couldn't help herself.

Some part of her suddenly wished she'd ended upon the rocks below. While merely hours before, she'd never felt more alive, more cherished, more complete, she now felt only an overwhelming emptiness in her heart.

Her father had come for her, after all.

Iain was uncertain how to feel.

In the space of a single day he'd discovered a brother, and then lost him. And in the course of the same day had come near to losing his son and the woman he loved, as well.

Later he would sort out his feelings for the brother he'd never claimed, and for the father who had denied them both. For now, his son was safe with Glenna. But while Page was safe from Lagan's fate, he was now in danger of losing her yet again. And this time he couldn't simply sweep her out of harm's reach.

More than aught, he wanted her to stay—and if she decided 'twas her heart's desire to do so, then her father's entourage along with David of Scotia's were not enough to prevail against him.

And if she chose to go, it would be the single most difficult thing he'd ever done, but Iain would let her. Ach, but he knew how important her father's acceptance was to her.

He could tell by the way she clung to him that she was afeared. He gave her ribs a squeeze when they neared the bluff top, and then handed her up into waiting arms. Kerwyn and Kermichil together hauled her up and onto her feet. And then with Angus's help, Iain climbed over the cliff edge, as well.

She looked so like a child standing there by the moonlight that Iain's heart wrenched for her. He knew this moment was difficult for her, and he wanted so much to whisk her away from her bastard sire, and keep her always from harm.

He couldn't do that, though. He knew that as well as she, and he was proud of her when she went to Fitz-Simon and stood before him. There were no embraces between them, but then Iain hadn't expected any.

He could scarce bear the thought of her leaving with her father. It wrenched at his gut, but he knew he wouldn't stop her. He wanted her to be happy. And Christ, if that meant she would leave him, so be it.

Though it seemed impossible to restrain himself, he did so, remaining behind her at a safe distance—safe for him, because he wanted to lunge at FitzSimon's throat and murder the bastard where he stood.

"I've come to take you home, daughter."

Page could scarce speak, so overwhelmed was she with conflicting emotions.

How long had she waited for her father to call her "daughter?"

An eternity too long.

And now he was here, speaking the words she'd so longed to hear, and all she wished to do was to slap his face. Aye, some part of her wanted to fall to his feet and thank him profusely, but some other wicked part of her wanted to deny him as he had done so long to her.

She straightened her spine and lifted her chin, demanding of him, "Why?" It was her right to know why he should change his mind. She wanted to believe he'd had a change of heart, but it was more like to be that he'd finally found some use for her.

He peered at the ground a long moment, and then again met her gaze. "The truth?"

"Aye," Page answered. "The truth."

"I did not believe you were my daughter. I thought you were Henry's bastard, conceived by my wife."

Her brow furrowed. She should have been shocked by his revelation, but wasn't. "I see," she said, and tried to find some comfort in his explanation. She found it only angered her all the more. "And now?"

"Your mother is long dead. I cannot make it up to her."

Page stood silent, listening.

"I never believed her, Page... but I confronted Henry at long last... when he came to take the boy. He swears to me that your mother was pure, and he never had carnal knowledge of her. I never believed her," he said again. "And I took it out upon you. For that, daughter, you have my deepest regrets."

Regrets? For a lifetime of disregard? For casting her mother away for a sin she hadn't committed?

Page remained silent.

"I just could not see what she could possibly want with me when she had England's king enamored of her, instead. I drove her away, Page. But I'll make it up to you—I swear it. I shall find you a fitting spouse, and make you the lady you deserve to be."

Page's eyes welled with tears. He was saying the things she'd so longed to hear. As a child. What she would have given to hear them spoken then...

At this moment... they merely confused her. She didn't know what to say. Didn't know what to do... nor did she seem to have a choice. Iain and his people had been generous enough to take her in, had embraced her these last days like one of their own... but only because her father had not wanted her.

And here he was, her father, willing and ready to take her home, it seemed.

"The MacKinnon's bride is a lady," someone suddenly proclaimed. Page turned and spied Broc stepping forward from the gathered crowd, his stance battle-ready. His expression, though obscured by the night's shadows, was unmistakably angry and full of challenge. She wasn't certain which she was more shocked by... the fact that he had claimed her as the MacKinnon's bride, or that he'd come forward to defend her.

Her brows knit suddenly, as the reason for his indignation filtered through her. Judas! Why hadn't she caught the slur in her father's words? She was a lady, indeed!

"Bride?" her father asked, oblivious to his own offense. "My daughter is no bride to this man!" His tone was contemptuous. "She will have better than a savage Scot."

"Aye," Angus argued, stepping forward, as well. "I say she is the MacKinnon's bride!"

"Aye," came a cacophony of voices from the gathered crowd. "She is the MacKinnon's bride!" and "Aye, she's the MacKinnon's bride, all right!"

Page could scarcely believe her eyes and ears.

"Is this true?" came a voice from the shadows.

Page searched out the speaker and found it belonged to a man still mounted upon horseback. He'd been watching quietly from a distance, and now seemed to be peering straight at her, waiting for her response... Nay, not her... She suddenly realized he was looking past her. She peered over her shoulder and found Iain standing guard at her back. He said nothing, seemed to be scrutinizing her, his eyes seeing only her, ignoring the surrounding crowd.

"My daughter is no bride to this barbarian," her father contended. "He stole her from me, and I would have her returned."

Stole. Returned. The words leapt out at her from her father's tirade.

Her gaze snapped back to meet her father's angry glare.

FitzSimon turned to regard the man on horseback. "I demand you command him to release her at once!"

"You demand?" the man asked from his vantage in the shadows.

"I did not come all this way to leave empty-handed," her father raved. "Release her to me, or—"

"Or what?" the man on horseback asked.

"Or I—"

"Iain MacKinnon?" the horseman asked, dismissing her father suddenly. "What say you to this? Is this woman your bride or nay?"

Page braced herself for his reply. She closed her eyes.

"Why do you not ask my lady?" he suggested.

Page turned to look at him in shock. He merely smiled at her, saying nothing. He nodded, urging her to answer the inquiry. And in that instant she understood love in its purest form. It was unveiled to her as it never had been before.

Her decision was clear: Choose a father who never once acknowledged her—cared so little that he never even bothered to give her a name—or choose a man with compassion enough that he would risk her anger to offer her one? Choose the one who rebuffed her though she was flesh and blood to him, or he who chose to take her into his fold, despite that she was a sour-mouthed wench and caused him more trouble than he'd ever bargained for? She smiled at the memory. He hadn't wanted her. She'd been cast into his unwilling hands, and yet he'd not turned her away.

She turned to meet her father's eyes.

"Tell him, Page," her father barked at her.

Nor, Page realized in that moment, had it been her father who had risked himself to deliver her from the jaws of death. It had been Iain's arms that had borne her to safety.

And it was Iain now who loved her enough to give her a choice.

"What say you, lass?" the horseman asked her.

She had no notion who he might be, but knew instinctively that he was someone of consequence. Even Iain, while not overly obsequious, seemed to defer to him. King David? It would make sense, Page thought, for her father would have gone to him for safe passage into the Highlands. Either David or Henry. But only David could ride with so few into these people's midst, and only a Scotsman would dare.

She turned again to address Iain, needing to know if he meant it true. He seemed to understand her silent plea, and she never needed to utter a word. He nodded, urging her to speak.

Page met her father's gaze once more and lifted her chin. Her lips curved into a smile as she declared, "I am."

"You are what?" her father snapped.

"The MacKinnon's bride," she said almost too softly to be heard.

"Nay! He's forcing her," her father declared, turning to address the horseman. "Did you see that?"

Page met David of Scotland's gaze, lifting her chin determinedly. "No one forces me," she assured him, her voice stronger.

"Speak it louder, Page," Iain whispered at her back,

and her heart flowered with joy as she'd never known before.

A smile burst upon her lips. "I am the MacKinnon's bride," she all but shouted.

All at once, a shout rang out. In unison, the clansmen cheered. Page felt her heart swell, until it seemed as though it would burst.

The horseman looked past her once more to Iain. "Is this true?"

Silence fell again. Iain stepped forward then, placing his arms about her in a protective embrace. "Aye."

"Well, then, FitzSimon," the horseman declared. "It seems to me your daughter is, in fact, the MacKinnon's bride."

Once again cheers rang out, and Page was scarce aware of the tirade her father began, nor even the quarrel between him and the horseman, nor the angry shouts of the MacKinnon men as they demanded he leave. She was aware only of the man at her back. She scarce knew it when her father stalked away and mounted his horse in anger. He spouted curses as he hied away, followed by an unsympathetic band of Scotsmen.

"You've not heard the last of this," her father declared. "I will demand satisfaction."

Page giggled softly. "He will, you realize," she warned Iain. "He does not like to be thwarted."

"So ye told me once before," he reminded her. "I dinna think he'll be back," he assured her. "Look at them," he urged her. "Ye've wormed your way into my people's hearts—sassy-mouthed wench that ye are. If he comes back, they'll flay him alive."

Page chuckled at his choice of words, remembering she'd said something of the same to him some time ago. Following his gaze to the angry horde of Scotsmen chasing her father from their land, shouting curses and threats at his back, she giggled at the sight of them.

Some part of her was sad to see her father go, for he was her father, after all, but the greater part of her felt only relief.

"I love ye, lass," Iain whispered in her ear, tightening the embrace. "Ach, I've somethin' for you," he revealed, releasing her suddenly. He searched through the folds of his breacan and drew something from it. Embracing her once more from behind, he offered her the battered remains of a yellow crocus. Her yellow crocus. The one she'd discarded in anger. He'd somehow found it, and saved it for her. "The moment I laid ye down upon that bed o' blossoms," he told her, "I considered ye mine. But I wanted to hear from your own lips that ye considered me yours."

Page was too overwhelmed to speak. "I am." Tears welled in her eyes. "I do," she cried softly.

"Say it again," he urged her, squeezing her gently.

"I am," she said with a contented sigh, "I am the MacKinnon's bride."

"That ye are," he assured her. "And I'll ne'er let ye regret it for the rest o' your days. I'll make ye happy, Page. I pledge to ye my love and my loyalty, and I wed thee here in the name of God."

Loyalty, she could well believe. "Love?" she asked him. "Truly?"

He turned her about to face him. "Dinna ye doubt it, lass." Grasping her arms, he shook her gently. "I love ye fiercely, truly, and gladly." And then he kissed her upon the bridge of the nose.

"And I love you," Page confessed. "I love you fiercely, truly, and gladly, too." And she did, without fear or reservation.

He lifted her up without warning, and tossed her over his shoulders.

Page squealed in surprise. "What are you doing?" she demanded in feigned outrage.

"I'm takin' ye home, lass... afore ye change your mind."

She laughed.

"Anyway, I'm a savage Scot," he reminded her. "We dinna want to be disappointin' your da."

Page laughed with scandalized delight.

"First," he declared, "you're goin' to be seein' to my son—assure him that ye live—and then I'm going to take ye to my bed... make ye sing me a sweet lullai bye."

And that he did.

And that she did.

A HEARTFELT THANK YOU!

Dearest Reader,

Great news! There is now an extended epilogue for The MacKinnon's Bride called MacKinnons' Hope. Throughout the years, I've gotten countless emails from readers lamenting the lack of an epilogue. Many reviews also shared that sentiment. But, at the time I wrote The MacKinnon's Bride an epilogue simply didn't fit the story.

So why an epilogue now, after all these years? In part, I wrote it for you. In part, for me—I wanted to revisit these characters and see them living happily. But if you're also following along in the Guardians series, you know these books are connected and take place during the same period. The new epilogue serves as a bridge to an upcoming story... maybe you'll guess who it's about?

Thank you from the bottom of my heart for reading The MacKinnon's Bride. If you enjoyed this book, please consider posting a review. Reviews don't just help the author, they help other readers discover our books and, no matter how long or short, I sincerely appreciate every review.

Would you like to know when my next book is available? Sign up for my newsletter:

❤️ Thank you! ❤️

TANYACROWE.COM/SUBSCRIBE

Also, please follow me on BookBub to be notified of deals and new releases.

Let's hang out! I have a Facebook group:

❤️ Let's Hang Out! ❤️

FACEBOOK.COM/GROUPS/TANYAANN
CROWE/

I'm also a member of the Jewels of Historical Romance. I hope you'll visit our Facebook group, the Jewels Salon. Read on for links to our Fabulous Firsts collections, two six book anthologies featuring starters for our most beloved series—each set is just 99c!

Thank you again for reading and for your support.

Tanya Anne Crosby

LYON'S GIFT
SNEAK PEEK

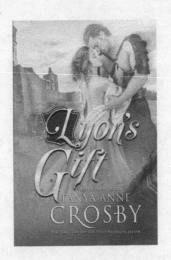

CHAPTER 1

"Twenty-seven," Baldwin announced, marching into the room where Piers sat poring over his new survey.

It was a lesson Piers had taken from old King William: one could hardly rule a land unless one knew precisely what one held to rule. Following William the Conqueror's example, the first thing he'd done upon receiving this fief was to survey his holdings, meager though they might be. And it was a good thing, as it seemed his stock was dwindling quickly. He might never have known until they'd been seriously depleted.

Thieving, conniving Scots.

"Twenty-seven," he exclaimed. Christ, but he didn't know whether to be angry or amused. At last count—only yesterday evening—the sheep had numbered thirty-four. "When did those whoresons have the occasion to rob me again? I thought I told you to set a man to guard those mangy beasts?"

"The Scots?"

"Them, too, cunning bastards. But I meant the bloody sheep, Baldwin. The bloody rotten mangy sheep! I thought I told you to set a guard for them?"

Baldwin's ears reddened. "Well..." His face twisted into an abashed grimace. "I *did* set a man to guard them, you see... but it seems I set a wolf to guard the sheep's pen."

"Wolf?" Piers lifted both brows. He couldn't wait to hear this one.

Baldwin winced. "I appointed Cameron," he said, looking shamefaced. "He was already keeping watch over his own sheep, you see, and I—"

"Cameron!" Piers exploded. "The arse who refused to leave his parcel and hut?" He tossed down his quill in disgust. "Damn it, Baldwin! Whatever were you thinking to put a thieving Scot to guard against his thieving kinsmen?"

"Well, I thought—"

"That he would give his loyalty to an Englishman over his own countrymen?"

Baldwin frowned. "Well, he did stay when the rest of them abandoned us," he pointed out.

"Only because he's a stubborn old coot who refused to leave his land to a bloody Sassenach. His own words, do you not recall? His behavior was certainly not born out of any sense of loyalty."

"Aye, but it's not what you think," Baldwin said. "He merely fell asleep, is all."

Piers sighed and slumped within his chair, smacking his head in exasperation against the high back of his seat. He rolled his eyes, then stared up at the ceiling, noting its rotten condition for the first time.

He frowned.

How had he missed that before now? His chamber was directly above. He was going to have to fix that bloody ceiling soon, lest he plummet through the floor onto the table in front of him and find himself fare for the band of misfit Scots who had remained with this ruined demesne.

"My lord?"

Piers turned his attention from the rotting floorboards and eyed his longtime friend with a mixture of bemusement and displeasure. It seemed to him that Baldwin had taken to behaving less like a friend and more like an underling, and though this new manner wasn't entirely without its merits, he was nevertheless uncomfortable with Baldwin's unexpected attention to the proprieties. He much preferred the drunken companionability he and his men had shared in the years before his enfeoffment.

Christ, but he'd never expected to find himself lord —or laird, for that matter—and he'd certainly never aspired to it. It seemed wholly unnatural to him now to be fussed over as though he were some grease-lipped lord casting dinner bones to his dogs. He was a commander first and foremost. It had been his skill at arms that had won him this little piece of Highland hell, and he didn't see the bloody need to change what had served him so well for so long. His men worked well beside him because they were foremost his fellows. He didn't want, or need, a bunch of knock-kneed lackeys running about according him undue honors.

"Sire?" Baldwin's tone clearly revealed uncertainty over Piers' mood. "What is it you'd have me do?"

"You might first cease to call me *my lord*," Piers suggested, his tone unmistakably provoked. "And *sire*, as well, as I am not your bloody father either."

Baldwin lifted his head in surprise. "Then what is it you'd have me call you... if not 'my lord'?"

Piers thought the answer rather obvious. "What is it you called me before?"

Baldwin cocked his head a little uncertainly. "Lyon?"

Piers responded with a droll grin. He'd been given the name by his men after a particularly bloody battle; they'd said he'd appeared to them coming off the battlefield, with his long, gilt mane of hair and bloodied face, like a lion fresh after its kill. It wasn't an honor he was particularly proud of, but he'd gotten used to the name after all.

Baldwin's brows lifted. "But you don't like that name?"

"I certainly prefer it to *my lord*."

Baldwin's lips curved into a companionable smile. "If that is your wish..."

"It is," Piers assured him. "I'm no different now merely because I have a parcel of land to piss on. Why should we resort to ceremony after all these years? I didn't like the damned name before and you hounded me with it anyway. Why not still?"

Baldwin nodded, his grin spreading from ear to ear. "I am relieved to hear you say so."

"Are you now?" Piers was relieved as well at having settled the matter once and for all. Now wasn't the time for maudlin expressions, as he still had these annoying, bare-arsed Scots to deal with.

And yet... strangely enough, though the Brodies had all but robbed him blind, it was a simple enough task to temper his anger against the thieving curs.

Why was that? he wondered.

Truth to tell, accustomed as he had become to the intrigues of court and the stealth of warfare, this matter of feuding seemed more like sport.

In fact, Piers could scarcely help but admire these Scots. They fought their battles fiercely, and by some strange code of honor that somehow appealed to him. They spat upon your boot; you drew your sword; they stole your goat; you stole your sheep; and so on and so on—though bloodshed seemed proscribed—and all of it done openly, as though thieving your good neighbor were the most natural and honorable thing to do. Thus far, not so much as a single beast had been harmed, though Piers had not enjoyed a moment's peace since first he'd stepped foot upon these Highlands.

It was more than apparent that a bond of blood was as binding as a Scotsman's honor would allow—that they defended kith and kin unto their dying breath.

It was also apparent that an outlander would always be just that... an outlander.

Well, Piers was perfectly accustomed to that. He didn't need their bloody approval. David of Scotia might, but he sure as hell didn't. He had grown up an outlander, didn't they know it; his father was a king and his mother a whore.

And while his mother had slept in a different bed many a night, Piers had slipped away and curled beneath a pew in the chapel to close his eyes and dream of all the things he wanted in life. And he had wanted so much.

He had wanted to go away and study in one of those places he'd only heard speak of... He'd wanted to read until his eyes went blind... He'd wanted to learn things, and do things, and see things.

He'd wanted to know why the sky was so blue and the grass so green. He'd wanted to know what stars were made of, and why they burned so brightly. He'd wanted to know why his veins were blue while his blood was red. He'd wanted so much more than a bed on a cold, hard floor and to stand alone behind invisible doors... watching other children at play.

Though, in truth, why should he have cared if the other children were outside playing and laughing? Thanks to his mother, he'd been able to study with the Archbishop of Canterbury and that had been no trifling thing. He'd had every reason to be grateful and no reason at all to yearn for something so negligible as dirty knees or silly games.

"Damn it all," he exclaimed, lifting up his pen and rapping the quill's end upon the wooden table. "We're going to show these bloody Scots that we can feud with the best of them."

And enjoy it every bit as much.

That's what it was going to take to win their alliance, he surmised.

Or not.

Either way, he would relish the sport.

Though at first he'd been taken unawares by their unanticipated raids, some part of him reveled in this honest form of warfare, where one's enemy stood up to be counted, and one's friends openly declared they'd as soon pluck out your eyes if they could profit from them. There was something particularly heartening in that unrelenting honesty.

Aye, he was perfectly pleased to play their games.

"These savages will not run us off this land," he vowed. "Damn you for a witless arse," he reprimanded Baldwin, though he knew his eyes didn't quite conceal the smile he hid. "I should take the price of those beasts out of your hide, you realize?"

Color returned to the tips of Baldwin's ears. "I wouldn't fault you for it, Lyon," he said, but neither did his smile vanish either. "So what would you have me do?"

"What else?" Piers grinned. "We steal the buggers back—and a few more for good measure."

Baldwin smirked. "If I didn't know better," he said, "I'd think you were enjoying this."

Lyon lifted a brow. "And you would probably be right," he returned, rising from his seat and taking his sword from where he'd placed it upon the table before him. He slid it into his scabbard and winked good-naturedly at Baldwin. "Now, let's go teach these Scots how to commit a proper thieving."

Keep reading.
Buy Lyon's Gift

CONNECTED SERIES
SERIES BIBLIOGRAPHY

Have you also read the Guardians of the Stone and the Daughters of Avalon? While it's not necessary to read these series to enjoy the Highland Brides, all three series are related with shared characters.

These books are ALSO AVAILABLE AS AUDIOBOOKS

THE HIGHLAND BRIDES

The MacKinnon's Bride

Lyon's Gift

On Bended Knee

Lion Heart

Highland Song

MacKinnon's Hope

GUARDIANS OF THE STONE

Once Upon a Highland Legend

Highland Fire

Highland Steel

Highland Storm

Maiden of the Mist

ALSO CONNECTED...

Angel of Fire

Once Upon a Kiss

DAUGHTERS OF AVALON

The King's Favorite

The Holly & the Ivy

A Winter's Rose

Fire Song

Lord of Shadows

THE MEDIEVALS HEROES

Once Upon a Kiss

Angel of Fire

Viking's Prize

REDEEMABLE ROGUES

Happily Ever After

Perfect In My Sight

McKenzie's Bride

Kissed by a Rogue

Thirty Ways to Leave a Duke

A Perfectly Scandalous Proposal

ANTHOLOGIES & NOVELLAS

Lady's Man

Married at Midnight

The Winter Stone

ROMANTIC SUSPENSE

Leave No Trace

Speak No Evil

Tell No Lies

MAINSTREAM FICTION

The Girl Who Stayed

The Things We Leave Behind

Redemption Song

Reprisal

Everyday Lies

ABOUT THE AUTHOR

Tanya Anne Crosby is the New York Times and USA Today bestselling author of thirty novels. She has been featured in magazines, such as People, Romantic Times and Publisher's Weekly, and her books have been translated into eight languages. Her first novel was published in 1992 by Avon Books, where Tanya was hailed as "one of Avon's fastest rising stars." Her fourth book was chosen to launch the company's Avon Romantic Treasure imprint.

Known for stories charged with emotion and humor and filled with flawed characters Tanya is an award-winning author, journalist, and editor, and her novels have garnered reader praise and glowing critical reviews. She and her writer husband split their time between Charleston, SC, where she was raised, and northern Michigan, where the couple make their home.

For more information
Website
Email
Newsletter